PALACE OF SILVER

A NISSERA NOVEL

PALACE OF SILVER

HANNAH WEST

HOLIDAY HOUSE ❧ NEW YORK

Text copyright © 2020 by Hannah West
Map by Jaime Zollars. Copyright © 2020 by Holiday House Publishing, Inc.
All Rights Reserved
HOLIDAY HOUSE is registered in the U.S. Patent and Trademark Office.
Printed and bound in February 2020 at Maple Press, York, PA, USA.
www.holidayhouse.com
First Edition
1 3 5 7 9 10 8 6 4 2

Library of Congress Cataloging-in-Publication Data

Names: West, Hannah, 1990- author.
Title: Palace of silver : a Nissera novel / Hannah West.
Description: First edition. | New York : Holiday House, [2020] | Summary:
"Corruption, uprisings, and a massive threat to elicromancy bring new
queens Glisette and Kadri to arms in this sequel to Realm of Ruins"—
Provided by publisher.
Identifiers: LCCN 2019013102 | ISBN 9780823444434 (hardcover)
Subjects: | CYAC: Magic—Fiction. | Kings, queens, rulers, etc.—Fiction.
Fantasy.
Classification: LCC PZ7.1.W4368 Pal 2020 | DDC [Fic]—dc23
LC record available at https://lccn.loc.gov/2019013102

To Dr. Johnny Wink and the Bugtruck

DEITIES OF AGRIMAS

THE HOLIES AND THEIR SYMBOLS

Eulippa. Lovingkindness. A broken-winged bird.

Atrelius. Courage. Sword and shield.

Mindaes. Moderation. Scales.

Orico. Generosity. Wine pitcher.

Hestraclea. Loyalty. Canine companion.

Kromanos. Diligence. Arrow and target.

Deliantha. Honesty. Candle and key.

Lerimides. Humility. Bowed head.

THE FALLEN

Nexantius. Vainglory.

Silimos. Apathy.

Robivoros. Depravity.

Themera. Cruelty.

PROLOGUE

Once upon a time, there were four queens.

The sheltered queen learned that she did not need magic to be brave.

The mortal queen learned that she was worthy of more.

The almighty queen learned that limitless power has its own constraints.

The last queen looked in the mirror and decided she would bend the world to her will.

ONE

GLISETTE LORENTHI
PONTAVAL, VOLARRE

A SIGH of wind snuffed out the campfire. The darkness in the belly of the forest was as dense as the black soil underneath my bedroll. I went rigid, listening to the rustle of footsteps and the rattle of rasping breaths. Enemies were near.

My elicrin stone held reassuring warmth from nestling against my breastbone. But magic couldn't guarantee my escape from the soulless creatures prowling in the shadows. When I opened my mouth to utter a spell, no sound emerged. No light burst from the stone. My head felt too heavy to lift.

A blight with sallow, sore-ridden skin and milky eyes approached, raising a jagged blade to ram it through my quick-beating heart. The creature drew so close I could smell its putrefying flesh, the scent of dark magic unbridled. Yet I couldn't react, couldn't move. I could only hope my death would be swift.

"Glisette?" the blight said in a cheery voice.

I gasped and heaved awake, terrifying my younger sister, Perennia.

Cold sweat dampened the satin sheets twisted around my thighs. Shafts of light from a flaming sunrise melted through gaps in the powder-blue drapes, skimming over gilded furniture and velvet upholstery. I was at home in the palace at Pontaval, not in the woods at night or in the throes of a bloody battle.

Months had passed since I'd helped to overthrow the Moth King, but the most harrowing memories of the journey still stalked my sleep.

"Sorry!" Perennia squeaked, holding aside the embroidered canopy that surrounded my four-poster bed. "Oliva said to tell you the mayors of the border towns have arrived."

With an irascible grunt, I swung my legs over the edge of the bed, brushing strands of blond hair from my face. "They're early."

"Yes."

"Was Oliva afraid to wake me?"

Perennia's honeyed curls bobbed as she nodded.

I could hardly blame my head maid, not after I'd accidentally unleashed a spell last week that had flung her across the room and into my open wardrobe. My heaps of flouncy dresses had padded her fall, but since then Oliva had been skittish when it came to waking me.

I pounced into action. A year ago it would have taken me hours to prepare for a social engagement. Sometimes I missed the simple luxury of pruning in the scalding water, dozing off as a maid's gentle fingers sifted through my long locks. Now I barely took the time to use a comb and mouth rinse before throwing back a swig of tea and hurrying off to whatever appointment awaited me first, pursued by Oliva and her flock of underling ladies-in-waiting. I could hardly even visit the lavatory alone for all the guards and servants tailing me.

Nothing had been the same since the day I told Uncle Mathis, in no uncertain terms, that I was stepping into the role of queen of Volarre and forcing him out.

One of the maids broke formation to scuttle ahead and open the door to the meeting chamber—I hadn't opened a door for myself in months either—revealing my chief advisor sitting at the marble-top table with a group of strange men.

"I present Her Majesty, Queen Glisette Lorenthi," he said.

As the mayors stood to bow, their gazes coasted over me, moving from the misty lavender chalcedony at my throat to the silver crown on my head, landing in unison on the scar that slashed over my right eye from forehead to cheek.

"Gentlemen," I said, scooping the skirts of my sapphire dress—a bit modest for my taste, despite the plunging neckline—to claim the head of the table. They took their seats. "Once again, I profoundly apologize for the decisions made by my uncle and elder sister, which brought food shortages to your towns. How are the assistance programs faring?"

"They're helping, Your Majesty," answered the man to my left, who looked too youthful for his silver hair. "The problem is that when Prince Regent Mathis tripled the tolls, the produce vendors who cross the border to our markets raised their prices."

"But we've decreased the tolls," I pointed out. "They're even lower than before Uncle Mathis raised them."

"Yes, Your Majesty," my chief advisor said, "but the vendors fear the crown might raise them again on a whim."

I was grateful for Hubert, who patiently filled in my gaps of understanding. My younger brother, Devorian, had been coached to take the crown while my sisters and I learned etiquette, languages, and, of course, elicromancy. As queen, I was forced to countervail my years of deficient governing studies with tireless initiative.

"I'll sign a decree guaranteeing that I will not raise the tolls for a decade," I said. "We'll have a ceremony in one of your towns."

"A bold idea, Your Majesty," Hubert said. "But it doesn't solve the immediate problem that many poor Volarians cannot afford food."

A blush of embarrassment bloomed behind my cheeks. In moments like these, I missed my old life—but not sprawling in the lap of opulence and reveling in a lack of responsibilities. Instead, strangely, I longed for my time trudging through the wilderness, scared, hungry, thirsty, sore, and wounded, but driven by a singular purpose.

The quest had been arduous, but with only one goal: deliver Valory Braiosa to the Moth King's court so that she could kill him before he destroyed Nissera.

The upheaval that necessitated the quest had happened so swiftly that I'd barely had time to second-guess my decision to join.

First, Valory had touched the Water—the ancient source of elicrin magic hidden deep in the woods—without permission from the Conclave. But unlike others who had tried before her, she did not die. Nor did she receive an elicrin stone, which would have bestowed upon her a magical gift. Instead, she had dried up the Water and gained a destructive power that looked nothing like elicromancy.

Meanwhile, my brother Devorian had come into possession of a pearl tablet inscribed with an arcane "awakening" spell written in an ancient, forgotten language. Though Devorian was an Omnilingual, the language was so strange that even he struggled to make sense of the spell. He convinced himself it would have the capacity to resurrect our parents from the dead.

Instead, it raised Emlyn Valmarys, an elicromancer tyrant from a dark age in history. He had been kept dormant for centuries when no one—not even an alliance of elicromancers, fay, and sea folk—could defeat him. His power allowed him to take other elicromancers' gifts for his own or lend them to his servants. He was invincible until the three groups devised a way to trap him in his mountain lair and keep him dormant using a contract engraved on the tablet.

A group of mortals called the Summoners had given Devorian the tablet to decipher without telling him what it would do. They wanted to resurrect Emlyn Valmarys so that he would offer them a reward of magic and immortality. Devorian was a foolish pawn who unwittingly did their bidding by speaking the spell on the tablet.

Valory accidentally cursed Devorian with a beastly form for his recklessness, demonstrating that her power could do more than just destroy. Then she crossed paths with Mercer, a Prophet from an earlier time. Mercer told her that Valmarys, whom he called the Moth King due to the tyrant's sigil, did not hold the power to give and take elicrin gifts on his own. Mercer's brother, Tilmorn, had; Tilmorn was a Purveyor, and the Moth King had taken him captive long ago. Now the Moth King was using Tilmorn's power to conquer the mountain fortress city of Darmeska and unleash havoc on the realm.

Mercer felt certain that Valory would be the one to defeat the risen tyrant at last, given her strange and unrivaled power. Thus we set out, the Moth King's servants hunting us while we hunted him. And as we fought, the Realm Alliance unraveled. The Moth King's servants captured and murdered many of its members, but spared Valory's family, who had joined forces with the Summoners in order to sow political chaos and make their own magical laws. My family had fallen under Valmarys's influence as well. Ambrosine and Uncle Mathis let the Moth King win them over with fine gifts, leading to crisis when they began overtaxing the kingdom to support the new heights of their lavish lifestyle.

Every corner of Nissera seemed to be caving in on itself. Yorth fell to plague, Volarre fell to greed, and Calgoran fell to corruption.

But we managed to deliver Valory to the Moth King's tower in Darmeska. While we battled his servants, she faced the tyrant himself. She stole his power and freed Tilmorn. And in the midst of the fight, she realized that the Water had given her more than just a gift for destruction and transformation—it had given her *itself*. The Water had always decided who was worthy of elicromancy. And now Valory had that power, carrying the Water's legacy. She was more than a mere Purveyor, like Tilmorn had been before she made him a Healer. She was more than a Neutralizer. She was the source of elicrin power.

On the heels of our triumph in Darmeska, we returned to our respective homes and punished those who had wronged the realm. Devorian supported me in pushing Uncle Mathis aside so that I could become queen of Volarre.

I had thought my trials were over. How was it that overthrowing a tyrant was somehow easier—or at least more straightforward—than taking up the scepter to rule?

"Theft and murder have escalated in our towns, Your Majesty," one of the mayors at the far end of the table said. "Our people have resorted to eating draft animals and seed grains. They're desperate for food."

I gulped, trying to remain calm so I could think. If the mayors hadn't arrived early, Hubert would have counseled me privately. But if he helped me now, my inexperience would be all too apparent.

A din from outside drowned my thoughts. "What is that shout-ing?" I demanded.

One of my guards hurried to the windows behind me. "There's a crowd approaching the palace gates, Your Majesty."

I rose and turned to see for myself, blinded by the brilliant sun glistening on the distant hills. I blinked the stars from my eyes and found a horde marching along the cobblestone thoroughfare, wind-ing uphill past shops and markets to our towering palace.

"Is it some sort of parade?" I asked, squinting into the distance. "Why was I not informed?"

"It's not a parade." Hubert sounded alarmed as he appeared at my side.

My stomach clenched. Even from afar, I caught angry flashes of farm tools and fists punching into the air, unintelligible chants and jeers. "It's a riot," I said.

The courtyard guards realized this before I did and slammed the wrought iron gates so swiftly that the silver-gilt lily emblems shivered. The loud clanging sliced through my skull, and when it faded, the words of the people's chant became clear:

No magic kings!
No magic queens!
Let mortals rule!
End the suffering!

The chant evolved into shouting as they slammed against the closed barrier, rattling the iron bars. With a boost, a young boy managed to scramble halfway up the gate and find a foothold on a silver lily petal. He threw his leg over to straddle the arch, his keen eyes searching the palace windows. Our gazes met. He slid a bulky stone from his pocket and reeled back his arm.

I jolted away from the window a mere half second before the glass burst, shards singing as they scattered over the floor.

Hubert clasped my elbow. "Get her to an interior room," he said to the guard.

"I need to speak to them," I insisted. "They're my people and they have grievances to air."

With a thunder of hooves, mounted guards cantered through the courtyard and lined up along the gates, daring the swarm to push through. One of the guards grabbed the boy by the wrist and yanked him from his perch. He hit the ground with an unsettling *whap* and curled into himself, writhing in pain.

"Stop!" I cried. "Hubert, make them stop!"

"Protecting you and the royal residence is their duty," Hubert said, urging me toward the door. "It is below the dignity of the crown to acknowledge the demands of subjects threatening your life. We must get you to safety."

"I'm an elicromancer, Hubert. I *am* safe." He couldn't truly understand what I'd endured, what I'd seen others endure. "No violence. That is a command."

"Your guards will do what they must," Hubert argued calmly. "I've served your family for many years. Your parents trusted me in these matters—"

"And look what happened to them," I snapped. The ice in my gaze was even more effective now than before I earned my scar.

Compunctious, Hubert bowed his head but didn't avert his

eyes. He lowered his voice, even toned. "That only reinforces my point. Like you, your parents thought their magic would keep them safe. And they were caught off guard."

The room suddenly felt too cramped, the air too warm, the riot outside as raucous as an unruly storm. Elicromancer-hating rebels had slain my parents during a diplomatic overseas excursion to Perispos. And now the crowd out there was clamoring for the fall of elicromancer rulers.

The reign of the Moth King had not been kind to mortals—nor to elicromancers who resisted him. But mortals couldn't see the latter fact. They only knew that their bellies had ached with hunger and their loved ones had fallen ill with plague, while Uncle Mathis and Ambrosine bled them dry with tolls and taxes. The glowing sense of appreciation for my part in overthrowing the Moth King had faded. Now all my people saw was a beautiful woman in a palace with a magical jewel at her throat, a woman resembling the elder sister who had failed Volarre; the only physical trait that truly distinguished me from Ambrosine was the gash across my eye.

I stormed to the exit, barely remembering to acknowledge the mayors. "Hubert will work out the details when the dust settles," I said over my shoulder. "My best wishes to you."

A fretful Perennia waited with the maids in the corridor, gnawing her bottom lip.

"Go to your room and stay away from the windows," I barked, sweeping past.

"What will you do?" she asked.

"Listen to them."

"They're not here to speak to you."

I ignored her as I marched back to my bedchamber.

"Where are you going?" she asked.

"To change." I flung open the door before a maid could do it for me. I stalked to my wardrobe, tuning out the deafening shouts from the distant courtyard. "We have to show them that we're not the vain little dolls they think we are."

My fingertips brushed delicate beading, silk ribbons, ruffles, lace. I yanked out a spring green gown and plucked wildly at its fabric flower embellishments, maiming petals and severing threads. "Do I own a single gown without frills?"

"Don't do that," Perennia said like a governess scolding a child smearing paint on the walls. She confiscated the garment. "Just order some plain new ones."

"That's the problem! Always more things!" I shouted. "Ambrosine betrayed the kingdom to bloat our family's wealth. I have to show all of Volarre that we are not like her."

"It's not about our wealth, Glisette, or finery, or beauty," Perennia replied. She draped the unfortunate gown over the back of a chair. I saw myself reflected in her face: ivory skin, long golden hair, sea-glass eyes, high cheekbones. But she possessed a softness that the other three of us Lorenthi children did not. "They're here to force you to give up your elicrin stone. They want you to become *mortal*. They no longer want all-powerful rulers. And who could blame them?"

"But I fought for them! I bled so they could live!"

As the words thrust out of me, violent memories returned, memories so horrifying that even my dreams didn't dare touch them. I winced against the recollection of people trampling one another to escape from Darmeska when I used my elicrin power to freeze and break the gates open; the bodies of the city's elders on display, feasts for carrion; the way the Moth King controlled the minds of Darmeskans from his tower, forcing them to terrorize their own people; the stinging cold of an arrow that should have killed me; and death's icy claws trying to drag me away.

Perennia caught my hands in hers. The mellow glow from her rose elicrin stone preceded the familiar peace and relief that snuck in when her Solacer power stole whatever dark emotions thrashed inside me.

"You made great sacrifices," she whispered. "But Ambrosine and Uncle Mathis hurt our people. Their mistakes shouldn't be your burdens to bear, but they are because you are a Lorenthi too, and you wear the crown. Going out there in plain garb isn't going to make a difference."

For the first time, I wondered whether the Realm Alliance had made a mistake showing lenience to Ambrosine and Uncle Mathis. Both had been put on magical probation and consigned to manual labor, mostly sorting and loading foodstuff for the assistance programs. While Mathis sullenly followed orders, Ambrosine refused to work. She was determined to be a thorn in my side until, ostensibly, I let her return to her old way of life.

But as I'd been riffling bleary-eyed through Uncle Mathis's documents days before my coronation, a solution presented itself. The king of Perispos had written to Uncle Mathis before the season of crises had begun, expressing an interest in marrying either Ambrosine or me. He had been widowed seven years earlier. Apparently, Uncle Mathis thought I would be suited to the task and had asked King Myron what bride price he was prepared to offer in exchange for my hand.

Upon reading the correspondences, I'd felt sour that I'd ever been treated like property, and then smug that I'd stripped Uncle Mathis of his power to do so. And then I'd grinned with relief and penned a missive to the king immediately. The Realm Alliance had approved, my sister had readily accepted the proposal, and I'd rejoiced to be rid of her. But Mathis, too embarrassed to continue his work, had fled soon afterward. We could have made a tracking map to hunt him down, but he wasn't worth the trouble. The restrictive enchantment we had placed on his elicrin stone wouldn't rob him of his immortality, but it would prevent him from using his magic to harm anyone. Besides, tracking maps were an archaic sort of magic, and they had limits; they would not work for anyone harboring malicious intent toward the person they sought, and if I got my hands on Mathis again, I might wring his neck.

Mathis and Ambrosine had stoked a fire of righteous fury in the hearts of our people, yet I was the only one left to burn.

Devorian broke through the gaggle of maids in the doorway and crossed the room to rip the drapes closed. Valory's unfortunate spell on him had at last worn off, but sometimes his eyes seemed to sparkle golden amber rather than blue green.

"You aren't going to dignify this, are you?" he asked.

"No," Perennia answered before I could, releasing my hand.

"Good." My brother raked a hand through his flaxen, shoulder-length waves. "It will blow over."

"So I'm to hide out until my people don't want my head on a pike?" I demanded.

"They don't want your head on a pike; they want your elicrin stone in a pit. All of ours." Devorian strode to my tea tray only to frown at the dearth of spirituous or fermented options. "It will take time, but when their situations improve under your rule, their ire will cool."

I sighed and sank into a chair, striking a woebegone pose before I checked myself and sat up straight. "Perhaps once I sign the decree restricting the border tolls, they'll—"

"You can't do that," Devorian interrupted, spreading margarine over a triangle of toast.

"What? Why not?"

"It's how the crown recoups investments. What if we must repair or rebuild a bridge and the cost of materials and labor has increased? No, no." He wagged his finger and took a bite. "Don't make promises you can't keep."

A growl rumbled in my throat. Though Devorian had abdicated his throne to me, the antiquated laws of Volarre still technically required a male principal ruler. That meant I was only the "provisional ruler" until I could revise the statute to the satisfaction of my father's senior advisors. Hubert supported me, but the other two were cantankerous old bats.

For this, I often found myself resenting Devorian, even when he was only trying to help.

I nearly asked why I would listen to the imbecile who had resurrected the Moth King, but bit back my retort as Devorian's wife entered the room.

"Are we in danger?" Larabelle asked. Her brown hair, which tended to adhere tightly to her scalp, needed fluffing, and her alabaster cheeks practically begged for rouge. She was lovely, but always quaintly styled, the daughter of a middle-class merchant. I would have intervened, but she disliked fuss on her account. Besides, Devorian might claw me to ribbons if I so much as changed a hair on her head, so fiercely did he love the pretty little mouse.

My brother's superior expression yielded to a smile so sickeningly sweet that he almost looked like a theatrical mockery of a doting lover. "No, my darling, we aren't in danger," he cooed.

"Are you hurt?" she asked, turning to me. "I heard—"

"Not at all." I waved to dismiss her concern and massaged my forehead. I had imagined ruling would be easy with Valory as queen of Calgoran and Kadri Lillis as queen of Yorth. The rest of the Realm Alliance members were friends, as well: Mercer Fye, Tilmorn Fye, Melkior Ermetarius, and Kadri's husband, Fabian Veloxen. With so many powerful, good people working toward a common cause, recovering and rebuilding should have been straightforward.

But all that power somehow amounted to weakness; we were so painstakingly careful not to overplay our hand.

I rose from the chair and parted the sea of attendants standing by, shooing them away. "You are all dismissed."

"You aren't going to the crowd, are you?" Perennia asked, but I didn't answer as I marched down the corridor, one of my heeled slippers catching on the sapphire carpet. I sped to a run and descended the curving staircase.

At last I shoved open the door to the gardens and pinned my hand to my ribs, taking in sharp breaths. The distant pandemonium was only a whisper from my quiet refuge of meandering paths and sculpted hedges.

But this wasn't the refuge I sought.

A materialization barrier protected the palace so that elicro-mancers could not pass through the walls using magic. Beyond the imposing garden fence hidden by stately hedges, I could slip away, fling myself through the expanse toward true solitude.

My heels clacked along the path until I stopped to kick off my slippers, sending one flying into a bed of peonies. I'd recently made the habit of tucking a pair of worn-in leather boots behind a potted lavender plant. I shoved them on, swung open the gate, and closed my eyes.

I spoke the materializing spell and whirled through oblivion.

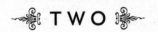

TWO

KADRI LILLIS
BEYRIAN, YORTH

THE letter seemed to sear my skin like a blazing coal.
I'd folded the crisp parchment into a tight square and tucked it into my skirt waist as though hiding it away might somehow make its truths untrue.

Tears gathered in my eyes as I drew my bowstring taut. The practice target was a blur of red and white, yet when I let the arrow slip, it struck the very center. My fraught mood made my form a little clumsy, however, and I felt the lingering sting of the bowstring slapping my unguarded forearm again. A faint, plum-purple bruise formed beneath my brown skin. I pressed it with the pad of my thumb as my brother's words slammed back against my chest.

I reached over my shoulder for another arrow, sliding the silky fletching through my fingers, hoping it would bring calm.

"Are you all right?" Falima asked.

I let fly and palmed away an escaping tear. "Yes."

"Did the letter from Rayed upset you?" my maid pressed. She slid her peach-colored summer scarf off her head, set aside her book of poems, and rose from the bench near the practice range. "What did it say?" she asked in our native Erdemese.

I turned but couldn't seem to meet her gaze, instead studying the limb tip of my beautifully crafted bow. "King Agmur didn't summon Rayed back to Erdem for just a short visit. He wants him to remain there permanently."

She frowned. "Did Rayed do something wrong?"

"No. Erdem is dissolving the position and closing the embassy here. There will be no ambassador to Nissera. My brother's not coming back."

"I suppose it's no surprise," Falima sighed. "Nearly every week there's a ship full of our people leaving for home."

"And I can't blame them. The horrors that befell this realm would drive even the bravest people to safer shores."

Falima didn't reply, but a crease of concern charted across her forehead. She had held me when I'd awakened from the fevered nightmares that forced me to relive the worst horrors from the journey to Darmeska with Valory, Glisette, and Mercer.

Falima could comfort me, but she couldn't understand what I had seen and felt: the blight disease decaying patches of my flesh, the sight of corpses murdered by the Moth King's servants rotting on public display, the fear that I might soon be one of them. Here in the palace, she had been shielded from the atrocities of the Moth King's short yet dreadful reign, from the plague raging outside the gates of these very palace grounds.

"Do you think your brother will find other employment?" she asked, always preferring to keep the conversation somewhat superficial. Her friendship was largely one of silence and secrets—rarely frank or frivolous confessions.

"He's already accepted a position in the trade ministry," I replied. "King Agmur is sending him on some mundane mission, which Rayed described to me in exhaustive detail, of course."

Falima chuckled, for she knew Rayed well, but I couldn't manage to smile in response. The reason I had become queen of Yorth—my purpose, my mission, despite the fact that I could not feel romantic love for my spouse and king—was to help my people. Many had journeyed from Erdem to Yorth expecting that magic would rid them of disease, hunger, and fear of harm. But they soon realized that life in Nissera was far from perfect, and that magic, like any other resource, was more easily accessed by the wealthy than the poor, despite the best efforts of the Realm Alliance.

And then the Moth King's evils had devastated the realm. Yorth was no longer safe. The life my people had sought slipped so far out of reach that they no longer had reason to stay.

And outside countries had lost faith in elicromancers' ability to keep their own kind in check.

And King Agmur wasn't only shuttering the Erdemese embassy and severing our diplomatic relations. He was challenging the legitimacy of our new Realm Alliance.

This was the bit of Rayed's letter that I couldn't bring myself to explain to Falima, the words that burned:

I know as well as you that many elicromancers are good, but King Agmur rightfully questions their ability to rid the barrel of bad apples before the rot spreads. He wants to scale back trade with Nissera until the realm proves politically stable.

Further diminishing the appearance of stability are Glisette's and Valory's dubious claims to their thrones. Glisette is only the "provisional ruler" of Volarre until her father's advisors consent to changing the laws. Valory seized her position in Calgoran through violence. As

far as His Eminence is concerned, Fabian is the only sovereign in Nis-
sera with a legitimate claim to his throne.

Sister, I know this is not news you wanted to hear. But King Agmur
is only trying to protect our people's interests. He will not recognize the
authority of the Realm Alliance until these issues are resolved and the
disturbances settle down.

In light of this news, have you reconsidered His Eminence's invitation?

Of course Rayed would remind me of that. King Agmur's invitation had been so insulting that I had not even mentioned it to
Fabian for fear of the repercussions.

Somehow, King Agmur knew that my marriage was "not in every
way legitimate," meaning unconsummated. Rayed fiercely denied dis-
closing this to him. The king said that if I desired, I could annul my
marriage to Fabian and return to Erdem to work for him as a top advisor. He said he would give me my own estate, which I would not have
to share with my brother or any other man. He claimed my passion for
helping the Erdemese people would be put to good use in my new role.

I had scrawled a scathing refusal within seconds, knowing Rayed
would rephrase the message before passing it along to his sovereign.
Yet the request had lingered in the back of my mind, itching with
possibility and making me feel restless. What if I could better help
Erdem's least-fortunate citizens by advising King Agmur? By leaving Nissera to its elicromancers and advocating for the voiceless
within my home country?

Footsteps crunched along the garden path. I turned to find the
redheaded kitchen maid, Trista, curtsying to me. "The tasting for
tomorrow's dinner is ready for you on the veranda, Your Majesty."

"Thank you," I said, and gathered my archery gear for Falima to carry inside.

Loosening my black hair from its braid, I walked the path that followed the back façade of the palace, which was perched on a cliff overlooking the sea. I gazed beyond the pale beach with its mosaic of rock formations to the ships bobbing in the aquamarine bay and wondered what it would be like to leave this home I had known since childhood.

But it was unimaginable. Nissera was my home, the other Realm Alliance leaders my friends, Fabian my husband.

And Rynna...

My spirit blazed as I thought of her yet again, the fay woman from Wenryn. In the midst of our terrifying journey, the others and I had found rest, healing, and protection at her people's forest dwelling. She was enthralling and sublime, ageless and ancient, witty and impish and charmingly imperious. Before her, I had never known anything so intense, so meaningful, though I'd cared for a handful of girls. There was the young envoy that used to escort Erdemese immigrants to our embassy when I resided there with my father and brother; Rayed used to tease me for how nervous I acted during our brief interactions. And then there was the niece of the palace pastry chef, who taught me to frost cakes before she left for work in another noble household. And finally, there was the daughter of the Perispi ambassador who had kissed me while we sunbathed on the beach. But upon turning sixteen, she had planned to serve as an altar attendant in one of the religious edifices back in Perispos, a role that demanded lifelong celibacy.

With Rynna, everything felt different, but she was still out of my reach. She belonged to the fay dwelling, a place I could only visit, a place I could never call home. When we met, I drank the nectar from the trees in Wenryn to purge my body of the blight disease. Rynna warned me I would feel a desperate longing for the fay land. Now homesickness was not only a wistful pining for distant shores and bygone days, but something far more profound; it was a soul-deep yearning for what could have been and would never be—a need to grasp everything wholesome and beautiful in this world yoked with an acute awareness that it was not mine to grasp.

I shoved aside my melancholy thoughts as I reached the tasting table on the veranda. The cook delivered steaming samples of the menu I'd requested for the Realm Alliance gathering tomorrow. We would watch the sun setting over the sea as we dined—Fabian's idea. The menu would be Erdemese, full of aromatic spices and earthy flavors—my idea.

Nothing brought me more joy than hosting my friends. Business took precedence, but after our agenda, we would eat and laugh and speak candidly of our dreams for the realm's future.

Our guests didn't usually tarry long. Even six months after the fall of the Moth King, there remained so much work to do. The elicromancers would materialize back to their homes after dessert. But that only made those moments with Valory, Glisette, and Mercer more precious.

I lifted the lid to the turmeric cauliflower soup, but my appetite balked at the thought of telling the others about Rayed's disconcerting letter. I believed in the work of the Realm Alliance. I believed we could make the benefits of magic accessible to the many instead of only the few, that we could restore balance. But a damaged relationship with Erdem, prominent ally, would present a challenge unlike any we had faced so far.

A hand reached over my shoulder and grabbed one of the savory lentil cardamom pastries. I smiled up at Fabian. "Sometimes I think your true elicrin gift is sensing the exact moment a plate of food touches a table anywhere in the palace," I teased.

"It's more of a skill I've developed," he managed to say through a mouthful, pulling out the empty chair across from me. The sunlight shimmered like brushed gold over his black hair and reflected in his bright green elicrin stone.

"Have you received any correspondences from Erdem recently?" I asked with a forced tone of nonchalance. I spooned some soup, almost too distracted to appreciate its flavors.

He shook his head. "No. But we do need to reply to Myron's invitation to visit Perispos during their upcoming religious celebration. We've sat on it for weeks."

I had grown up knowing Erdem's neighbors in Perispos practiced the Agrimas religion, but I struggled to believe in something that could not be proven. Here in Nissera, magic itself took the place of religion: it was ancient, revered, coveted, and feared. Instead of prayers, people found comfort in spells and charms.

Likewise, most Erdemese citizens collectively shrugged at organized religion, much to the chagrin of the nearby Perispi. Many believed that kind deeds would ensure prosperity in the afterlife, but we exalted our lore and family histories more than any moralizing texts.

"We declined Myron's last invitation," Fabian said. "Should I tell him the truth, that you dread sea travel?"

"No," I sighed. "We'll ask to use Valory's portal box when she returns from answering that distress call."

"I can kindly refuse, if you'd like."

"But should you?" I asked, searching his slate-gray eyes. The bone structure of his suntanned face was so refined that he seemed chiseled of stone. The physical tasks of seafaring that he so enjoyed had carved lean strength into his frame. For years I'd tried so earnestly to admire his physique the way I'd felt I was meant to.

"I don't know," he admitted. "My mother would have known."

I reached over the platters and gripped his hand. "She and your father would both be proud of how we've handled ourselves."

"No, they would be proud of you, Kadri," he said. "Of your bravery."

Squeezing tighter, I tried to infuse him with confidence that he had been wholly forgiven—by me, by the others, by his parents before they died.

"I should have been here," he whispered. "I failed everyone."

"You didn't know," I assured him, as I had so many times since I'd returned to him.

Both were true: he had failed, and he hadn't done so knowingly.

The rogue wave had been one of the first harbingers of the Moth King's rise last year. It had crashed ashore during Fabian's birthday celebration, which took place aboard his anchored ship in the bay. Fabian had acted nobly, intending to sacrifice his life to save others, until a mysterious girl saved *his* life at the final second.

If the story had ended there, he would have remained a hero. But when the blight plague assaulted us from the other direction, he failed to understand that it marked the advent of an oppressive darkness. He had caught wind of the sickness that struck his city but underestimated its deadliness—and overestimated the old Realm Alliance's power to squelch the crisis.

Instead of taking bold initiative, he'd become infatuated with the girl who saved him and whisked her out to sea to avoid prying eyes. I could hardly blame him. I'd glimpsed her once and seen enchanting blue eyes, a coconut-milk complexion, and hair fairer than frosted glass. She disappeared when she learned Fabian planned to marry me. Later, I learned she was a sea maiden who had helped translate the lost language on the pearlescent tablet Devorian had broken. In exchange, she took a beautiful human form through the combination of Valory's power and a sea witch's magic.

Fabian confided in me that her oddness and childlike demeanor had dashed his hopes for a passionate dalliance. He preferred more worldly-wise women.

And *I* preferred he be a bit more discreet about his affairs.

I hadn't needed to flaunt his mistakes to rebuke him. His jarring homecoming from the sea had been rebuke enough. Not only did he return to a city in chaos, with both of his parents presumed dead and no Realm Alliance left standing; but I, his betrothed, appeared to have fled to Erdem for the sake of my safety.

Now he knew the truth: I had nearly died facing down the evil he had failed to recognize as a threat until it was too late.

Fabian squeezed my hand in return and offered a frail smile. "I wouldn't last a day without you."

"No, you wouldn't," I said playfully, and reached for a shrimp. "Oh, that's divine. I think just a bit more cumin, don't you? And seeing it now, I'd prefer the gold glass plates to the blue ones."

"How do you focus on these things?" Fabian asked, shaking his head. "I can't seem to concentrate on anything constructive. Sometimes I sit in the study for hours, wondering how everything went so wrong and whether it could happen again."

A cool breeze rushed over us, tugging at the table linens and streaming my raven hair over my face. "Nissera has to move on," I said, looking over the jewel-blue sea. "It has to heal. We're the leaders now. We're the ones who have to stitch everything together with smiles on our faces, no matter what challenges arise."

I resituated my wind-tossed skirt, and the corners of the folded letter pressed against my skin. "Speaking of challenges," I continued. "I received a letter from Rayed. It contains less-than-ideal news."

"When did you start phrasing everything so diplomatically?"

"When I was crowned queen and had no choice."

"Fair enough," he said, popping a shrimp into his mouth. "What's the matter?"

"Our alliance with Erdem is under strain. They look at us and see unmitigated disasters, young and inexperienced leaders. If we don't start thinking like your mother and father, we could lose the favor of Perispos too. The economic crisis Ambrosine and Mathis Lorenthi caused will be nothing compared to losing trade partners."

My tone intensified toward the end. The lenience the Realm Alliance showed Glisette's sister and uncle had agitated me from the start. A prescient regret had haunted me during their hearings. But I let the others sentence them without speaking up. I stayed silent because Rayed had also made grave errors, which we had informally pardoned. His intentions were far more innocent, and anyone with half a heart could understand why Rayed helped the Calgoranian traitors—they had threatened my life if he refused.

But one could also argue that Ambrosine and Mathis didn't *mean* to cause any harm. In fact, they had argued that for themselves quite deftly. The pursuit of justice so easily became a slick slope into a valley of moral ambiguity.

Thunderclouds passed through Fabian's eyes. "So King Agmur does not respect us."

"He respects you. He says your claim to Yorth's throne is the only inarguable one."

"It's insulting," he said, though he looked a tad relieved. "He should know better than to disregard elicromancers. Does he not know what we can do if our relations sour? Does he not fear us?"

"Oh, Fabian," I sighed, molding my hand to his cheek. "After what we've endured, can't you concede that no elicromancer is invincible?"

"Even Valory?" he asked.

I swallowed hard and broke our gazes. "Probably even her. Regardless, the Realm Alliance cannot antagonize mortals, even mortals who insult us. We need to repair the relationship as best we can. Promise me you won't do anything rash until we've spoken with the others?"

He hesitated before nodding. I knew he wouldn't lie to me. "I promise."

Excusing myself, I went inside, crossed the pearlescent and bronze tiles of the banquet hall, and journeyed upstairs to my suite, adjacent to Fabian's for appearance's sake. It was large and resplendent, with embroidered silk cushions, sheer fabric dividers, and pierced metal lanterns reminiscent of typical Erdemese décor.

I glanced to make sure Falima wasn't there before I approached the jewelry case on my vanity, opened the bottom drawer, and removed the wooden slat concealing a silk-lined compartment.

My violet-and-blue elicrin stone winked at me from its hiding spot.

Withdrawing the crystal-like gem by its gold chain, I stuffed the letter from Rayed in its place. Fabian could never learn about the king of Erdem's invitation.

I didn't used to have so many secrets. Just one, which I had never guarded closely. Fabian and I were content to let people see what they wished when they looked at us. Some saw a happy couple in love, yet others surely saw a royal man-boy chasing skirts while his wife suffered in silence. Some believed we were simply willing to share our intense romantic love with others. And some knew the truth: we were friends who had struck a beneficial bargain.

Our union was an act of diplomacy. The engagement had pleased his parents, and I didn't mind Fabian's dalliances with beautiful girls so long as they didn't jeopardize my status. I would be able to assist my people as queen, and Fabian would not force me to perform any duties I did not wish to. We were each other's shields from excessive scrutiny, from people trying to dictate our lives and futures. It wasn't so much a secret or a lie as an innocent omission of the truth.

But this—accepting an elicrin stone from Valory—was a secret. A heavy one, which I both feared and relished.

Immortality. Status. Equality. That was what she had given me. She was now the steward of elicrin gifts, and she had confiscated this stone from an elicromancer who had abused her power.

At first, I had rejected the stone. If she turned one mortal into an elicromancer, where would it stop? How many more mortals would come to her begging for power and eternal life?

But Valory had insisted it was a simple, small gift: the gift of perfect marksmanship. Compared to others, it was trivial, and she had jested that my marksmanship was near perfect anyway.

We both knew that the gift would make some things easier and others more complicated. And for that reason, I could not publicize my possession of it yet.

The elicrin stone was slender, nearly cylindrical, and easier to hide than most. And Valory had taught me a concealing spell, though I wasn't yet comfortable using it.

I slipped on the chain and tucked the powerful jewel into my bodice, sheltering its warmth against my skin.

THREE

GLISETTE
THE BRAZOR MOUNTAINS

HE mountain air tasted of freedom, and the sharp-sweet aroma of pine needles and snow. A chilling breeze snaked up my sleeves and made me shiver with delight.

When I opened my eyes after materializing from the palace, the late-morning sky over the Brazor Mountains was a canvas of periwinkle and ruby red, streaked with feather-thin clouds. I stood upon a ridge overlooking the vast fortress city of Darmeska, and the iron-and-glass monstrosity of a tower that loomed over it: the Moth King's lair.

It was an obscene imprint that a now-deceased oppressor had inflicted upon a graceful landscape—a reminder that one could overthrow evil, yet still reside in its shadow.

I filled my lungs with the crisp wind and trod through the thawing spring snows toward a ledge. Settling down, I dangled my legs over the yawning chasm below. The danger of it made my blood course like a wild river through my veins, made me feel alive.

But it wasn't the only reason I came here. A strange sense of loss had lately carved out a pit between my ribs, and I'd found myself thinking wistfully of my adventures with Valory, Kadri, and Mercer. Before Devorian had unleashed the dormant tyrant on Nissera,

I had hardly cared about anything besides my siblings and the luxuries we enjoyed as royalty.

The quest had changed everything. It had awakened something within me, a sense of higher purpose. And while being queen of Volarre offered me that purpose, I couldn't shed the trappings of my old life that had begun to chafe. I held court, heard petitions, received foreign dignitaries, signed decrees, and attended every Realm Alliance meeting in Yorth; yet at times, I felt less important to this realm than I had while tromping through the woods in filthy garments.

"Interesting choice of retreat."

The familiar, deep voice made my already pounding heart quicken its cadence. I cast a glance over my shoulder and saw a lean, tall figure with sandy hair loping toward me: Mercer.

The pang of delight I felt was something of a reflex. I'd fallen a bit in love with him over our journey, and for a month or so after its conclusion, I believed that the emptiness inside me was missing him, the wound of wanting what I could never have. But my feelings had ebbed and blurred, and I realized that the emptiness was something far more frightening than desire. I had discovered my truest, bravest self on that journey. And now I feared losing her.

That was why I came here.

As for my pattering heart and whirling butterflies, well…Mercer was just so viciously *handsome*, damn him. One of his eyes was as white as bone now, with a tiny black dot for a pupil, but somehow it hadn't diminished his beauty.

"I followed your materialization trail," he explained, hunkering down next to me.

"Then I suppose you arrived at the palace around the time the commotion began," I said, propping my palms on the cool rock. "I'm surprised you made it inside without my people ripping that off," I added, jerking my chin toward the dappled, gray-green elicrin stone hanging from a dingy cord around his neck.

"I found another way in. Are you all right?"

The question cut straight through my armor of dark humor. "Just a bit rattled," I said with a slanted smile. "I think the mortals fail to understand that even if we gave up our elicrin stones, Valory would stay the same. She can't give away what she is, not like we can. It's better that the rest of us retain our power, in case she..." I trailed off, remembering that I was speaking to her lover.

"It's all right," he said. "She and I have discussed the same thing. We've seen what power without accountability looks like. No one is capable of doing much to mitigate..." Now it was his turn to trail off. He sighed. "It's strange to be back here. I can't say I care for it."

"Why did you come? You would have seen me at the Realm Alliance gathering tomorrow."

Mercer looked at me, one eye warm golden brown, one shocking white. "I had a vision last night."

"Oh? Dreaming of me, are you?" I teased.

"It was about your sister."

"Perennia?" The protective mother wolf in me raised her hackles in alarm.

"No. Ambrosine."

I relaxed, tipping my head back so the morning sun could splash its warmth over my face. "Does the king of Perispos want to send her back on the fastest ship in his fleet?"

"Perhaps," he admitted. "But I've seen something more worrisome."

I arched a brow.

He draped his forearms over his knees and gazed at the tower's soaring height. "At first, I saw Ambrosine in a dim room." He squinted, as though struggling to recall a fading memory. "There was an enormous mirror. Hours passed, and your sister stared into it without looking away."

"That sounds highly typical."

"She spoke to it," he added.

"To herself, you mean?"

"She replied to unuttered questions and laughed at silence. It was as though someone was there, but I couldn't see or hear anyone. I think you should go to Perispos."

"You expect me to neglect my crushing list of responsibilities to journey to a place beyond my materializing range because my elder sister won't stop admiring herself in the mirror? She can do it forever for all I care. At least she's not making anyone else's life miserable like she was before."

"I know it sounds trivial, but it *felt* sinister."

"Weren't you just saying a few weeks ago that your visions have been showing you several conflicting possibilities instead of one imminent future?"

He nodded. "But it didn't start then. I haven't told Valory, but it started when she embraced the full power of the Water."

"I don't understand."

"She's a dynamic, unpredictable force in the world. It's as if no future is set in stone."

"You think she's that powerful?"

"Don't change the subject. My visions may be more confusing than ever, but I know without a doubt this one about Ambrosine was a warning."

I worried my lip. We had restricted Ambrosine's use of magic to a brief list of approved spells and enchantments. She could brighten her elicrin stone to see in the dark, test her food and drink for poison, shield herself if someone tried to hurt her. The enchantment we placed on her stone before she departed would alert us if she tried to use it for anything else.

"Could she defy her probation?" I asked. "Without using unsanctioned magic to remove the restrictions?"

"You mean...without using dark elicromancy?" Mercer asked. "Do you think she *would*?"

"Devorian has already shown a proclivity for forbidden magic. My siblings and I are 'contumacious and curious,' as our governess used to say. I wouldn't be shocked if Ambrosine had found a way to break her probation."

"I don't know." He pursed his lips. "I wish I could tell you more. My visions don't always—"

"Yes, I know, they're minimally helpful, quite persnickety, and getting worse every day."

Mercer grunted out a laugh. "Fair. Do you trust me enough to go merely because I've asked?"

I slid a skeptical glance his way, pretending to consider, before rolling my eyes in resignation. "Yes. Why can't I use Valory's portal box?"

"She hasn't returned from answering that mysterious call for help. She's so confident now that she just...left last week without telling me where she was going. I'm beginning to worry."

"Worry? About Valory Braiosa?" I asked.

"Believe it or not," he admitted.

"She'll be back soon. And meanwhile, when I get seasick, I'll be thinking of you."

"As long as I've appeased my visions," he said, rising to his feet.

"What about the Realm Alliance meeting?" I asked, pushing myself up after him.

"Send Devorian in your place. He's wised up since he wreaked havoc on the realm."

"But I may need him as a translator. My Perispi is stale."

"You've bragged before that your Perispi is impeccable."

I scowled.

"Are you that desperate for a reason not to go?".

"You know what happened there, don't you?" I asked, my voice a little hoarse. "My parents?"

Mercer nodded solemnly. His broad hands rested on my shoulders. "But King Myron executed the murderers. He promised that Perispos would leave its superstitions about elicromancers in the past. Isn't that why he wanted to marry you or Ambrosine? To symbolize that his kingdom no longer held any prejudice against our kind?"

"Yes, but we haven't exactly sent our best." I kneaded my temples. Just a moment ago, I'd longed to flee far from the palace in Pontaval, but now I only wanted to return to my bed and sink into it like a sugar cube melting in warm tea. "What if I find that Ambrosine has somehow worked around her probation? Isn't it better if Valory goes when she's back, to confiscate Ambrosine's elicrin stone if needed?"

"You agreed—we all did—that Valory should wield her power over others as seldom as possible," Mercer said, dropping his warm hands from my shoulders. "If she goes to Perispos, it will provoke unease and alarm. If you go, it will look like nothing more than an overdue family visit."

"I suppose I could bring Perennia with me to ease the tension. Ambrosine adores her as much as I do." I crossed my arms and turned a flat expression to the snowy mountain spines snaking off into the distance. "Perhaps a voyage will cool my people's anger—as long as they don't think I'm absconding."

A dimple hollowed out in his right cheek. "You, running away from a fight? Never."

I gave him a wry smile. "I'll throttle you if you've sent me to Perispos over nothing. Give my best to the others."

"Stay safe."

In a whisper of wind, Mercer was gone.

The solitude was less alluring than it had seemed moments ago, and the enduring tower a great deal more ominous.

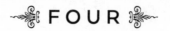
GLISETTE
PONTAVAL, VOLARRE

THE next morning the courtyard was almost shockingly quiet. When I'd returned, Hubert reported that the riot had been "handled." Out of fear of what that meant, I posed no further questions.

But now, as the soles of my silk slippers whispered across the stones, I wondered what might have happened to the boy who had been yanked from his perch by one of my armed defenders.

"My father enjoyed traveling to Perispos before he lost his ships in the wave," Larabelle said, cradling a hefty tome as she and Devorian waited to see us off. "He used to bring gifts like black truffles and olives and beautiful paintings. They were such treats for my sisters and me."

I had tasted black truffles and olives brought from Perispos, and I cared for neither, nor did I much care for the muted, dusky color palettes of the paintings my parents had received as gifts from Perispi nobles. But Larabelle was only hoping to put me in a sunnier mood about the impending journey, so I offered her a smile. "We'll be sure to bring you some."

Larabelle blushed and offered me the book. "I found this in the library. It's about the Agrimas religion. Devorian said you stopped your Perispi language and culture lessons after your parents died. I thought you might want to brush up."

"Lovely," I said, accepting the gift and staggering a little with the weight of it. "I *so* enjoy reading about how elicromancers were spawned by an evil deity."

"Clever as she is, Glisette never learned the words 'thank you,'" Devorian said derisively. His soft waves were bound with a bit of blue fabric, and he looked so much like Father—except that Father was never derisive.

"Is that why some of them hate us?" Perennia asked. "They think we spawned from an evil being?"

"Only a few zealots still believe that," Devorian explained. "Most are very accepting. One of my former lady callers"—he paused to glance down at Larabelle, who gave him a charitable half smile—"said that her family was more devout than most, but even they viewed Agrimas as more of a tradition than religion. Not to say they were completely without prejudice; she said imagining their disapproval of me made our tryst all the more thrilling."

"Is that necessary to your point?" I demanded. Devorian's magical gift of omnilingualism had made it easier for him to sample faraway places without leaving his den of debauchery. I'd always known how he busied himself in the nearby abandoned palace before Valory cursed him with a beastly form, but I didn't want to hear the particulars.

"I'm merely saying you'll be welcomed warmly, and everything will be fine," Devorian said, tugging on one of Perennia's curls. "And don't let Glissy fool you. Perispi language and culture used to be her favorite subject. I once caught her reading a book about Agrimas that hadn't even been translated into Nisseran."

"I was fascinated by how gullible people can be," I explained.

"Their simplistic creed of virtues and vices sounded like a tale to make children behave."

"We should be going," Perennia said, squinting at the sun. "We don't want to miss launch."

I sighed and looked at Devorian. "Use the hand mirror locked in Father's desk to tell Ambrosine we're coming, but be sure to put it back. I want her eyes and ears nowhere near state business."

"Of course," Devorian said, understanding the need to be careful. Ambrosine could still access any mirrors she had enchanted. She had taken one with her to communicate with us, and we had destroyed all but one here. We rarely used it.

Perennia and I passed through the open courtyard gates. We would materialize to the eastern shore and board a ship to Perispos. Mortals thought materializing solved every inconvenience, but materializing great distances to unfamiliar lands was too dangerous to attempt. If we found ourselves in the middle of the ocean and somehow lost our elicrin stones in the commotion, we would be stranded.

Oliva shuffled forward to hand off our velvet-coated suitcases. We kissed Devorian and Larabelle farewell and materialized to a predetermined location, atop a green hill overlooking the eastern port city of Eriewal.

The sun burst through dramatic clouds and the distant gray sea swayed, smacking the rocky bases of the rolling hills. Salty air was sharp in my nostrils.

"Why in the world would I want to lug this monstrous thing around?" I asked, shifting the weight of the book to retain a tenuous hold on my suitcase. "It'll sink our ship straight to the seabed."

"You're such a sorehead this morning!" Perennia extracted the book from my grip as though it were a living thing I had mistreated.

Someone cleared his throat behind us. We turned to find four royal guards bowing their heads. Hubert had arranged our travel accommodations via magical missives, and he must have asked for local escorts. I scowled as one relieved me of my light burden. I then started along the uneven path winding downhill to the dock market. Perennia and the guards followed.

Our ship was called the *Soaring Heart*, and from here I could see the majestic vessel rocking gently in the bay, its mighty masts jutting toward the clouds. As we walked through the market toward the docking slip where a ferry waited to bear us hence, subjects recognized us and stepped aside, presenting bows and curtsies. The aroma of brined fish and the whining of a fiddle plucked at my nerves.

We passed a shop selling wood paintings of me and my siblings, inferior likenesses of the official portraits displayed in the great hall back home, which the mediocre artist must have had occasion to study. If I had known back then that I would be queen someday, I would have worn something more subdued and austere than the circlet of pearls and layered lilac gown.

But I didn't have much time to regret past wardrobe choices. Something hot and wet struck me across the jaw.

I used my fingers to scrape away what appeared to be meat pie filling and pastry crust. Gasps sliced through the sudden silence. Two of my escorts hedged in around me, tense and tall and suffocating, so I could not see where the next pie came from, only where it exploded: on the face of my portrait hanging in the shop doorway.

The other two escorts shoved through the crowd and grabbed the perpetrator—a middle-aged woman with a tired face and the sinewy arms of a hard worker. She held her chin high as they dragged her toward me.

"That's for the children who starved because of you and your family," she spat.

Indignation, embarrassment, animus boiled in my blood. *Slap her face*, a vicious voice inside me said. *Toss her in prison or lock her in the pillory.*

But with a pang of shame, I thought of the young boy who had thrown the rock at the window, the way my guards had rushed to defend me, no questions asked. They would slay this woman on the spot if I commanded it.

It was a power I was duty-bound to wield with compassion.

But that didn't mean I had to roll over like a submissive dog.

I slid my thumb down my cheek, gathering warm filling that smelled of black pepper and cloves, which I made a show of sucking off while staring at the woman. My guards each sported one rapier and one dagger, and I reached for the nearest one's dagger, sliding it from the scabbard engraved with our kingdom's lily crest.

The people in the crowd gasped again. Perennia uttered my name in a cautious tone. Since I'd pulled the blade out facing down, I twirled the weapon's handle over my fingers to deftly reverse the grip, something I'd casually practiced but wasn't sure I could do without flubbing it until that very moment. I took one step, then another, until I towered over the insolent woman, who appeared more ill at ease with every beat that passed.

But I didn't press the blade's edge to her throat as my pride desired, nor did I take it to one of her knobby fingers, greasy from the pies, as Uncle Mathis might have done. Instead, I turned and strode back toward the portrait of me, smeared with oozing filling, and dragged the blade over the wood and cheap paint until a gash marred one eye.

When that was done, I lightly tossed it back to my guard. He caught it by the handle, sheathing it along with the brief flicker of surprise that crossed his face. The crowd gave me a wide berth as I walked away.

On the ferry, Perennia sat silent and tense at my side. After we reached the merchant ship and strode up the gangplank, crew-members waved us past the captain's cabin to the private guest cabin. It was installed with a desk, a dining table, and a curtained bed tucked into an alcove. Six windows curved with the shape of the ship's stern, looking out on the gyrating sea.

I sighed and dropped my belongings beside the bed, eager to access the cruet of brandy on the dining table. Perennia sank onto the mattress and hugged Larabelle's book to her chest, staring at me.

"What?" I asked as I splashed brandy into a pear-shaped crystal goblet. "Did you think I was going to execute her?"

"No," Perennia muttered. But I wasn't convinced. She pried open the dense book and began to read. I took a few swigs and looked outside again, thinking how long a fortnight would feel undulating over an endless sea.

"That's interesting," Perennia mused after what seemed a long while.

When she didn't elaborate, I indulged her. "What?"

"In Perispos, they build edifices to honor both the good and evil deities, whom they call the Holies and the Fallen. The Holy edifices are on top of hills and the Fallen edifices are underground."

"Yes, I've heard. Quite fascinating."

"The Holy edifices are for praise and prayer, but the Fallen edifices are for self-reflection," she explained, disregarding my sarcasm. "The former feature murals depicting joy and redemption, and the latter, suffering and carnage."

"And elicromancers spawning from demons, I suppose?"

Perennia frowned. "Why are you acting this way?"

"Why aren't you? This nonsense inspired those zealots to kill our parents." My tone had gone so cold so as to become brittle, and it broke over the last two words.

My younger sister furrowed her fair brow. "Just because some believers interpret the holy text that way doesn't mean the whole religion is worthy of ridicule."

I plunked down my goblet, already feeling the warmth of the spirit settle in my chest. "You are more forgiving than I am. I've no curiosity about their edifices or their deities. I only want to make sure Ambrosine hasn't set her new kingdom on a course for disaster. And then I want to go home."

"Home, where everything is going so well?" Perennia asked.

I wanted to bristle at the irony in her tone, yet I knew she wasn't using it to wound, as my other siblings and I often did. She watched sadness clear the bitterness from my expression. She stood.

"Don't," I said from across the cabin, splaying a hand to stop her from using her Solacer power to relieve me of my taxing emotions. "I don't need you to take this away."

She set her brow in determination, but merely strode to the dining table and sloshed brandy into another crystal goblet. "When Father was troubled, I used to hear Mother tell him this: 'It's easy to find fault with whoever wears the crown, but harder to wear it.' You've taken on a role that has never been easy for anyone, Glisette. And it will be even more difficult if you let your prejudices stand in the way of ruling justly. Mother and Father wouldn't have wanted us to judge an entire religion based on the actions of a few." She raised her goblet of amber liquid. "To finding your stride as a benevolent queen."

I clinked my crystal against hers and swallowed the rest of my serving. Perennia took a sip and grimaced in disgust. "How do you drink that, and so early in the morning?"

I smiled a little as she forced herself to drain her serving, finishing it off with a gag. She crossed back to the bed and settled in to read while I stared at the rising sun sparkling over the waters.

At last I heard the distant hollers of crewmembers and felt the boat gently shift. "I think we're leaving," I said, but turned to find Perennia asleep sitting up, the book sprawled on the coverlet beside her. The brandy must have gone to her head.

I tented my fingers against my smile for a moment, hoping to hide it should she notice me staring tenderly at her. But she didn't awaken. I padded toward her, shedding my lightweight spring mantle to spread over her shoulders.

As I pulled away, an illustration within the book caught my eye. It was a crude relief printing depicting miserable humans writhing in darkness, their mouths open wide with tormented screams I could almost hear. In the background stood four shadowy figures.

It took a few beats for what I'd learned in lessons to return, sloshing a little with the brandy. I didn't even need to squint and read the script at the foot of the illustration that provided the names for each Fallen deity. I remembered.

The first was *Themera*, meaning Cruelty. She wore a crown of knives. The second was *Silimos*, or Apathy. A thin veil covered her emaciated form. The third went by the name *Robivoros*, or Depravity. Teeth grew from unnatural places all over his sinewy body. And the fourth was called *Nexantius*, or Vainglory. His flesh sparkled like diamonds, but his face was featureless, a reflective mask.

My gaze traced the final masculine silhouette. Nexantius, the Fallen of Vainglory, was the one who was believed to have spawned elicromancers. He was, in their view, our creator. That was how the Perispis viewed us: superior, mighty, boastful, conceited.

And Ambrosine would do absolutely nothing to convince them otherwise.

It was hard to swallow around a growing lump of regret. I had been so ready to rid Pontaval of my sister's overbearing presence. I knew she might try to bleed the king dry with her love of fine things, but I hadn't pondered how her moral shortcomings might undo Perispos' acceptance of our kind.

I snapped the book shut and determined not to think of Fallen deities.

I didn't know much about sea travel or navigation, but I could feel the pull of the wind's might, our vessel resisting the north-easterly blasts that tried to push us off course.

Slipping out the door of our cabin, I made my way up to the quarterdeck, past sailors tugging and tying ropes, to where the stocky young captain stood stiffly at the ship's wheel. He bowed his head as I joined him, and I returned the gesture.

Hooking a hand on the railing to keep my balance, I turned away from Volarre's green shores to the rising sun.

"Admiring the view, Your Majesty?" the captain asked.

"Something like that," I said, and released the railing to splay my palms at my sides. I could feel the power stirring in the depths of the elicrin stone resting against my sternum. My breaths and the wild winds became one, together, the same, and the air grew bitter and chilling.

The captain shivered as my icy gale swept over us, driving into the sails until they swelled, until we were gliding easily and speedily downwind. The icy wind laced over my scalp. My golden hair blinded me as it thrashed like the Volarian flags fixed to the masts.

When the wind fell still, the sailors stared at me, huddling into their coats. I heaved out one last sigh. When I turned, we could no longer see Volarre's shores in the distance.

"Fetch me if you need further assistance," I said, and strode back to the passage leading belowdecks.

❦ FIVE ❦

KADRI
BEYRIAN, YORTH

AN hour before the other Realm Alliance leaders would arrive, I donned a leaf-green skirt with a matching midriff-baring bodice and bundled my black hair into a high knot. I set my emerald-studded crown on my head and felt silly somehow, like a child playing dress-up—or maybe that feeling resulted from the elicrin stone hiding beneath my collar.

I descended to the veranda and surveyed the table set for seven. A bittersweet mood swept over me. On the one hand, the lingering sense of victory was empowering. We had survived. We had conquered. We had begun rebuilding.

On the other, the road to recovery seemed littered with stumbling blocks.

I realized I was gripping the back of a chair so tightly that my palms had begun to sweat. Releasing it, I turned to cross back through the banquet hall so I could greet the guests as they arrived.

But I halted after only one step, my heart bobbing into my throat like a buoy that had been shoved underwater.

A guest I did not expect stood before me like an apparition, escorted by the head maid, whose mouth hung ajar as she took in the fay's willowy form and tapered ears.

"Rynna," I breathed.

She looked different. Instead of sage green, her eyes gleamed deep lavender blue, reminding me of my secret stone. Rather than fawn colored and traced with green veins, as I recalled in my fond imaginings, her skin shone golden. Freckles splashed across her nose and cheeks, matching the rich tawny of her hair. Straying far from her forest home seemed to have caused her adaptive features to undergo their seasonal change from spring to summer early.

"I'm sorry to come unannounced—" she started, but I rounded the table and trapped her in my arms, shaking with disbelief. She laughed near my ear and returned the embrace. "I hoped you would be glad to see me."

"What are you doing here?" I asked, putting enough distance between us to peer at her face, but not enough to lose the fragrance of sunshine on grass and heady tree sap. She smelled like Wenryn.

"I have business to bring before the Realm Alliance."

"What sort?" I asked, surprised that she would want anything to do with the Realm Alliance. The ancient fay lived in seclusion and secrecy. I hadn't even known they still existed until they sought out our small troupe in the forest.

"The urgent sort," she answered. "And when I share it, we'll be able to talk of nothing else. So, why don't you show me the shore and tell me how queenship is treating you while we wait for the others to arrive?"

I resisted the urge to interrogate her, seeing as these moments might be the only pleasant ones we shared.

"I'll set another place," the head maid said before ducking her head and scurrying away. With a crooked smile, I recalled how unsettling our group had found the presence of the ancient fairies at first. They had seemed almost menacing, but quickly proved to be true allies. I would have died were it not for their healing nectar. And without Rynna and Theslyn's help storming Darmeska, Valory might never have reached the Moth King's towering lair.

I pivoted to link arms with Rynna, who stood a palm's length taller than me, and steered her toward the stairs that would deposit us on the beach.

"How *is* queenship treating you?" Rynna asked, sending a sideways smile my direction. Her wardrobe was a bit peculiar. She wore a typical loose-knit green garment and boots, but she also sported unseasonable cloth gloves.

"It's..." I thought of the letter hiding in my jewelry case, the magical stone reposing under the hollow of my throat. "Complicated."

"You always knew it would be."

"Yes," I admitted. Out of habit, I clung to the broad balustrade and kicked off my sandals when we reached the last few stairs, which high tides had eroded and discolored. I sauntered to the water's edge, letting the evening tide brush over my toes. To the ankle was as deep as I ever dared go. Thinking of creatures residing in the murk of the ocean gave me gooseflesh. I had learned of the existence of the sea folk—and monsters of the deep that even they feared—and now there was no returning to blissful ignorance.

Rynna removed her left glove to grasp a handful of sand, letting it slide through her fingers.

I had dreamed of our reunion every day. I had rehearsed the

encounter again and again, fantasizing of losing myself deep in the forest, believing she would find me even if I couldn't find her. But I hadn't expected her to come to the palace at Beyrian and didn't quite know how to conduct myself.

"Isn't it marvelous?" I asked, gesturing at the view as though she were a visiting diplomat whom I was meant to regale with prosaic chatter.

She swung her gaze back to me and tilted her head in unabashed admiration. "It is something to behold."

My knees went feeble. Unable to resist, I paced back to her, laced my fingers through hers, and tugged her into the shade alongside the staircase where no guards or meddlesome maids could see us. There, needing no further encouragement, she splayed her gloved hand along my bare side and stroked my bottom lip with her opposite thumb. Her mouth closed over mine, light as the brush of a bird's wing at first. My lips hungrily responded, and soon her lithe body pressed flush against mine while I grasped a silky handful of her hair.

"I missed you," I whispered against her lips.

"And I missed you, my mortal dear." She played with a strand of raven hair that had fallen from its knot. "But you're not so mortal now, are you?"

"How did you know?" I asked, releasing her to press two fingers against the stone hiding under the loose fabric of my bodice. "Is it so obvious?"

"I sensed it. Was it a gift from the all-powerful queen of Calgoran?"

"Yes. One I might be ashamed of accepting, even if it means I'll get to live a long time like you."

Rynna gave a melancholy half smile. "Even elicromancer lives are short compared to ours. They kill one another off or grow tired after a century or two."

"I may not keep it that long," I sighed. "I'm not sure the Realm Alliance can afford more controversy."

"What's the matter?" she asked.

"Our foreign allies don't want to associate with a realm whose most powerful citizens can bring plague and devastation on a whim. Nissera is recovering the best we can, but the ruler of my home country is inventing excuses to sever diplomatic ties. If he learns that Valory is giving out elicrin stones to mortals, he will have even more reason to."

A voice carried from the veranda, soaring above the whisper of the waves. "Kadri!" Fabian called. "They're here!"

"Coming!" I called back, and pressed my lips to Rynna's for one last, long gratifying kiss. "We'll have more time together after dinner," I said, kicking up sand as I returned to the foot of the stairs and wriggled back into my sandals.

"I'm not certain we will," she said.

"What's wrong?" I asked.

She removed her remaining glove. A textured gray crust coated the back of her hand. Peering closer, I noticed that it looked similar to the leafy lichen I'd seen sprouting from tree trunks in the woods.

But this seemed to be affixed to her flesh, or even...growing from it.

"There's something dark where the Water used to lie," she said gravely. "Something has taken its place, and it's destroying the forest. It's destroying *us*."

She scratched at the base of the thumb where the growth met bare skin. She plucked away a tiny leaf, but grayish-red blood bubbled up in its place. I gasped. By the set of her jaw, I could see it was painful.

"That's what happens when we try to remove it," she said, answering my unspoken question. "A few have bled to death trying."

I stared, too horrified to say anything. The ancient fay were supposed to be untouchable, sheltered from the problems that rattled the rest of Nissera. "What could it be?" I finally managed. "A remnant of the Moth King's power? A disease? A curse?"

"We don't know. But it's made Wenryn uninhabitable," she explained, forcing her voice to remain even as she slid both gloves back on. "Our fruits and grains spoil before we can eat them. We can't sit idle for even a moment; the growths only spread faster. Those of us who were able to departed from Wenryn, but Malyrra was too weak. She stayed behind. Theslyn is leading the others to safety."

"What about the nectar?" I asked, sorrow crushing my chest at the thought of Wenryn being invaded, changing and darkening. "It healed me from the blight disease."

"It's soured," she said. "I hope you elicromancers are able to stop this. We can't seem to."

The way she so casually counted me among the elicromancers struck fear into my heart. This wouldn't be like the journey north, when I followed along and fought when necessary. No, I was a leader now. Ridding the forest of this foul intrusion would be as much my responsibility as everyone else's.

"You came to our aid when we needed you." I took her gloved hand in mine. "The Realm Alliance will help save Wenryn and your people."

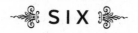

SIX

KADRI

BUT the Realm Alliance was short two of its members today. There were so few of us to begin with that the absence of both Glisette and Valory made the pit of fear inside me yawn wider. Something felt *off*.

Glisette had departed for Perispos, dispatching her brother to the meeting in her place. After several days, Valory hadn't returned from answering the distress call that even Mercer knew nothing about.

It was nearly impossible to muster concern for Valory's safety now that she was so powerful. If anything, I was irritated by her ill-timed absence. She did have a prophetical lover in Mercer, after all, and should have known this meeting would be important. And even though she couldn't materialize, she could use the portal box King Tiernan had given her to arrive just as swiftly.

Her truancy left six of us, seven including Rynna, scattered along the first row of seats in the meeting chamber overlooking Beyrian Bay: Mercer; his brother, Tilmorn; Fabian; Devorian; Valory's cousin Melkior; and me.

The other tiers of benches rising from the circular center of the room remained empty. The rest of the former Realm Alliance, those who had not been murdered by the Moth King, had fled back to their towns or countries of origin.

Even Rayed had left. Erdem had given him no choice.

Eventually, we would need to invite more leaders back into the fold: mortals, nonroyals, foreign diplomats, and advisors with governing experience. Yet the hidden rifts and deep-rooted deceit in the former Realm Alliance, which the Moth King had gleefully exploited, gave us pause. Our new administration was too new, too fragile to make the mistake of allowing an untrustworthy person into our ranks.

While Rynna explained the plight of her people, I studied my comrades' faces. Mercer was a tense shadow perched on the seat nearest the wall of windows, the setting sun skimming the top of his tousled dark-blond hair. Next to him, Tilmorn cut a similar, but bulkier, outline. They both absently stroked their chins, and though I had to squint against the light, I found identical consternation carved into their foreheads. Surely, *surely*, one of these elicromancers would recall something pertinent from their dense elicrin history books. Surely one of them would recognize the growth on Rynna's hand as an obscure curse that could be broken, or a matter of magical botany with an antidote—perhaps a potion brewed during a full moon and boiled with the bones of an enemy, or some other archaic elicrin nonsense. But they remained silent.

I toyed with my bangles as Rynna concluded, "It has not worsened since I left the rotting area of the woods. But the rate at which the ruin has taken over our forest troubles me. We already lost the northern stretch to the Moth King's fires. We can't allow this to invade what remains."

"We should have anticipated this," Mercer said grimly. "Whenever deep magic is eradicated, it leaves a gap, a hollow place of power. It presents an opportunity for another supernatural force to establish dominion. It's just like—"

"Otilien's Shrine," Tilmorn finished, exchanging a look with his brother.

"It's an old story from our region in the mountains," Mercer explained to the rest of us, "about a warrior who defended his village from invaders. After he died, the village built a shrine to honor him, a statue that wore his armor and stood over his grave. Before the dry season or on the eve of battle, the villagers would spit on his helm and polish it for luck. They prospered for decades. But when Otilien's son was preparing to die of old age, he asked to be buried in his father's armor. The villagers reluctantly honored his last wishes. The very night of the son's funeral, a storm destroyed their crops. Lightning struck Otilien's shrine. It cracked the sepulchre and toppled the statue. The villagers dug up the armor, but it had lost its power. Season after season, the land refused to yield. Outsiders pillaged until nothing was left. The villagers believed their home was cursed and eventually abandoned it. It's one of many stories our elders told to teach us not to disturb powerful magic."

"So you're saying that when Valory accidentally dried up the Water, she left an empty space that would inevitably be filled?" I asked.

"Yes. By something more sinister," Mercer clarified. "By the laws of magic, a broken blessing becomes a curse."

"More sinister than a pool that kills someone if they aren't magical enough?" I scoffed.

"How do you know its point of origin is the Water pit?" Melkior asked, training his regrettably rodent-like eyes on Rynna. He tapped his knee with a removed expression while he spoke. There was something squirmy about Melkior, but if Valory trusted him, then I did too. The alliances in this room had been forged in fire and were iron-strong.

"Theslyn saw it there before it spread," Rynna replied. He encountered the pit not far from our dwelling. It used to lie in the burnt stretch of forest, but it's moved closer."

"At least *that* is not abnormal," Melkior said. "The Water has always moved to protect itself, to remain secret."

"I think, this time, it moved so it would have life to feed on," Rynna replied. "Whatever inhabits the pit now couldn't flourish surrounded by scorched earth."

"So, what do we do?" Fabian asked.

"We should help Wenryn's people first and then try to stop the invasion of their lands," I said. "Can you heal her, Tilmorn?"

After the Moth King's fall, Valory had taken Tilmorn's elicrin gift and given him Melkior's, changing Tilmorn from Purveyor to Healer. In turn, she had stripped Knox Rodenia of his gift and made Melkior an Empath in his stead. Unfortunately, the Moth King had targeted the Healers in Nissera so that the blight plague could run rampant. As far as we knew, Tilmorn was the sole remaining elicrin Healer, a demanding role that Melkior was relieved to turn down. So many desperate hopes rested upon Tilmorn's shoulders each day. Today, they were mine.

"Whatever this is may not submit to elicrin power," Mercer warned delicately.

But Tilmorn rose to his impressive height and strode forward. Even the lissome, tall fay looked diminutive as Tilmorn approached her and cradled her hand in his. He made a brief study of her ethereal features before blinking down at the lichen growing on her otherwise perfect flesh. Rynna watched him, head cocked, eyes radiant as violet gems splashed with starlight. A prick of envy pinched my navel. But as a bright light swirled in Tilmorn's smoke-gray elicrin stone, Rynna slid her eyes to meet mine, quirking up the corner of her mouth, and my grudging feelings subsided.

But then she cried out in agony and tore her arm free of Tilmorn's hold, collapsing to the floor. I ran to her.

She whimpered as I peeled her hand away from the afflicted flesh. "I can feel it deepening its hold," she said.

Nothing had changed that I could see, but the terror in her eyes was a dagger twisting in my gut. I had survived the blight disease. I knew how it felt to fear my own body, to sense a wrongness taking hold.

Tilmorn clenched his giant fist, staring at it as though it had betrayed him.

"What do we do?" I asked. I despised the desperation in my voice.

Mercer stood and strode to the mosaic sea serpent coiled at the center of the tiled floor. "We should materialize to the woods and study its source."

"And risk exposure to it?" I asked.

"Unless you've a better idea." Tilmorn hiked up a brow and the faint, shiny scars marring his skin caught the light.

I didn't know what to say. We didn't even bother to reach an official consensus before the boys began to gather the weapons they wore out of habit and don their spring cloaks.

Fabian's mother, Queen Jessa, had so gracefully commanded the powerful people who used to occupy this room. Yet here we were, acting on rash ideas, no strategy in sight. Glancing up at the rows of empty seats where many noble leaders once sat, I wondered whether we would ever truly fill those spaces that death had left vacant.

I wondered whether King Agmur was right to doubt our competency.

I nearly admonished Mercer and the others for being so impetuous. But this was *Rynna* at stake. And Wenryn. So I was silent.

Mercer pecked a farewell kiss on my cheek and followed Tilmorn, Devorian, and Melkior as they flung open the chamber doors. They would materialize as soon as they passed through the magical barrier, beyond the front gates that faced the city.

"Be careful!" I called after them, feeling like a young girl excluded from a rough-and-tumble boys' game. As far as they knew, I possessed no elicrin stone and could not come. Fabian brushed a kiss on my temple and followed the others, his steps confident.

When I could no longer see him retreating, I reentered the meeting chamber. Rynna stood with her back to me, looking east over the bay. I felt yanked in two directions; I wanted to stay and comfort her, bask in her presence to ease the dark fear squirming in my heart. But I also wanted to join the others and defeat this scourge through outright determination.

Huffing a decisive breath, I turned and started the journey back to my upstairs quarters, pacing past servants lighting lamps in the corridors. Rynna followed me.

"What are you doing?" she asked.

"I'm going with them. I'm going to materialize."

"Have you even learned to do that yet?"

"No." I checked to make sure my room was empty and locked the door behind Rynna. I shoved aside the beaded crimson curtain of my boudoir and yanked open the bottom drawer of my wardrobe, tossing out undergarments as I hunted for the volume of basic elicrin enchantments Valory had given me. Rynna caught a lace corset, eyeing its rigid shape with a mixture of intrigue and mistrust.

"I understand that you want to take action," she said. "But this is dangerous."

"How hard could it be?" I asked. "You say the spell and you imagine where you want to go." I hauled out the heavy book and plopped it on my desk. It exhaled a puff of dust as I began to riffle through pages of Old Nisseran spells. I had a proclivity for languages and already knew many of the spells by heart, though I'd have to ask Valory about the pronunciation of the more complicated ones.

I located the materialization spell: *aphanis od.* I'd never heard any of my friends say the spell aloud; Valory had explained that competent elicromancers could communicate with their elicrin stones using thoughts, that a stone could learn to anticipate the will of its wielder. But of course I had to memorize basic spells before I could even dream of that. Meanwhile, she had promised we would tell the others everything soon so that they could teach me to materialize.

She hadn't warned me not to try it on my own. She would never expect me to do something so rash.

I shuddered, recalling Valory's assigned Neutralizer, Brandar, who had been torn to bloody shreds by a materialization trap laid by the Moth King last year. Those who had seen him draw his last breaths could hardly bring themselves to describe his final state.

Rynna let out a shaky breath and swayed back a step, grasping for the bed frame behind her, nearly sliding off the silk coverings as she lowered herself onto the mattress.

"Rynna?" I cried, hurrying to her side. Her sun-kissed skin paled, and her violet eyes cooled in hue.

"I'm so tired," she said.

"Do you need fresh air?" I hurried to the balcony doors that opened to the warm night and the vast expanse of starlit sea. "Or hot tea? I can send for tea or dinner."

Rynna's eyelids flickered closed, and she slumped onto her side. I sat with her and tugged the knit blanket from the end of the bed up to her waist, stroking her hair and, for my own satisfaction, lightly tracing the velvety skin of her tapered ear.

"Don't try to materialize," she whispered. "Stay with me."

I weighed the risks. Of course it was silly to think I could materialize to the middle of the woods, at night no less. Sometimes I tired of being the only powerless mortal in the group—but I couldn't let my envy win out. I needed to learn elicromancy properly, patiently, as my friends had. Even Valory had continued to toil and study long after she failed to display a natural magical gift.

"I'll stay here," I promised Rynna. I looked out at the twilight, a deep dread climbing like wild ivy between my ribs. "I hope they come back soon, with answers. And in one piece. Or five pieces... you know what I mean."

Rynna chuckled at my anxious rambling. That made me smile. Though she had seen me at my most vulnerable, I hadn't seen her like this, almost childlike.

While she rested, I tried to resist glancing at her growth to see if it had spread. I hid the book again, deposited my crown in its velvet case, sent for tea and soup, and asked the cook to keep dinner warm for the others. They would be hungry when they returned.

The sustenance restored some hope and courage, but I couldn't coax Rynna to swallow a single bite. I drank fragrant tea and curled up beside her as she slept.

When would they come back? What would they discover? Why hadn't Valory resurfaced after leaving for her mysterious mission?

What if we couldn't stop the invasion of Wenryn?

What if it spread through the whole realm unchecked, like the blight disease?

My dozing mind was cruel. Nightmares hounded me: Fabian and the others returning with horrific growths, blood seeping through lichen on a rotting tree stump, the drained pit in the woods deepening until it became a bottomless abyss.

A soft knock made me jerk awake. With a light leap and a few soft steps, I answered, expecting news of the boys' return.

Falima stood outside, hands clasped and brown eyes wide. "I need to speak with you. Alone."

"Have the others returned?"

"I haven't heard any news."

I blinked away the sleep in my eyes. "What's the matter?"

Falima cast a wary glance down the hall and spoke in Erdemese. "It's about the... gift that you received."

I gaped in surprise. A typical lady's maid knew her mistress's secrets, but I thought I had managed to keep this one to myself. "You know?" I asked.

"Yes, and I'm not the only one," she whispered.

"Who?" I asked.

Falima rocked a step closer and whispered, "We shouldn't talk about it here."

"Are you worried someone will hurt you?" I clasped her elbow. "Falima, what do you know?"

She grasped my sleeve. "Please, come with me to the terrace, where we can speak alone."

With a last look at Rynna, I closed the door and followed Falima down the hall to the lounge. This was where Fabian and I ate our meals together when he was landlocked due to weather or business. Sometimes I read books or penned letters while he studied maps and newfangled nautical instruments. Occasionally, he forced himself to frown over administrative documents while I simplified their contents to tether his wandering attentions.

The lounge lamps had been extinguished, but I could easily navigate my way through the dark room to the moonlit terrace. Falima worried her small hands as we emerged in the night, the corner of her headscarf trailing in the wind.

A briny ocean breeze mingled with the spicy, clovelike scent of pink dianthus beds bordering the terrace ledges. The familiar fragrance dispossessed me of the fresh memory of Rynna's more intoxicating one, so that as I drew even with Falima I wondered whether Rynna had truly come or I had dreamed her.

"What's happening?" I demanded. Without the warm glow of

the glass lanterns that usually lit the terrace, I could see nothing but Falima's wide, fearful eyes. "Has someone threatened you? Tried to extort you? Give me their name. I'll see to it."

She hesitated. I shook her by the shoulders. "I won't let anyone hurt you. Please, tell me!"

Falima parted her lips to speak, but her eyes darted over my shoulder. I felt the warmth of another presence behind me, a breath tickling the hairs at my nape.

I whipped my head around just as a hand attempted to close over my mouth. The brief warning from Falima allowed me to push away the wrist, duck under the arm, scramble to the balustrade, and turn to face my attacker head-on.

SEVEN

KADRI

H E was a swift shadow, already covering the ground I'd put between us. Without a weapon, wearing a long skirt and sandals, I was no match for an armed fighter. The elicrin enchantments I'd studied became a snarled web of nonsensical words in my mind.

The flash of a curved blade foretold a violent death, a quick death. In despair, I closed my eyes so I wouldn't see it coming.

But the whir of steel slicing through air ended with a shrill clang, weapon against weapon. When I dared open my eyes, I found Rynna gripping an ornate display sword, which she must have dislodged from a plaque on the lounge wall. The old but well-kept blade chimed as she slid it away from the curved saber she'd blocked before it could strike me dead.

I looked at the attacker. He wore black garments that left only the upper half of his face exposed, but even that small glimpse of him chilled me to the marrow. His eyes glinted like obsidian pebbles, reflecting sharp spears of moonlight.

Rynna reeled back to take him down, but he thwarted her with ease. Falima pressed into the far corner of the balcony where the balustrade joined the palace wall.

My mind stuttered until I grasped at the memory of an elicrin spell, Old Nisseran words that would summon magic from my stone. I scrambled to pull the jewel out from my collar, glared at the attacker, and shouted, *"Matara liss!"*

The heat of supernatural power thrashed through my chest and erupted from my elicrin stone in a stream of white light. But the shaft of hungry fire I directed at the man instead split into four distinct flames and flew to the glass lanterns hanging overhead, catching them alight. My inexperience had rendered the fire enchantment harmless.

By the lanterns' glow, I caught sight of another figure in black creeping over the balustrade. A grappling iron clung to the stone lip of the flowerbed.

I swore. I was unarmed, helpless, and inept at wielding the magic I'd had to practice only in secret. I had survived worse—had held my own amid the chaos of the full-scale, bloody battle at Darmeska's gates—with my weapon of choice: the bow and arrows Rynna and Theslyn had crafted specifically for me.

Now I was empty-handed.

But another sword hung on display in the lounge. While Rynna fought the first attacker, I dashed through the open door and leapt onto a velvet chair, reaching for the sword of King Nicolas Veloxen. The emerald eye of the sea serpent hilt glittered at me as I ripped it off the wall. I burst back onto the patio and hoisted the heavy weapon high to block a strike from the newcomer that was so fierce it made my teeth rattle. I reeled back and stabbed at his middle.

I felt power muster in my elicrin stone again, and miraculously, my blade pushed through his flesh and lodged under his ribs, prying a guttural cry from his lips.

He staggered back. I yanked the sword clean, stunned by the effectiveness of my marksmanship gift.

Rynna was parrying with her opponent, and Falima still cowered in the corner behind them. Why hadn't she run to find a guard?

Rynna's opponent bared his teeth and slammed a fist into her side. She howled, and when he withdrew, I saw a row of metal spikes protruding from a four-finger ring on his knuckles. The points dripped with Rynna's blood.

I heard myself yell her name as if from a distance. The fay's sword dropped hilt-first to the stone underfoot. Blood seeped between her fingers as she swayed on her feet.

Her opponent used my horror to fling my heavy sword from my hands. I staggered back, broke a sandal strap, and fell hard on my hip. I had no option but to grasp Rynna's fallen sword by the sharp end, which I did with a yelp of pain, slicing open the creases of my fingers.

But I wasn't quick enough. The attacker's curved blade brushed my throat, rendering me motionless. I tried not to tremble as its edge skimmed upward, hugging my flesh, as delicate as a barber's razor. I dropped the bloody sword tip as the cold steel forced my chin upward and my gaze with it. He continued to drive my movement until I shifted cautiously to my knees.

"What do you want?" I asked, watching two more identically dressed shadow-men climb over the balcony. Their garb concealed their features, though I could tell their brown complexions more or less matched mine. Who were these men?

Out of the corner of my eye, I saw Rynna stumble back and lean against the wall. If she survived, the palace physician could tend to her until Tilmorn returned. Perhaps Mercer had foreseen this attack and would lead the others back from their mission to aid us. Maybe they were on their way, would arrive any second.

The man didn't reply to my question. The tip of his saber traveled down to my collarbone and snagged on the chain around my neck. He lifted the elicrin stone until it was dangling in front of my face, the point of his blade between my eyes. How had he known?

"Your scarf," the man said in Erdemese, beckoning Falima with his free hand, the spikes of his rings still wet with Rynna's blood.

Falima unwrapped her scarf with shaky hands. She surrendered it but kept her distance. Why was she still here? She could have escaped during the fight.

The chain rubbed my skin raw as the man snapped it.

He caught the elicrin stone in the scarf, staining the peach fabric with blood as he wrapped it and tucked it inside a leather pouch on his belt.

"Give this one a quick and merciful end," he said to the others with a nod toward Rynna.

"Don't touch her," I growled in my first language.

"They have to bring you to Erdem unharmed!" Falima blurted out. "You can strike a barg—"

One of the fighters hit my maid hard across the face, cutting her off.

The realization made my rage burn hotter than a forge fire: Falima had lured me into a trap. She had knocked on my door to recite lines and lead me into danger.

But my anger toward her paled in comparison to my fear for Rynna.

"I'll go willingly," I breathed. I jerked my head in Rynna's direction. "If you leave her be, I'll do whatever you ask."

"No, Kadri!" Rynna barked. Though she did not speak the language, she seemed to understand the tone of the interaction enough to realize what I was offering.

The man, who was clearly the leader, dropped his blade from my throat. "You have a deal."

I gulped in an overdue breath of relief.

"To your feet," he ordered.

Rynna struggled to straighten as well, but the leader turned his blade on her instead as a warning.

The other two men advanced toward me. Within seconds, I was bound and gagged and utterly at their mercy. One shoved me toward the balustrade.

I offered Rynna a farewell nod that I hoped would encourage her. The wound wasn't fatal. She would survive.

An arm dense with muscle reached around me to seize the rope attached to the grappling hook. With three slapdash motions, one of the men in black tangled me up and slung me over the balustrade, gripping me under one arm. He held a clamp in the other. Squeezing the release lever, he pushed off the craggy cliffside with the soles of his boots, and we soared downward until we landed upon soft sand.

He slackened the rope and I stumbled forward, tripping and falling flat. Through the sting of sand in my eyes I saw the bodies of two royal guards just paces away. Blood stained their emerald tunics.

A hard wrench of my elbow set me back on unsteady feet and

propelled me toward an oared vessel poised in shallow waters. The boat rocked as my captor pulled me aboard and sat me down. Soon after, another shoved a grim-faced Falima down beside me with such bruising force that she struck her jaw on the thwart before struggling to sit up.

The leader followed swiftly behind. "You warned her twice, the first time with your eyes," he said to Falima in a chilling tone as he sat down. The others began rowing us into deeper, darker water, undoubtedly toward a larger ship waiting in the infinite night. "You cost me one of my men. You are fortunate that King Agmur asked us to treat you both with kindness."

King Agmur.

"Ironically, the bargain you suggested did none of you any good." He raised the fist with the protruding spikes, eyeing the weapon with pride. "Venom from the eastern coilsnake."

Bile rose in my throat. Rynna had lived peacefully and quietly for hundreds of years and this was the inglorious end she would meet? Bleeding, poisoned, sick…and for me? Tears burned my eyes, but I blinked them away to glare murderously at the man across from me. He sheathed his weapon and removed the scarf hiding the lower half of his face. I took in the shadowy eyes, the black beard…and the necklace with a snake fang cast in silver.

Terror gutted me as I realized who he was: the leader of the *Jav Darhu*, the Red Fangs, infamous Erdemese mercenaries who tortured and murdered at the whim of whoever stuffed their coffers. If you owed a debt you could not repay, if you had wronged a wealthy and vindictive family, or if you had simply bedded the wrong person's spouse, there was always the possibility that the infamous Captain Ardjan Nasso and his Jav Darhu would pay you a visit.

Many immigrants who came to the embassy in Yorth had fled our home country because of the lawless mercenaries. These victims had trembled in fear standing before my father, as though wary their stalkers might leap out from behind his cluttered desk.

But as far as I knew, the Jav Darhu had never pursued a target beyond the mountainous border Erdem shared with Perispos, much less across the Mizrah Sea.

Until now.

❖ EIGHT ❖

GLISETTE
PERISPOS, TWO WEEKS LATER

OUR carriage sped past sunflower fields and vineyards bordering the road to Halithenica like the green-and-yellow patchwork squares of a nursery blanket. Spindly cypress trees peppered the rolling countryside, trailing off toward a forest in the distance. I longed to take my aching legs on a tour of the landscape, to pluck sweet grapes from their vines and wander through towering sunflower stalks.

The fortnight at sea had been mind-numbingly dull. After a few days tossing in the waves, only the occasional storm or molten red sunset had sparked any sense of wonder.

"There's the palace," Perennia said, pointing out the carriage window as the road wended. "That dome at the top is the largest Edifice of the Holies in all of Perispos. Citizens can climb the stairs and say their prayers atop the tallest summit in Halithenica."

I hunched to peer out her window and found the palace overlooking the sprawling royal city. I groaned. "Can we please just materialize? It will take us a mortal lifetime to get there."

"You want to arrive looking like the entitled elicromancers they think we are?" Perennia asked.

"I don't have the energy to fool them. I'm your queen and I order you to materialize with me."

"We're not that far." Perennia settled the matter by opening her beloved book to a page with a folded corner.

"What if Mercer is right?" I asked, looking beyond the red-tiled roofs of the city to the countless tracery windows and turreted walkways of the domed palace. "What if Ambrosine has begun to court darkness?"

Perennia closed the book. "We can pull her back from the precipice."

"Maybe you're right," I agreed. "Even if she has strayed, she is our sister."

She nodded, her flaxen curls bouncing. "We must do what we can to reason with her."

As the road dipped, the city submerged beneath a hill until only the magnificent Edifice of the Holies jutted above thick grasses awash in sunlight.

"But if for some reason you were forced to confront her..." Perennia added, to my surprise. I did not think she wanted to consider the possibility. "You would prevail."

"Why do you say that?"

"She fights only for herself. You fight for more than your own happiness. That gives you a power she cannot match."

Pride swelled in my chest. I wondered what Mother and Father would think to see me now. Before they had been murdered here in this very land, the last request I'd made of them was to bring me a pair of white leather slippers from Halithenica. Father had asked Ambrosine and me to make sure Devorian attended to his studies in their absence, and Mother asked us to confer with the head maid to oversee the domestic duties. Ambrosine had acquiesced with a saccharine smile—she loved being the most responsible in their eyes.

But I had groaned. I had recently completed my tenure at the elicromancer academy in Arna and wanted to do nothing but host celebratory parties and gossip with the daughters of favored courtiers.

"The staff shouldn't need us breathing down their necks to do their jobs, and Devorian's nearly a man," I had argued, shrugging against Father's farewell embrace. I scowled as Mother brushed a loving kiss on my cheek. "I'm no one's governess teaching them their letters."

Too often, I staved away my regret over that final farewell by dreaming that Mother and Father looked down upon us from the land of light.

But if that were true, they would see Ambrosine as well. They would know that her tendencies toward cunning and vanity had trampled her virtues. They would know she had afflicted our people with poverty and starvation. And it would break their hearts.

At last we entered the city of Halithenica, coasting under an arched stone gate with a marble relief of eight celestial figures in rippling robes. The inbound road diverted around a plaza with a fountain sculpted into the likeness of a broad-shouldered man tipping a pitcher, which gushed forth water for children to drink and splash at one another.

"That's Orico, the Holy of Generosity," Perennia explained. "His statue was placed here at the entry to make visitors feel welcome. The other seven Holies are scattered throughout the—"

I cut her a look that said I would fling her beloved book out the door.

"Sorry," she finished.

The buildings were arranged in a tight but orderly grid, and a network of bridges intersected a river meandering through the city. Many people swept bows and curtsies as we passed. Young children skipped around, tossing sunflowers into our path.

"How kind!" Perennia waved at them.

"It's a relief to be shown a bit of respect," I muttered, donning a neutral smile.

The cheerful crowd lined the streets all the way to the palace, where purple flags embroidered with the kingdom's tree symbol flapped in the breeze. Before long, guards in elegant purple livery summoned us through the gates. When I stepped out of the carriage, I looked up at a façade of clean white and glossy black stones. Spiraling columns, niches for gaudy statues, and domed towers gave the palace an outlandish grandeur.

But nothing was quite as gaudy as our sister who awaited us.

Ambrosine stood in a billowing crimson gown with two straight, solemn rows of guards branching out before her. The seams of the close-fitting bodice cut around her hips and exploded into layers of fiery skirts, with an endless train furling out behind her like a tulip petal. She wore a gold necklace so large it was nearly a mantle, and her luxurious blond waves had been smoothed into a dramatic high plait and topped by a coronet. Her lips gleamed the startling red of a fresh blood drop.

"Dear sisters!" she called, splaying her hands in greeting. She perched on the final step, and it took a few beats for me to realize she meant for us to approach her.

Perennia smiled encouragingly. Together, we crossed the

courtyard while the attendants transported our luggage. Ambrosine bent to bestow kisses near our cheeks, more sound than substance.

"I trust you received a friendly reception from my people," she said over the distant thunder of approaching hooves. She looked over our heads. "Ah! The huntsmen have returned!"

I turned to find a small band of riders accompanied by panting hounds. Braces of rabbits and fat pheasants bounced from the saddles, as well as bags of packed and quartered game meat. Three men dismounted upon entry to the courtyard and led away the hounds and horses.

But the dark-haired leader cantered onward and slung down from the saddle to approach us, his shoulders rigid. Bold brows, black as coal smudges, gave emphasis to brown eyes that skimmed over me with what felt like anger held in deep reserve. Why a stranger from a foreign land would regard me with such cold disdain, I couldn't fathom.

"What did you bring us, Severo?" Ambrosine asked gleefully.

The young man took a square stance and met her giddiness with proud stoicism. "A red hart for the upcoming Sun's Benediction festivities," he declared. "And, as you see, fowl and rabbits for tonight." He spoke in a rolling, rustic accent that revealed only an intermediate grasp on Nisseran—how I might sound trying to speak Perispi after not having lessons since my parents died. Without a trace of emotion, he added, almost too late, "My queen."

My eyes strayed to the dark blood seeping through the game bags borne by his patient horse, then moved on to the many weapons arranged on his person: a bow and quiver lashed to his back, knives of various sizes fastened at his waist and thighs. He sported a weatherworn leather jerkin, and as he casually gripped the hilt of his hunting knife, I noticed rough calluses on his hands and dried blood under his fingernails. Back home, noblemen did their own hunting as a matter of sport and status while their servants performed the dirty work of field dressing their kills, but perhaps the lords of Perispos hired commoners to do both.

"I would expect nothing less of the royal huntsman," Ambrosine replied in an oily tone, as though she loved nothing more than lavishing praise upon this handsome yet prickly fellow. He stalked away to untether the bloody packs, saying nothing more.

"Where is King Myron?" I asked Ambrosine.

"And the princess?" Perennia couldn't bring herself to say "your stepdaughter." Judging by her recent conduct, Ambrosine was in no condition to care for anyone other than herself. But surely Princess Navara did not require my sister's care anyway, not with her flocks of maids and tutors. From her perspective, Ambrosine was probably nothing but a porcelain figurine making frivolous, featherbrained demands from the king's side.

"Regrettably, my husband is ill with digestive woes today," Ambrosine answered. "But you'll meet the sweet little girl at dinner."

She lifted a finger wearing a gold filigree claw-tip ring and used it to stroke the scar that sliced down my cheek. She executed every movement with a strange self-awareness, as though she were sitting for a portrait and experimenting with gestures to find the most flattering pose. I resisted the urge to swerve from her cool touch.

When she dropped her arm and straightened, I realized that she still had not dismounted the final stair. My instincts screamed a refusal to allow her to tower over me; I joined her at her level. With a tight smile, she immediately turned and ascended.

"I've spared no expense arranging your accommodations," she said as we followed her indoors, chaperoned by two guards and two servants. "And my court will feast tonight in your honor."

Perennia gasped as we entered the foyer. A richly colored mural sprawled across the domed ceiling. Shades of saturated purple created a velvety backdrop for countless stars that seemed to sparkle in the soft beams from the high windows. "The Eight Holies," Perennia said, twirling in place to study the ring of divine figures in golden robes. "This is breathtaking work."

"Come, come!" Ambrosine said without looking up, ascending another set of black and white stairs, this one leading to a long hall of mirrors. Gilt moldings scrolled along the white walls and framed the silver glass panels. Mirror mosaics covered the arched ceiling like diamonds. "When I arrived, the palace sorely needed renovating. So many faded frescoes and chipped sculptures. This area, at least, has been much improved. Myron and I have been bickering over the foyer."

"Were these your personal touches?" I asked, gesturing at a mirror and meeting eyes with my reflection. I looked even more ill at ease than I felt.

"Yes. They bring in more light than the drab paintings that had hung here before. You would have hated them, Glisette. So many bleak colors and morose deities no one in Perispos prays to anymore."

From the long corridor branched many others, and though I stole only glimpses of them, I realized all were lined with mirrors. My head whirled as my eyes tried to make sense of their optical tricks.

"Your people know about your gift for mirror manipulation," I said cautiously. "Might this intimidate them?"

In a flurry of untamed skirts, Ambrosine stopped short. The servants and guards halted several steps behind us, their expressions blank. "Why would it intimidate them? I'm their sovereign. I care for them. My power is their power."

"Which I hope you've not found a way to use," I said in a careful tone. "Considering it would take dark elicromancy to break the restriction we imposed."

"I haven't," Ambrosine said, jutting her chin in defiance. "I wouldn't want to cross the Empress of Elicromancy who presides over us all."

"Valory?" I chuckled. "Don't let her ego hear that."

"It's hardly a joke." Ambrosine clasped her hands and stepped back toward me, her gaze sharp and bright. Out of the corners of my eyes, I found fragmented reflections of us staring each other down. "Valory could destroy us all with the flutter of an eyelash. How do you sleep at night?"

"I trust her. She loves Nissera and its people."

"But you don't trust me." Ambrosine arched a brow, challenging me. "That's why you're here."

"You're right," I said, my features icing over. "It is."

"*I'm* here to visit with my sisters," Perennia insisted. She stepped between us and took each of our hands. "We haven't been together in months, and you two are already fighting."

"Oh, Perennia, dear . . ." Ambrosine's tight, angry smile returned, more of a sneer this time, exposing a glint of teeth as she held my gaze. "You'll know a fight when you see it."

I sensed the presence of a baleful power, like sudden storm clouds slithering over a crystal summer sky. In the corner of my eye, Ambrosine's mirrored face looked more sinister than taunting, its shadows deep and alive, racing off into an infinity of reflections. I feared that if I turned to face the image, I would be frightened by what I saw.

"You were showing us to our rooms," I reminded her, escaping Perennia's grip to contain the shudder I could not allow either of them to notice.

Ambrosine patted Perennia's hand. "Yes. You will be impressed."

In strained silence, we continued down mirrored corridors, past servants who swept such obsequious bows that their noses nearly brushed the floor. My lip curled in disgust. We had banished Ambrosine to a foreign kingdom to quell her sense of entitlement, to make her feel small and force her to start over. Yes, she had wed into privilege and power, which was more than she deserved, but I thought she would be kept in check. King Myron loved his country and many of its traditions. Why hadn't he resisted my sister's imperious charm?

"I'll leave you to rest and tidy yourselves for dinner," Ambrosine said, clasping her hands again—the sanctimonious gesture of a gracious host who had been slighted. "I do hope everything is to your liking."

With that, she swept away. Her guards followed. One of the servants opened the door and stepped aside for us to enter.

First, I noticed the view of the back façade of the palace. Broad windows overlooked a sun-drenched hillside and a gradual staircase leading up to the Edifice of the Holies. Dozens of acolytes, mostly elderly and hobbling, some aided by younger hands, made their ascending pilgrimage.

When I turned my focus to our quarters, the servants had already deposited our baggage and left us. I found an abundance of boxes with white ribbons.

"Look," Perennia said, lifting a box of pastries from the night table. "Your favorite."

"Rose-pear tartlets," I said with surprise. I picked another package and untied the ribbon. A lace-embellished yellow ball gown moved like liquid through my fingers. "For you, I suppose," I said. "Your favorite color."

"And for you." Perennia held up a subdued blush-pink gown with brighter pink fabric lilies cascading down its train. She draped it over her forearm and opened another tiny box. "Oh! A figurine of Eulippa. These are sort of like charms. They're supposed to help you exhibit the Holy virtues they represent. This one is Lovingkindness."

Disinterested in her trinket, I opened the lid of a box on the bed and nearly gasped. "Beaded white leather shoes."

I couldn't bring myself to reminisce aloud about the final request I'd made of Mother and Father, but Perennia was well aware of the symbolic gesture. "Is she taunting me?" I asked.

"You are relentless," Perennia groaned. "Ambrosine is flawed, but this demonstrates thoughtfulness. She's not so broken that she cannot be mended."

"A few gifts can't undo what she's done—"

"I'm not saying they can, Glisette! But neither will your derision and suspicion." She thrust the pink gown on the bed and tossed the cast-iron Eulippa figurine on top of it. "Take that. I think you need it more than I."

My younger sister scooped up her new yellow gown, marched to the lavatory, and slammed the door.

NINE

GLISETTE

SUNSET seeped across the sky like spilled wine.

A silent maid finished fastening the hooks along the back of my bodice with deft fingers. I faced the mirror to find a ludicrously billowy gown that belonged on a doll rather than a young woman. The flowery neckline cut too high for my liking, so high I could have inhaled fabric petals with one sharply drawn breath. My own face glared at me, scarred and grim and utterly at odds with the juvenile garment.

"Oh, Ambrosine," I grumbled, smoothing down the voluminous sleeves to no avail. But the idea of Ambrosine giving me a gift, even one I despised, made my chest cramp with remorse.

I shuffled to retrieve the figurine that had lain facedown on the bed since I'd yanked the gown out from under it. It was no bigger than a fairy charm that Nisserans might hang over a threshold or bury in a garden. But I could clearly make out a depiction of a woman holding a hand to her heart. Her other hand cradled a bird with a broken wing.

"Look here." The maid spoke Nisseran with a Perispi accent, pointing to a discreet pocket sewn into my waistline. "Every garment made by Perispi hands has at least one pouch sized for a Holy effigy."

I swallowed my pride and slid the effigy into the pouch. "Like this?" I asked.

The quiet woman nodded, pleased. "Your Majesty, you look..."

"Like strawberry frosting on a cake," I filled in with a wry laugh.

A friendly light flooded her formerly opaque gray eyes. "Cake is never a bad thing."

"How did you learn Nisseran?" I asked.

"I'm a scholar. I was Princess Navara's tutor in languages and diplomatic studies." The woman's smile flickered. I refrained from asking why she no longer held that post. "Some say that giving the effigy a rub every now and then makes it more effective."

"I'll remember that. My elder sister tests the limits of my every virtue."

The lavatory door swung open. Perennia shuffled out. Her dress was also a bit *much*, with several draping tiers and a tie around her waist that erupted into a giant bow at the back. She turned around to show us the buttons she couldn't reach. Before I could gather my skirts to go help, she looked over her shoulder and said, "Hesper, isn't it?"

"Yes, Your Majesty," the maid answered.

"Would you mind?"

Hesper assisted while I marveled over Perennia's ability to learn the woman's name despite spending the better part of the last two hours sulking in the lavatory. I'd only managed to evict her for a quick refreshing.

"It seems you overlooked a gift," Hesper said as she slipped the last button through the eyelet. She nodded to another small box waiting on the table by the mirror. Perennia swished over to pick it up.

"Another Holy figurine," she said, showing us. I squinted to see a male figure bearing a sword and shield.

"Atrelius," Hesper said. "Holy of Courage."

"I had no idea Ambrosine was so interested in your faith," Perennia mused as she studied the trinket.

"Here." I stepped forward to feel along her waist for a hidden pouch.

"What are you doing?" she demanded. But when I snatched her figurine and slipped it snugly inside, she said, "Oh...thank you."

"Shall we?" I asked.

In more companionable spirits, Perennia and I followed Hesper down several stories to the reception hall. The black-and-white-tile motif continued throughout the palace—as did Ambrosine's mirrors along the walls. We entered a deep hall with arched ceilings and marble moldings of stern faces and flowers. At the far end, a set of stairs led up toward twin thrones bathed in moonlight from high clerestory windows.

Before us stretched one endless table heaping with fresh food and festooned with olive branches. The guests bowed their heads and smiled as Hesper escorted us to the farthest end and seated us at the left and right hand of the head chair.

"Glisette," Perennia whispered over a platter holding fragrant roasted rabbit and leg of lamb. She indicated something over my shoulder.

I'd been eyeing a rosemary loaf drizzled with olive oil, but I tore my attention away to follow her gaze. An enormous family portrait hung on the wall. Ambrosine alone commanded the eye. The artist portrayed a beauty so fierce it verged on formidable. She wore a coy smile and her eyes came alive as though animated by some sorcery. Her fluid silver gown with sparkling embroidery must have taken ages to render, but the skill applied to her perplexing expression was unmatched.

An odd chill licked up my nape. Minutes seemed to pass before I could release her painted gaze and focus on the other subjects of the portrait.

King Myron stood at a stately distance from his new wife. Grays were strewn through his black hair, and solemn wrinkles creased his handsome olive complexion. His daughter, Navara, sat in a chair at Ambrosine's other side, her hands crossed primly in her lap, her brown eyes vacant.

I'd been under the impression that the princess was only a year or two younger than Perennia, but perhaps my memory failed me; this portrait depicted a child, with fleshy cheeks and ribbons in her lusterless black hair.

I turned back to exchange a troubled look with Perennia, but an announcement diverted her attention to the entrance. The herald declared the arrival of Princess Navara Vasila who, after a suspenseful pause, stepped into view.

A gasp gushed out before I could stop it. The heir of Perispos was hardly a child. In fact, she wavered on the cusp of womanhood. Her velvety black hair tumbled in curls down her back and captured the light like pitch catching aflame. The comely shape of her lips struck me with envy. Thick lashes fanned out from bottomless topaz-brown eyes.

The portraitist had *lied*.

But the lie didn't begin and end with the brush; it clung to Navara in person in the form of childish trappings. She wore a white linen smock with a ruffled collar and lace trim. Sky-blue ribbons frolicked amid her bouncing curls and her warm olive cheeks looked like they'd been rouged by a heavy-handed player in a traveling troupe.

The next announcement sliced through a room so quiet I could hear a man several seats down from me swallow.

"Her Majesty, Queen Ambrosine Vasila."

My sister entered like a blaze of fire. Her garment looked as if molten gold had been poured over her body, like battle armor meant to expose rather than protect. The metallic bodice carved inward at her navel so that from ribs to thighs, her flanks were bare. She wore a black cape that trailed behind her like a silk shadow, and her pale hair had been plaited, dusted with sparkling minerals, and topped with a crown of jagged obsidians. Indrawn breaths of admiration swelled around me, echoing, consuming all other sound.

I toyed with the ruffles at my collar. Ambrosine had made sure I looked puerile and harmless—like a dandified princess overshadowed by a glorious queen.

When Navara took her seat at the opposite end of the table, Ambrosine raised her goblet and tapped it with a clawed ring. "To my beautiful sisters. I know I speak on behalf of both my husband and my new daughter when I say that I hope you regard our kingdom as a second home, and its fine people as friends."

A taut moment of silence stretched until it was clear she had concluded, prompting the man next to me to call out "Hear, hear!" with great gusto. Others followed suit. Pleased, Ambrosine gestured at the food, and every person at the endless banquet table began to fill a plate and converse animatedly.

Veiled dancers emerged to clap and twirl, and the crowd applauded. A nervous jester performed, and they laughed. Ambrosine sipped wine and carved rodentlike nibbles of food, chewing mechanically as though it disgusted her, then smiling to keep others from noticing. I tried again and again to capture Perennia's attention, to commiserate, to communicate that I sensed something strange. But she was determined not to look at me.

I'd come to the feast hungry, yet the tart lemon flavor of the stuffed grape leaves on my plate tasted like sour bile.

I dropped my fork, unfurled a hand over my belly as though I'd eaten my fill. Stealthily, my thumb and index finger found the iron figurine in my pocket and rubbed it for good measure.

It's in your mind, Glisette. You haven't forgiven her, and that's making you see darkness and ill intentions that don't exist.

But what of Mercer's prophecy?

I caught Ambrosine watching me with a cryptic smile.

When the unbearable feast drew to a close, Perennia and I followed Hesper back through the maze of reflections. Earlier, in the daylight, the mirrors had seemed to open up infinite passageways. Now, in the dim light of the sconces, I felt trapped, watched on every side.

"I'm disappointed that Navara and I were not able to become friends tonight," Perennia mused. "Perhaps over the coming days we can—"

"Something was wrong with the portrait," I interrupted, the words festering inside me.

"Glisette..." Perennia sighed.

"Do you not agree?"

"It was strange. But that doesn't mean anything. Not everything *means* something."

"The artist went mad," Hesper whispered without looking back. "He left the queen's eyes unfinished for as long as he could, until she demanded he finish. He finally did. That very hour he hiked up to the edifice and leapt to his death."

"Hesper!" Perennia cried. "That's nothing more than a salacious rumor, surely!"

"I do not repeat rumors, Your Highness," Hesper answered, grave. "I was there in the edifice saying my prayers when it occurred. Many of our people have renewed their pledge to the faith in recent days."

A cool touch stroked the back of my wrist. I jolted in terror before realizing it was Perennia, reaching to entangle our fingers. I clasped her hand in mine.

When we arrived at our quarters, Hesper stopped and turned, the shadows toying with her dark hair. "Good night, and may the Holies bestow blessings on you."

When the door shut, I kneaded my temples and strode to the window, gazing out at the edifice stairs. I had known visiting Ambrosine would be strange, but I hadn't expected to feel so uneasy. I hadn't seen any indication that she had broken any rules or caused any harm. And yet...

And yet everything felt wrong: the missing king, the subdued princess, the mirrors, the portrait, the fraught mood haunting this place.

Mercer's vision hadn't shown him much, yet he had sensed something deeply sinister. Now I understood. In spite of Ambrosine's logical explanations for everything disquieting, I was not reassured.

"What's the matter?" Perennia stopped wrestling with her ridiculous gown to ask.

"Pack your things. I'm sending you home in the morning."

"What? No! We just arrived!"

"I should have come alone."

"Whatever you need to do, I can help," she said, seizing my wrists. "I'm an elicromancer too, and old enough that you can stop obsessing over my safety and think of me as an ally. I want to join the Realm Alliance in a few years, but how will I ever be of use if you don't let me take risks?"

"Bringing you here was risky enough, Perennia."

"You don't believe Hesper's ridiculous story, do you?" she demanded.

"Of course not."

"Then why are you sending me home?"

"Because it's what I've decided," I said, in my most queenly tone. Perennia could sense its gravity. She ripped at the buttons of her bodice until she was able to shimmy out of the gown and throw herself onto her bed.

I dragged in a long breath. The figurine seemed to weigh heavier in my pocket.

I fished it out and frowned at it, noticing a tiny, messy inscription engraved into its base. I squinted and turned it in the light to make it out.

Edifice. Midnight.

I clenched it in my fist, made sure Perennia hadn't seen, and hurried to rip off my travesty of a gown.

✦ TEN ✦

GLISETTE

THE servants had extinguished the lamps and retired. As I scaled the staircases leading upward, only the soft illumination of my elicrin stone kept the shadows at bay.

The palace was predictably laid out, but the mirrors transformed the corridors into a maze of unexpected turns and unwanted company. Several times, my own reflection tricked my heart into pounding like a battering ram against my chest.

Who could blame me, when Ambrosine and I looked so alike?

At last I encountered an antechamber with marble columns leading to a grand staircase flooded with moonlight. I ascended to find an enormous domed terrace covered in cool-hued mosaics. An altar with carved figures stood at the center and a series of open arches provided panoramic views of the city. The edge called to me and I crossed the empty edifice to lean against the hip-high railing.

The night sky was a tapestry of silver stars and wool-gray clouds. A soft wind brushed along my skin, and for a moment it felt like Mother's gentle fingers, the breath of Father's lighthearted laughter. I could understand why people came here to renew their hope, to ask questions, to feel small.

But the wind kicked up and I grasped the railing to keep from swaying. Chilling notions seeped through my thoughts like cold water through fissuring ice. The invitation could have been a trap meant to send me to the same violent end as my parents. I thought of the artist who had thrown himself to his death after painting Ambrosine's likeness—and imagined my mysterious caller shoving me over the edge.

I heard soft footsteps and turned to find a raven-haired figure carrying a flickering candle.

"You came," Navara said.

"Princess," I breathed in relief. Instead of the unflattering frock, she wore a dress as dark blue as the night. I looked to see if any guards accompanied her, but found only Hesper, who knelt in obeisance to her beloved deities before rising to stand at Navara's side.

"You gave us the effigies," I said.

"Yes," Navara replied. "The queen asked Hesper to leave her gifts in your room. We added two of our own. I hoped that you or your sister would receive my message, but also that the Holies would give you the compassion to hear my plight, and the courage to help me liberate my father and my people."

"From what?" I asked warily.

Navara did not reply. Instead, she took a deep breath and turned to look up at the carvings of the Holies, her eyes the brown of dates. "My mother was devoted to Agrimas. Father less so. His views mirror those of his people. The legends of our deities feel like nothing more than tales sometimes."

She circled the altar, studying the figures. "But my mother was devout. It grieved her to find the edifice empty when she came to say her prayers. So she set out to renew our people's commitment to the faith, and our people loved her enough that her devotion sparked an awakening." A wistful smile crossed the girl's face as she stopped before me again. "She was so kind. She represented every Holy virtue, but Lovingkindness most of all."

Hesper bowed her head in reverent sorrow.

"When she fell ill," Navara continued, "she grew weak and had to be carried to the edifice on a litter. My father tried to convince her to travel to Nissera to see an elicromancer Healer. She refused, believing that Eulippa would take pity on her and Hestreclea would honor her loyalty. At first her fellow devotees continued to flock to the edifice and pray for her. But when it became clear that prayers for her health would not be answered, they abandoned the faith again. People began to speak fondly of her beauty and kind spirit as though she was already gone. They preferred to remember her as she was. Even my father."

Navara stared at her toes, tears glittering like dewdrops in her thick lashes. She looked so young and fragile until her eyes shot up to meet mine, deep and determined. "She said the Holies would not look kindly on this city turning their backs on the faith again. She said that I would live to see the wrath of the gods fall upon Halithenica." She paused. "And their wrath has come."

"What do you mean?" I whispered.

"One of the Fallen deities walks among us," Hesper answered. The candlelight sculpted her narrow features.

"The Fallen?" I repeated, remembering the illustration of bloodshed and chaos in Perennia's book. A skeptical laugh slipped out.

"You cannot deny that an unholy presence accompanies the queen," Hesper said. "You said you sensed something strange about the portrait."

"Yes, the fact that Ambrosine treats her stepdaughter like a child to try and stifle a beauty that rivals her own."

Navara blushed and ducked her head, but Hesper lifted her chin. The compliant attitude befitting a ladies' maid had vanished; the fire of a challenging scholar's spirit flared in her gray eyes. "Nexantius, the Fiend of Vainglory, would do just such a thing."

"Of course," I snapped. "The one who spawned elicromancers, seeing as we're inherently vain and power hungry?"

"No." Princess Navara shook her head. Her denial resounded through the edifice. "We know what you did to save Nissera. That's why I thought you could help us. It's why I thought you *would*."

"It was you who unleashed her upon us," Hesper added. "You unburdened yourself of your sister at our kingdom's expense. It is your duty to liberate us."

"Hesper," Navara chided. She stepped forward to seize my hand, her grip firm and desperate. In her other hand, the candlestick trembled. "The final chapter of the Book of Belief warns of a time when the Fallen will take on flesh and enter our world. They've been waiting for their moment and the vessels to make it possible. They will bring scourges on mankind. Once all four arrive, it will signal the beginning of the end."

"Of what?"

"Humanity."

"I'm sorry, I don't believe—"

"Please, listen," the princess pressed. "There's a missing section of the final chapter: a sealed apocryphal scroll, which only the high priest and the king are allowed to see. It's rumored to contain guidance for banishing the Fallen. The high priest kept it safe and secret, but he died suspiciously over a month ago now. The day after his death, the queen questioned me to make sure I didn't know what it said. I think she wanted to destroy it and bury any knowledge of it."

"Are you implying that she killed your priest?" I asked in disbelief. "You don't know my sister. She's not a murderer, and she has no interest in your religion."

"The priest was one of only two people who knew how to banish the Fallen, and now he's dead," Hesper said. "The other is the king, and the queen has locked him away and corrupted his mind."

My skull prickled with the onslaught of a raging headache.

"Regardless of what you believe, my father is in peril," Navara said. "I haven't seen him for weeks except when she trots him out to sign royal decrees. When I try to find his quarters, the mirrors confuse my mind and I wake up in my bed as though I never left."

"What the queen has become is not natural," Hesper said. "Her servants told me she does not eat her food, and when she must eat for appearance's sake, she vomits. She is obsessed with infantilizing the princess and dresses her like a child. She ended our academic lessons and reduced me from tutor to maid. She wants to smother the princess's growth in every way."

Navara swallowed hard and released my hand to trail a finger along her throat. "I wore my mother's ruby necklace when I sat for the painting. It was foolish, but I wanted to defy her in some small way. When the queen saw it, she tore it off...and ate it."

"Ate it?" I half laughed through my growing despair. "I've never heard of such a thing! Do you have any proof to support these bizarre accusations?"

"Do your own instincts not offer proof enough?" Hesper asked. "Does the testimony of the Princess of Perispos not hold weight?"

"She's probably already destroyed the sealed scroll," Navara said. "Without you, without elicromancers, there is no hope for us. You have to believe us."

I massaged my temples, buying time to think. My relationship with Ambrosine was fractured beyond repair, but Perennia believed she could change. If I confronted Ambrosine with false accusations, the sister I truly cared for might never speak to me again.

But if I didn't confront her, and the claims were true…

"Invite Ambrosine here," Hesper said after a moment, as though inspiration had struck. "She cannot cross the threshold of the edifice. It's a sacred place, and she is unholy."

"It's true," Navara added. "It's why we asked to meet you here."

The princess paced to the other side of the edifice, bending to set her candle on the floor and dig her fingernails into a crevice between two tiles. She dislodged one and set it aside. "It's why we've used it as a hiding place for the paintings and statues we were able to salvage when she ordered the guards to burn them."

She pried away another tile. Hesper hurried to help. By the time I joined them, I was looking down into a cellar of artworks that had been hastily wrapped in flour sacks.

"This is part of the scene from the main corridor on the first floor," Navara said, handing me a chipped portion of a fresco that depicted a human reaching up toward one of the Holies while in the grip of a shadow creature, a Fallen whose face and body must have belonged to another damaged shard. "And this is the only portrait of my mother we were able to save. The queen even toppled the statue of her in the rose garden." Navara uncovered the top half of a large canvas. Though the candle flame didn't offer much light, I could tell in the low gleam that the king's first wife had been a great beauty.

"She ordered your mother's portrait burned?" I asked, wondering what I would do without the glorious renderings of Mother and Father that graced the halls of our home. Would their images slowly slip from my memory like plucked flowers shedding their petals?

"All of it," Hesper answered. "Everything reminiscent of our queen whose presence brought warmth and light to these grounds before the impostor brought her darkness."

"What about the foyer ceiling?" I asked. "Perennia said it's a mural of the Holies."

"She was about to destroy it too, until she heard you were coming," Navara replied. "She couldn't undo the damage and desecration, but she could make you think my father still had some say in what happened under his roof."

Could this be true, or was the princess enlisting the help of her favorite tutor to purge the palace of unwelcome change? To paint Ambrosine's unabashed self-centeredness as something darker?

But then I remembered Mercer's prophecy.

"Please, Your Majesty," Navara begged, dropping to one knee in front of me. "I was nothing but welcoming, yet she despised me the moment we met. I don't *want* her to think of my beauty as a threat. I don't care about my beauty at all. I'll show you."

With wide eyes asking permission, she reached for the dagger I'd belted at my waist. My muscles stiffened, alert as she slid the sharp blade from its sheath, but I let her proceed. She gathered a handful of gorgeous hair and sawed until a flood of black tresses fell to the floor, some of them wistfully riding the wind into the cellar of sacred items. She grabbed another thick handful.

"Let me," I said softly. She turned over the blade and I circled her to gather what remained. In one motion, I cut it to a blunt edge that rested at her jaw. Sheathing my knife, I circled back to face her.

"I should have done this weeks ago," she said, her eyes filling with tears as she touched her shorn locks. "I should have disfigured myself so that she would not take her wrath toward me out on Father, on our kingdom, on our faith."

"Princess!" Hesper cried, clearly disturbed by the suggestion, but Navara ignored her.

"Please," Navara begged again. "Only you are powerful enough to fight through her dark enchantments."

I bit hard into my bottom lip. They were right: this was my fault.

This rebuke could not be like the last one. I couldn't make the same mistake of showing mercy. I would have to confiscate Ambrosine's elicrin stone and drag her back to Nissera for another trial before the Realm Alliance.

"So you will help us?" Navara asked.

"Help you with what, darling girl?" asked a calm, lyrical voice from the shadows of the edifice entry.

ELEVEN

AMBROSINE
TWO MONTHS AGO

HOW could someone so beautiful look so unhappy?" Myron's finger curled under my chin and lifted it until our eyes met.

I didn't want to answer. I didn't know how. So I urged his mouth toward mine, slid my tongue along the inside of his lip. Myron was an attractive man—older than I would have preferred, but a skilled lover and a distraction from the boredom overtaking my mind.

The only other cure was basking in the admiration of his people. But they had grown accustomed to my beauty. They no longer gasped and fawned over me. They no longer spoke Nisseran in my presence, instead droning on and on in Perispi with no regard for my lack of understanding. Sometimes I wished I had paid closer attention in lessons, but I always envied how naturally Glisette picked up Perispi, how relentlessly she teased me for guessing wrong answers. Even Devorian didn't do that.

Lonely, powerless, overlooked. Queen or not, I had come to realize I was nothing but a jewel in the king's pommel. The best I could do was to be a sparkling jewel that pleased and dazzled him, one too rare and precious to replace.

I pulled back, molding my body to the chaise, trailing one hand along the silk collar of my dressing gown and tugging at his belt buckle with the other.

"Not now, my love," he said, bending to plant a kiss on my forehead. "Navara will never forgive me if I miss the Day of Holies ceremony in the city square."

"She's a demanding child, isn't she?" I remarked before I could stop myself, but I managed to temper my irritation enough to sound fond of her.

He laughed. "Demanding yes, but a child no longer. Men young and old have taken to ogling her. Are you sure you don't wish to come and protect her by holding their gazes captive?"

A tendril of delight unfurled in my belly at his flattery. "I'd rather hold you captive," I purred.

"Later, my queen," he promised, pressing a kiss on the back of my hand. "I know it's difficult for you to understand the customs of my people, including our many, *many* religious holidays—"

"There's practically one every fortnight," I grumbled.

"—but perhaps you could try. The philosophy of the faith is based on self-examination: what we aspire to be and how we fall short. If you think of it that way, it doesn't seem so ridiculous." Tenderly, he brushed a lock of hair from my face. "It would mean so much to Navara if you went to the edifice to pray with her, or if she knew you made a habit of going downstairs for reflection hour every seventh dawn."

"Reflection hour?"

"Come. I'll show you. You're usually sleeping, and I don't like to disturb you when you look so peaceful."

With a scowl of reluctance, I accepted his hand and allowed him to lead me across the expanse of our private chamber. Morning sunlight poured through the vivid colors of the stained-glass figures of the eight Holies, four goddesses and four gods. Though I had never made a direct effort to learn them, I knew all of the Holies by name, virtue, and symbol. If I cared about them, or pretended to care, perhaps I might not feel so lonely.

Myron shoved aside a rich tapestry of frolicking deer, revealing a door in the wall.

"I never noticed that," I said. "Why is it hidden?"

"I had the servants cover it before you arrived. I didn't want to frighten you."

"Frighten me?" I chuckled. "I'm an elicromancer. I have little to be afraid of."

Even as I declared this, I thought of how weak and helpless I'd felt standing in chains before the Realm Alliance, subjugated by that insolent little bitch. No one, *no one*, was meant to have so much power. And then Valory had the audacity to pretend to be generous for not ripping the elicrin magic from my chest, an act that would have been as ruthless as tearing out my heart.

Instead, they put a probation spell on my elicrin stone. If I tried to call on my power to do anything more than light a fire on a cold night, they would punish me.

My teeth clenched with that steady rage that resided like a living thing inside me, moving under my skin. Sometimes, when I was alone with Myron or walking in the city, I felt almost happy. And then the anger would strike, and I would think of Glisette, who used to be my companion in everything before she sneered at me, at our past, and became so proud of her metamorphosis—and of that hideous scar. So what if we had always been a little vain and a tiny bit selfish? Our redemption was that we loved and defended each other no matter what. Why was she so ashamed of that? Of me?

Because Valory proselytized her, the anger inside me hissed. *Sweet and impressionable Perennia got caught up as well, and Devorian is just happy to be in his normal human state and forgiven for his transgressions.*

But there was no forgiveness for me. What did I do that every other ruler doesn't? Raise taxes and tolls? Myron did so twice each year, and his people loved him.

After the carnage in Arna, I should have been grateful Valory didn't snap me like a stick. But I simply couldn't muster the gratitude.

"This place serves a unique purpose," Myron explained, gripping the door latch. I realized I'd been clutching my elicrin stone and released it.

"How so?" I asked, more polite than interested.

"The Edifice of the Holies honors the virtues. But the Edifice of the Fallen reminds us that virtues do not exist in a vacuum—the absence of a virtue is a vice. The room is empty but for a mirror, which invites the visitor to examine his soul and the evils he has committed." He turned the knob and revealed a dark stone stairway spiraling down. "It is an unsettling place, meant to cause discomfort with oneself."

"On second thought, I'll go to the ceremony."

Myron laughed again. "You don't have to go anywhere. You can go back to bed if you like. But promise me if you go down there, you'll remove your elicrin stone."

"Why?"

"We're supposed to enter naked and smeared with ashes, for humility's sake. You are meant to leave all your earthly trappings behind, anything that could obstruct an honest view of yourself." He gathered my hands. His were always warm. "And, though my people are no longer so prejudiced against elicromancers, I don't want to give them any reason to think you're desecrating a holy place."

"How would they know? Do other people go down there?"

"No. This edifice is ours alone so we can reflect in private. But if you respect our people's traditions, it will show. They will see."

"Everyone else goes naked in a public edifice?" I asked doubtfully.

"Many go in rags. Either choice is acceptable."

The distant roar of music and cheers floated up from the streets. "Speaking of traditions…" I said.

"Right, I should be off. If you go, take a light so you don't harm yourself."

After he departed, I turned to stare into the pitch-dark passageway that awaited me.

I rolled my eyes and slammed the door shut, floating toward my vanity set with a sigh. "Show me Perennia," I said. But when the glass rippled, the other side was dark, just as I expected. My siblings had smashed all of the enchanted mirrors at home except a handheld one, which they kept locked in a dark, quiet room, ignoring me until it suited them. Only Perennia dug it out to visit with me once each week. We weren't scheduled to speak today.

I groaned and swiped my hand to clear the view in the mirror. My expression was bland, my normally bright eyes spiritless. I was bored of everything, even trying on gowns and jewels—so bored I thought about donning something appropriate and participating in the holiday celebration.

But then I remembered what Myron had said about the underground edifice. *I didn't want to frighten you.*

Intrigued, I returned to the tapestry and swept it aside. I could use a little adventure.

"*Carathin har,*" I whispered. My elicrin stone illuminated. Myron said not to bring it downstairs. But he also said to bring a light, and I could barely use it anyway thanks to my probation. I knew he wouldn't *truly* mind.

I started down the tight spiral stairwell, my lacy hem gathering dust. Minutes seemed to pass before my dizzying path straightened. At the end of a narrow passage waited a cool chamber, so dark I felt blind gazing into it.

A bowl of ashes sat on a table just outside the edifice, next to a tinderbox and a candle. Giggling at myself for playing along with such silliness, I shed my dressing gown and dipped two fingers into the bowl, shivering as I drew lines of ash along my eyebrows and cheeks, then down my neck, around my bare breasts, and around the weight of my elicrin stone between them. I picked up the candle, said "*Matara liss,*" to catch it aflame, and stepped into the edifice.

Iron sconces hung on either side of the interior of the archway; I used the candle to light the torches and faced the chamber with a stifled gasp.

The opposite wall held a giant gilt mirror, and every remaining fingerbreadth of the walls and ceiling were covered by a horrifying mural, saturated with lurid detail.

The theme was clear: the four Fallen reigned over their miserable supplicants in the underworld, no redemption in sight.

The ceiling alone depicted humans living on earth. Here, their "vices" seemed, in some ways, harmless. It appeared this played out as a prologue to what lay beneath: judgment for their choices.

In one corner people indulged in rampant debauchery at a feast, spilling wine, fighting over food, engaging in carnal acts. On the walls below their feet, naked worshippers wailed in a grimy pit, gaunt with starvation and sprouting animal features like horns and claws. Amid them hunched Depravity, Robivoros, a creature with sharp teeth—in both of his mouths. The second maw was where his stomach should have been, and with it he feasted on a corpse.

In the next corner stood Cruelty, Themera, a beautiful woman in black wearing a dark smile and a crown made of knives, each point skewering a human skull. Her worshippers wept blood on a ravaged battlefield. The living humans above were shown torturing young children and beggars.

Opposite her was Apathy, Silimos, a withered woman wrapped in a translucent cocoon, her empty, staring eyes covered with a veil of cobwebs. Her limbs were twisted and rigid with the stiffening that comes soon after death. Those who had fallen prey to her lived in a gloomy, rotting forest. Some were intertwined with the trees, so they could no longer move, and covered in moss and mold—yet their eyes remained awake and alert. On the ceiling people lounged in languor, playing cards and ignoring a blazing fire ravaging the fields outside their window.

And lastly, at the far-right corner stood Vainglory, Nexantius. The tall, muscular figure was formed of the purest silver and wore a mask of mirrors that revealed only the attractive structure of his face and his glowing silver eyes. He stood on a pedestal amid a swathe of starry darkness, gripping chains attached to jeweled manacles that held prisoners captive. The damned souls wore crowns of jagged diamonds that dug into their skin and sent rivers of blood down their faces.

In their previous lives, his prisoners dripped with expensive jewelry and lifted golden trophies. One man sat on a throne of contorted human bodies, grovelers who gazed on him with admiration even as they bent over backward to bear his weight.

The scenes were terrifying...and impossible to look away from.

As I circled the room, I caught sight of my reflection in the mirror and turned to fully face it. The dark streaks of ash looked like war paint. Accustomed as I was to dressing like a spring flower, I had to admit I looked beautiful this way: bare and formidable.

I softly traced a hand from my cheek to my lips, down the line that ran sternum to navel with a brief detour over my elicrin stone, forbidden in every way. I looked so exquisite that even the darkness around me began to scintillate.

A sudden draft extinguished the torches.

Ambrosine.

I not only heard the whisper in the wind but *felt* it: a cool shiver slithering over my naked skin.

"Who's there?" I asked. "Myron, are you toying with me?" I looked over my shoulder at the stairwell but couldn't see anything. The idea of playing games in the dark frightened and exhilarated me. Though he had a sense of humor, Myron always struck me as the tame, rule-following type. I smirked thinking of him prowling in the dark, pretending to devour me like a fallen god claiming his wicked worshipper.

Aren't you a magnificent creature?

The voice hummed in my head, deep, glossy, and most certainly not Myron's. The latent magic in my blood stirred slowly, like a cat stretching awake from a nap. The cool glow of my elicrin stone, to which my eyes were still adjusting in the absence of golden torch-light, swirled and writhed.

I faced the mirror again. The reflection of the edifice had vanished. A nebulous, starry night stretched out around me and my eyes glowed an otherworldly shade of silver. The ash marks on my skin sparkled like diamond powder. A nearly translucent figure in a reflective mask imposed over mine.

"Who are you?" I asked, rocking a step closer. "Are you...?"

I am, the being answered, and again the words poured through my mind, more thought than sound.

I laughed. Someone was trying to deceive me with illusions of noise and light. "Myron didn't mention that the Edifice of the Fallen housed a real, live Fallen deity. Do you visit every acolyte who ventures down here?"

I've not visited a mortal in centuries.

"And that remains true," I replied. "I'm not a mortal."

Of course you're not. I sense the power you hold. A beat passed. *Where is your husband, the king?*

"Oh, peeking through a hole in the wall somewhere, ready to tease me the moment I believe this is real."

The silver figure laughed a knowing laugh. I didn't like it.

Come closer, Ambrosine, and inspect the mirror. There are no clever deceptions here.

I took a tentative step forward. The figure pressed his hand against the other side of the glass. The tip of my forefinger stretched toward him, and his image grew more substantial the closer I drew, while mine faded away. His eyes sharpened behind the holes of his mask. The irises glowed silver, the space around them a fathomless black.

Our fingertips touched, and before I could squeal in shock, he snatched my hand and twisted me around, drawing my back flush against his cool, solid form. The glass, the only barrier between us, had ceased to exist. His icy hands trapped me like bars of a cage, one loosely gripping my throat while the other spread flat over my middle, thumb caressing my navel, fingers splaying dangerously close to the powerful knot of nerves at the base of my belly.

I didn't want to defy my probation. I imagined myself in chains before Glisette and Valory again, explaining to them that I had tried to use my power against an apparition in a mirror—when manipulating mirrors was *my* gift. It would be downright embarrassing.

"What do you want?" I asked. "Who are you?"

You know my name. Even though I still sensed more than heard the words, the whisper of his cool breath brushed over my ear. The finger that rested at my throat moved down to stroke my elicrin stone. My gaze shot to the mural, to the Fallen of Vainglory.

This was no ruse; I could feel the diamond-dusted darkness of this being's power. Whether fallen deity, ancient specter, or distant cousin of my own kind, he was mighty.

Why do you detest the king's daughter?

"I don't." The lie trembled out of me.

I'm here to give you everything you desire. You don't have to lie to me. You can let me inside. There's nothing you can say that will drive me away. Do you hate her because she is soon to be lovelier than you, the loveliest of all? Or is it her piety?

I scoffed. "Don't try to burrow under my skin."

But hat's what I'm asking for: a way under your skin, an anchor to the mortal world, a home to inhabit, one that can hold the breadth and power of all that I am. No creature like you has ever stepped into my temple. I only need you to say yes.

"Why would I?"

Because I will help you. What do you want? I can obtain it if you let me. If you want to subjugate the king and his guards so you can kill the princess, I can give you that. I can give you far more, but it's a beginning.

"I don't want to kill her. I'm not a murderer."

Then what do you wish to do with her?

"Nothing. I only want to be unequivocally considered the most beautiful woman in existence for all of my days."

Oh?

"But not just beautiful…I want to be so beautiful, it terrifies people," I whispered, surprising myself. "True beauty is fierce. That's why my sister likes her scar. I want to be as fierce as I am lovely, and for everyone who looks at me to fear me."

Beauty alone is not what strikes fear. What you want is power. But you have that already. You are of ancient, magical stock. What stands in your way, splendorous queen?

He spun me back around, graceful as a trained dancing partner, but kept my hand in his plated grip. The muscular shape of his body swelled through the mirror, as though it were molten metal and he, a model, shaping its mold. His bright silver eyes seemed to carve rivets into my very soul.

What stands in your way? he repeated.

"Valory Braiosa," I whispered. "By a fluke, she is more powerful than any other elicromancer. There is no one able to hold her in check."

Together, we will rival her in power, Nexantius said, stroking my hair. *Together, you and I will cut her down.*

TWELVE

GLISETTE

THE night seemed to darken as Ambrosine leaned against the entry to the Edifice of the Holies, wearing a revealing black nightdress confected of sheer lace. Her eyes appeared to shine silver.

I shifted my stance to shield Navara and Hesper.

"Why do you look so nervous?" Ambrosine asked, her claw-tip rings toying with the ribbon closure of her gown. "Like foxes prowling in a vineyard."

"Come here, Ambrosine," I said evenly.

"You don't command me any longer, Glisette."

"One step over the threshold. That's all."

She cocked her head. "This place is considered sacred by my new family and my people. I do not wish to defile it with my unbelief."

She pronounced "defile" with relish, as though the word tasted delicious. Then, turning a patronizing smile on Navara, she added, "I know how your mother valued faith, dear girl."

"Where is my father?" Navara demanded.

"He's resting. How many times do I have to tell you that he's feeling unwell of late? He is a proud man and will allow only his wife to see him in such a condition."

"You're lying!" Navara lunged, but I shoved her back. "If I find out you've harmed him in any way, I will—"

"You'll what?" Ambrosine asked. "Cut off your nose to spite your face, just like your hair?"

"That's enough," I said, squaring my shoulders so that Ambrosine could plainly see where my loyalties resided. "This game you're playing must end. Enter the edifice or take us to the king."

A grimace tightened Ambrosine's features. I didn't believe in this lore of the Holies and the Fallen, but her hesitance to take even one step into the edifice needled me with doubt. Her narrowed eyes shot up to the altar, down to the missing tiles and the treasures Navara had scattered on the floor. As she realized the princess had tricked her, her nostrils flared.

"Right this way," she said, collecting herself, and turned to descend the steps.

Navara started to follow, but I grabbed her by the elbow and swung her around. "Stay here, both of you," I ordered. "You're right: Ambrosine doesn't want to come in here, for whatever reason. You'll be safer here than anywhere else."

Hesper nodded. I could trust her to protect the princess.

By the time I jogged down the steps, I saw only a streak of golden hair trailing around a corner.

"Keep up!" Ambrosine called.

Turn after turn, I glimpsed enough of her to continue pursuit: the hem of her gown, a lock of hair, her swiftly retreating reflection. The concept behind the mirrors became clear. They didn't just feed her vanity; they helped her maintain control by sowing confusion.

The mirror illusions became more artful the longer I pursued her. They created a labyrinth of infinite, nonexistent corridors and stairwells. The pounding in my head grew unbearable as I struggled to make sense of them.

And then I lost her. Maybe I'd taken a wrong turn. I retraced my steps and came face-to-face with a mirror. A pang of panic made my limbs feel weak. I could have sworn I'd come from that direction.

I swallowed my fear and spun in place, determined to make sense of this maze. Navara stood at the far end of the hall.

"I told you to stay in the edifice," I whispered harshly, but the princess didn't acknowledge me.

"Father, please!" she cried in Perispi, gazing beyond me, or maybe through me. Her hair was long again, and she wore a ruby necklace like the one she'd described. "Please help us!"

I turned around to see an image of King Myron, unkempt and unwell, sobbing on the floor of a dark room painted with appallingly violent murals. From my studies and Perennia's reminder, I recognized his surroundings as an Edifice of the Fallen, the underground counterpart to the beautiful temple I had just left behind.

Myron's eyes were bright silver, rimmed with dark circles, and wild with madness. He was only a reflection, or even an illusion. Was his torment real? There were three of him, then a dozen, and all around him Navara screamed for help while duplicates of me watched in bewilderment.

"Come find us," a calmer, feminine voice said behind me. "Please, Myron, my love."

I looked over my shoulder and found an enchanting woman with black hair—the same face from the portrait Navara had showed me. It was Navara's mother, the dead queen.

Either Ambrosine had found a way to break the enchantment on her elicrin stone, or she truly had tapped into a dark power.

"I can't!" the king sobbed. "You're not here. You're not real."

"What can I do to make you believe I'm real?" she answered, with sorrow that sounded convincing.

"Ambrosine!" I called out, tempted to smash through the glass and put an end to this eerie sensation that I was seeing a ghost. "Where are you?"

The woman dropped her expression of despair and stared at me. "I'm only doing as you asked." Ambrosine's voice emerged from her lips. "I'm showing you the king. Now you can tell Navara he's alive and assuage her fears."

"You're torturing him!"

"I could do worse."

"But you haven't."

"I'm keeping him for legitimacy's sake. A revolt against my rule would be a waste of my attentions. I'm busy with other undertakings."

"What other undertakings?"

The image of the woman faded, replaced by Ambrosine wearing revealing battle armor that no warrior would ever wear. "I hate seeing you act like a pathetic shell of yourself, Glisette," she said, dodging my question.

"I could say the same to you," I said. I took a step closer. This could be the last chance to reason with her, to remind her of who she used to be—the last chance to keep this encounter as civil as Perennia hoped it would be. "Your sharp thorns used to protect something good and sensitive. I don't know when you changed. Was it Mother's and Father's deaths that shriveled your soul? Or was it riches beyond your wildest dreams? Was it the Water drying up? Fear over the changing politics of power? When did you become someone our parents would be ashamed of?"

A flash of teeth let me know I had struck a vulnerable place that no armor could protect. "At least I'm not the slavering sycophant to a Calgoranian bitch born with no magic," she barked. "They would be ashamed of you, not me."

She had finally dropped the insouciant act, as I'd hoped. Maybe I could still reach her. "This is about Valory?" I asked, ignoring the dangling bait that would drag me into an argument I couldn't win. "This tantrum, this torment of your new people, is all about her? You call me a sycophant, but I'm not the one obsessed with her power."

"Maybe you should be. Immortals know that even the best of intentions turn rancid with time and invincibility. The only way to stop people like Valory from claiming absolute power is to use *our* power to restrain them."

"Perhaps you don't recall that Valory and I were doing exactly that while you enabled the Moth King in his quest for chaos. We restrain elicromancers *after* they use their magic for ill. Valory has done nothing wrong, unlike you."

"She killed her own family."

"They were traitors and murderers."

"She took justice into her own hands. It's only a matter of time before she runs afoul of the Realm Alliance and throws off the shackles of her conscience."

"Is that how you see one's conscience? As a restraint?"

"I'm not going to argue morality with you." Ambrosine's countenance darkened. "This is about survival, about protecting Devorian and Perennia. We can't guarantee their safety when a creature like her exists. But I will save this world from her. My plan has already been set in motion, but I want you to help me. Help me and be even stronger than Valory. You are no one's right-hand woman, Glisette. You deserve better. You deserve *more*."

"What are you planning?" I asked.

"You must trust me," she said. The mirror rippled and stretched with her movement like a bubble too strong to burst as she reached out her hand, offering it to me.

I considered deceiving her to decrease the intensity of the situation, to lessen the danger for others who could be caught up in her wrath and sacrificed to her temper. But I could not pretend I didn't hear the poison lacing her every word, a toxic brew of arrogance, fear, envy, and acrimony that she hoped to make me swallow.

Elicrin magic pounded through me, warm and urgent. The hairs on my forearms prickled.

"You're asking me whom I will serve," I said. "You're asking me to choose between you and Valory. But my answer is neither. I serve light over darkness, goodness over wickedness. You cannot understand that because you only serve yourself."

Ambrosine bared her teeth, ready to retort, but someone else spoke first.

"That's not true. She serves her new master."

Hesper emerged from the shadowy space between two mirrors, clenching an effigy in her fist. She must have quietly followed me here. "I can see him behind her eyes. Vainglory does not hide for long. It cannot resist showing itself when invited."

Holding out the effigy, she closed her eyes and began praying in Perispi, beseeching the Holies to give us the strength to defeat Nexantius.

Ambrosine twitched and sneered as though repulsed. Her pupils enlarged and the irises flooded with luminous silver.

"Stop!" she yelled, her high-pitched screech entwined with a velvety male whisper.

"Hesper, let me handle this!" I raised my voice over hers, trying to contain my panic, but she only prayed louder.

"Stop it!" Ambrosine screamed. To my horror, she stretched the fluid mirror to knock the figurine from Hesper's grip and raked her claw-tipped rings across the woman's face.

I roared while Hesper shrieked and sank to her knees. Blood trickled through the cracks between her fingers as she clenched her wounds.

My shock fueled the spell that sent two glowing whips hurling from my elicrin stone. They were meant to wrap around Ambrosine's wrists, but she stepped back into the safety of the mirror. They struck the glass and dissolved to glimmering dust.

Ambrosine laughed. Again, a deeper voice braided through hers.

Waves of dread roiled through me. My sister was a formidable enough opponent, but she had struck an unholy union with this creature. Who knew the scale of their combined power?

I had to face them both. Ambrosine had squandered the redemption we'd given her. She had misspent our mercy and, instead of reforming her ways as Perennia probably still hoped, she had tormented innocent people. She had opened her body and soul to something even more wicked than herself.

I would never be able to drag her back to Nissera in chains.

The only choice was to destroy her.

But not here, in this maze of mirrors, where she held an undeniable upper hand. I had to escape, draw her out.

"*Sokek sinna*," I whispered to generate an enveloping shield.

Hundreds of reflections of the shield glowed back at me in the darkness, encouraging me. I knelt beside Hesper to cover her with my shield and help her stand. "We have to get back to the edifice. Is Navara still there?"

She peeled her hands away from her rent flesh and managed a nod. One of her eyes was a bloodied mess. Even a fine physician would not be able to salvage it. I tried not to cringe or think of how close I had come to such a devastating injury myself in my battle with the blights last year.

"Keep close to me," I whispered, leading the way back down the passage.

But now ... it was solid. Closed off. Another mirror.

This was no maze.

It was a prison.

Hesper whimpered through her blood-slicked hands. I turned in place to find a way out.

Instead, I found likenesses of my parents.

My heart thundered with longing, joy, loss, despair. I'd known Ambrosine was capable of cruelty, but this was beyond cruel.

"How could you turn your back on your own sister, Glisette?" the likeness of my mother asked.

"We always taught you that family comes first," my father added in his typical stern tone.

"Father would never say that," I said, feeling as if my heart had been torn. "He was a king. His duty required putting his people first."

"We told you to take care of each other," Mother continued. "You have lost your way, my darling. You've lost sight of what truly matters."

"Ambrosine!" I roared. "Don't be a coward, hiding in your mirrors. Face me!" I stood and smashed my fist into the glass, shattering it, revealing the wall behind it that had been stripped bare of its art. "Fight me!"

In the next mirror, Mercer appeared. Ambrosine only knew him from her hearing before the Realm Alliance. He didn't look quite the same; she had made his eyes blue instead of brown and had misrepresented his elegant chin, making his jaw almost comically masculine.

"Glisette," his unconvincing likeness whispered. "I'm finished with Valory. What she is, is wrong. It's not natural. But I fear her retaliation if I tell her it's *you* I want."

"*Erac esfashir*," I whispered. A blast of power from my elicrin stone shattered the mirror so my bloodied knuckles didn't have to.

"Fight me!" I screamed again. "Your tricks won't work."

"Glisette!" a voice behind me called. "Help me!"

I turned to find Perennia cowering in a prison cell, bloodied and wearing filthy rags. "Valory's coming to take my power," she whispered, trembling, tears blazing trails down grimy cheeks. "She's going to kill me."

"*Erac esfashir.*"

The bubbly sound of children's laughter floated around me. I turned again to see Ambrosine and me as young children, playing in the garden while Mother sat in the shade with a chubby infant Devorian. Ambrosine was braiding flowers into my hair, as pale and soft as the pear tree blossoms overhead.

"*Erac esfashir.*" The happy image burst into fragments.

This time, when I shattered the mirror, it revealed a long, dark corridor—a way out.

I turned to look for Hesper but found I was alone. A few drops of dark blood dappled the carpet.

I launched into a sprint. Gold-clawed fingers jutted from every mirror lining my path, nicking my face and tearing my clothes like branches blown by a treacherous wind. Retracing my steps was impossible, but I stumbled upon the antechamber: the way to the edifice.

Erecting my shield again, I drove on. Frightening images with silver eyes pursued me, but I was so close now, could see the marble stairs awash in moonlight...

And a lifeless body sprawled across them.

Hesper's limbs fell limp and contorted, as though she'd been shoved backward down the stairs. Her dark hair had slipped loose from its bun and spilled around her, damp with blood seeping from her skull. I heard Navara's sobs resounding in the temple, broken up by appeals to the deities she worshipped.

An elegant shadow waited on the top step, blocking the entrance to the edifice, her wicked eyes gleaming. "So, it's come to this," Ambrosine said.

"You brought us to this," I spat.

The silver in her eyes slid down her face, forming a swirling metal mask under her eyes and over her cheeks. It spread to her neck and chest and arms like plating, armor that embraced her shape.

The creature facing me was far more powerful than the Ambrosine I knew how to fight. But I prepared to strike anyway, the magic in my blood rising to the challenge.

"Umrac korat!" I called, using a slashing spell. I expected Ambrosine to react with a shield, but she merely raised an arm to deflect. It bounced off of her armor and shot back at me. I barely jumped aside. It skimmed over the back of my hand, drawing a thin line of blood.

Then I registered the gasp of pain from behind me.

Ambrosine's eyes widened with shock.

I followed her gaze, turning to find Perennia, the color draining from her lily-white face. A red bloodstain bloomed on her nightgown, crossing from shoulder to hip like a sash.

My whole future, my world, balanced on the point of a shard of a glass. I waited for Ambrosine to reveal this as another of her disturbing deceptions. But the bloodstain only spread and grew. Perennia dropped her chin to stare down at the wound, stunned.

"Perennia!"

I used a levitation spell to catch and cradle her just before she slumped to her knees, hurrying to gather her small warmth in my arms.

"Get help!" I turned to scream at Ambrosine.

She gaped at me briefly. The metal plating on her flesh receded. She stepped over Hesper's corpse and hurried to do as I'd commanded.

I would kill her. I would drag her to the edge of the edifice, throw her off, and never feel a shred of remorse.

But for now, I bunched Perennia's nightgown against the wound I was too afraid to examine. I had to stop the bleeding. "Hold on," I said while my sister drew desperate, shallow breaths.

A gentle hand touched my shoulder. "Let's bring her up to safety," Navara said. "Just in case."

The blood soaked through the fabric, seeping between my fingers. I refused to believe this could be the end. I rested my cheek on the crown of her head and, with a shuddering cry, shed tears into her hair. After a moment I nodded and lifted her with the whisper of an incantation.

In the edifice Navara spread out the flour sack that had covered her mother's painting. Gently, I set Perennia down and cradled her head in my palm.

"Is my father alive?" Navara asked.

"Yes, he's alive," I whispered back numbly.

"I'm sure the physician will be here soon," Navara said, but I didn't miss how she pursed her lips until they drained of color as her eyes skimmed over the blood.

"I love it up here," Perennia said, her eyes tracing the stars. "This is a good place."

"Perennia, you wouldn't dream of leaving me, would you?" I asked through an aching sob. "That's not what you mean, is it?"

"This isn't your fault," she said, sputtering for breath. "Promise that you will save her. She needs love to come back to us."

"You're not—"

"*Please*. Promise."

"I promise."

She drew in a long, convulsing breath and released it.

The last one she would ever take.

Her head drooped back, heavy in my hand. The soul behind her eyes vacated like mist in the sun.

My younger sister was gone.

And the last promise I made to her was a lie.

I would never be whole. There was no coming back, no escape, no healing, no light, no hope in this forsaken wasteland of a world. I begged for her to return, screamed at the stars, blasted away the altar until only crumbling stone remained, and screamed again. Tears blinded me. Navara tried to be comforting, but I felt her tense with fear as she held me.

Ambrosine had returned with a young woman, who looked upon the carnage with a neutral expression before she bent to shoulder the weight of Hesper's body.

"What have you done?" I asked Ambrosine.

"What have *I* done?" Ambrosine demanded through her tears. "This was *your* fault! You murdered our sister! It was *your spell*!"

In my imagination, I rose. I let my rage build up like a column of fire around my spine. I released enough power to rip the skin from her bones.

But in reality, I collapsed and curled against my sister's body, holding her cool hand, weeping until I felt my soul might retch out of me.

Navara stayed with me, clasping Perennia's other hand, for what seemed like hours.

Eventually, the sound of footsteps broke through the silence of our sanctuary of mourning.

"What are you doing here?" Navara asked the newcomer.

I heard what sounded like a weapon swiping through the air, preparing to strike.

I accepted the darkness.

And the darkness came.

When I awoke, my head pounding, it took all of three seconds to recall what had come to fruition.

Perennia was gone.

The tears began before I could pry my bleary eyes open. Everything felt wrong. My hands were heavy. The air smelled like damp soil.

"Glisette!" the harsh whisper cut through the hums of insects. I turned to my right and found Navara tied to a tree a few paces away.

"What's happened?" I mumbled, barely managing to evict the words through the thick taste of grief in my throat.

"We have to escape, now, while he's gathering firewood."

"What?" I asked, the word muddled by the dryness in my mouth.

"Use magic to cut our ropes. Then we can go back to the palace to kill the queen and save my father!"

I tried to blink the fog of confusion away. Everything felt wrong. Perennia couldn't be gone.

"We don't have long!" Navara pleaded.

I took stock of my surroundings. A dappled gray rouncey stood tethered to a nearby tree, and a hazy memory returned to me of jostling along its back. A ring of stones encircled a neatly arranged pile of firewood nearby.

Dew soaked the seat of my tunic dress and the tan breeches I'd donned to meet my mystery caller. Aches and bruises throbbed throughout my body, most acutely at the back of my head. My hands were bundled uselessly in my lap and my back rested against a mossy tree. I felt an odd weightlessness, a tickle of air around my neck where a cool metal chain should have rested.

My elicrin stone was gone.

"Do the magic! Hurry! I hear him coming!" Navara whispered.

"It's gone," I said. "My elicrin stone."

"Gone? You mean she took it before she sent us out here to die?" Navara cursed in Perispi. "Of course she did. We're finished."

Without my elicrin stone, grief was simply despair. The plans for revenge that took shape in my tortured dreams disintegrated like cinders in the wind.

The approaching footsteps were so deft and quiet that I didn't notice the huntsman until he reached the campsite, carrying a bundle of split wood. He neatly arranged the logs atop the heap—a pyre far too large for cooking or warmth on a mild spring day. It had to be for another purpose.

When he finished he turned to face us, the severity of his expression revealing his intentions.

Deft as a hawk, he reached for the hunting knife at his hip, unsheathing the keen-edged blade.

THIRTEEN

AMBROSINE
SIX WEEKS AGO

THE serrated edge of my knife scraped against the porcelain plate, drawing the attention of Myron, his commander, and his high priest. They had nearly finished their meals despite their fluid conversation in Perispi, while my stomach revolted at the roast duck drowning in tangy olive sauce.

But I couldn't carve the bites any smaller. I would have to eat. Already, Father Peramati regarded me with a hawkish stare. We barely spoke each other's native language, but I felt as though he could peer through tissue and bone to my soul. The notion made me squirm.

I forced down a nibble. It tasted mushy, flavorless, inedible. I knew I would spend my evening vomiting into the commode.

An insubordinate maid had told Myron of my sickness and he had rejoiced, believing me to be with child. Nexantius had mocked him in the privacy of our entwined thoughts. His laughter had filled my head while I reluctantly crushed Myron's joy.

Before, I would have been pleased to deliver news of a pregnancy, knowing nearly everyone in our kingdom would delight in me. No longer would I feel forgotten and small. Everyone would fret over me and they would once again appreciate my beauty and consequence.

But that was before. Soon I wouldn't need their approval or their admiration.

Instead, I would have their fear and respect.

You will, indeed, Nexantius said, stirring inside me, the whisper of his thoughts brushing against mine. *As soon as you agree: two men at this table need to die.*

He had been silent since our argument, when I had first realized there were conditions to our arrangement—which he had withheld from me at first.

I refuse to hurt Myron, my thoughts hissed back at him. *And I will not kill the priest so long as Valory has the power to punish me. Give me victory over her first.*

They are the only two in this entire kingdom who know how to stop us. There are only two who have read the sealed scroll. Nexantius no longer whispered, his voice pouring through my mind like viscous honey. *The priest is clever; he will soon find out what I am, what we are. We will fail before we've even begun.*

What do he and Myron know that others don't?

Nexantius didn't answer.

Do you not trust me? I asked. *I have opened myself to you. I have increased your power. Can you at least tell me your plan for Valory Braiosa before I risk her wrath by shedding innocent blood? She could stop us with far less effort than Myron or the priest.*

Again, silence. I set down my utensils and made fists in my lap. Even when he had abandoned me to the quiet of my thoughts, Nexantius still resided within me. I felt his visceral repulsion of the many depictions of the Holies that graced the palace. His voracious cravings for precious metals and gems roiled in my belly.

I raised one fist to rest it under my chin, touching my tongue to the gold setting of my amethyst ring. Myron had gifted it to me on our wedding day. The metal tasted more decadent than warm pastry, the jewel sweeter than pomegranate arils. My teeth could miraculously cut through both like a knife through butter.

But even after dinner, when I was alone—more or less—I could not succumb to the Fallen's appetite. My jewelry case had begun to look bare. Myron had noticed my lack of baubles, and I had already dismissed two maids over false accusations of theft.

We needed to act, and soon.

"Thank Orico for this delicious meal," Father Peramati said in Perispi, tossing his silk serviette onto the table.

Before I could stop myself, I sneered. The names of the Holies grated my ears. Their countenances stung my eyes like the midday sun. Right now, the pious, unctuous Holies of Generosity and Moderation gazed down upon us from a marble relief above the mantel. I ground my teeth, tempted to pluck up a candelabra and smash the sculptures to bits.

Commander Larsio caught on to my distaste. In the flickering light, I failed to decipher the pensive lines crossing his face. "You are not enjoying the meal, my queen?" he asked in Nisseran, his voice as neutral as his steady hazel eyes.

"My wife has been unwell in recent weeks," Myron replied. I heard worry tighten in his throat. He translated for Father Peramati. But I no longer needed a translator with Nexantius inside me. His caressing whispers kept me apprised of important conversations.

"Should we also thank Orico for the blessing of a growing

family?" Father Peramati asked, his smile warm with wine. But the joy didn't touch his eyes.

"Not just yet, Father," Myron answered.

I forced myself to take another bite.

"I will pray you recover soon," the priest managed in Nisseran, but his oily tone made it easier to imagine him praying that the statue of Myron's first wife would fall and crush me on my next stroll through the rose garden. He had advised Myron against marrying me and did not bother to hide his opinion that our union was an abomination.

"Forgive our thoughtlessness in excluding you, my dear," Myron said. "Commander Larsio was just telling us that the Segona boy would make a fine successor for him."

"I don't disagree," I said. "Severo is a gifted huntsman. My father always said that hunting requires both strategy and skill, and I'm certain those come in handy in military service." I sipped my wine and met the commander's steady gaze. "But surely you're not thinking of retiring, Commander? You've more black hairs than gray."

"We mortals must plan ahead, Your Majesty, for our time is limited," the commander replied, his burly hands stiff on either side of his empty plate. "With Nissera's leadership changing, I would like to pass the torch to someone levelheaded and clever, who follows orders without regard for personal cost. Severo Segona is loyal to crown and country."

Loyal to the crown... Nexantius purred, his words tickling my spine at the base of my skull. *We could use him, and the commander. Their might and skill could be ours.*

Father Peramati spoke again. "A good commander and a strong

army mean nothing if our people stray onto paths of vice and destruction. We are only as strong as our faith."

The priest rambled on. My stomach churned, rebelling against the meager nibbles I'd forced down. The fire crackled in the stately hearth despite the mild spring evening.

"I think I'll withdraw to bed," I said, sliding back my chair. The taste of acid snuck up my throat. Saliva pooled around my tongue. I needed to escape the stifling dining room.

"May I say a blessing for your health?" the Father asked, feebly pushing away from the table. He never called me by any reverential title. In Perispos, the crown and the faith were nearly coequal powers; the crown held only the slightest edge.

"I suppose," I managed. If he were quick about it, I'd escape the torment of this dull evening. I would find something small to settle my stomach: a silver sugar spoon or a gold knob from my wardrobe.

The Father hobbled toward me. I sighed and swung my purple skirts to face him. His failing vision made his stare no less cutting as he squinted up at me and pressed the tips of eight fingers on my forehead—one for each of the Holies, Myron had explained to me before we'd received our wedding blessing. Back then, the experience had been mildly uncomfortable, breathing in the Father's sour breath, crouching on my knees in my delicately embellished gown and veil at the foot of the altar in the throne room.

But now, in reaction to the Father's touch, lightning rods of pain shot through my skull. I closed my eyes and winced, repressing a howl of anguish.

"Orico," he began, and my belly lurched violently while the pain seared fiery paths through my brain. "Hestreclea. Eulippa." Another lurch. My mouth filled with acid again. *No, no, no.* "Lerimides—"

I wrenched back, but I couldn't escape in time. I gagged. Black bile issued from my lips. It spattered onto the Father's cream and gray vestments, spilling down my chin and the neck of my gown.

Shaking, hollowed out, I wiped my mouth with the side of my hand, used the other to mop the foul-smelling sick from my sternum. So far, I'd been able to control myself, vomiting only in the privacy of my rooms, keeping even my maids at a distance, cleaning up after myself. They heard me wretch, but they didn't see the dark substance that scraped its way up my raw insides anytime I had to eat and pretend I was still...still what?

Human?

I looked from Myron to the commander, finding identical looks of horror and concern—and for the first time since this had begun weeks ago, I truly felt the horror too. My eyes met the old priest's. They held a gleam of grim recognition.

He knows. He knows. My inward whisper became a silent scream.

Nexantius tugged at me from inside, hooking my navel, urging me away.

I may have apologized before I stumbled out of the dining room and began to run down the echoing corridor. It seemed only seconds and yet far too long before I reached the privacy of our suite and mumbled something about a spill to a maid who fussed over me. Somehow, I got rid of her and locked the door.

Relieved, I set my back to the dense, smooth pine, swallowing the wretched taste in my mouth. After a few heaving breaths, I marched to my dressing mirror.

"What are you?" I asked through clenched teeth. My reflection was fearsome, vicious, but not in the way I desired. I looked unkempt and overwhelmed, haunted and harassed, a wild animal pursued to the point of desperation. "I don't believe in the priest's drivel. The only true power in this world is magic. So why did his prayer do that to me?"

Magic is not so narrow a thing as you imagine, Nexantius replied. He did not show himself to me in the glass. For a moment, I wondered whether I'd simply gone mad.

"I did not agree to this!" I whispered, dismissing his words. "The tiresome pretense, the sickness, and worst, the way the Holy statues and Father Peramati hold power over me. There's already someone lording power over me. You were supposed to change that."

And I will. We have a plan.

"We?" I asked.

The others and me. We abide within the same universe of darkness, banished and cursed. But not for long.

A shiver frolicked over my scalp. *The others.*

The Fallen's image manifested in the mirror, taking my place. A tremor nearly buckled my knees; he radiated power, beautiful and mighty enough to resolve the nauseated ache in my belly and inspire a different one at the apex of my hips and thighs. He tilted his masked head, silver eyes as sharp as weapons, vigorous muscles taut but calm.

A knock rapped on the door, and in turn my heart beat against my chest. "Who is it?" I called.

"The physician, Your Majesty, here to examine you," the guest announced in a muffled voice. "Your husband summoned me."

My hand flew to the damp spot at my neckline. "I'm feeling better. I just need rest."

A pause. "Are you certain, my queen?"

"Yes."

The king is solicitous, Nexantius said when the physician departed. *He's a problem.*

I swallowed and again faced the glorious godlike being. "You want me to kill him for showing concern?"

You won't have to lie and pretend. Nexantius shifted closer, strength rippling beneath his silver skin. Though the mask covered his face, I could see enough to know his beauty might be too much to fully comprehend. His hair was as dark as the blackness around his silver irises. The angles of the mask suggested perfect symmetry.

Kill them both, and you won't have to eat and make yourself sick. You can destroy every likeness of our enemies and spit on them. You can do whatever you want, and no one will stop you. You are dragging your feet and bringing misery on yourself.

While the Fallen's words coiled around me, my mind traveled back to the airless dining room, to the priest's haughty eyes, his tendency to let everyone near him roast like pigs on spits simply because he was frail and apparently too stupid to have heard of a wool mantle. Though I'd resisted in theory, I *could* see myself hurting him, clamping my fingers around his wrinkly wattle and squeezing until fear filled his eyes.

"Is there any other way for Myron?" I asked.

I suppose there is a way to inoculate him without killing him. I don't prefer it. But if you insist—

"I do insist."

Nexantius laughed, low and tantalizing. It rumbled through me. *Fond of your mortal king, are you? And he is fond of you. We can use that.*

Myron entered the suite with a sigh. As he unlaced his jerkin, he noticed me reclining on the embroidered cushions of the bay window seat. He broke our gazes and continued yanking the laces loose. "The physician said you sent him away."

"I'm feeling better."

He stopped and turned to me. "There's something wrong. We can't simply ignore it."

"There is something happening, but there is nothing wrong," I said, rising from the window seat. I'd disposed of my soiled dress, bathed away the dried crud, brushed out my clean hair, and sprayed perfume in the air. In order to make Myron believe my deceptions, I needed him to forget the alarming aspects of what he had seen.

When I approached him, I gathered his hands in mine. "I don't need a physician, but I will be needing a midwife."

"A midwife?" he repeated, joy and confusion at war on his face.

"I didn't think I was with child, but now I know I am." The smile I gave him would put the stars to shame, but faking it withered something wholesome inside of me. I mourned it for only an instant.

Myron laughed and swept me up in a kiss. "But shouldn't we be even more concerned, then, about your condition?"

"This *is* my condition."

"But…the black…" He gestured at his own clean collar, grimacing.

"Oh, that," I said, and laughed it off. "I snuck down to the kitchen before dinner and ate black truffles. A woman with child has strange appetites, they say. While my mother carried Perennia, she desperately craved brined red onions. It's what brought me to realize."

The furrows of disbelief and concern lifted away from Myron's face, leaving a joy so pure that the withered bud inside of me shuddered. He kissed me again, and I forced an enthusiastic response.

Go on, Nexantius said, his seductive growl of a voice licking at my nape. *He's resting in your palm.*

"Come," I said, and interlaced my fingers with Myron's. I led him to my mirror and positioned him beside me. "Won't we make a lovely family?" I asked, stroking his arm as I rested my head on his shoulder. "When your new son or daughter looks at you, they will see a man who leads his country with strength and mercy."

He shook his head in disbelief and turned to me. "I'm to be a father again. And again and again, I hope."

"I hope so too." I crinkled my nose in a show of bashfulness. "Please apologize to Father Peramati for me. I can't bear to face him myself."

"He will understand." Myron cupped my chin. "And he will rejoice with us."

My gaze dropped to the floor. "No, Myron. He will think our child is an abomination. I'm sure of it."

"Of course he won't."

"Why do you let him undermine you?"

"He tells me the truth as he sees it. He's one of the only people who does."

"As he sees it?" I echoed. "Why should what he sees matter? You are the king."

"And good kings do not rule alone, my beauty," he said, stroking my hair. "Wise men seek the wisdom of others."

"But is *his* the wisdom you require?"

Gently, Nexantius coached.

"The faith and the crown are two branches of the same tree," Myron answered, "reaching for the heavens while bearing nourishing fruit for our people."

"But your people are disillusioned with the faith," I reminded him. "Even you are. You perform the motions for Navara's sake, and the poor girl only cares because she misses her mother. You've helped usher in an age of intellectualism and acceptance. Father Peramati is rigidly traditional. You can't forfeit progress because of dusty old laws and a dusty old man."

Myron's brows knit together. "It's true that the edifices are empty except on holidays. It's why Father Peramati has invented so many more in recent years. Nevertheless, it would be inappropriate for me to diminish the power of the faith in any way."

"The queen of Calgoran may be the most powerful elicromancer this world has ever seen. She could conquer beyond Nissera." The words tasted worse than vomit, all the more vile for their truthfulness. But I held the delicious secret inside me: Valory's reign would be temporary. Nexantius had a plan, which he would share with me as soon as Myron and Father Peramati were no longer a threat. "We must employ delicate diplomacy with the Realm

Alliance to maintain our standing, and that can't happen while anti-elicromancer Agrimas zealots hold power here."

I took his hand and pressed it to my belly. "You are a forward-thinking king. Wise, fair, and moderate. You are humbler than most men would be in your position."

The reluctance in his eyes melted. I hadn't known how badly he desired a child, how easily this would work.

We will show him what he wants to see.

I turned my husband toward the mirror again, shifting one step behind him. My elicrin stone remained unlit and lifeless against my skin, but I felt the power of the Fallen moving in and around me.

Myron's reflection changed ever so subtly, the progression as natural as blood rushing to the cheeks in a moment of pleasure.

It showed a man who stood a thumb's width taller and broader. His mildly thinning black hair thickened, the gray hairs darkening to charcoal. His skin looked young and ruddy, his face more solemn and handsome. I squeezed his upper arms as I peered around him, noting that the mirror made them look firmer and mightier than they felt.

"If your forebears had the power to write these laws," I whispered. "You have the power to *over*write them."

I stoked the charred logs of a steady fire and saw the inevitable sparks. Within the king's eyes, a new hunger and pride glistered bright, the color of steel.

Soon it would consume him.

❧ FOURTEEN ❧

KADRI
HALITHENICA, PERISPOS

WITH every bump in the road, I felt less like a person and more like a sack of potatoes.

Though I preferred jostling on land to swaying at sea, the musty enclosed wagon was hardly a material improvement over the dank ship cabin I'd left behind.

But only a few wooden boards separated me from freedom, rather than an entire sea.

And the ropes binding my hands. And the caravan of mercenaries with curved swords and poisoned knuckle spikes. And Falima.

I'd not seen much of her until we reached land, when my kidnappers had told her to ride in the wagon and keep an eye on me. My anger was nested so deep that I had said nothing when she climbed in with me. I'd only spat in her face.

From what I'd seen, our escorts handled her like a second sack of potatoes. Neither of us had been given a change of clothes. I still wore the emerald skirt and bodice I'd donned for the Realm Alliance meeting, now grimy and stained with rings of sweat, and Falima wore the same dark mustard dress. From the looks of her, I doubted her bathing ritual aboard the ship could have been much more sophisticated than mine, which involved a bucket of seawater and a grimy bar of soap. The chafing rope around my wrists seemed to be the only difference in our treatment.

The wheels hit a rut, and the bruised back of my head bumped the board behind me again.

"I'm sorry things had to happen this way," Falima said quietly from her seat across the wagon.

I bit down on my chapped lower lip. My outrage had not cooled over the days it took to reach land, but I'd learned to make room for it. There had to be a reason I was alive and mostly unharmed. King Agmur and the Jav Darhu *wanted* me that way. As long as that remained true, I knew I could escape somehow from whatever they had planned for me. I would fight to see Rynna again, assuming— and I did assume—that she had survived.

But Falima's hollow half apology stoked that smoldering outrage to a crackling flame.

"You're sorry?" I demanded. "I don't think you are. But you will be."

"I had no choice but to obey my king."

"No choice," I repeated. "The defense of a coward."

I used *arajir*, one of the most humiliating insults in the Erdemese language. It implied both cowardice and the act of disgracing oneself with shameful deeds.

Falima didn't take it well. Though she'd never been an emotive person, she did locate the nerve to lean forward and dole out a half-hearted slap that stung a little.

"You can't hurt me," I said. "You've done your worst already."

Without replying, she fell back against her seat.

"How long have you been King Agmur's informant? How long have you known about my elicrin stone?"

"A few months."

"What does King Agmur want? I refused his invitation, so he decided to drag me to Erdem by force? Wars are started over less."

"He didn't intend for us to be treated so badly."

"You don't know what he wants, do you?"

She averted her eyes. "At first, he only wanted information from me, anything damaging or compromising I could provide."

"Why?"

"I don't know," she whispered. "But when he found out Valory Braiosa had given you an elicrin stone, he wanted you in Erdem immediately. He tried asking first, in the letter."

"Does he not fear the retaliation of elicromancers?"

"Maybe he thinks he can convince you to stay. You know Fabian would let you leave without trouble, if that's what you wanted."

I didn't like that—the way she talked about my marriage like we were still companions. But she was right.

I sighed and peered out the open slat at the undulating hills of Perispos, the fields of sunflowers that taunted me with their cheerful, sun-drenched faces. Halithenica was famous for its rolling landscape and mild weather. I always admired the towering cypress trees, olive groves, and fertile vineyards. I could see the splotch of green that marked the Borivali Forest about five leagues south of the capital. Even the Jav Darhu might have trouble finding me if I could somehow escape into its shadows.

A corner of my heart fantasized about crossing the border into

Erdem at the end of this horrible journey, smelling the aromatic spices at the market in Doghan, clapping along to the plucky tunes that, back in Nissera, barely received more appreciation than a copper thesar given out of pity. And I'd be happy to see my brother again. I could have used Valory's portal to visit him at any time, but I couldn't bring myself to return to my first home. Perhaps I had always feared that I would want to stay, or that my heart would break leaving again.

More powerful than my sudden homesickness was my need to be home in Nissera, to reclaim the hours of Rynna's company I had lost.

If she survived, that cruel voice of reason reminded me.

The road took a rising turn. My tiny window peeked out at a hilltop estate nestled near a vast vineyard, striped by orderly rows of grapevines. The wagon slowed to enter the winding drive, guarded by men armed with daggers, who swung open an iron gate to admit us.

Falima looked around, baffled, while a fearful hope fluttered through my belly. A change of surroundings might mean more possibilities of escape. Mercer said Glisette had come to Halithenica to visit Ambrosine. The longer we stayed, the better chance I had of reuniting with her.

"Why are we stopping?" Falima wondered aloud, as though we were friendly strangers sharing a coach by happenstance. "We're barely outside Halithenica. It will be days before we reach the border of Erdem." She licked her lips, nervous. "Maybe we're just resting here for the night."

That seemed unlikely. Plenty of daylight remained for us to cover more ground, and a curious exchange at the docks earlier had already led me to wonder whether previous arrangements had changed. While Captain Nasso's crew had transferred me from ship to wagon under cover of predawn darkness, a pair of unarmed men approached the captain and offered him a rolled missive. The desperate bud of hope that the letter might somehow grant me salvation disappeared when Captain Nasso burned the missive in a vagrant's cooking fire.

Now, as we rolled up the smooth drive, I thought I recognized the two mysterious men amid a cavalcade of servants in rust-colored garb emerging from the estate house, shielding their eyes from the sun. The wagon jerked to a stop, and my heart jolted along with my bruised body; this might be my only chance to flee.

The metal latch scraped, and the wagon door squealed open. I winced against the sunlight. One of the mercenaries yanked me out by my elbow and forced me to stagger along the pebbled drive.

I mentally rehearsed my escape, but my undernourished body protested, the fatigue from sedentary days and nights on a stinking cot. These people were trained killers, and I knew nothing about the company they kept here in Perispos.

Unless I regained my strength soon, I would not escape using speed or force.

I would need wit and caution.

Or powerful friends.

How I would love to see Glisette or Valory annihilate Captain Nasso and leave nothing but scorched earth. Even the Jav Darhu had to know they didn't stand a chance against experienced elicromancers.

My friends would find me. Maybe Mercer would have a vision, or maybe they could locate me by other means. I'd once heard

Glisette describe how to make a magical tracking map with supplies I'd never even heard of. It sounded like a tedious, fickle endeavor that could take weeks due to the necessity of a full moon's light. But surely they had already started and would be on their way to recover me soon.

Until then, wit and caution it is.

The people awaiting us wore fine clothing and jewelry, even those who appeared to be household staff. Gold and copper embroidery adorned the necks and hems of their uniform tunics and dresses. At the apex of their casual formation stood a broadly built Perispi man with golden olive skin, dark waves, and a coarse, graying beard.

"Where are we?" Falima asked, her sandals scuffing as she hurried to catch up.

"We received a higher bid for the delivery of Kadri Lillis," the man who handled me replied to her.

My heart sank like an anchor. At least King Agmur had wanted me alive and well. What did this man want?

"A higher bid?" Falima repeated, alarmed. "You mean she's not going to the king anymore?"

"No," the man said simply, and that one word on the back of my neck sent shivers down my spine.

"You were supposed to take me to Erdem with you," Falima said, brown eyes wide with panic as she drew even with us. "I don't have coin. I don't have anywhere to go!"

Captain Nasso stalked around the front of the wagon and spoke to her in a menacing, low voice. "You're making a scene in front of our hosts. We will take you to Erdem as promised, but we will go when our business is finished here. If you don't like that, you are free to leave."

The captain smiled as he turned to shake the broad man's hand.

"The rumors about you are true, then," the stranger said in non-native Erdemese, a Perispi accent noticeable. He wore a wide grin. "The Red Fangs always deliver…unless one client poaches another's prey!" He busted into a hearty laugh.

Nasso smirked. "We never claimed to be men of honor."

"No, you did not," the master of the estate agreed, still chuckling. His brown eyes found me, looked me up and down. "She's rather worse for wear. I heard King Agmur asked you to treat her according to her status."

"Her status is a hostage," Captain Nasso replied. "She is alive and unharmed."

The man frowned at this, but his face lightened as he gave me another quick study and decided that my wretchedness was either immaterial or easily curable. He called over his shoulder, "Lucrez! Why don't you take our guest to bathe and make her presentable for the meal?"

The request rubbed me the wrong way, like an unwanted touch. His use of the word "guest" was cold comfort. If I couldn't leave freely and flee home to Rynna, my standing had not changed.

In response to his call, a curvaceous woman emerged from the shade of a nearby pergola, carrying a tabby cat and looking bored, as if we were statues in a garden she'd toured a thousand times. The persimmon gown that bared her brown midriff reminded me of home in a way even my custom-made garments in Yorth had not; I could tell she was my compatriot before she responded to the lord's summons spoken in Erdemese. I wondered if I could make an ally of her.

"Cut the queen's ropes, please," the master of the estate said to my escort.

The mercenary who restrained me hesitated.

"By all means!" Captain Nasso said with a dismissive gesture. "Our work is done. Lord Orturio can treat her as he pleases."

My teeth locked together in anger, but I didn't want to sacrifice the freedom I'd just been granted.

The man cut the ropes. I resisted the urge to rub the raw skin.

"Speaking of comfort," Nasso said to Lord Orturio, "they say you are generous with your finest vintages."

Lord Orturio laughed again. "Follow me and I'll prove them right."

As the men turned to enter the estate, Lucrez dropped the cat and motioned me through another entry. The cat flicked its tail and moseyed away.

Wondering what awaited me on the other side of the studded pine doors, I reluctantly followed.

The interior was rustic but elegant, with wood-beam ceilings, religious tapestries, and iron chandeliers. The jovial voice of our host echoed through the halls—I heard something about a wheel of cheese, and my stomach grumbled—but we journeyed away from the noise to a second-floor bedchamber with a stunning vineyard view.

"You will sleep here," Lucrez said, though for how long she did not specify.

A maid with fair skin, ruddy cheeks, and short red curls curt-sied to me before pouring bathwater into a marble tub.

"Why am I here?" I asked Lucrez.

"You'll have to ask Rasmus," she replied.

"Who?"

"Rasmus Orturio. The master of the house."

"Is he your husband?"

"No."

"He doesn't fear the king of Erdem's wrath?"

She gave a harsh laugh. "Rasmus is the richest winemaker in Perispos. He doesn't fear other rich and powerful men."

"So am I to be his wife?" I asked, sweeping my gaze over the iron four-poster bed with flowy curtains and a luxurious pile of pillows. "His mistress? A stolen trophy to anger his rivals?"

"As I said, you will have to ask him. Bathe while I fetch my cosmetics."

Lucrez sashayed out and closed the door behind her. I hurried to peel off my filthy clothes and tried to bathe quickly, though the maid had other ideas in mind, scrubbing me with the cloth so patiently I could have slapped her out of blinding, ravenous hunger. But the warm water soothed me, and by the time she rubbed balm on my tender, broken skin, I pondered delaying any attempt of escape until their hospitality helped me recover my strength. As long as the hospitality remained this benevolent.

As the thought of escape crossed my mind, I wondered about my elicrin stone. Would it be turned over to my new "buyer" or brought to King Agmur?

"Do you know why I'm here?" I asked the maid in Nisseran. As the daughter of a foreign diplomat, I'd been proficient in Perispi since early childhood, but perhaps it would be wise not to reveal this; the people of the household might be less careful with their words if they believed I couldn't understand.

My guess about her nationality was correct; the maid replied in Nisseran, "Forgive me, Your Majesty, but I'm not supposed to fraternize with you."

"Hurry," Lucrez said, returning to steer me to a vanity. "I still have to get ready."

Unlike the maid, Lucrez was almost violently hasty in beautifying me. She dusted my cheeks with a rouge of ground flowers and painted my eyes so carelessly that I feared for my sight. The thick fragrance of jasmine and nerumia flowers clung to her silken hair, which tickled my shoulders as she worked. "There are clothes for you in the wardrobe," she said when she'd finished, and left again.

My bruises protested as I hauled myself to the wardrobe and opened it to find bright colors, decorative borders, accents threaded in silver and gold. I chose the most subdued bodice and skirt set I could find in case I decided to attempt escape: maroon with a lavender shoulder sash and silver beading.

After I had dressed, the maid beckoned me to follow her.

As we descended to the first floor, I memorized what I could of the estate's layout, grateful for the sunlight pouring over pale stones, giving me a clear idea of my surroundings. Tucking away the thought of escape for now, I entered the boisterous dining room.

Chandeliers illuminated paintings of an ancient war Perispos had waged against Erdem to try to convert our people to Agrimas. The Perispi army attempted to conquer the city of Doghan to establish an edifice at its heart, but Erdem crushed the Perispi invaders and executed their commander. These paintings depicted the commander as a martyr, his death as a tragedy, and the Erde-mese soldiers as an angry mob. The Holy of Loyalty opened her arms to welcome him to the afterlife.

What did it matter that historical records showed the "martyr" was no hero, but a monster who committed vile acts against vulnerable women while destroying a city not his own? What did it matter that the war was more about controlling the trade of precious spices than religious conversion? It was a legend now, and legends lived on regardless of inconvenient truths.

Tearing my eyes away, I searched the faces in the room and found no sign of Lucrez, or Falima, for that matter.

Lord Orturio sat at the far end of a long dining table, Captain Nasso opposite him. The other mercenaries gathered along the flanks, mingling with five Perispi men I did not recognize. One of them resembled Lord Orturio, but older, heavier, and gray-headed.

Wine had thawed the mercenaries' formidable demeanor, and none of them seemed to care that the same person they treated like dirt had managed to recover her dignity. I was only a job to them, a task to be completed with minimal inconvenience.

"Please, sit over there," Lord Orturio said, gesturing to a seat near the windows. The shutters were propped open to permit a warm midday breeze. "Help yourself."

As I obeyed, I realized how much self-restraint it would take not to wolf down the spread of cheeses, galantine, olives, jellies. I consumed a desperate bite of cheese with a soft yellow rind, sighing as the tangy taste coated my tongue. By the time I had piled enough food on my plate to quell the storm of hunger, tantalizing flute notes pierced through the conversation.

Captain Nasso rubbed his hands together in anticipation. "Is this the entertainment you promised?"

Orturio nodded once, a twinkle in his eye.

In the corner, musicians had taken up instruments: a goatskin tambourine with brass cymbals, a goblet-shaped drum, and an eastern lute. After a few bars, the music changed, its dynamic turning dark and persuasive. A sensual shadow appeared in the doorway, softly gyrating her hipbones. It was Lucrez, wearing a traditional Erdemese folk dance costume of black and flame-red fabric. The cropped vest chimed with disc ornaments, and chains of silver fangs encircled her bare belly—a tribute to Orturio's honored guests.

The provocative drumbeat guided her articulations of chest and hips. A few of the men whistled as she entered and whirled around the table, pausing to strike poses and shimmy her ornaments in their faces. Normally, I would be too fascinated to tear my eyes away. One of my most vivid memories from Erdem was watching folk dancers perform in King Agmur's court, and afterward, telling my father I wanted to be a dancer someday. He chuckled and said I was meant for greater things, and I never spoke of it again. Of course, I eventually realized I didn't want to *be* one of them so much as wanted to *kiss* one of them. I also enjoyed the spectacle of Erdemese folk dance for its own sake, but not right now; I took the opportunity to continue appeasing my appetite.

When Lucrez reached the man sitting next to me, I dropped the handful of olives I held. The fragrance of jasmine and nerumia flowers washed over me again, and suddenly I wanted to weep. I missed home—all of my homes. Nissera, Erdem, Wenryn. But here I was, under a stranger's roof, unsure of my status, splitting the difference between captive and guest, elicromancer and mortal, queen and inconsequential victim.

Lucrez stroked the face of the man beside me before moving on, sliding her hand along the back of my chair on her way to the next mercenary.

"Don't pass her up," Orturio called over the music, and Lucrez looked at him, her come-hither mask carefully held in place. I clenched the arms of the chair in fear. Did he know something I would rather have kept secret from him, something he might use against me?

"She's a guest," he added to justify the request. Or was it an order?

Lucrez smiled obligingly and slid next to me, continuing her skilled dance of alternating percussive and fluid movements. A piercing whistle of appreciation hurt my ears, and the others erupted into cheers. Lucrez responded to their encouragement by posting one hand on the back of my chair and pressing closer to me, closer than she had with any of the men, but not close enough to touch. She slid her free hand through her hair, opening up so the audience could see her movements. My breath hitched—she was the best dancer I'd ever seen, and also terribly beautiful. But sudden, hot tears stung the bridge of my nose.

No, you can't, I scolded myself.

But I felt so lost, so far from everything familiar and yet, in the presence of this Erdemese beauty who smelled of memory and simpler days, somehow closer than ever.

I tried to swallow the tears. Lucrez met my eyes, her expression the same as it had been with the others—an emotional performance

I found unconvincing while the men ate it up and yearned for more. A realization registered in her painted brown eyes, and with an assertive punch of her hip, she glided away from me as gracefully as she had come. She moved on to the next guest and drew his sword, dancing skillfully with the weapon.

I breathed deeply until the tears subsided.

By the end of the meal, I wished only to climb into a soft bed and sleep so that I could approach my captivity with a clear head tomorrow. It dragged until exhaustion weighed down my eyelids, but no one dismissed me.

"Kadri Lillis," Orturio said as I began to nod off. I remembered where I was with a clench of panic.

"Come with me to the wine cellar," he said, beckoning me. "Where only my guests of honor go."

⚜ FIFTEEN ⚜

KADRI

A PRICKLE crawled down my nape as I reluctantly followed my host and captor.

The music dimmed. I was alone with the master of the house, and I did not like it. And yet I had been no safer in the dining room with the mercenaries. Lord Orturio could have violated or murdered me, and Captain Nasso would have simply watched.

We approached another studded pine door. Orturio withdrew a ring of iron keys from an interior pocket of his vest and selected one with a swirling filigree head.

"Why do you outbid the king of Erdem?" I asked.

"My other guest of honor will explain," he said in Perispi. I realized too late that I had let surprise show on my face—now he would know for certain that I spoke the language of this country.

When he turned the knob, a draft licked over my skin, tracing my wounds with cool fingers. Closed stone stairs led to a dim underground space. I feared whatever awaited me down there, but I also feared the drunken men in the dining room, aroused by Lucrez's performance and craving fare beyond food and wine.

"Come, a sip of renowned Casiani Trescara will help you recover from your harrowing journey," Orturio said, gesturing for me to descend first. "Captain Nasso has heard I'm generous with my best wines, but that's a myth I perpetuate. I save the best for conducting serious business."

"If outbidding the ruler of one nation to kidnap the queen of another isn't serious business, I don't know what is," I replied without moving.

Orturio laughed. "I have heard you were clever. I anticipate a productive partnership. But I don't do business without a goblet in hand. Come."

Business. Perhaps there was a chance to secure my freedom without the risk of Lord Orturio sending the Jav Darhu to drag me back or kill me. But what did he want? Who awaited me on the other side of this door? What was so valuable that he would pay a fortune to undercut King Agmur?

It's too high a price for simply bedding me. Isn't it?

The thought of him pinning me down with those brawny, hairy forearms and trapping me under his body made a cold stake of fear pierce my ribs. What if he considered my disinterest in men an entertaining challenge, or an aberration to be suppressed or eradicated?

Regardless, overpowering him—and whoever else awaited me—could be no more difficult than taking on the rowdy lot of inebriated murderers upstairs. So I descended. The powerful smell of fermenting grapes pervaded the air.

I heard Orturio follow me and lock the door behind him.

At the bottom, I found a dirt cellar containing oak barrels and large wooden vats. Their enormity made the arched ceiling feel low and confining, but the cool air kept me from spiraling into a panic—until I noticed a figure sitting at a table.

Sconces splashed light on a male face I recognized. With shoulder-length pale hair, exquisite cheekbones, a thin nose, and flawless cream skin, the man looked like an even less approachable facsimile of Devorian.

Mathis Lorenthi.

I shut my gaping mouth to prevent every curse I knew from spilling out. "You? You're behind this?" I stalked down the dirt aisle and showed him the bloody lacerations encircling my wrists. "You fled the Realm Alliance's punishment so you could hurt more innocent people?"

Mathis's shapely lips melted into a diabolical smirk as my breathless interrogation hung in the air. "We did not arrange your kidnapping; we intercepted it. And it's not my fault you saddled me with a punishment I could escape. You should have confiscated my elicrin stone and thrown me in prison. The probation was bewilderingly naïve."

He swirled and sipped from a glass of ruby wine, groaning with relish. Mathis was an Amplisensor, an elicromancer with the gift of enhanced senses. Any touch, taste, scent, sight, or sound he chose to perceive with his gift became exponentially more potent. He used it to amplify music, art, sex, and cuisine... and to manipulate others so he could enjoy his lavish lifestyle without interruption.

"There's no need to convince *you* of the naïveté," Mathis continued, tracing a graceful finger around the rim of his glass. "You wanted a more severe sentence, but you were the token mortal in the council chamber... or so most of your friends believed."

I glared at him, my tongue on fire with a thousand scathing rebukes. "You think you're clever for noting my displeasure? You didn't intend to starve and kill your own people, so my friends balked. But I believe negligence and greed are no better than cruelty and malice, and your heart is home to all. They should have carved out your power and ripped the privilege of immortal life from you."

My tone was biting and indignant. I had forgotten for a moment that compliance might be my sole means of escape.

The elicromancer shifted to cross his legs. The movement made the specks of gold within his clear elicrin stone twinkle, but not as brightly as the cunning in his oceanic eyes. "So, we can agree that the Realm Alliance made a poor decision?"

I did not like the idea of agreeing with Mathis Lorenthi. For as long as he had been a prominent political player in Nissera—since the death of Glisette's parents—Mathis had been manipulative. While defending himself at trial, he had somehow succeeded in making us all feel like clueless children who had bested the Moth King through sheer luck and reckless bravery.

I smoothed the ragged edge from my voice. "I'm not going to agree with every decision the group makes. That's how it works when you value differing opinions instead of hibernating in comfort and gorging yourself on riches you didn't earn."

There my composure went again. Thankfully, neither man seemed to care.

"But you did not voice your differing opinion," Mathis said. "Isn't that the purpose of the Realm Alliance?"

I shut my mouth. I would say nothing of the reason I'd kept quiet: the Realm Alliance had pardoned Rayed for the betrayal he was forced to commit.

Forced to commit? Inwardly, I recoiled from my own hypocrisy. I had just called Falima a coward for claiming she had no choice.

I glanced back at Lord Orturio. Arms crossed over his tree trunk of a chest, almond-shaped brown eyes calm, he watched me. "Come, sit. This doesn't have to be so unfriendly," he said in Perispi. He stepped around me to approach a shelf holding an oak cask with a spigot. I hadn't noticed until now that the wall behind Mathis had a marble shrine depicting the Holies.

Orturio opened the cask spout and filled a goblet with wine. "*Casiani* was my mother's family name. *Trescara* is the grape. Casiani Trescara is"—he held the jeweled red wine to the light—"liquid riches."

As though offering a vessel containing a piece of his soul, Orturio placed the goblet at the empty place across from Mathis. When I didn't accept it, Orturio threw his head back and released a booming laugh. "Oh, for Holies' sakes!" He took a swig and replaced it. "I would never poison wine. Making it requires too much sweat and fervent prayer."

I pulled out the chair opposite Mathis and perched on its edge. Orturio filled another goblet for himself and settled down to the tune of creaking wood.

"Why am I here?" I asked again. I looked at Mathis. "Why are *you* here?"

"Let's start with me. I traveled abroad to find allies who would help me undermine the Realm Alliance." He finished his wine and stood to help himself to more. No doubt, he was an expensive houseguest. "Orturio and I found each other. Together, we campaigned to convince the king of Erdem that your group's authority is null. It was not a difficult task, considering your husband is the only ruler in Nissera with a legitimate claim to his throne. As a woman, Glisette's claim is no more legitimate than mine was as regent. And Valory Braiosa is the 'queen of widows,' who seized leadership of Calgoran by murdering half the men in her family."

"You snake." His words echoed Rayed's letter almost exactly. King Agmur wouldn't have cared about obsolete Volarian laws until Mathis pointed them out and told him he *should* care. And yes, Valory had not tried the traitors in her family before executing them, but trials would inevitably have led to the same result.

"That statute is antiquated nonsense," I said. "It's a thin excuse for a foreign ally to withdraw support for Glisette. As for Valory, her claim is legitimate. King Tiernan made her his heir apparent while those traitors were torturing and killing him."

"That is what she and her odd little cousin Melkior claim," Mathis sneered. "They were the only witnesses to such a historic transfer of power."

I narrowed my eyes at him. "Undermining our influence will help you claim the throne of Volarre. I understand that part. But why does this involve me?"

"King Agmur instructed Falima to seek damaging information about the Realm Alliance, which could further cast its competency into doubt," Mathis explained. "But when he learned that you, a mortal, possessed an elicrin stone, he went rogue. His fear of Valory Braiosa turned to ambition. He hoped you would be able to persuade her to give elicrin stones to him and a few select nobles. He was ready to lure you to his side with promises of peace, prosperity, and equality for everyone in Erdem. He would also promise to recognize the Realm Alliance again if you could help him obtain elicrin power. When you rejected his invitation, he sent the Jav Darhu, the only people he trusted to kidnap an elicromancer."

"Are you saying he had me kidnapped, wounding one of my friends, in order to *win me over?*" I didn't want to specify the nature of Rynna's importance to me, but all the same, my voice cracked in aguish and anger. A sob built in my throat. The horrible irony of it all made me want to knock down every barrel in this cellar, storm upstairs, and strike the cruel Captain Nasso with my bare fists until his self-assured face looked like an overripe fruit.

"King Agmur thought he had paid the Jav Darhu enough to secure royal treatment on your behalf," Orturio said in Perispi with a shrug. He swirled his wine and inserted his nose in the glass before taking a drink. "But they don't take any special orders that could slow down the mission or cut into their profits."

"So you intercepted my kidnapping because you did not want King Agmur to become an elicromancer?" I asked in Perispi.

"That's one reason," Mathis replied in the language of his host, his Perispi accent positively atrocious. Apparently, even the best language tutors that a royal purse could buy could not guarantee competence. "But I also could not allow the Realm Alliance to negotiate back into his good graces."

I laughed, nearly hysterical. "You wasted your resources bringing me here. Valory would never agree to make him an elicromancer."

"So he was wrong to think Valory Braiosa's scruples were negotiable, just like the tyrant she overthrew?" Mathis asked in Nisseran.

"She's nothing like the Moth King."

"Did Emlyn Valmarys not reward the loyalty of his mortal servants with elicrin gifts?"

"Yes, but—"

"And Valory Braiosa gave you yours in secret, without consulting the other members of the Realm Alliance?"

I didn't answer. The night she'd given me my elicrin stone, the desire to use my new magic for good had overpowered my unease about outside perceptions.

"Publicly, she claims to comply with your noble majority votes," Mathis said. "Privately, she's doling out elicrin gifts to mortals."

I tried not to reveal how deeply his comment burrowed under my skin. "You've prevented King Agmur from making me a means to an end. Am I free to leave at will?"

"In due time," Orturio said. "But I hope you'll consider our interference a favor—a favor you might see fit to repay."

Of course. My freedom would come at a cost. I should have known.

"What do you want?" I asked, steeling myself for the possibilities. Did they plan to extort me? Use me like the Ermetarius men had used Rayed—as a precious Realm Alliance vote that could be cast in their favor when they needed it?

"Your help rescuing my princess from the tyrant queen, as a start," Orturio said.

Tucking away my surprise, I set my full goblet to my lips and let the robust flavor swirl over my senses. "What has Ambrosine done now? Emptied the royal vault? Taxed the poor people out of hearth and home?"

"She has subdued the king and usurped his authority," Orturio explained. "She murdered the high priest. She is changing laws to sunder the faith from the crown. She is imprisoning dissidents and persecuting Agrimas believers."

I stared at him. "That can't be true."

"Oh, it is," Mathis said. "*And* she's taxed poor people out of hearth and home. *And* demanded the edifice tithes as repayment for centuries of support from the crown."

Guilt bored into my belly like a corkscrew, but Mathis wasn't exactly trustworthy, and I knew nothing about Rasmus Orturio. "The Realm Alliance would know if that were true," I said, jutting my chin in defiance.

"Oh, would you?" Mathis laughed into his goblet. "Because you have so much experience maintaining foreign contacts and alliances? Because the myriad problems within your own realm aren't keeping you occupied?"

"Ambrosine is vain and greedy, but she didn't challenge Devorian's claim to the throne despite being the eldest child. And when he abdicated, she didn't try to stop you from taking over as regent. She's never been power hungry."

"People change." Mathis brushed the rim of his glass again, insouciant.

"How would she even accomplish those things? We restricted her magic just like we did yours." I gestured at his gold-flecked elicrin stone.

"The locals have some superstitious theories," Mathis explained. "But I think she resorted to dark elicromancy to seize what she desired. Her poor husband or the priest tried to reign in her frivolity, and she simply would not be denied. It's a family trait." He smiled as though it were something to be proud of.

"How could Myron allow this?" I asked, shaking my head. How did the Realm Alliance not know? Why did no one ask us for help?

A cold dread turned in my stomach. Perhaps I already knew the answer to that. We had already failed to hold Ambrosine accountable once. The people of Perispos did not trust us to save them.

"Myron is a castrated king," Orturio answered. "He still signs decrees, but only at her behest."

He swilled the rest of his wine and pushed back from the table. "Perhaps it's better for you to see than hear. Come."

Sleep seemed ever out of reach as our open-top carriage sped away from the estate. Orturio had bound my wrists again, though thankfully with soft strips of cloth this time.

I watched the countryside roll by and found it difficult to believe that a reign of terror had fallen over this kingdom. Serene, crisp green hills billowed toward woodlands to the south and toward the outline of the city proper and the palace in the northwest—where Glisette was just out of reach. If only she knew. She would come for me and punish anyone who had laid a finger on me.

Soon the taste of smoke coated my tongue. The light wind carried a haze that stung my eyes. Through it, I saw a town of red-clay roofs rising up from the slope of a valley. A structure of jagged, blackened stones overshadowed the other buildings on the square.

"Is that an edifice?" I asked Orturio.

"It was. Now it's a pile of stones."

The taste of ash thickened as we rolled into town, greeted by the wary stares of locals and sun-withered vagabonds. The ruins surrounding the edifice looked more dismal the nearer we drew. My lungs itched with the urge to cough.

The driver eased to a halt in the edifice courtyard.

"Did she do this?" I asked Orturio as we debarked from the carriage and hiked over heaps of gray rubble and shards of stained glass. Only the skeleton of the edifice remained standing. So badly, I wanted to see Glisette, to know she was all right, to ask her how this could have happened without our knowledge. But Orturio instinctively knew I had thoughts of escape. He followed close behind, cloaking me in his large shadow.

Inside the edifice we encountered utter devastation. Everything not made of marble had been burned to crisps. Chunks of structural stones had warped in the heat and crumbled.

I picked my way over the wreckage to the pale altar, smudged with black marks. Falling debris had broken off an arm of the Holy of Honesty. I couldn't recall her name, but I remembered why she held a key in one hand and a candle in the other: it symbolized that no truth could stay locked away or obscured forever.

I spotted the broken hand holding the key and bent to retrieve it.

We should not have shown Ambrosine mercy. But Glisette had seemed so thrilled at the thought of sending her far away, and Valory had wanted to prove she could be merciful. I'd hoped that the measures would be enough to restrain Ambrosine.

But clearly, that hope had been in vain.

"The priest, the altar attendants, a few townspeople, and even one of my brethren died," Orturio explained.

"Your brethren?" I asked, breathless with disbelief.

"My organization fights for the preservation of the faith. The high priest recently gave us an ancient religious artifact of immeasurable value. He wanted to keep it safe from the queen. We believe she killed him trying to obtain it. So we planted a rumor that it was hidden here and hid a fake instead, hoping she would come and we could ambush her. But she only had interest in destroying it. She sent soldiers to torch the place and everyone inside without even searching it."

"Why?" I asked, despair over the Realm Alliance's mistake weighing heavier with every ash-ridden breath I took. "What grudge does she hold against Agrimas?"

Orturio had let me wander deep into the edifice unaccompanied. Now he approached me and motioned for me to give him the broken bit of statue. Confused, I offered it to him, but he did not take it. Instead, he loosened the tied cloth around my wrists.

"You are free to recover your strength and leave if you wish," he said. "Or you could atone for your role in pardoning Ambrosine Lorenthi. You could the join the Uprising. You could become our agent and return to the Realm Alliance to affect meaningful change. You could make it your mission to prevent your powerful allies from bringing yet another disaster on defenseless mortals."

Orturio set something cool and hard in my palm. When he lifted his hand, I found an iron figurine. It was the Holy of Loyalty.

"King Agmur promised you peace and equality for Erdem's mortals, but he wanted an elicrin stone in exchange. We promise you peace and equality for all mortals…and we only want your allegiance."

"We want to return to a simpler time." Mathis ambled gracefully through the wreckage and fixed me with a calculating stare. "Before Queen Bristal, before the academy, before magical and royal bloodlines intertwined, elicromancers nearly went extinct. The remaining few minded their business in the mountains. Mortal kings reigned. There was order."

I narrowed my eyes at him. "You would give up your elicrin stone to be a mortal king?"

"To bring peace, yes. We want all elicromancers to surrender their stones, and it starts with us, when we're ready."

"There was peace and order before the Moth King too," I argued. "The Conclave set laws for elicromancers. They confiscated elicrin stones when necessary, and the Realm Alliance held them accountable. There was balance. That's all the new Realm Alliance wants."

"None of that prevented the Moth King," Mathis pointed out.

The reek of soot stung my nostrils. I looked around at the ravaged edifice. Mathis was right—if elicromancers could have solved the world's problems, they would have already. Queen Jessa, as the brilliant former leader of the Realm Alliance, would have. But even she couldn't keep her own kind from using their powers selfishly. Even elicrin Healers charged a gold aurion just to disappear a wart from a finger because if they deigned to heal every disease or injury, they would have to sacrifice their time and luxury.

Maybe elicromancers' chance to prove they could rule justly had already passed. Maybe it was time to step aside, regardless of our good intentions.

The uncertainty must have shown on my face. Orturio's eyes sparked like flint as he said, "Show your loyalty to your true people. Use your influence to advocate for defenseless mortals."

He closed my fingers into a fist around the Holy of Loyalty. "Help us end the chaotic reign of elicromancers forever."

❧ SIXTEEN ❧

GLISETTE
EARLIER THAT DAY

HE huntsman's knife flashed in the daylight falling through the trees. He took one menacing step, then another, his soles silent on the bed of moss and strewn leaves.

"Wait, no! Please!" Navara begged through tears of desperation.

But every plea I nearly mustered died in my throat. What was the use of living now? What did I have to protect, to cherish, to fight for?

My family had nearly unraveled when news of my parents' deaths reached our ears. And since that day, Devorian's and Ambrosine's selfish choices had tugged on every loose thread until only Perennia and I remained tightly woven. Without her, all was lost. Ambrosine had severed the cords of sisterhood in every direction.

If I survived this, Devorian and I would grieve together, dine together, discuss insipid diplomatic affairs, but things would never be the same. Ghosts would abide between us, in the empty seats, within the wardrobes of unworn dresses, behind the faces of our loved ones in every portrait.

The huntsman took a third step, shifting a calculating glare from Navara to me. Perhaps he had not yet chosen which of us to kill first.

"My father has always treated you kindly, Sev," Navara said, trembling. I remembered more Perispi than I thought, grasping her meaning. "He compensated you and your father fairly. You remember taking me on my first hunt, don't you? When I was eleven and you were fifteen? Father only brought me to make me feel important, and you played along like he asked. You let me think I killed that quail. But when I cried over having killed it, you told me the truth."

The huntsman listened, pausing mid-movement like a predator whose prey had glimpsed him prowling in the shadows.

The tendons in his hand and forearm swelled as he tightened his grip, preparing to bleed us out like swine. How fitting that Perennia and I would both die in this forsaken country, just like Mother and Father.

"*Giavna, giavna, Severo!*" Navara sobbed. It was one of the first words I'd learned in lessons: *please*. I'd heard it only in the context of mundane, polite exchanges, such as *Please pass the tea*.

"Kill me, if those are your orders," I managed to croak through the grief that clamped around my throat. "But spare your princess."

I closed my eyes and waited in darkness for the brief, horrible pain, and the peace that I hoped would follow after.

The huntsman roared, but the strike didn't come. I dared open my eyes and saw him stab his deadly blade into a mound of mossy soil.

Navara expelled a gasp of relief.

The huntsman raked stiff fingers through his hair. "She wants proof," he said. "She will kill my family if I don't deliver it by nightfall."

"What kind of proof?" I asked in Perispi. Aside from my elicrin stone, which she'd already stolen, any trophy he could present as evidence of my death would be a grisly one. The possibilities turned my stomach. My sister had become a monster. "A tongue? A hand? A head?"

"She asked for the princess's lungs," he answered, and added a word I didn't recognize: *taolo*.

"What is *taolo*?" I asked.

"Liver," Navara supplied breathlessly.

"And from you"—he looked at me—"hair ripped out by the roots."

I wanted to laugh despite the grim situation. Ambrosine was too craven to even request more than a lock of hair from me.

"That coward," I muttered. Tears blurred my sight. I leaned my pounding head back against the rough bark and licked the salt from my dry lips. "Kill me. Use whatever you need from me as proof for both of us."

"There has to be another way!" Navara said, but the appeal sounded halfhearted. She was noble and sweet, but only human. Of course she didn't want to die and have her corpse carved up and brought to Ambrosine as some morbid memento of triumph.

I ignored her and spoke to the huntsman. "She won't know the difference."

Even as I said it, something inside me thrashed with the blind will to survive, but fled as soon as Perennia's name whispered through my mind, a lonesome autumn wind dragging along shriveled blossoms.

"No!" Navara cried. "I can't face her alone. I need you."

"You do realize I just offered to serve up my bloody guts to save your life?" I said, a hysterical laugh threatening to break loose. "Now you're begging me to help you destroy her? You can't have it both ways."

Navara stared at me, at a loss.

"Do we have a deal?" I asked the huntsman.

He nodded solemnly.

"My friends can help you," I said to Navara. "Send word to the queen of Calgoran. Tell her everything."

The princess's throat bobbed, but she, too, gave a small nod.

I looked back up at the huntsman. His features may as well have been carved of marble for all they revealed, but in his eyes, determination battled doubt.

He was accustomed to watching creatures accept death when they stared into his eyes. A strange understanding seemed to settle between us. I wondered why the Agrimas teachings did not name a Holy of Mercy. My grief-addled mind imagined him as a statue in the Edifice of the Holies, draped in white, swiftly putting suffering creatures out of their misery.

Steeling himself, the huntsman took up his knife once more. "It will be quick," he promised.

I shut my eyes again and waited for the slice of the deadly blade.

"I can fool her," I heard the huntsman say.

I blinked my eyes open. An odd anger pounded at my chest, which made an unseasonably cold wind nip at the ends of my hair. Normally, that anger would transfer to my elicrin stone if I allowed it, brightening the misty chalcedony with power, which I could direct as I wished.

Now that anger would fuel the raw magic that had lived inside me before I received my stone—the unwieldy magic that didn't ask permission and was no slave to my better sense.

"Stop toying with me!" I shouted, and suddenly I wanted to live, in spite of everything.

"I'm sorry," the huntsman said. He lowered the knife. "I don't want to do this. But if she knows I'm lying, she will kill my family. That's why I . . . otherwise I wouldn't . . ." He trailed off. "All I need is a lock of your hair. I'll let you go, and I will hunt for the other parts. But you cannot show your faces."

"We won't," Navara vowed, lifting her stately chin. "We'll stay hidden. Your family will have nothing to fear, Sev. If we come back, it will be with an elicromancer army."

"Can you survive out here?" he asked.

"No," Navara said.

"Yes." I spoke over her.

"Take my pack," he said, tossing it at my feet. "Go deeper into the woods, where the foresters will be less likely to find you. The hair?"

"Just give me a moment." I closed my eyes and tried to fortify myself, but a fiery pain tore across the left side of my scalp before I was ready, adding to the throbbing in my head. I brayed and struggled against my bonds, wishing my hands were free to massage the tender area. A thousand curses formed on my tongue, but my better judgment told me not to insult the hunter who had just agreed to find other prey.

"It hurts more when you expect it," he said, grasping a bloody clump of golden hair. He slipped it into a pocket and severed the ropes holding Navara hostage. As she worked to untangle herself, he sheathed his knife and retrieved his mount, disappearing amid the dense trees.

Navara finally broke free. She clambered the few paces toward me and worked at the knots in my rope.

"What do we do now?" she asked in Nisseran, giving my tired mind a respite.

Crawl in a hole and die, I thought. "First of all, where are we?"

She paused, eyes searching the woods. "I don't know. South of Halithenica. Woods this dense are a few hours' ride from the city gates if you're traveling light. Sev must have led his horse for it to take so long."

"I think Ambrosine drugged us," I said, tasting the pungent residue of a veracamum root elixir. Ambrosine had once recommended it to help me sleep in the weeks following Mother's and Father's deaths. "I don't remember anything."

"Neither do I," Navara said. She gritted her teeth as she tugged on the impossibly tight knot in my rope. When she at last pulled it loose, the whole knot slipped out as though it should have been easy.

I squirmed to shake off the ropes and pulled a hand free, gently kneading the fresh bald spot on my scalp. At first, Ambrosine's request for my hair seemed silly, but now I recognized her insecurity. She couldn't abide the notion of eviscerating me, but she wanted to rob me of some trivial representation of the beauty she always feared would surpass hers.

What would Ambrosine say to Devorian when she sent him word? Would she tell him the truth or lie and tell him this appalling tragedy was every bit my fault?

The recollection of Perennia's dead weight in my arms made suffocating despair hedge in around me, crushing my chest, weakening my knees until even walking felt impossible.

But the idea of my sister's funeral taking place on foreign soil, without me, made intolerable fury flame up around my broken heart.

A few moments ago, I'd wanted to die. But now I wanted to kill Ambrosine first.

I scooped up the huntsman's pack and found only a bit of water sloshing in a skin, a flint stone, some dried berries, a string, and a slender boning knife. I took a sip of the water and passed Navara the rest.

She brushed the dirt from her skirts out of habit and accepted it. "What should we do?"

Without my elicrin stone, and without knowing how long it would take for my Nisseran friends to hear news of last night's tragedy, there was only one path for us to take.

"We hide," I answered. "We survive."

"Hide?" Navara repeated. "Hiding won't save my father or my kingdom."

"Neither will getting your lungs and liver carved out," I reminded her.

"But—"

"We aren't strong enough to defeat her!" I barked, my voice hoarse. "Listen, it's only temporary. Until help comes."

Navara's blazing eyes searched my face as though the answer might be hidden there. "We can sneak into the palace. She thinks we're dead. She won't expect us."

"She might," I said, and sighed when her eyebrows dove together in question. "Even if the huntsman manages to convince her with his proof, my elicrin stone will tell her I'm alive the second she touches it. It will always have a desire to return to its living master."

"Then why—?"

"I had to let the huntsman believe his plan would work so he didn't go through with murdering us."

The hopeful bravado that inflated her chest drained away, leaving her hunched and small. "He was trying to protect his family. Now they'll be in danger."

"We need to protect ourselves," I reminded her. "We need to find water and food. We need to get away from where the foresters can find us. I'll try to catch a quail or rabbit to sell somewhere for more supplies while you stay safe wherever we camp. You're too recognizable."

"But we promised Sev we wouldn't let anyone see us."

"We have no choice. I can't hunt with a boning knife."

Standing seemed an unconquerable chore, but I managed. The meager contents of the pack jostled against my hip as I started off south, deeper into the woods. Navara followed.

"Can we send word to one of your friends? Don't elicromancers have a way to send magical letters that travel faster?"

"Yes, but the network needs to be established first by an elicromancer who can forge missive channels between earthly places. Nissera has countless channels, but Perispos never allowed the Realm Alliance to establish them here."

"Oh."

She fell silent. I made note of everything I saw as I walked, to moor myself to the physical world instead of drowning in the pool of emotions brimming inside me, dense and dark as tar. *One foot. Now the other.*

Tree to the left. Rock to the right.

A girl you need to keep safe, behind you.

Navara yelped, and I turned to find the hem of her dark-blue dress already tangled in a nest of thorns.

I trudged back and knelt to unsnarl them from the delicate fabric, but that wouldn't stop it from happening again. "I'm going to cut your skirts." I dug for the sheathed boning knife. "You can take my boots to protect your legs."

"What about you?" she asked, grasping my shoulder for balance.

"I'll be fine." When I finished, the ragged hem hit midway down her calf. Tiny beads of blood dotted the scratches around her ankles. She wouldn't make it ten more steps without me.

"Your Majesty...Glisette...I'm sorry," she said. Her touch on my shoulder was soft. "If I hadn't asked you to meet me—"

"It's not your fault. It's mine." I cut her off, more curtly than I intended. "Ambrosine should never have set foot on Perispi soil."

"Perennia didn't deserve—"

"Let's move on." I sheathed the knife and traipsed to a nearby boulder to tug off my boots. Navara removed her silk slippers. Both of us looked ridiculous after the trade: me in breeches and dainty slippers and she in black leather boots paired with a short, tattered dress. But on we walked, listening for the trickle of a stream.

"I can't believe my father fell under the spell of a usurper," Navara said after a time. "Is she holding him prisoner? Is he suffering?"

"She's keeping him in the Edifice of the Fallen," I said. "She's created mirror illusions that seem to have warped his mind." A shudder crept up my spine as I recalled the guileful deceptions she had shown me.

"Has she hurt him?" Navara asked. She sounded unprepared to hear answers to her questions.

"Not physically."

"So, when we have more elicromancers, we'll be able to defeat Ambrosine and save him?" Navara asked, rustling as loudly as a wounded animal behind me. "Without a doubt?"

"Yes."

"Even though she's possessed by Nexantius?"

I ducked under a low branch and thought for a moment. "Whatever Nexantius is—and I'm not saying I believe in your Fallen gods—Valory Braiosa's power surpasses his. That I can assure you."

⚜ SEVENTEEN ⚜

AMBROSINE
ONE MONTH AND ONE WEEK AGO

HE old man looked small and frail standing at the foot of the dais, surprise deepening the feathered lines on his forehead. Myron had summoned the priest to tell him that his advice would no longer be welcome concerning military or diplomatic affairs. Myron explained that he was not repudiating the faith but giving it independence from the crown. An official decree would be coming forthwith.

Myron's tone, as ever, remained civil, but the priest looked like a kettle ready to shriek. I almost laughed at how the red sunset glow streaming from the windows resembled flames around his feet.

At last Myron dismissed him with a stern "Good night, Father." The old man shot a withering look my way. He turned and stormed from the receiving hall, his gray robes rippling behind him in spite of his hobbled gait.

Before he passed the guards at the threshold, he stopped, pivoted, and said, "She will destroy you and this kingdom."

The echo of the priest's words had not yet faded when I felt Nexantius's command like a stern tap on the shoulder.

It's time. The secret of our destruction must die with him, and with Myron's grasp on reality.

"I know that was a difficult decision, and you have much to

ponder," I said to Myron, resting a hand over my womb. I'd learned how easily the simple gesture reinforced my deception. I relished the blithe fondness it immediately brought to the king's face. "Shall I leave you to your thoughts?"

"I did have my doubts about this," Myron mused, ignoring my question. "But the way Father Peramati disrespected you just now dissolved every one. No one who is prejudiced against elicromancers should wield political power. Your parents' murders will be the last act of senseless violence committed against elicromancers in my kingdom."

Hurry.

I reached across the space between our twin thrones to take his hand. "I think I'll take a sunset walk in the gardens."

"I'll send truffles up as a treat upon your return," Myron replied, patting my hand. "Be sure to wear a cloak."

His warm attentions had delighted me, but over the course of a week, they'd become cloying. Fortunately, I could already see Nexantius's power taking hold of Myron's mind. Myron spent more time gazing into mirrors, succumbing to the little fictions they showed him: that he was stronger, younger, more regal, more virile. The more attached he became to these perceptions, the easier it would be to entangle him in a world of pleasant fantasies, to set him aside without causing him undue harm.

"You are such a dear." I planted a kiss on his forehead and gathered my skirts. "I will see you when you come to bed."

"I'll count the minutes, my darling," he sang.

My doting smile faded as soon as I showed him my back.

When he could no longer see me, I charted a course from the

ground floor to the priest's lofty quarters. He lived in an apartment beneath the Edifice of the Holies. Every morning at dawn, the old man unlocked the gates at the crest of the edifice staircase and admitted the few staggering worshippers making their pathetic daily pilgrimages to pray for health or wealth or a herd of a sheep.

Tomorrow, he would not.

I reached a sunset-striped landing and caught the priest scurrying out of sight on the third floor. This level held the family's private corridors, but our guards didn't bat an eye at his presence. I hurried after him. The eastward path he had taken led only to the princess's bedchamber, library, and recreation room.

Do not let him speak to Navara, Nexantius warned. *He will pass on the sacred knowledge of the apocrypha to her. He will tell her how to destroy us. We must destroy him first.*

I moved silently, a wolf in the night, gaining on the old man by covering more ground in one step than he could in three shuffling strides. A belt of lamplight burned bright beneath the door of the princess's bedchamber. The priest stopped and knocked, half glancing over his shoulder, as though afraid to face the falling darkness.

The door cracked open. A perplexed lady's maid greeted him. "Father?"

"I must see the princess," he whispered. "It is most urgent."

The maid yielded to the princess's strict tutor, Hesper. "She's reciting her nightly scriptures, Father. She hasn't missed a day since her mother died."

"Father," I said, "surely you see why it's inappropriate for you to call upon the young princess at this late hour."

At the sound of my voice, the priest turned, dark eyes blazing with a premonition of his death.

I thought he might try to shove his way in or ask the tutor to pass a message to Navara. But he had to know that once the secret left his lips, it would endanger others. So he ran.

He tried to sprint but only managed an uneven trot. Wary, the tutor closed the door.

I resumed my pursuit.

Father Peramati stumbled onward, rasping for breath. A smile pulled at the corner of my mouth when he tripped on the staircase leading to the top floor and issued a panicked cry.

Don't let him reach the edifice.

Why not?

We cannot enter.

He slipped out of sight. The pursuit became more of a hunt than a game, and I quickened my pace. Elaborate columns and skyward windows turned the edifice antechamber into a maze of sanguine sunset light and stretching shadows. Slow as he was, the priest wouldn't have had time to slip through the oak double doors leading down to the clergy quarters, and he certainly wouldn't have had time to scale the dozen steps to the edifice. He was hiding from me.

"Oh, Father," I sighed, circling in place. "It was not my idea to kill you. *He* insisted. You know who 'he' is, don't you?"

A shadow moved at the far end of the antechamber. The priest doddered out from behind a column, making a break for the edifice. What exactly did he plan to do? Remain there until I lost interest? He had to know he had reached the end of his road.

I sprang into action, catching up to him on the stairs and clawing at the back of his stiff collar. He toppled backward, striking the steps with a thud and a feeble croak.

A dark bloodstain fanned out from the back of his head. Shallow breaths rattled from his wrinkled lips. His eyes followed my every movement as I knelt over him and wrapped my fingers around his throat.

Like a baby bird, he felt warm and fragile. His heartbeat fluttered frantically underneath the parchmentlike cocoon of skin.

I squeezed.

He flinched but did not fight back. I had broken him.

His tongue jutted out, grotesque and porous. He seemed more creature than man as he gasped for breath. I hadn't spent much time around aging mortals with wrinkles and bald patches. By the time my parents died, they looked no older than they had when I was a toddling child, their skin supple and their gleaming hair pure wheat-gold.

A glaze passed over the priest's eyes as his thrumming pulse fell still. His dying breath seemed to last a lifetime of its own, a long, slow hiss of wind.

I rocked back on my heels and studied my work. The task had been even easier than I had expected. I had always been capable of wounding well enough with words. I had never needed to use my hands. But now they felt strong, powerful, invincible.

The priest's knobby fingers unfurled, revealing an effigy in his palm. He probably thought it would protect him. I noticed a gold ring on his other hand and gleefully worked it off his fleshy knuckle.

I set the ring against the tip of my tongue, emitting a groan of pleasure.

Amid the winds blowing through the edifice, I heard the padding of soft footsteps behind me.

I snapped my head around and found the altar attendant clutching a candle snuffer, watching me. Dark curls framed a comely face, but she wore a frock in the plainest shade of gray. It was the only garment I'd ever seen her wear. She had come in and out of our bedchamber with the other servants about once a week, but only recently did I realize she had been descending to the Edifice of the Fallen to replace the bowl of ashes and wipe dust from the mirror.

The girl was just performing her nightly chores. How must I have appeared to her, hunched like a beastie from a children's tale in the falling dusk, prying gold from a dead man's fingers?

I stood and straightened, ashamed that anyone had seen me in such a state. Horror writhed inside me, as though my heart had decayed and maggots had come wriggling in the darkness to eat their fill.

And yet, the only guilt I felt was for not feeling guilty at all. The old man's death did not sadden me. A hidden part of me had always known myself to be capable of such violence.

"Don't be afraid," I said to the altar girl, Nexantius animating my tongue with the Perispi words I needed. "Speak of this to no one, and no harm will come to you."

The girl's throat bobbed as she swallowed. "What do I say about him?" She gestured at the dead priest.

"He fell and broke his neck. You were the only one present."

After a prolonged silence, she nodded.

"I take it you weren't close?" I asked.

"He rapped my knuckles when I overslept. He said Kromanos blesses servants who rise before dawn to do holy work."

"And do you enjoy this 'holy work'?" I asked.

She opened her mouth and closed it, considering. "I didn't choose to be an altar girl. I'm paying off my father's debt. He stole from the edifice tithe box on a holiday and gambled it away." She looked at me sideways. "Forgive me, but the priest told me that you speak very little Perispi and were reluctant to learn. How are you speaking to me now?"

"He underestimated me," I replied. "What's your name?"

"Damiatta."

"Damiatta." I clasped my hands and studied her. "Let me see you without that ghastly garment."

Instead of demurring like most celibate altar girls might, she lifted her frock and let it float to the edifice floor, unashamed.

I stroked my chin as I studied the shapes filling out her pale undergarments. She was beautiful, but hardly spectacular. Even if I adorned her in fine clothes fit for my right-hand woman, she would never outshine me.

"Serve me instead and consider your debt repaid," I said. "Every luxury that I enjoy will be yours."

"It would be my pleasure, Your Majesty," she said, curtsying. We smiled at each other.

"My first request is that you clean up the priest and prepare him for a funeral. You will stay an altar girl until he's nothing but a brittle crisp on a pyre. After that, you will serve as my right-hand woman."

"Yes, Your Majesty."

"But first, tell me everything you know about the sealed scroll. Where is the priest hiding it?"

"He would never tell a lowly altar girl where the apocrypha is hidden," she answered.

For a beat, I doubted my decision to spare her. With the right threat, I could make a loyal lackey out of anyone. Perhaps she was not worth my time.

"But last night, Father Peramati asked me to summon the huntsman, Severo Segona, for an urgent errand," she added. "He gave him the scroll to spirit away. He said even the king wouldn't know where to find it."

"Interesting," I said, pleased. "Any idea where he might have taken it?"

"The Father has connections to a group of religious radicals called the Uprising. I think he may have sent it to them for safeguarding. He normally uses me to pass along messages, but he wanted someone quick and dangerous for this, in case anyone tried to intercept."

"Quick and dangerous," I mused, rolling the gold ring between my thumb and index finger. "Move the body out of sight for now. Then summon the huntsman to the priest's private quarters."

Your first execution. How does it feel?

I feel . . . riveted.

Nexantius responded with a low laugh and stroked one cool

finger down my back. He was everywhere, inside and around me, yet still barely a breath across my flesh.

A knock sounded on the door. Propped up on the priest's writing desk, I crossed my legs and rearranged my black skirts until they revealed everything up to bare thighs. "Come in!"

Severo Segona cracked open the door and peered into the fire-lit room cramped with bookshelves and Agrimas iconography. When he saw me, his gaze snagged everywhere I expected it to.

"Where's Father Peramati?" he asked.

"Saying his nightly prayers in the edifice. Come in and shut the door, Severo."

After a brief pause, he did as I asked. I held out the wooden chalice I'd filled with red wine, propping the other hand on the desk cluttered with inkwells, leafs of parchment, and wooden scrolls. "Drink with me."

He hesitated before crossing the room to accept the wine, his brown eyes luminous.

"Your Perispi has improved," he said.

I tossed my cascade of hair to one side, exposing a bare shoulder. "I've been practicing."

He smiled. He was delicious. Every time I saw him, I couldn't help but imagine caressing his loose coils of black hair, his pronounced cheekbones, his soft and full mouth. The same fingers that had just wrapped around the priest's wattle now found their way around the distinguished curve of his upper arm. "Do you find me appealing to look at, Severo?" I asked.

"I think you know I do."

Even though the words were reluctantly spoken, I sighed at

the pleasure of hearing them in his husky voice. I hooked my leg around his.

"King Myron has been kind to me and my family," he said, planting his chalice on the desk without taking a drink. Wine sloshed over the lip and stained a leaf of parchment. "If I had known this was the reason you called, I wouldn't have come."

He sounded like he meant it, yet he didn't move away.

"What my husband doesn't know can't break his heart," I whispered. "Besides, aren't forbidden things more tantalizing?" I knocked an open inkwell out of my way so I could lean back on my elbows. It spilled over scattered pieces of parchment, blotting out whole pages of writing. Severo didn't stop me as I slid my hand from his chest to his solid abdomen. Where Myron had become cushy from middle age and endless meetings, Severo's body had been neatly hewn by his job of spilling blood and rending flesh.

A primal part of me wanted to see him at work.

I reached for his hand and brought his callused palm to my lips. His deep sigh made desire shudder through me.

Don't lose track of your purpose, Nexantius said.

"I heard the priest sent you on an errand last night," I said. "Whom did you meet?"

"So this is why you summoned me." Severo yanked his hand away. "You could have asked me. My loyalty is to the king, not the priest."

"It's not why I summoned you. I've wanted to do this since the moment we met." I took his hand once more, dragged it along my parted lips again, and then began to guide it elsewhere....

"No!" Severo barked, nearly upending the desk as he broke away from me. "I will not betray King Myron. He's a good man. And you're a fool for not respecting him."

Indignation burned through me at his double-sided insult. Not only did he dare to reject my bold advances—he was calling me names as well. I could not permit that.

I glared at him. "Tell me where you went and whom you met."

"I refuse to speak to you again without the king present." He marched to the door and flung it open.

"Your family," I called after him, sitting up. I waited until he turned around and faced me, a budding horror overtaking his expression. "Your siblings, whom Myron has taken such excellent care of..."

The heels of my slippers clinked on the stone tiles as I slid off the desk and strode toward him. "Unless you tell me where you went and whom you met last night, I'm afraid grave misfortune might befall them."

His top lip curled, but he stifled his outrage just as he had stifled his desire. He was not as susceptible to carnal cravings as I had hoped. "I met an old man outside of Enturra," he said. "I didn't recognize his face. I barely even saw it. I hope your inquest is worth threatening innocent children."

He walked out and slammed the door.

Seething, I stared after him for a long moment before I picked up a Holy statuette and smashed it to bits against the wall, releasing an unbridled screech. I tore handfuls of parchment and thrust the shreds away from me, yanked books off the shelves and smeared fresh ink over the pages.

I stared at the destruction I'd caused. My hands shook as I

realized how difficult it would be to frame the priest's death as an accident with his living quarters in such disarray.

What had I done? Why had I threatened Severo's family? He and I had become friendly. He was reserved from the start, but he had warmed up to me. We had even laughed together last time I saw him.

There was no going back to who I was before tonight. The blushing princess who cared more about the regalia of wealth than the power that secured it, who could claim ignorance when she made selfish mistakes... She was a husk, a specter, a fading note of a sweet melody from a simpler time.

"I've done as you asked," I said aloud to Nexantius, my voice hoarse from shouting as I broke and destroyed. "The priest is dead. Make good on your promise. Tell me how we will destroy Valory Braiosa."

The others and I have waited long for an opportunity to claim worthy flesh vessels, Nexantius replied. *You opened the door for me...for us. The others want worthy vessels too.*

"What does that have to do with Valory?"

She would make a fine vessel.

Envy stabbed me like a thorn. "I offered you myself so that I could become more powerful than she, more powerful than anyone. If one of the other Fallen claims her body and mind—"

Don't worry. We shall conquer her will. She will cease to exist. And when all four of us have claimed vessels, scourges will beleaguer our enemies. You will sit on your throne with unmatched beauty and power—as long as no one finds the sealed scroll. No one can know how to stop us before we've accomplished our goal.

"Is that a promise?" I asked, my desperation grating even my own ears. "If I do everything you ask, what I seek will be mine?"

I promise, my magnificent darling, Nexantius replied. *Help me find vessels for the others before anyone thwarts us. Then you will reign sovereign over all.*

EIGHTEEN

GLISETTE

MY head ached. Hunger groused in my gut. But I pushed us deeper into the rolling forest of oaks and evergreens toward safe shelter.

We had replenished the skin with stream water and foraged wild olives that were hard and bitter. Plenty of juicy meals on four legs had crossed our path, but I didn't know how to catch the creatures without hunting weapons.

Mercer had once rigged a rabbit trap during our journey through the Forest of the West Fringe. But we'd moved on so quickly that he'd disassembled it before it had a chance to prove useful. I'd watched closely enough to feel I could brave an attempt as soon as we found a safe place to rest. I needed daylight, and somehow the sun was already sinking, deepening the blue sky to a melancholy violet.

"Another quail!" Navara whispered, as though alerting me to its presence might allow me to shapeshift into a hunting dog who could catch it between my teeth.

"I think we'll need to stop soon," I said. "We'll settle for berries and mint leaves tonight. I'll set a rabbit snare, and we'll see if it's worked in the morning."

Navara groaned. "Then we should sleep soon. The sooner we

sleep, the sooner we'll have a rabbit to eat." She said this as though the snare might set itself, as though sleep alone would bring breakfast frolicking onto our plates. For all the valor she showed defying Ambrosine, she was a rather helpless traveling companion.

But I was grateful for her juvenile grumbling; it reminded me of my immediate goals: find food and shelter. These dominated my thoughts, shoving darker matters mercifully aside.

"That hollow between those boulders should do," I said, pointing to a mass of mossy rocks. "Why don't you gather leaves for bedding? I'm going to set the snare."

Try *to set the snare*, I thought, but I didn't have the heart to tell the poor girl it might not work.

While enough light remained, I searched for a rabbit path. Mercer had said they tended to use the same paths every day, noticeably shaping the brush. I wandered around, studying the undergrowth until it was almost too dark too see, and settled on a spot for no reason except that I was running out of time. I rigged the snare with pine saplings and hoped it might miraculously bring us an early catch.

With a deep sigh, I traipsed back to the rock shelter, ducking into the passageway. At the other end, the rock covering disappeared, revealing a patch of velvety black sky teeming with stars. Navara lay curled up on her side in the twilight.

I rubbed my eyes and dropped down beside her.

"I was afraid you wouldn't come back," she mumbled, half-asleep.

"Well, I did," I whispered, and drifted off as soon as my sore head touched the ground.

The scent of rain filled the air the next morning. I blinked awake and saw somber clouds drifting over the opening in our shelter.

Wonderful.

The nervous feeling in my belly became a pit of dread. Maybe I didn't know how to survive in the wild. Maybe I only knew how to follow. Maybe we would wander in circles until we starved while perfectly edible creatures loped about.

Or worse, maybe I would survive unharmed. Maybe I would defeat Ambrosine and return to a world without Perennia. Maybe I would let the people of Volarre down just as I had let her down. Maybe I didn't deserve to lead when I couldn't even protect the most precious thing in my life.

Maybe you should just let yourself...die, a small voice said. *Valory will come and fix it all eventually. This world doesn't need you.*

"Have you checked the snare?" Navara asked sleepily, wiping her short, messy hair from her face.

But she *needs me.*

Grateful to have a task to silence my insidious thoughts, I ducked under the passageway and went out, hoping against hope that I had caught something.

My soles crunched the briars and saplings as I approached the snare and found a full-grown brown rabbit squirming to break free.

Elation and relief washed over me like a cleansing tide. But then my empty stomach sank. It seemed I had made the loop too large, catching the rabbit by the hindquarters instead of strangling it and giving it a quick death, free of suffering.

How long had it struggled in fear?

I tugged the knife out of my pocket and forced myself to catch the frantic creature by the hind legs. As quickly and decisively as I could, I sliced the poor thing's neck to sever an artery, hoping its light would burn out quickly. But it twitched as it bled out, and I gritted my teeth through the onslaught of tears. A slight chill laced the morning breeze as I waited for it to die.

When at last it did, I used my bloody knife-holding hand to palm away the tears, took several deep breaths, and stalked back toward the cave just as rain began to fall.

Navara gleefully gathered kindling and worked to light the fire. I put aside my emotions and dragged the boning knife, once again poorly suited to the task, along the rabbit's flesh to skin it. When the animal was gutted and ready to cook, I turned around and found Navara still struggling to light her poorly assembled kindling.

"Let me," I said, prying the flint stone and rock from her fingers and rearranging the kindling. When the fire caught and seemed healthy enough to need only a little tending, I barked, "Surely you can handle it from here," and stalked back to the privacy of the rock shelter.

I'd barely reached its welcome shadow by the time a violent sob wrenched my body. I staggered into the shelter, dropping to my knees and issuing a silent scream.

How had an innocent life found itself the victim of a cruel, broken world?

Perennia. Perennia. Perennia. You're gone.

A frigid wind swirled through the shelter, scattering leaves and carrying the taste of bitter winter, of snow and ice. I wept and wept, my shoulders shaking with sobs. I wept until I wretched up the berries and sunflowers seeds that had failed to sustain me, and wept even more, without holding back, refusing to care about the consequences of the stinging cold I was provoking.

When I woke, walls of glimmering ice surrounded me. The world sparkled in clean, pale colors.

Maybe I had died. This seemed like a faraway place, a place from a dream. I felt safe in this peaceful palace of silver.

But then I remembered Navara, the rabbit, my unrestrained power. I remembered weeping myself to sleep in a den of rocks in a foreign forest.

I gasped, realizing what I'd done, and my exhale clouded the air.

My aching bones creaked as I pushed myself up. The snow underneath me was deep enough to drown my ankles as I stalked toward the mouth of the shelter and ducked to pass through, looking at the world on the other side in disbelief.

Glittering, white winter cloaked the forest. A frozen creek cut through clumps of fresh snow, and little flurries dusted down like powdered sugar.

"Navara?" I called. My voice echoed in the eerily quiet woods.

"I'm here," she said hoarsely. I turned to find her huddled up under an icy ledge near the ghost of the campfire, shivering, her hair damp and clinging to her face.

"Are you all right? I'm so sorry." I almost gathered her in my arms to warm her, but I realized I was soaked to the bone.

"You wouldn't wake up," she said reproachfully through chattering teeth. "When I tried to wake you, it got worse."

"I'm sorry," I repeated, softer.

"I saved you some of the rabbit." She unwrapped what was left of the juicy meat on a stick, which she'd tried to shelter in a layer of her skirt. It must have taken a great deal of self-restraint not to devour what remained.

"Thank you."

"Ambrosine will have no doubt we're alive now," she said.

I licked my lips and reached for the skewer of rabbit meat, hunkering down next to her. "I'm afraid not." My teeth tore the flesh and the flavor burst on my tongue. I couldn't speak, couldn't think again until I'd finished the last bite.

"Do you know how far this spread?" I asked, gesturing.

"Much farther than I could go without worrying I'd get lost."

"Maybe the sun will come out and melt it before anyone else sees," I said optimistically, but I knew how powerful I was. I couldn't help thinking of villagers who would have to strive to forage and hunt in this weather, their crops ruined and plans waylaid.

Not that we would be any better off than they were. I dreaded the inevitability of our tamed hunger roaring back in just a few hours.

"What do we do now?" Navara asked. She'd asked me the same question yesterday, but at the time, I had been focused on our most urgent needs. Now we had to face the inevitability that Ambrosine would hunt us down.

"You might be better off going it alone," I said. "I can't seem to lay low to save my life, and you're the beloved princess. I'll bring you to one of the outlying towns, where you'll find a sympathetic soul to offer you food and shelter. You can hide out until this is finished."

Navara glared at the fire. "No. *We* are supposed to go back and finish this. *We* are going to save my father and my kingdom, and avenge your sister's death."

The word *death* bit, stung, tormented.

"You're not abandoning me like some useless rag," she commanded, but her tone softened as she said, "and you're not going to let yourself die out here."

I looked at her, surprised by her intuition, but the sound of hooves in the snow drew our attention. Startled, I stood and seized the boning knife, pinning it against my thigh.

I noticed the dappled gray rouncey trudging through the snow from the north before I recognized his fur-clad rider: the huntsman.

"She's sent him back to finish his work," I said, shoving Navara behind me.

"He's here to help," Navara argued, and stepped away from my protection. Land of light, this girl was more naïve than Perennia. How would I keep her alive?

But I saw that furs spilled from the huntsman's saddle bags, and that he had not drawn a weapon. Had he come to bring us aid? Or was this a trap?

"Did you hope to get us all killed with this?" he demanded, slinging his lean weight down from the saddle. "I told you to hide."

"It was an accident," Navara said. "She can't—"

"Without my elicrin stone, I have no control," I said over her.

"We shall have to retrieve it, then," he said irritably, his breath pouring like smoke from his nostrils.

"How did you find us?" I asked.

"I tracked you from where I left you until the snow covered your trail. Then I went against the wind because I knew it would lead me to you."

"You know about my—?"

"Everyone here knows what the royals of Nissera can do. They will know who caused this." He stalked past us to kick snow over the pitiful remains of the fire. "What's more, the queen is saying you killed your sister and kidnapped Princess Navara."

Rage wrapped around my every nerve. "As though I would murder my..."

I couldn't bring myself to utter the words: *murder my own sister.* But why was I shocked? Ambrosine had thought I was dead, unable to return and tell the sordid truth behind her lies. What difference did it make to her if my reputation died with me?

"She's offering a reward for your capture and the princess's safe return." The huntsman returned to his horse to gather the furs. "She didn't think she would have to pay it, of course, believing you dead. Now she'll know the truth. It's a good thing I left before the snow reached Halithenica." He handed the princess a fur cloak before roughly tossing one my way. I caught it with a scornful glare. "And there's something else: I saw your brother arriving at the palace as I was leaving."

"Devorian?" How had he arrived so fast? How had word reached him so quickly? Perhaps Mercer had seen another vision and sent him here to chase after me. Perhaps, too late, he had foreseen the fate that would befall Perennia.

The hope brought on by Devorian's nearness dissipated as swiftly as it came. What if he believed Ambrosine's lies about Perennia, about what I had done?

"Why didn't you tell him what had happened?" I demanded. "He could have helped us."

"I didn't know if I could trust him," the huntsman replied, his expression carved of stone. "We need to move quickly. The town criers will have spread word to even the outlying villages by now, and every poor soul the queen has overtaxed will hope to earn a bounty by handing you over."

"Where are we going?" Navara asked, rubbing her arms for warmth. I envied her the sturdy leather boots she'd borrowed from me; her flimsy slippers were soaked through.

"To gather my family and hide," he said, casting a determined look over his shoulder. "We have no choice."

❧ NINETEEN ❧

KADRI

THE next morning was so pleasant that when I first blinked awake, I wondered how I had reached this unfamiliar paradise. The shutters stood open, admitting jaunty bird chirps and the scent of spring rain. Yogurt with pomegranate arils and a pan of joyful egg yolks in sauce sat on my nightstand.

But when I rocked up onto my side, I yelped at the tenderness of my bruises and the scabs circling my wrists. The memory of yesterday reeled back with its pressing questions:

Why hadn't the all-powerful Valory stopped Ambrosine?

Was Rynna alive?

What exactly did Lord Orturio and Mathis want me to do? Convince the others to relinquish their elicrin stones or abdicate their thrones?

Join the Uprising, Orturio had said. *Help us end the chaotic reign of elicromancers forever.*

We'd left the ravaged edifice behind, and sleep had claimed my exhausted body on the journey back through the hills and the towering cypress trees. Everything between then and now was a haze.

They hadn't demanded an answer from me yet, but the weight of their request made me drop back onto the mattress.

Their examination of how much political power elicromancers deserved—or whether they deserved any—did not disturb me. It was a question for the ages, one that I had hoped the Realm Alliance would address in due time.

What *did* disturb me were the echoes of a past tragedy, the specter of violence shadowing Lord Orturio's convictions.

I could recall the precise moment I had learned about the assassination of Clovis and Mauriette Lorenthi during their visit to Perispos. I'd been reading poetry on the terrace at the Erdemese embassy in Yorth, the sun shining so bright that it made my hair hot to the touch. That night, we were supposed to host the family of the Perispi ambassador. I looked forward to seeing his pretty daughter, Talva, the one who would eventually become an altar attendant.

Father summoned me inside to tell me the news: mere mortals had managed to kill two elicromancers abroad. The incident rocked diplomatic relations, and the Perispi ambassador cancelled dinner that night. Father even speculated that the ambassador and family might have to leave Nissera.

But then King Myron proclaimed that he had put the "anti-elicromancer rebels" to death. He said that they had acted alone. The political storm dissipated. Selfishly, I was relieved that Talva would stay.

Could those rebels be connected to Orturio's uprising? Could they have operated in secret for years without King Myron discovering them?

The prospect frightened me immensely, though it struck me as unlikely. Orturio seemed willing to manipulate and deceive, but he had not implied a penchant for bloodshed. Besides, Mathis Lorenthi was a scoundrel, but he wouldn't align himself with his own brother's murderers.

Mathis's presence was perplexing. Toppling the Realm Alliance would make it easier to reclaim his crown. On the other hand, why take political power away from his own kind?

We want to return to a simpler time, he had said, a time when mortal kings ruled. During his trial, he had lamented that his second-born niece had returned from war believing her valiance gave her a right to rule. He stressed that only Devorian could exercise a claim to the throne. He said that we were undermining his authority, that we were lawless juveniles, that Glisette had no right to change the laws that prohibited her reign.

His nostalgia, I realized, had nothing to do with wanting the world to be fairer to mortals—of course it didn't. He wanted to return to a political age when a young woman would have no power to oust him, when women like Glisette could be kept in check and made docile by society. In that world, he believed, she would plan parties, attract suitors, and eventually marry off. She would have no interest in power. The benefits of wealth, beauty, and prestige would be satisfying enough, and resistance against oppressive conventions would be futile.

Mathis would need to sacrifice his elicrin stone and immortality to live in that world. In his eyes, it was worth it to bring Glisette down, to bring all of us down.

But did that make him wrong about the Realm Alliance?

What if the kings and queens of Nissera were mortal again? Would they better understand the plights of those who endured illness and poverty? If magic played no role in politics, would grave ruling errors—like sparing Ambrosine the punishment she deserved—have such horrible repercussions?

What if I returned to Nissera and convinced my friends to confiscate or surrender every elicrin stone? What would Valory do, with nothing *to* surrender? Agree to never use her power unless the kingdoms of mortals collectively agreed it was necessary? That didn't seem so terrible.

But the thought of giving up my elicrin stone so soon after obtaining it made me feel as territorial as a feasting wolf fending off circling crows. Valory had done a kind thing, offering it to me. She knew that I felt different, helpless, less useful, when every other member of the Realm Alliance, even my husband, possessed eternal youth and immense power. And she knew that Rynna aged as slowly as the ancient trees of Wenryn.

I believed I had good reasons for accepting the elicrin stone, and that Valory had good reasons for giving it to me—not that she needed any. The Water had dried up, transferred its power to her. The source of elicrin magic had changed. Why wasn't the world allowed to change with it? Why couldn't people merit magic with deeds and integrity rather than heredity and birthright?

Overwhelmed by my whirling thoughts, I tossed off the bedclothes and shuffled to the open window. Workers wearing airy clothing scattered across the endless rows of grapevines while gray clouds drifted across the sky. The wagons of the Jav Darhu had departed. Falima had gone with the mercenaries—to what fate, I didn't know.

Grimacing against the aches in my body, I staggered to the wardrobe. I needed to reclaim my elicrin stone and find Glisette as soon as possible. Maybe she and I could confront Ambrosine together, confiscate her stone, and take her back to Nissera to face the Realm Alliance once more. Or maybe Valory would reach the palace before me and handle Ambrosine. Then I could help the others stop the spread of the forest's deadly rot.

Someone knocked softly on my door. The Nisseran maid with short, curly hair came in. "Lord Orturio would like you to join him in the dining room at your leisure," she said with a friendly bow.

"I'll be down shortly," I assured her, and she gave me a lingering look before she bowed again and closed the door.

I scarfed down my cold breakfast, exchanged my nightgown for a mauve linen dress, and descended to the dining room.

Without the mercenaries, the expansive room was strangely quiet. Mathis, Orturio, and the Perispi men from last night huddled around the table, including the older man who resembled Orturio, except that his broad build had drooped into a more pendulous shape. Everyone sported varyingly troubled expressions, save for a young man with a wave of pomade-slicked hair who leaned back in his chair, picking his teeth with a knife. Cordial glasses accompanied the spattering of teacups.

Even Mathis looked morose. The complacency I'd considered a permanent facial feature had slipped away.

Orturio poured a cup of stout tea from the tray, which he passed along to me as he gestured for me to sit.

I opened my mouth to refuse, to thank him for his courtesy, to tell him I had to be going but that I would take their concerns into consideration. They had said I was free to leave.

But before I could speak, he said, "One of my informants has sent word that your friend Glisette Lorenthi has killed her own sister, and that she and Princess Navara Vasila are missing."

I blinked at him. "She killed Ambrosine?"

Though it must have been a heartbreaking choice for Glisette, I had to admit the unexpected news brought me relief.

But three words demolished that relief: "Not Ambrosine. Perennia."

It was Mathis who had uttered them.

"Perennia?" I sank into the seat Orturio had offered me. How could this have happened? Glisette would rip the world apart to keep Perennia safe. Even Ambrosine would never hurt her youngest sibling. She was so lovely, a gentle soul adored by many, like her mother. If these tidings were true, this was a tragedy of the worst kind. "That's not possible."

"Ambrosine is claiming that Glisette went mad, murdered Perennia, and kidnapped Navara," Mathis explained. "It's obviously a lie, but she's holding a funeral today. She must have a body."

"We are trying to find out the truth," Orturio said. "But the queen has turned our palace informant, an altar girl named Damiatta who previously worked for the high priest."

"How do you know she's turned her?" I asked.

"We tested her loyalties by lying about the location of the religious artifact the queen sought. The queen sent soldiers to burn it down the next day. Damiatta thinks we believe someone else in our ranks betrayed us, but we told only her."

"And despite her betrayal, you remain in contact with her so you can continue misinforming Ambrosine," I guessed.

Orturio jabbed a finger at me, staring at me with heavy-lidded eyes. "Clever young woman. That's why we need you." He tossed back a clear spirit and slammed it on the table so hard I wondered how the dainty glass didn't shatter. "Princess Navara is our first priority. We've dispatched word to our contacts; nearly every priest and altar attendant around Halithenica will be watching for her. But if it's true that Glisette Lorenthi has indeed gone mad and poses a danger to Navara, we may need your help securing her."

"It's *not* true," I insisted. But with Perennia gone, I didn't know what Glisette would do or how desperate she had become.

Only last night, I thought I had needed Glisette to rescue me. I longed to return to Nissera without even glancing back over my shoulder, but I couldn't leave her to suffer alone.

If it was true that they had a whole network of agents looking for Glisette, there was no sense in wandering off on my own to search for her. I didn't even know where to begin.

"I will help you secure the princess—" I started.

"Holies bless you," the older relative interrupted. "Without her, our cause would be dead. We must do everything we can to protect her from the witch behind the palace walls."

"We will, Uncle," Orturio assured him.

"But," I continued, "I want to send a letter home to Yorth, and I want my elicrin stone."

"The first request I can grant," Orturio said, splashing more liquid into his cordial glass, sending a caustic whiff of it my way. "But the Jav Darhu refused to turn over your elicrin stone before they departed. They say I failed to specify that demand in our negotiations. I tried to make them reconsider, but arguing with them is never wise."

Another wave of loss washed over me. But Valory could give me a new stone, or take mine back from those vicious murderers and exterminate them like vermin in the process. "How long do you think it will take to locate the princess and Glisette?" I asked. I wanted to weep with grief for Perennia, with worry for Rynna and Glisette, with anger at my helplessness.

"Possibly tomorrow morning, depending on Lucrez," Orturio answered. "There's a young man—the king's huntsman—who has earned the queen's trust. Lucrez has been warming him up as an unwitting informant. She'll go to him tonight. If he doesn't freely offer her the truth, we'll send Viteus and the boys."

I figured I knew what he meant by "warming up," but I didn't know what "sending Viteus and the boys" meant—until the young man picking his teeth slammed the legs of his chair back down and dragged his thumb along the hooked tip of his knife. "Just tell me when and where," he said.

It seemed the Uprising did resort to violence. Perhaps I was right to suspect a connection to the radical rebels who killed Glisette's parents. But if the young man they planned to hurt held Ambrosine's trust, maybe such measures were warranted.

"What did you mean when you said that your cause is dead without Navara?" I asked.

"We want to depose elicromancer rulers and make sure worthy mortals take their place. Navara has been divinely appointed to lead Perispos. Ambrosine Lorenthi's crown belongs to her."

"Navara's mother was my cousin, a daughter of the noble Casiani family before she wed the king," Orturio's uncle explained proudly. "She was far too good for Myron the Appeaser, but Navara is family.

And more than that, if she dies—Holies forbid—the queen will hold the only legally legitimate claim to the throne."

"Which will complicate efforts to rally the people behind a worthy replacement," Orturio added.

"And then the great religion of Agrimas will dwindle to memory in a kingdom oppressed by elicromancers," the uncle continued, dropping his voice an octave, his dark eyes narrowing to slits. "It will be as our ancient prophets forewarned...." He gestured grandiosely at the heavens. "'The rulers of the earth will bend the knee to the Fallen gods, and the pure-hearted will be slaughtered in droves. The four scourges of the Fallen will descend on mankind.'"

Mathis took a deep swig of tea to fortify himself.

"What are the four scourges?" I asked out of curiosity. Mathis cut me a glare of annoyance.

"Robivoros will afflict us with a taste for human flesh and murderous impulses," the uncle said, trembling with conviction. "Nexantius will drive people to madness by showing them that which they long to see in their reflections until they become blind to everything else. Silimos will bring a scourge of mold and rot that spreads until it infests all life it touches. And Themera will cause her victims to sweat and weep blood."

"A scourge of mold and rot?" I repeated, remembering Rynna's description of the spreading infestation in the forest back home. "The Agrimas holy text says that?"

"Indeed." Orturio pushed back from the table and approached a shelf of tomes bookended by wine jugs, choosing a dense volume with bronzed fore-edges. "It's in the last chapter of the Book of Belief."

I accepted the book, flipping through until something odd caught my attention. "Why are there so many blank pages with only the symbol of a"—I peered at the faded ink of the stamp—"four-horned ram?"

"It's represents the sealed scroll," Orturio explained. "The law stipulates that only the high priest and the king can know its contents. Anyone else who reads it will be struck dead."

I thought I caught Mathis spitting tea back into his cup across from me, trying not to laugh.

"So the whole section was left out of the text?" I asked, brushing the symbol.

Orturio nodded. His eyes looked like a lamp wick catching fire in the dark.

"Does the ram symbolize the four Fallen?"

"Yes. Goats are stubborn, impulsive, malcontent, and devious. Everything the Holies are not."

I shivered, realizing a draft had crept into the room. Our breaths became visible, and everyone looked at one another in confusion.

A sudden gust of freezing wind rattled the open shutters on their hinges and jiggled the teacups on the lips of their saucers. A few of the cordial glasses toppled and rolled off the table, chiming softly as they broke on the floor.

Viteus jumped up to look out the windows, blocking my view. "It's snowing."

"Snowing?" Orturio laughed. "It's nearly summer."

Viteus stepped aside so we could see.

The poor grapevines quavered in the mighty wind. Iron-gray

clouds swung low and heavy laden. A churning winter storm blew in from fields already cloaked in white snow.

"Impossible." The table rocked as Orturio stormed to the window. "We didn't prepare for this. It will ruin the harvest!"

I watched as workers rushed to cover the grapevines. A few recognized that as a fool's errand and herded bewildered livestock toward the stables.

It made no sense. The weather here was moderate. Snow fell occasionally in the middle of winter, but not at the end of spring. Moreover, it had been pleasant only moments ago, patches of rainclouds the only omen of ill weather to come.

This storm was not at all natural.

It was Glisette. And Glisette would not do this on purpose.

Something had indeed gone terribly wrong.

Stunned, I scampered to my chamber to clear the way for servants frantically lashing down the shutters and hauling firewood stores inside. The icy wind howled through every crack and crevice as I ascended the stairs.

I didn't notice I was still holding the Book of Belief until I had to drop it on the bed and dash to wrestle my shutters closed.

By the time I succeeded, I was soaked and covered in gooseflesh. Trembling in the cold, dim room, I listened to the distant shouts and orders, the sounds of a household swallowed by pandemonium.

The redheaded Nisseran maid admitted herself, carrying a torch to light the fire across the room.

But she didn't kneel at the hearth. Instead, she grabbed my elbow, her green eyes wide and flickering with urgency. "You need to escape now, while chaos is your friend. The gate guards left their posts to help the workers."

"Escape?" I echoed.

"They think I don't understand Perispi, but I've learned more than 'dust this' and 'mop that' since I arrived," she whispered, casting a fearful look at the closed door. "Orturio has your elicrin stone. It's in the cellar."

I set my jaw and launched off the mattress, ready to demand what belonged to me. With my elicrin stone, I wouldn't have to wait for the Uprising's help to search for Glisette. I could go out on my own without fear of dying of cold. I would have fire at my fingertips. Maybe I could find her even faster than they could.

But the maid pushed me back with shocking vehemence, her short curls adhering to her cheeks. "Your elicrin stone isn't worth it."

"I need it," I argued.

"How do I make you understand?" She raked a hand through her wild hair. "My brother and I came here last year to escape the blight disease and started asking about work as soon as we arrived. Within a few days, he was doing some sort of dangerous work for Lord Orturio. All I knew was that I'd be a maid in his household. A few months ago, my brother confided that he knew too much and felt he was in danger. Then he disappeared. He would never have left me with no explanation." She shook her head. "Never."

"Are you saying—?"

"Orturio killed him," she whispered, the shadows on her face deepening in the torchlight. The clouds had darkened the sky so abruptly I could almost believe night had fallen in the middle of the day. "He doesn't let people walk away. You give him what he wants until you can't anymore, and then you face his wrath. When the Uprising decided to intercept your kidnapping, I heard him say to the others that he hoped you would be useful to him, but if not, he planned to kill you so there would be one less elicromancer in the world. He saw you as the most likely to turn against your fellow elicromancers... and if you refused, the easiest to pick off."

The cold sensation her words caused cut much deeper than the biting wind. I braced myself against one of the iron bed posters. Orturio had nearly succeeded in manipulating me with his exhortation about protecting mortals. And if he found out that he had failed...

The notion of being the "easiest to pick off" was as embarrassing as it was terrifying.

"Hurry!" the maid said, pushing me toward the window. I thought about taking something from the wardrobe, but I hadn't seen a cloak earlier. I opened the shutters and faced the roaring wind, peering down at the grass and stone path directly below my window. Of course, there were no helpful hedges outside my room, nor was there even a balcony or ledge I could use to lower myself before making the jump.

Before I could think twice, I mounted the window frame and leapt.

✠ TWENTY ✠

KADRI

WHEN I hit the ground, an excruciating pain stabbed through my ankle. I heard a sickening pop as it twisted beneath me.

I crumpled. The wet wind tore at my hair and dress. Groaning through my teeth, I peered across the vineyards. The snow swirled, thick enough now to obscure my view of the road and blur the figures of the workers trying to salvage their master's crop.

I struggled to stand. I didn't think any bones were broken, but placing weight on the injury made me yelp with regret.

Limping, shielding my face from the violent winds, I started a desperate trek toward the snow-covered clusters of red grapes and beyond them, the fence that marked the boundary of the estate.

A fierce grip on my arm jerked me back and made me howl with pain. Terror thrummed in my veins.

"What are you doing?" a woman's voice demanded. Fingernails dug into the flesh of my forearm. I turned to find Lucrez. The winds thrashed her raven hair and the corners of her cloak, within whose folds she sheltered the tabby cat from yesterday.

"Come inside," she barked at me, looking up at the windows. "And hope no one else knows you were trying to escape."

The distant baying of guard hounds made arguing seem futile. I let her usher me back to my room, wondering whether I would leave this place alive.

Lucrez promised to bring me a pain tincture. When she left the room, I heard shuffling in the corridor. "You could have killed her," Lucrez reprimanded in hushed tones. I heard the maid utter a meek, indistinguishable reply.

A moment later, the latter came to light my fire and departed without looking in my direction.

Dejected and shivering, I slid off my shoes and curled up on the hearthstones, my ankle throbbing mercilessly. The wet tabby cat sidled over to me with a grouchy expression and nestled up against my thigh.

Some time passed before Lucrez returned with a tray bearing a clear tincture and hot tea. She carried a pair of keys dangling from a scarlet ribbon, which she used to lock the door from the inside. Turning to me, she sighed. "I didn't take you for an idiot."

"I'm an idiot for wanting my freedom?"

Lucrez crossed to the fireplace, her damp teal and gold skirts swishing around her ankles. "Orturio's uncle saw you outside, but no one saw you jump," she said. "I convinced them that you were out looking at the storm and that you twisted your ankle on the way back up the stairs. But Orturio is suspicious. You need to be careful and do as he says. That's the only way you will escape."

"That's not what the Nisseran girl said."

"I'm smarter than she is." Lucrez set down the tray and sat cross-legged beside me, stroking the cat between the eyes.

"Are you trapped here too?" I whispered.

"I can leave whenever I wish," she said.

"You don't wish to?"

"I have no reason to. Not all of us are born to ambassadors and betrothed to princes. This is a better life than any I've led."

Lucrez didn't look more than a few years older than I, yet she spoke of her past as though she were a wise old woman looking back on decades of suffering.

I wanted to ask her why she had come here from Erdem, what happened in her past that made her want to leave it behind. Instead, I asked, "Where did you learn to dance so beautifully?"

She smiled and the little jewel stud in her nose twinkled. "I danced with a famous traveling troupe in Erdem. We performed at all kinds of events, from street fairs to lavish private banquets. And every year, we danced in the heritage parade outside the palace."

"You danced with the Shamra Yartziza?" I asked in awe.

"You've heard of them."

"I used to watch them in the parade. My brother would lift me on his shoulders so I could see. One year they danced with snakes. It was amazing."

She laughed. "That was before my time. Swords were the fashion when I joined."

"I wish I could have seen that. Why did you leave?"

Lucrez poured a cup of tea without meeting my eyes. I smelled the comforting scent of cardamom. "Many reasons. Our manager treated us like whores and kept most of our earnings for herself. She encouraged us to get close to the guests and perform private dances for them, but when I..." Lucrez seemed to remember that she had been serving me tea and set the full cup in front of me along with the tincture. "When I became romantic with the son of a rich man who hired us to entertain his guests, I found myself with child. I thought the son cared for me, but he wanted to pay me off so that no one would know it was his. I saved the money and danced for as long as I could. Eventually Madame noticed and dismissed me."

I swallowed the tincture and took a warming sip of tea. "What did you do?"

"One of the other dancers told me that the king of Perispos was looking to hire court dancers. This was after his wife died. He was in a lonely spell and needed entertainment. I used the secret payment from my lover to travel to Halithenica and secure the services of a midwife. What remained was just enough to allow my son and me to survive until I could audition for the king. He hired me, and I danced in his court for years. The pay wasn't much, but it put food on our plates."

"Did Lord Orturio poach you as well?" I asked. "Does he make a sport of outbidding rulers?"

"Actually, no," she said, pausing midstroke. The complacent cat opened its yellow eyes, looking surly again. "The new queen dismissed me."

"Ambrosine? That's not surprising."

"You know her well, I suppose?"

"Well enough to guess that she dismissed you for being too beautiful."

Lucrez chuckled humorlessly. "Perispi people value modesty.

The dancers wear veils to offset any enticing movements. We performed many a routine where we prayed to the Holies or suffered due to a life of promiscuousness." She rolled her eyes. "It's embarrassingly theatrical, and not in a 'snakes and swords' sort of way. At the king's wedding feast, I played a virgin dancing with each of the Holies before removing her veil for her husband. Minutes after I revealed my face, I was ordered to leave. The queen had not enjoyed my performance."

"Oh, Ambrosine," I muttered. "True to form."

"But Orturio is well connected. When he heard that the queen had ousted the best court dancer, he thought I might be a valuable tool." Lucrez traced a swirl of beading on her skirt without looking at me. I wondered if she was manipulating me now, using kindness and the affectation of honesty to win my trust. But I needed to hope that she was good, to trust that the pain tincture I'd just consumed was only that—a tincture. "He provides for me. He even paid for my son to return to Erdem and enlist in a scribe apprenticeship. Sami loves to read and practice his handwriting. He's written letters to say how happy he is, bunking with other boys and learning every day."

She smiled again, and the joy in her clove-brown eyes could not be a farce; if she was manipulating me, it was with the truth.

"I'm not saying Orturio is an upstanding man," she continued, dropping her voice to a whisper. "But…he follows his own rules. Do you understand?"

"I'm sorry, no."

She scratched her chin, seeming to think of a careful way to say what she meant. "You will doom yourself trying to run. The guards or the dogs will stop you. You have to negotiate with him, offer something of value. He will honor the terms of a deal. He's a businessman, through and through."

"But his business is violence and secrets..."

Taking the empty tincture glass, she looked sidelong at me. "Then make it yours too."

Tray in hand, she slipped out the door and locked it behind her.

⋙ TWENTY-ONE ⋘

GLISETTE

T
HE lights of Givita, the huntsman's village, burned like beacons against the gray dusk.

Nothing sounded quite so appealing as a toasty fire and a hot meal. The huntsman had brought us nuts and jerky, but the effort of plodding for hours through the snow—while restraining my emotions—made my appetite unable to be sated by such modest morsels.

The emotional effort was no small feat. The ache of my ever-present sorrow maintained the cold bite in the air, preventing the treacherous snow and ice from thawing. At least I wasn't making it worse.

Navara rode on the rouncey's back, piled in furs, while the huntsman and I walked alongside her. Navara had given me back my boots and offered to let me ride. But I wasn't certain I could trust Severo, which made me loath to accept any more charity.

We eventually reached a dirt road bordered with tree stumps and fresh footprints. *Firewood,* I thought, swallowing the guilt that had gnawed at me all day. *Last night, these people never would have dreamed they'd need so much of it.*

In the village ahead, smoke poured out of clay chimneys that jutted from thatched roofs, blending with the night clouds. The roads had become slush, rutted with the tracks of people tending to business before hurrying to their homes to close and latch the shutters. The lamplighter had done his duty, at least, and by the shuddering lights, a few wayward souls shuffled about, sniffling in the sudden cold.

"Maybe I should stay in the woods," I said. "I don't want to endanger anyone else."

"You pose more danger when you surrender to grief," Navara said, and once again I was surprised by her discernment. "Maybe some creature comforts will help?"

I wrapped the fur cloak tighter around my shoulders, ignoring the musty smell. The temperate weather in Perispos had clearly consigned it to disuse. "Perhaps."

We stopped at the edge of town. "I'll bring you one at a time," the huntsman said. "The queen's reward is for both of you. People will be looking for a pair."

He fitted his boot in the stirrup and swung onto the saddle in front of Navara before taking over the reins. Of course, it was only polite to take his princess first. The horse looked like he needed a meal and a rest almost as much as we did, but he trotted obediently down the road, turning left at the first corner and disappearing from sight.

I folded my arms and sank onto a stump, letting my head droop a little with the urge to doze off.

Glisette.

I felt the harsh whisper whisk along my nape, colder than the already chill air.

I whipped around. Had Ambrosine's soldiers or foresters found us? The thought made my exhausted muscles tense in fear. I searched the snow-cloaked shapes of the woods and found no one, nothing, not even a creature scurrying into the brush.

Fatigue and grief could play tricks on one's mind. I knew that. But for reasons I couldn't name, the chilling memory of Ambrosine's silver eyes and the strange, deep voice emerging from her lips came back to haunt me.

With one last glance back at the woods, I hurried to meet the huntsman as he cantered through the icy slush. He offered me his gloved hand. I accepted it and mounted my foot in the stirrup, all too aware that I'd been tossed over this selfsame saddle like bagged quail yesterday.

I sat back, squeezing my thighs so that I would not sink against the huntsman. But the short ride inevitably jostled me closer to his solid human warmth, and I realized for the first time how truly cold I was.

"Our shelter is not far," he said in my language. My mind was too tired to do the work of rapidly parsing the meaning of Perispi words, and I was grateful for the sympathy.

We passed the snow-drenched village square, a hilltop edifice nowhere near as grand or large as the one at the palace, and a frozen watermill. Then we abruptly arrived at a quaint residence with animals crowded in a cozy stable and warm light shining through cracks in the warped shutters. Flowers in the beds beneath the windows had withered in the cold.

I dismounted before the huntsman could offer a hand to help, but he was quick to steady me when I wearily stumbled over my feet. As soon as I felt his touch on my elbow, he pulled away, making me doubt I'd felt it at all.

"You can go inside," he said, leading his steed to shelter. "It's safe."

I didn't have the will to question his assurance, but my nerves hummed as I approached the door and stamped muddy snow from my boots. My thumb paused on the latch before I found the courage to enter.

The savory scent of a warm meal greeted me first, disarming me completely. An angry bear could have been waiting for me and I would have swooned heart-first into the warmth of that room.

It was a small cottage with a high vaulted ceiling and a loft. A wooden dining table bearing many a nick and score stretched toward a hearth and kitchen with pots and pans on pegs. Dark heads bobbed around the room. One of them belonged to Navara, who sat in the chair closest to the hearth with a hunk of bread and a bowl of what looked like hearty meat stew. A thin woman who I guessed to be Severo's mother bent over the fire, stirring the contents of a heavy pot suspended over the flames.

The heads stopped bobbing for a moment to regard me. I realized I was letting a draft fill the room, and quickly shut the door behind me.

"I'm sorry," I said in Perispi, wringing my damp sleeve in my fist.

The woman straightened and turned. "Oh," she said, waving me inside. "Um, please, come in."

Wary, I shuffled to an open seat at the table, absorbing the expressions of the children gathered around it. The smallest was a little girl, perhaps four or five years old. The oldest was a boy about Navara's age.

"There's plenty of stew," the woman said, and turned to one of the younger girls. "Eleni, please get another bowl."

Staring at me all the while, she did as her mother asked.

As I drew near the firelight, the woman's eyes widened. She grasped the bowl with tense fingers and looked from Navara to me in perplexed awe. She must not have previously recognized the princess with her cropped hair and desperate hunger, but she did now. The huntsman had been correct that we were too easy to identify as a pair: the lovely, kind princess and the fair, imposing foreign queen.

The woman plunged into a curtsy. "Forgive me. Sev told us to expect company, but he did not extend the courtesy of telling me who. I would have"—she gestured, frazzled—"prepared more suitable accommodations."

"This is far better than suitable," Navara assured her. "We've been wandering in the wilderness. Your hospitality alone is a luxury, and this stew is as delicious as anything the palace cooks ever prepared for me."

Gracious. Artful. This princess knew how to interact with her people.

The woman seemed near to tears. "My name is Melda Segona. I'm Severo's mother, and these are his brothers and sisters." She pointed to each of the children. "The girls from oldest to youngest are Stasi, Leda, Eleni, and Margala. The boys are Jeno, Lukas, and Narios."

The children regarded us with a range of expressions, from awestruck to mistrustful. "Mama, is that the princess?" the youngest girl asked.

"Eat your dinner. It's almost time for bed."

"Are they sleeping here?"

Without looking at us, the mother said, "Yes, Margala. You'll share a bed with Leda tonight."

The door swung open. Severo came in and stamped the snow off his boots. His mother shot him a discreet look, as if to say *you didn't bother to tell me* royalty *was coming to stay the night?* He cocked an eyebrow at her and tromped past me toward the fire.

"You don't want to take that wet thing off?" he asked me over his shoulder as he warmed his hands.

"Oh." I realized I was still wearing the fur, damp from snow. I shrugged it off and his mother hung it on a line of garments following the steep staircase to the loft.

Severo filled a bowl with stew and passed it to me before serving himself. The huntsman dropped into it with the familiarity of someone who belonged.

I began to devour the stew, savoring it bite by delicious bite. Melda bustled about while we ate, collecting and folding laundry.

Navara and I both started another helping. The mother sent the boys to bed and they trampled up to the loft like a herd of cattle. There, they whispered and chuckled until the eldest of the three boys chided them.

The two eldest girls, Stasi and Leda, were tasked with carrying a sloshing pail of hot water into their shared bedchamber for our baths. Margala took Navara by the hand, and I followed, leaving Severo and his mother speaking softly in the kitchen.

Without a hearth of its own, the girls' bedchamber was cold. There were three narrow straw mattresses piled with tattered quilts. Dolls and spinning tops littered the floor, but Stasi, who was twelve or thirteen, said, "Pick those up, Eleni." The second-smallest girl gathered them and dumped them in a toy chest while the two older girls poured the steaming water from the pail.

The copper bathtub was little more than a pail itself. Navara had already started unlacing her ravaged gown, and I felt I deserved at least the punishment of staying filthy a bit longer for the havoc I'd wreaked. I let her go first.

"Your hair is so lovely," Leda said, touching the ends of one of my long golden waves. "You look tired. You can sit down."

She pulled my arm and brought me to sit on the edge of the nearest mattress, where she continued playing with my hair, much to the sorrow of my tender scalp. The two younger girls climbed up to join her. "How did you get that scar?"

"Leda," the eldest warned while she bent to soak a cloth. The tub was small enough that Navara had to hunch rather than sit.

"It's all right," I said. My mind felt like that frozen watermill, unable to turn and find the right words in Perispi thanks to crippling exhaustion. "I was fighting creatures that wanted to kill me in the woods."

"Those woods?" Eleni asked, the whites of her eyes showing as she pointed vaguely in the direction of the forest.

"Oh, no, far away from here."

Navara yawned loudly, and Stasi shook out a clean nightgown for her. I unlaced my tunic and waited for the girls to refresh the water. They didn't.

"It will get cold if you don't hurry," Stasi said. She beckoned me over.

Hiding my surprise, I crossed the room and wriggled out of my boots and breeches. Despite the secondhand bathwater and unaccommodating tub, I felt at home among the sisters, who went about their business climbing under the covers and whispering.

Stasi wrung out the cloth over my shoulders. "You're not even shivering," she said. "You don't mind the cold?"

"Maybe not as much as most."

She passed me the cloth. "I know the queen's men are looking for you," she said, quietly so that the other girls couldn't hear. "I'm surprised my brother brought you back here."

Guilt closed like a vise around my heart. All day, I'd been thinking of Severo—Sev—as the callous hunter who had kidnapped and nearly killed me. But now I realized he was the older brother who'd risked everything dear to him by keeping Navara and me alive and bringing us to this safe haven.

Boots scuffled outside the door, followed by a light knock.

"Come in!" one of the younger girls called. Sev swung the door open before anyone could retract permission. I happened to be in the midst of bending over to scrub my dirty feet. He swiftly turned away.

"Leda!" Stasi scolded. "Why did you tell him to come in?"

"I'm sorry! I wasn't thinking."

"You never are."

"More blankets," Sev said, thrusting the folded quilts in our direction without looking. Eleni scurried to accept them. Sev slammed the door.

The other sisters looked at Leda. "I said I was sorry!" she whined. Eleni burst into a laugh, leading the others to laugh, and I found myself chuckling a bit too.

But grief slammed back full force. I could imagine Perennia

here, giggling with these girls. They'd want to play with her hair too, and she would probably encourage them to braid it while she told them stories of lavish balls and sumptuous gowns that would dance through their dreams. She would recount child-friendly versions of my perilous journey that would leave them believing that good always triumphs over evil.

But there would be no triumph here, at least not for me.

While dripping wet, I tugged on the clean nightgown and wool stockings waiting for me. Burrowing into the straw mattress next to Navara, who was already asleep, I covered my head with the quilt and listened to the creaks and rustle of the girls blowing out candles and settling snugly into their beds.

Chill air hissed through the warped shutters. What if my power acted while I slept, when I could not control the turmoil inside me? Would I lead Ambrosine straight to this cottage? Or was she already on her way after realizing Severo had not fulfilled his duty to her?

A band of yellow light glowed beneath the door, and soft footsteps padded in the kitchen. I needed rest, but I also needed a distraction to dull the immense pain before my eyes closed in sleep. Perhaps I could sit by the fire and wait for the flames to thaw my power into submission. I would assure Severo's mother that I would leave in the morning and no longer put her family in peril. Perhaps with a proper disguise—unremarkable commoner clothes, a scarf over my head and face, which the cold readily excused—I might be able to get a message to Devorian at the palace. Maybe Severo had a contact there who had not succumbed to Ambrosine's influence.

I rose from bed, taking care to tuck the covers back around Navara's shoulders, and slipped out the door.

But the shadow thrown into relief in the firelight was not Severo's mother tidying up before retiring. It was the huntsman himself, staring into the fire. He held a mug of frothy ale.

"I'm sorry," I said, turning back toward the room.

"Do you need more quilts?" he asked impassively. "You can take mine from upstairs."

I shook my head. "I'm afraid to sleep," I said, surprising myself by admitting it aloud. "I might make it colder if I have bad dreams."

Setting his jaw, as though to show this was an act of mere decency and not of kindness, Sev dragged a chair close to the hearth and gestured for me to sit. I folded my arms against the chill and shuffled forward, suddenly aware of how threadbare and damp my linen nightdress was.

"I feel the need to apologize," he said, unable to meet my eyes.

Not exactly an apology in and of itself. "For barging in on me bathing?" I asked disingenuously. I was going to force him to say what he meant. "It's all right. I have nothing to hide."

He seemed taken aback by my brassiness, his ironclad expression giving way to amusement. But he immediately banished the rogue quirk at the corner of his mouth.

He spoke carefully, in Nisseran. "I'm sorry I injured you."

"And almost killed me."

"Yes, that. Does your head hurt?"

"A little," I admitted.

"Let me see." He clanked his mug on the table.

I turned in my chair so that his fingers could part my hair and brush over the contusion. He remembered the spot where he'd ripped a lock out by the roots, and examined that, too. Despite the soreness, his touch didn't hurt.

"You ripped my hair out for nothing," I said irritably.

"If you had lain low like I said, it wouldn't have been for nothing," he replied, slipping back into Perispi. "Here, hold it like this."

He handed me a section of thick hair and went to rummage through a cupboard, producing a bottle of salve and a ratty but clean washcloth. He returned to dab at the wound.

"It's a good thing Ambrosine was too cowardly to kill us with her own hands," I murmured.

He finished his work and put away the salve, throwing the cloth into a wicker basket. He turned abruptly and raked back his springy dark curls. "I didn't want to do what she commanded. I was protecting my family."

I sighed as though a deep enough breath could fill the cracks in my broken heart. "I would have done the same."

I reached for Sev's mug of ale. I was owed a nightcap at least.

"You won't like it. Our neighbor Yannis makes it."

"Don't presume to know what I like." I took a sip and nearly spat it back out, but let it pool in my mouth until I found the fortitude to gulp it down. "That's awful."

A dimple formed in his right cheek, though nothing else about his face signaled a smile. He dropped into a seat at the table. The firelight glistered in his dark eyes, and his long eyelashes cast shadows across prominent cheekbones.

"How often do you come here?" I asked. "Is it a long way from the palace?"

"I try to come once every few days. When Jeno and Stasi are old enough to take care of the others the way my mother and I do, I'll feel better leaving them for longer. But that doesn't matter anymore. I won't be going back to the palace after today."

"Is it safe here?" I asked. "Now that Ambrosine knows you didn't kill us?"

"I've told very few souls where we live, and I know how to make sure no one follows me. We'll be safe for one night."

I nodded. "If you say so."

"You speak Perispi well," he said. "Your Nisseran accent is light."

"My brother is an Omnilingual, and I had a very strict governess. I also entertained many a Perispi guest until my..." I trailed off and cleared my throat. "How did you learn what Nisseran you know?"

"My father was the royal huntsman before me, and he would take me on outings. When King Myron entertained prominent Nisserans, they liked to go hunting. To our people, it's not a sport. It's putting a meal on the table. But we were expected to help entertain the guests by leading them to quarries and letting them make the kill. King Myron let me join the princess's language lessons so I could become a better host."

"Did you ever take my parents?"

"Yes," he said. "Your father was a skilled hunter. And he could not stop singing the praises of his 'beautiful, intelligent' daughters."

"Trying to capture the king's interest, no doubt," I scoffed. "Did you meet my mother?"

"No, but I know that during her visit, she used her magic to help Halithenica's crops thrive after a season of heavy rains."

My power had done the exact opposite. I took a regretful swig and passed him back the ale. He scratched his chin and took a drink. Impressive, how he didn't grimace. When he set the mug down, I caught him looking at my scar.

"Lovely, isn't it?" I asked.

"I expected worse." He smiled. "It's strange. The description the town crier gave was something like 'blond hair, fair skin, and a horribly disfiguring scar.' But..." He gestured at me, bewildered.

"Sounds like Ambrosine," I sighed. "That's an advantage, I suppose; if she has all of Halithenica searching for someone with a disfigured face, perhaps no one will recognize me."

"Perhaps," he agreed.

"Do you have any friends you still trust at the palace? Anyone who could help you get a message to my brother?"

Sev pursed his lips. I noticed that the top lip was thicker than the bottom, which leant his mouth a natural pout when he wasn't looking grim. "It's hard to know, considering everyone remaining at the palace fears her," he said.

But he hushed when someone knocked three times on the front door.

TWENTY-TWO

GLISETTE

WE both froze. The visitor knocked again, more urgently.

"The cupboard," Sev whispered, pointing to a door in the kitchen. I stood and tread carefully over creaky boards, looking back at him for reassurance before wedging myself in among jars and depleted flour sacks.

Through the crack, I watched Sev lift an axe from high pegs on the wall. His grip flexed around it as he strode across the room and opened the cottage door just wide enough to look outside.

"Oh," he said, swinging it wider.

"Three knocks," a woman said. "Didn't you know it was me?" She had an Erdemese accent. She removed the hood of her cloak, revealing onyx hair and stunning features. Her complexion was a warm brown rather than the medium olive of most Perispi people.

"You can't be too careful." Sev ushered her inside and replaced the axe on the pegs. He seemed to trust her, but without an invitation, I didn't dare emerge. "What are you doing here?" he asked. "You didn't come in the cold just to bring that, did you?" He indicated a laden sack in her hand.

She shook her head. A jewel sparkled in her nose. "No, I'm here on business."

"Sit down," Sev said. "Have some ale for warmth."

"Yannis's ale? No, thank you," she laughed. I had to work a little harder to understand our common tongue through her accent. Thankfully, she sat facing me, which allowed me to read her lips.

"I came to tell you that the Uprising plans to question you about the princess's whereabouts," the stranger said. "You need to flee."

"I don't know anything—"

She put up a hand. "I don't care what you know. I only care that you and your family are safe. The Uprising knows the queen used you. They're very protective of the princess, and they will torture you if they think it will help them find her. They consider you an elicromancer sympathizer, just like your father. Maybe you could give them enough to stay valuable and alive. But it's a trap. Once you give something to the Uprising, there's no going back. You're loyal to them or you're dead."

Elicromancer sympathizer. Uprising.

My exhausted mind managed to make the connection: this had to be the same group who had killed Mother and Father.

But King Myron had told us that the anti-elicromancer rebels had been swiftly tracked down and executed. He said he personally oversaw their executions.

Were there others? How big was the Uprising? What had Sev's father done to earn their ire?

"They are more powerful than you know," the stranger went on. "And they have eyes and ears in places you would never expect. Your family needs to flee as soon as possible."

"Who are they, Lucrez?" Sev asked. "Is it Rasmus Orturio? It was his brothers the king executed after..."

Sev trailed off, and I knew why: to spare me the mention of my parents' deaths, the details that had been scrubbed, neatly packaged, and dispatched across the sea so that my brother and sisters and I might have closure. I had never asked for the names of the rebels; they hadn't mattered. I thought they were all dead, everyone who'd plotted such senseless violence.

"Orturio has never been involved with the Uprising," the woman called Lucrez replied. "He isn't radical like his brothers were. He made his own path."

Sev cocked his head. "You work for Rasmus Orturio and live under his roof. You know so much about the Uprising's movements. And yet you claim the two have no relationship."

"He keeps his ear to the ground, and so do I."

"What about the rumors?" he asked. "That Orturio killed his first wife for not being pious enough, that he killed his second wife for prying into his business, that he kills people for knowing too much—"

Lucrez bleated out a laugh. "You sound like a gossiping hen, Sev!"

"What am I supposed to believe? You've told me nothing about the Uprising. How will I know who to run from, where to go?"

"You already know where to go: your father's cabin in the woods. It's the only safe place. And you don't need to know anything about the Uprising except that they won't hesitate to kill you and your family."

Sev quietly pushed out of his chair and crossed the room, drawing near enough to block my view.

"You can come out," he said.

Wary, I stepped out of hiding. The woman's mouth dropped open.

"This is Lucrez," he explained. "She's a friend from the palace. She was a dancer in the king's court before your sister dismissed her. Lucrez, this is—"

"The queen's sister, who has a bounty on her head? Who brought winter to Halithenica and spoiled the summer harvest?"

My better instincts told me to apologize and promise I would make things right. But instead, I retorted, "Pleasure."

"Likewise," she said, but her tone was playful. "Oh, Sev. Don't tell me this means you're harboring someone else..."

"Then I won't tell you."

Lucrez shook her head. "You make it hard, trying to protect you."

"She ordered me to kill them both, Lucrez. What should I have done?"

"Why was your father called an elicromancer sympathizer?" I asked quietly.

Sev hesitated, staring into the fire for a moment before he said, "After the Uprising murdered your parents, King Myron sent his huntsman to track down the murderers and bring them back for execution."

I swallowed, trying to find the words to speak. "Your father... avenged my parents' deaths?"

He led me back to the table and hunkered down, sliding his ale in front of him, but he didn't drink. "He died in a hunting accident just days after. I have no proof, but I always suspected other members of the Uprising killed my father and made it look like poachers."

Eyeing Lucrez, I took the seat next to Sev.

"The Uprising has grown smarter and more secretive since," he explained. "They have resources, funds, information. There haven't

been any more public assassinations, but elicromancer sympathiz-
ers go missing sometimes. A few years ago, one of the king's advisors suggested asking the Realm Alliance to send a Healer to stop a
raging cattle disease. He disappeared."

"Why do they hate us so much?" I asked, but I didn't need to
hear the answer. I thought of our legacy of destructive dark magic:
the Moth King, Tamarice, Ambrosine, and now...me.

"The Perispi people would rather see Navara crowned as queen
rather than submit to your sister's rule," Lucrez explained. "But
the Uprising wants to take it further. They want to kill *all* elicromancers and their allies, to purge the earth of what they consider
unholy magic."

"They resent King Myron for straying from the faith and marrying an elicromancer," Sev said, and he tucked his hand in his vest
pocket in a way that made me think he might be hiding an effigy
there. "They want to make sure Navara takes the crown and honors
her mother's legacy. They want to manipulate her into becoming a
punisher of the unfaithful."

"These people are cruel, violent radicals," Lucrez added, and
I thought I noticed a tiny tremor run through her shoulders, but it
might have just been the firelight. "They'll use Navara's faith and her
mother's legacy to twist her mind, maybe even torment her if they
must, until she is both their servant and savior. When she's ready,
they'll kill the king so she can be crowned and carry out their agenda."

"News will reach the Realm Alliance soon, and my allies will
come to our aid," I said. "Valory and the others will easily overthrow Ambrosine, even with that... *thing* inside her. We will quash
the Uprising and help Perispos recover."

"Thing inside her?" Lucrez repeated.

I noticed Sev's hand slip back into his pocket, rubbing the little effigy out of habit.

"She was hardly my sister anymore when she left for Perispos," I said. "But a dark power has set upon her since she arrived."

"I saw something in her eyes that worried me," Sev said. "I thought I was imagining things at first. And then the king retreated in supposed sickness, and the high priest took a fall and died—"

A bump and a thud overhead made the three of us jolt in unison.

"Narios," Lucrez whispered with relief. The youngest boy stood at the top of the stairs, massaging his tired eyes. "Come here. I have something for you."

The boy flashed a toothless grin and tiptoed down. When he reached the bottom, he ran to embrace Lucrez. She smiled and combed his rumpled hair out of his eyes. "Have you behaved lately?" she asked.

He nodded emphatically. Sev raised an eyebrow to contest, but his doubtful look was good-natured.

"Good," she said with a tap on Narios's nose for emphasis. She dug into her satchel and pulled out a lumpy paper package tied with twine.

"Honey chews!" he exclaimed.

She shushed him, still smiling. "You have to save enough to share with your brothers and sisters."

"Even Sev?" he asked, concerned, already ripping at the twine.

"No, not Sev," she laughed, and kissed his cheek. "Have a few, and then back to bed with you, darling."

I couldn't quite discern what Lucrez meant to this family, or to

Sev. She was beautiful, her hair richer than black velvet, her body ample and shapely. She was older than Sev, though I doubted that would blind him to her allure.

She looked at Narios as a mother might, with adoration and pride, but with a tinge of sadness pinching her brows.

He ate four sweets in a blink and attempted to tuck the rest in his nightshirt before tiptoeing back toward the stairs. Sev made a chiding noise. Narios shuffled back, dejected, and handed Sev the bag.

"Good night," Sev said.

Narios pouted his way up to bed. Sev tucked the candies at the top of the cupboard. "Like wolves on a carcass if they woke up and saw him eating those."

"I'm sorry. I can't resist," Lucrez chuckled. She dove back into her satchel and extracted a few small bags and jars. "I brought some jam and olive oil and grain," she said. One of the purses jangled, sounding suspiciously like coins, and I wondered if she had to hide the money to make Sev take it.

"Thank you," Sev said.

"I should be going. Do the right thing for your family. They need you."

"We already planned to leave at dawn."

"*Before* dawn," Lucrez instructed.

She gathered her empty satchel and lifted the hood of her cloak.

"It is Rasmus Orturio, isn't it?" he asked as she reached for the door. "The leader of the Uprising?"

"No, I swear to you he has nothing to do with it. The sins of one's brother are not one's own." She looked at me meaningfully. "Or sister."

"And you can't tell me who is involved," he stated flatly.

"I like my head attached to my body."

"I could find out another way," he answered, taking a swig of ale.

"But you won't because *you* like my head attached to my body. Good night, darling."

She left us alone, in silence but for the crackling of fire.

"Shouldn't you have told your family to pack already?"

Sev stood and locked the door. "My mother knows. She'll be awake well before dawn preparing. But the children would get too excited and restless. They need sleep."

"And it's safe where you're going?"

"You mean where 'we' are going?"

"You want me to come?" I asked, incredulous. "Why?"

"You heard Lucrez. If the Uprising catches you, they'll torture you to find Navara. And if Ambrosine catches you, you'll be no safer. We all need to stay together. For the sake of the resistance."

"Resistance?" I repeated.

"People will soon be desperate," Sev said. "Your sister has raised our taxes. She burned down an edifice. Everyone in Halithenica and the outlying villages knows something is wrong behind the palace walls. Your elicromancer allies may come and liberate us, but until then, these people need something to put faith in."

I rubbed my temples. "I wish I could help, though I only seem to make things worse. I'm useless without my stone."

"You *can* help," he insisted. "Navara's not a leader yet. But she could be. Why let the Uprising mold her into *their* queen when we could make her a symbol of hope for all people?"

"I'll put you in danger. There's a price on my head."

"And on Navara's. And probably on mine by now. So we'll hide. We'll get more help."

"Help from whom?"

"The king's commander resigned from his post in protest," Sev said. "He couldn't refuse to follow orders the king had signed even though he knew Ambrosine had written them, so he retired instead. He's been hiding from her guards, but I know where to find him. He could help us mount a resistance."

"Mortals can't defeat her," I argued. "What's the point of mounting a resistance?"

"If your friends come, that's fine. But what if they don't? At least this way, we'll have hope. We'll fight." The shadows shrouded his handsomely carved features in mystery, but a rebellious spark flared in his brown eyes as he said, "We'll create an uprising of our own."

TWENTY-THREE

AMBROSINE
ONE MONTH AGO

"SIT up straight, dear," I said, snapping my fingers in Navara's face.

She huffed—the brat—and wiggled a bit, barely improving her posture. Casting a glance at the empty chair beside us, she asked, "Why isn't my father here yet? We can't start without him."

"He will have a separate sitting with the artist when he recovers his health. We must do our part to ensure this will be a grand family portrait." I lowered my voice, eyeing the artist mixing his paints in the far corner of the drawing room. "Don't you want your younger brother or sister to know what you looked like as a little girl?"

Disdain simmered in her doe-brown eyes. She pinched the exaggerated blouson collar of her plain dress and said, "I'm not a little girl. You could be my sister, and my father could be your father."

As I had feared, Myron had been too thrilled by the pregnancy to keep the news from his daughter. I had asked him not to tell a soul until it had progressed healthily, hoping to buy myself time. But he viewed Navara as the exception to that request. And ever since, she had shown me nothing but spite. Such a jealous creature.

Outside of telling our secret, Myron had obeyed me. I had utterly bent him to my will after just a few days of toying with his mind and investing in his madness. To truly lift him from reality, I had begun replicating visions of his late wife based only on her portraits and statues. Seeing her brought back to life gave him more joy than even the prospect of me bearing his child.

At first, it had bruised my heart to learn that he would never love me as much as he had loved her—that bringing a child into the world with me failed to delight him as much as the ghost of his first wife.

But his obsession gave me the permission I needed to trap him in darkness and continue with my plan. He wasn't miserable. No, he was in paradise down there in the Edifice of the Fallen, surrounded by visions of his first love.

And he would do anything I asked just to see her again.

I had tested this theory by parading him in front of the court to sign a decree I had authored. I made sure to do it while Navara was busy on an outing with her tutor.

It was an innocuous first proclamation: banning religious iconography in the palace. Already, workmen were busy chipping away at the drab frescoes and dragging away the earnest statues.

"All of our family portraits have a Holy statuette in the background," Navara said, as if reading my thoughts.

"We must respect your father's decree," I chided. "The faith and the crown must have their independence, or corruption will rot our great kingdom from the inside out. Father Peramati shamelessly manipulated Myron."

"And he was not the only one," she growled. "I know you're not pregnant."

"You have no way of proving that," I whispered into her ebony curls, checking to make sure the artist's ears hadn't pricked. Hunched over his paint mixtures, he gave no sign that he could overhear our conversation.

Navara twisted in her chair to look at me. The princess truly was a beauty. The dusky-rose tinge of her full cheeks and lips complemented the richness of her dark eyes and hair. I'd never seen such an elegant chin either. If the artist did too fine a job rendering her into paint, I would ask for revisions. I would accuse him of endowing a young girl with sensual characteristics.

"Time will prove it," Navara replied, facing forward again. Her fingers found a hard shape under the collar of her dress. The pale fabric couldn't hide the brilliant red of her mother's ruby necklace.

Ah. A small act of protest. She planned to hide it until the artist had already begun and we could not flinch for fear of ruining the tableau. How daring.

"In time, proof won't matter." I grasped the chain of her necklace. With one hard yank, I broke the clasp. Navara gasped.

By the gem's weight and vibrant hue, I knew it would taste better and satisfy me longer than any I'd yet tasted. Making sure the artist was distracted, I set it on my tongue and took a bite. It felt like digging my teeth into a smooth, perfect strawberry. Unable to stop myself, I emitted a quiet moan of pleasure.

Navara stared, transfixed and horrified. I watched her through the slits in my eyes as I finished the decadent feast and licked my fingers.

The door opened. Damiatta peeked her head into the drawing

room. I motioned her inside. She wore one of my more modest black gowns with elegant embellishments.

Father Peramati had underestimated Damiatta's intelligence and potential. I would not make the same mistake. Already, the former altar girl had served me well, spreading the lie of the priest's tumble down the stairs. Now he was a pile of ashes in the royal crypt. His quarters looked orderly and untouched.

"The king seems to be improving," she said for Navara's sake. "I just cleared his dinner. He says he wants to see his wife again."

"Very well," I said, knowing which wife she truly meant. "This may take some time, but I'll visit him after."

"There's one other thing, Your Majesty." She motioned me aside and we huddled in the corner. Navara sat still, clearly shaken.

"My contact in the Uprising told me that the sealed scroll is hidden at an edifice in a village—"

"Send soldiers to burn it," I interrupted.

"The village?"

"The edifice."

"The commander won't allow that."

"Then let him tell me so himself," I hissed. "Draw up the command. Myron will sign it."

She nodded and left the room.

Nexantius would have made me strike with more precision. But this morning, he had stepped away from my mind to confer with the other Fallen. Just like the last time he had departed, I still felt him anchored in my soul, though I was glad to be rid of his voice in my head for a short while. He would want me to personally retrieve the scroll and kill anyone who might have lain eyes on it. He had nearly convinced me to kill Navara until we learned she had no inkling of the scroll's contents.

This quest to find the apocrypha was inconvenient and, frankly, mundane. According to Nexantius, it contained the truth about how to defeat the Fallen. But tracking it down had become a waste of time and resources, and it seemed to me that he was using it as an excuse to delay our plans for Valory.

I had already risked everything killing the priest. Burning the edifice would have to suffice.

I inspected my reflection in the mirror and experimented with different poses. My silver dress was a work of art in and of itself. The royal clothier had worked night and day, glaring at the tiny glass beads by flickering candle flame. The result was a fluid master-piece that danced with fragments of light.

The silence in my head suddenly crackled like the charge before a bolt of lightning. Nexantius had returned.

Silimos is waiting, he said. *The chasm vacated by the Water allowed her a passage into your world, but she needs a living vessel.*

Does this mean—?

Silimos will trap your enemy Valory Braiosa, holding her hostage until she cares for no one and nothing...until she is a willing vessel. She will become callous, impassive, lazy, the worst queen this world has ever known. We will stake our claim to the kingdoms of men and she will not stop us.

Restraining a smile, I took my place for the portrait and rested a hand on Navara's shoulder. I felt her trying not to squirm under my touch.

The artist turned around and studied us. He peered into my eyes and shifted a step back in surprise. "I mixed shades of green and blue for your eyes, my queen, but now I see that's not quite right. They're more of a gray...no, silver. Pardon me for a moment."

❧ TWENTY-FOUR ❧

KADRI

BY nighttime, snow fleeced the vineyards, but the storm had abated.

I didn't know if it meant that Glisette had defeated whatever darkness she had faced…or something much worse.

Tucked into bed with the cat, I read the final chapter of the Book of Belief between bouts of sleep brought on by the tincture. The figurative, flowery language frustrated me. I encountered obsolete words retired from everyday Perispi vocabulary and found no further descriptions of the scourge of mold and rot that had brought to mind the infestation in the Forest of the West Fringe.

The meatiest parts must have resided in the blank pages, untranscribed, scrawled only on a sealed scroll.

Regardless, I felt silly for thinking the fictional scourges and the forest rot could be related in the first place. Never in my life had the teachings of Agrimas resonated with me, beyond their encouragement of self-edification. But even clear and simple principles could somehow be warped to suit a selfish agenda. Loyalty to the wrong causes was hardly a virtue.

Embittered and wracked with pain, I flung the book at the nightstand, startling the cat and knocking over the effigy of Hestreclea that Orturio had given me.

I climbed out of bed and limped to huddle by the fire again. I couldn't help Rynna. I couldn't help Glisette. I was trapped here, held hostage by a powerful man who had only spared me thus far because I had agreed to help him.

I'd learned from the Moth King's rise to power how quickly a small insurgency could grow. If Ambrosine's reign stoked outrage among the remaining Agrimas faithful, the Uprising might expand from a secret sect of radicals to an entire country bent on our destruction. Elicromancers could defeat a mortal army from Perispos, but such a war would be costly in terms of mortal life and would tear down whatever trust remained between the two sides.

A loud crash jolted me out of my thoughts. Lord Orturio had been too distracted by his misfortune to pay me much mind today.

I heard a distant hum of voices in spite of the late hour. One of them was no more of a lazy purr: Mathis. Wincing at the pain, I limped to the door and crouched down to look through the keyhole, straining to make out figures in front of Lucrez's chamber across the dark corridor.

"Tomorrow, Mathis," Lucrez said.

"Let me just get a peek of what I have to look forward to," Mathis said, sliding the sleeve of her black dress off her shoulder.

"Are you mad? I just came home empty-handed and had to tell Orturio that my informant fled Givita for the woods before I got there," she whispered as he kissed up her throat. "His harvest has been destroyed, and he's been drinking heavily. He broke a chair when I told him, for Holies' sake! Do you really want to stake a claim to me right now?"

"Absolutely, more than ever." I grimaced at the hungry way his top lip moved away from his teeth like a horse biting off blades of grass.

"Why right now, tonight, when you haven't come to me in weeks?" she asked, pushing his blond head away. "Is it some sort of revenge, reveling in his misery? I won't be used like that."

"Revenge?" Mathis asked, looping his arms around her waist and yanking her close. "Whatever for?"

She did not adopt his playful, mischievous tone. "Your brother."

I bit my knuckles to hold back a gasp.

"His brothers killed my brother, and the king killed them for it." Mathis recounted this dismissively, as though it were old, boring news. "We're more or less even, don't you think? Please, spend the night in my room. The thought of you juicing an informant made me wildly jealous, and now I must have you."

Lucrez sighed. "After he goes to bed. It shouldn't be long now. He's had the strong spirits."

Mathis lifted her hand and kissed her palm as if to devour her flesh. "I'll see you soon."

He left. I sat back on the floor to process their conversation. I had not been wrong to make the connection: the Uprising had murdered Clovis and Mauriette Lorenthi.

Footsteps padded closer. My heart beat against the base of my throat, but the sound of skirts swishing and keys chiming told me it was only Lucrez. She had been the keeper of the keys today, unlocking my door only to allow an unfamiliar maid to collect my laundry and used dishes. I hadn't seen the Nisseran maid since before noon, when she lit my fire.

Lucrez paused outside. Then she inserted her key into the opening. Perhaps she thought she'd forgotten to lock it.

But she turned it the wrong way. The click was succinct and unmistakable. She was intentionally *un*locking it.

When she swished away, I returned to peer through the keyhole. She went to her bedchamber across the corridor and walked directly to her nightstand. Very deliberately, she set her keys in the top drawer. She closed it and returned to shut her door, but the scrambled sequence made her intentions clear: she wanted me to see where she kept her keys.

My mind turned like the tumbles of the locks that held me captive. Was this an invitation to steal the keys? She had called me an idiot for trying to run and said I wouldn't earn my freedom that way. If I couldn't escape with the guards and dogs prowling outside, what was the point of offering this to me?

My elicrin stone.

The cellar.

The thought burned me up with excitement and hope, but fear consumed both. If Orturio caught me, the consequences would be dire. But I needed my elicrin stone to break free without getting torn apart by the dogs or freezing to death in the snow. I needed it to find Glisette and Princess Navara before the Uprising did.

I didn't believe an anti-elicromancer rebel who belonged to the same ruthless organization that murdered Glisette's parents would spare Glisette if given the opportunity to kill her. And if Orturio knew that she had generated the storm, he would be even less inclined toward mercy. Under normal circumstances, Glisette could squash Lord Orturio like a beetle, but these didn't seem like normal circumstances.

I needed leverage. I needed strength. I needed my elicrin stone.

But neither of the ordinary keys on Lucrez's ribbon matched the distinct key Orturio had used to unlock the cellar door. The key I needed was enormous with unique swirl filigree.

Think. Think. What does she expect you to do?

One of her keys probably fit the exterior locks, permitting her to run errands like the one Orturio had given her tonight. If the other fit both her door and mine, it might be a master key for the interior locks. Except the one protecting Orturio's underground trove of "liquid gold."

Orturio probably had the only key to the cellar. With the master key, I could sneak into Orturio's chamber and steal it while he slept. The very notion made it hard to swallow.

Panting, grumbling breaths heralded the men's drunken journeys to their bedchambers. I quieted my own until I heard the last door slam.

A few moments later, Lucrez left her chamber in a red nightdress. She didn't lock it behind her.

The only sound I could hear was blood rushing through my ears. Three times, I flinched to act and changed my mind. Then, finally, I stood, wincing at the pain in my bruised, swollen ankle. If I didn't go now, I might never get another chance.

Muffling the sound of the door latches with my sleeve, I limped directly to Lucrez's nightstand and opened the drawer. Amid bottles of perfume and cosmetics, there they were: the keys tied to the red ribbon. I felt a rush of triumph, but I wasn't even a quarter of the way to finding my elicrin stone and escaping.

Light footsteps pattered through the hall, and I heard someone blowing out the lanterns. I hobbled back to my chamber and quietly shut the door. Clutching the keys to my chest, I sank onto my bed.

I waited until everything fell still, and waited longer.

Eventually, I mustered the courage to venture back across the corridor to make sure one of the keys worked in both my door and Lucrez's. It did—the interior master key.

Limping gingerly on the cold stone floor, I knelt to peer through keyholes into firelit rooms. If it weren't for the chill, I doubted the fires would be blazing so brightly, aiding my search. I only had to look into two rooms before I recognized the bulky outline and wavy hair of Lord Orturio, asleep and heavily snoring. He had not even dressed for bed, instead shedding only his boots and outer layers.

I extracted the master key and held my breath as it slid comfortably into the lock. Though I'd expected it, the muffled click almost made me leap out of my skin. I opened the door and slipped inside.

The master's bedchamber was decorated in deep purple and dark wood. Opaque curtains were draped around the bed and tied to the posts, giving me a bit of secrecy.

I tiptoed to his nightstand and carefully slid the drawer open. There were pieces of parchment and an Agrimas prayer book, but no keys. Clenching my teeth, I closed the drawer and looked around.

The silk-trimmed gray jerkin he'd worn this morning lay over a purple armchair at the far side of the bed. I tread lightly over the rugs and paused behind the bunched curtains of the canopy bed, feeling safe and hidden. Finally, I convinced myself to reach for the jerkin. I took a step out from my refuge and patted the right pocket. I felt the lumpy, hard shape of his key ring.

Instead of extracting so many clanging bits of metal, I swiped the entire garment, but the other pocket gaped open. Two coins tumbled out and hit the rug with a muted clang.

Orturio's snore cut off. I jumped back behind the curtain with the garment.

I heard the covers swish as Orturio stirred. The bed frame groaned with his shifting weight. I thought for sure I would see his thick legs toss over the edge. But a few beats later, the snoring resumed.

After I snuck out and closed the door, I clenched the outline of the large cellar key through the fabric. *One step closer to freedom.*

Tucking Lucrez's keys in the empty pocket, I folded the jerkin over my arm and tiptoed downstairs to the dining room. It was empty, but embers blazed in the hearth grate. A bronze oil lamp sat on the mantel. I breathed the fire back to life just enough to light the lamp's braided wick.

My stocking-clad feet were numb by the time I limped to the studded door leading to the cellar. The largest key on the ring fit gloriously into place.

The lamplight barely penetrated the cavernous dark of the stair-way leading underground.

I locked the door behind and me and doddered down. When I reached the dirt floor, I removed my socks and left the jerkin behind. Bare feet would be easier to wash without anyone noticing.

Finally, I faced the darkness. A jolt of fear worked its way between my shoulders. I took a step, raising the lamp to search by its pitiful glow.

What exactly was I looking for? A hidden door? A hollow barrel?

Mathis's appearance had distracted me from absorbing details yesterday, but I at least recalled the layout of the cellar. It was long and narrow, with two or three rows of vats and barrels on either side of the main aisle. On one end lengthwise, there was the table and the marble shrine. On the opposite wall, I remembered seeing a door large enough to accommodate the transfer of large equipment.

This door I found easily. It was barred from the inside with a heavy plank.

I peered through the crack around the doorframe—how I tired of looking at the world through openings in walls and doors, wagons and ship cabins—and found an outer cellar flooded with moonlight. It contained a large mechanical winepress and a sorting table lined with buckets. But more importantly, it opened up to the outside on the far end, where two hound dogs sprawled on the ground, their ribs rising and falling in sleep.

One of them lifted its head and stared in my direction.

Breathless, motionless, I waited. It would but take a single loud bay to stir the household.

The dog dropped its head, deciding there was no threat after all. I shuffled back from the door, tucking the knowledge of this potential escape route away.

I crossed to the shrine at the other end of the cellar. I thought of my own hiding place for my elicrin stone back in Beyrian: inside my velvet-lined jewelry case, where my most valuable possessions resided alongside letters from people I loved, including an old one from my father that had browned and crinkled from the oil on my fingers. People tended to hoard their most sacred things in one place.

Sacred.

The glow of the lamp shuddered over the shrine with sculptures of the Holies, surrounded by carved foliage and woodland creatures. Placing the lamp on the table behind me, I ran my fingers over the minute artistic details of each deity.

Which virtue did Orturio admire most? Loyalty, to his country and his faith. I tried to pull on Hestreclea and her dog like a lever, hoping she would reveal some kind of hidden compartment. When it didn't work, I felt silly for trying.

But there was something so purposeful about this shrine and its location in the house. Orturio spoke of the wine he created here like a besotted lover extolling his lady's virtues.

I traced my fingers over each statue, tugging and pushing and pressing. I very nearly laughed at myself. One chance to steal the key from the dozing giant to find my elicrin stone, and here I was prodding statues, squandering this dear opportunity.

But when I pushed the Holy of Courage's shield, I heard a little clink. Elated, I wedged my fingernail into a minuscule crack around the shield boss.

It popped open like a lid. My mouth fell agape.

A tiny keyhole stared at me.

Elated, I clumsily searched on the ring for the smallest key and shoved it in. With a resounding clunk, the lock turned, and I dragged open the entire marble panel, which was surprisingly lightweight. It was a veneer for this secret wooden door.

Even before I reached back for the lamp, I noticed glimmers of reflected light, as well as a faint, strange odor, nearly masked by overbearing amounts of rosemary and sage. When I slung the lamp around and lifted it high, I nearly gasped at all the treasures hidden in this secret cellar.

There were gold statuettes, chests brimming with coins, and countless scrolls with jewel-encrusted rollers. This vault preserved a heritage whose keepers feared it might vanish to dust without their efforts.

There were also enormous varying gems that could only be elicrin stones, still set in silver and gold medallions, once worn by elicromancers who had relinquished them or been murdered.

If the Uprising was collecting masterless elicrin stones, clearly they understood the limits of Valory's power: she could only give elicrin magic to mortals if there were elicrin stones to fill with gifts. The Water had dried up—there would be no new elicrin stones. If the Uprising bought and stole as many as possible and hid them, they could keep Valory's power in check.

It was a clever strategy, one Valory and the others would need to hear about as soon as I escaped with my elicrin stone, reunited with Glisette, and returned home.

I lifted the lamp and limped into the room to look at the collection, deeply dismayed that mine didn't seem to be among them. The others would be of no use to me.

A viscid liquid squelching between my toes distracted me from my search. I lowered the lamp and saw what looked like congealed, dark blood that had seeped out from a barrel.

The lamp nearly slipped from my fingers. I placed it on a shelf.

Surely this was some wine-related substance—perhaps grapes pressed with their red skins still on. But the faint musky odor I'd noticed upon opening the door, which I detected again, begged to differ.

I grabbed a wooden mallet sitting on the barrelhead and tapped lightly underneath the rim until I could pry it off.

When I glimpsed the contents, my stomach lurched, and I tasted the medicinal tincture spilling back up my throat.

It was the Nisseran maid—her *corpse*. Contorted and mangled to fit inside a wine barrel.

My insides turned watery with horror, and I realized how very real the threat of death had been since our wagon rolled down the drive to this estate. Here I was, sneaking, stealing keys out from under Orturio's nose as carelessly as if playing a game of hide-and-seek.

Had Orturio learned that the maid had tried to help me? That I had attempted escape because of what she had confided to me? Would I be the next to face punishment?

I felt the urge to undo everything, to lock this door and wipe the blood from my feet, return the keys—land of light, how stupid had I been?—and flee back to my bed and comply, comply, comply to save my life.

A door on the upper level opened and closed. My heart felt like it might punch through my chest.

I reset the lid on the barrel as securely as I could, picked up the lamp, and stepped outside the secret room. My hand shook as I reached to close the door, and I accidentally flung the keys onto the ground. They landed in blood. I cursed and scooped them up.

I used my stockings to wipe blood from the keys first, then my bare feet. I whimpered in anticipation as I staggered up the stairs, slowed down by my injury. With every step, I expected to see a light shine through the crack under the door, a large shadow moving.

Hoping the sound had been the mere stirring of a restless sleeper, I waited a few minutes before opening the cellar door. I limped to the dining room to replace the lamp on the mantel and traveled upstairs in the pitch dark, pausing outside Orturio's chamber. Fear froze my hand on the latch, but the urge to be back in the safety of my private chamber was too compelling; I opened the door and hurried to replace the jerkin with the key ring safely in the pocket.

At last I returned to Lucrez's empty chamber to replace her keys. Afterward I perched on the edge of my bed, panting, my ears as keen as a fox's.

Wiping away a hot tear, I threw my bloody stockings into the fire.

❧ TWENTY-FIVE ❧

KADRI

THE maid screamed in my feverish nightmares. My ankle throbbed, and the pain fused with the shadows and fire of my tormented dreams.

I awoke coated with sweat. My ankle hurt even worse than it had in sleep. Slivers of dawn light pushed through thin cracks in the shutters.

And someone was shouting.

"I didn't lie!"

It was Lucrez.

"You told me that the huntsman and his family had already fled when you arrived," Orturio said.

By his dangerous, unsteady tone, I guessed that the spirits from last night hadn't quite worn off. "You said you broke in when no one answered and found the cottage empty. But I sent Viteus to catch anything you might have missed. Do you know what the neighbor said when Viteus questioned him this morning? He said that someone let you in and you stayed for several minutes."

"It's not true!" Lucrez cried. "The neighbor knew he had to give Viteus *something*, or he'd kill him. So he made it up. Who wouldn't?"

"She didn't go to get information from the huntsman," Viteus spat. "She went to warn him we wanted it. She's a traitor."

His declaration was followed by a hiss of pain and a clatter. He was hurting her.

"Lucrez," Orturio said, and his tone chilled me. "If you have betrayed me, I will let that boy of yours starve in the streets."

"No!" she shouted, pleading. "No, I never would. I know what is at stake. You are so generous with me and Sami. Viteus is too violent to make a good interrogator. People lie and tell him whatever will stop him from hurting them."

"That's not all the neighbor told me, Orturio," Viteus said, clearly relishing this.

I heard a passionate tremor in his voice. Was it resentment? Envy? Did he long to bring Lucrez into his bed, and she denied him? Was he envious of their master's favor?

"He said he saw the huntsman bring two other young women into his home. One was blonde. She had a scar."

My pulse thrashed like drums of war. Glisette. Glisette had been in the huntsman's village—the huntsman who had earned Ambrosine's trust.

The desire to escape nearly choked off my breath. These people did not deserve influence over their princess. The Uprising was twisted, violent, uncompromising.

Stifling a moan of pain, I managed to climb out of bed and watch through the keyhole. Lucrez's door was only partly ajar, but I could see her on the floor in the scarlet nightgown she had donned to meet Mathis, blood dribbling from the ink-dark line of her hair.

"I've taken such good care of you," Orturio growled. "Kept you from starving. Sent your boy off to learn and have a future. Do you realize your betrayal could cost the princess her life? She, who the Holies have ordained to lead my people back to the faith?"

"Severo Segona told me the queen threatened to kill his family if he did not murder the princess," Lucrez said.

A name. Lucrez had mentioned the village, and now I had a name. Was it the huntsman's?

"That's why they fled, not because I warned him about the Uprising," she continued. "He *saved* the princess. He's keeping her safe. Isn't that enough reason to spare him?"

"This is not your first act of duplicity, is it?" Orturio asked, ignoring her. "It's not the first time I've sensed you sneaking about. But last night, you were careless. You let the huntsman's neighbor see you, and I found blood dried on my keys. Did you take them while I slept?"

My skin prickled and my mouth went dry.

"No, I know nothing about that," Lucrez said.

Viteus forced her to her feet and held a knife to her throat. Her expression was defiant.

"You betrayed my trust and tried to lie when you were caught," Orturio said. "That is unforgivable. But I might forgive you, if you tell me where the huntsman planned to take the girls. Did he tell you?"

"No."

"Are you sure about that?"

Viteus dug the knife in at the edge of her collarbone. She sucked in a breath and said through her teeth, "He told me nothing."

The following pause was the tensest I'd ever heard. "Take her outside and deal with her as you dealt with the other snake in the grass," Orturio said. "Once a traitor, always a traitor."

"They were going to a hideout in the woods," Lucrez yelled, frantic. "A place that belonged to his father. I have no idea where it is. He never told me."

Orturio seized her jaw, forcing her to look him in the eyes. "Take her outside."

"No!" Lucrez screamed as Viteus jerked her by the elbow. "Please, Rasmus!"

The urge to confess to stealing the keys rose hot and dangerous in my throat. But Lucrez had damned herself regardless.

Claiming responsibility for stealing the keys would not undo her fate. It would only damn me along with her.

In my imagination, I screamed at these beasts to unhand her, sent arrows through their chests, and relished their suffering. But the image of the maid's grisly remains seared my thoughts like a fresh brand, reminding me of my helplessness. I could barely draw breath around the fear that filled my core.

Orturio walked away, leaving Viteus to drag out a thrashing Lucrez. What I wouldn't give to have even the innate, unruly magic that Glisette possessed without an elicrin stone.

"What's going on?" I heard Mathis demand.

"It's none of your concern," Viteus replied. Mathis roared with rage and erupted into a sequence of offensive spells, but no magic came. The Realm Alliance had taken his elicromancy from him but for a few measly tricks.

When nothing worked, Mathis shoved Viteus back and tried to rip Lucrez free of his grip. Viteus stumbled and nearly fell, flinging

Lucrez to the floor, but he caught his balance and bounded back to bury his knife in Mathis's flank.

I gasped. Mathis groaned. Viteus yanked out the knife, leaving Mathis pressing the wound in disbelief, blood trickling through his fingers.

Viteus dragged a struggling Lucrez down the hall. Mathis choked and staggered away.

Not long after, I heard Lucrez's distant scream get choked off.

I pressed my eyes closed. Warm tears streamed on my cheeks. I wept for Lucrez and wished for her to find the land of light. I barely knew her, yet I knew she lived in passion, in danger, in sacrifice.

Eventually, a maid entered and offered no comfort beyond another pain tincture and a tray of oats and fruit. "You'll dine with the master this evening," she said. "He wanted me to tell you that he values your willingness to help secure the princess."

She seemed resigned, disconnected. Perhaps she did not want to grow attached to someone who might be executed before her very eyes, lest she herself be executed for showing too much sympathy, like the Nisseran maid whose name I hadn't even learned, the other "snake in the grass."

The new maid opened the shutters to a beautiful day before bustling out. She locked the door on her way out. Clicking locks were the heartbeat of this dreadful house.

Mere seconds later, someone slipped a piece of parchment under my door. Wary, I slid it toward me, finding a message in Nisseran.

I wish I could do more to help you, but I watched them kill the Nisseran girl for trying to steal your elicrin stone for you. I'm sorry for my part in bringing you here. I knew that Orturio's brothers killed my brother, but I didn't know he was a murderer like them. He told me we would not use violence to overthrow elicromancers.

I know you borrowed Lucrez's keys and that you found the maid's body. Look again—your elicrin stone is with her.

Hurried hoof beats struck the stones of the drive. I launched toward the window and saw Mathis riding away, a streak of blond hair and bloody bandages.

That selfish bastard. He had dragged me here and left me behind to face Orturio's wrath. The tip he shared was enough to satisfy his pathetic conscience, but it would mean nothing if I didn't get a chance to search for the elicrin stone again without meeting the same fate as Lucrez.

As I watched the note from Mathis burn, I let that one glimpse inside the barrel come back to me as vividly as my horror-stricken memory would allow. There was so much blood it was hard to distinguish anything, but I had seen something at the bottom of the barrel.

An idea sprang from the depths of my despair, and the thrill of revenge already throbbed under my skin like the first bold, dangerous notes of a folk-dancing song. I swiped one of several perfume bottles from my vanity tray and went to the lavatory to pour its contents into the commode. Back in my room, empty bottle in one hand, I sniffed the clear liquid in the tiny tincture glass. It smelled more pungent than my earlier doses. Perhaps both the maid and I would be safer if she kept me drowsy and docile. Carefully, I poured the tincture from the glass into the narrow opening of the bottle. I couldn't afford to spill a single drop.

I didn't breathe again until I had finished and put the stopper back in the bottle. I set the empty glass on the nightstand—I would have to endure the pain of my injury—and tucked the perfume bottle under the mattress, climbing onto the other side of the bed. I stared at the wall and pretended to sleep, listening to melting snow drip from the roof.

❦ TWENTY-SIX ❦

KADRI

Y plan was not foolproof, but it was less clumsy than my plan to steal Orturio's keys, which would have resulted in my demise had Lucrez not been guilty of her own insurrection.

Not long after the incident, I saw Viteus and two other men leave on horseback. Orturio must have sent them out in pursuit of the princess.

Their absence could strengthen my odds. As far as I knew, only Orturio, his uncle, and the household servants were currently under this roof.

For dinner, I chose a dark-brown dress with cream brocade on the sleeves and a tight bodice that allowed me to hide the perfume bottle against my bosom. Without the tincture, my sprained ankle hurt worse than it had yesterday. But it would be worth the pain.

When Orturio sent for me, I took a moment to breathe and center myself.

Down in the dining room, I found him looking disheveled, distracted, like a man who had lost everything. His uncle was there too, which I'd hoped wouldn't be the case, but I had factored the possibility into my plan.

Thankfully, they were drinking the clear spirits. Everything hinged on it.

Orturio gruffly beckoned me into the room without even glancing up from the map he was perusing. Gone were the canny pleasantries, gone was the zealous look in his eyes and his poised sense of control. Orturio was a desperate man who would cling to the hope and future his divinely appointed princess symbolized.

The kitchen staff served lamb pie, potatoes, and stuffed dates. I was the only one who took up my utensils.

"Tell us about Glisette Lorenthi," Orturio said after a time, still studying the map of Halithenica and its surrounding villages.

"What do you want to know?" I asked. My voice sounded meek, but exhilaration coursed through my veins.

"Why would she cause such devastation?" He gestured at the window. The clouds had cleared, and the night was full of stars. But the snow had only begun to melt, and the breeze carried a bit of a bite. The workers had spent the day shoveling snow away from the damaged vines.

"I don't think it was intentional," I replied.

"Then how did it happen?"

"Well, her younger sister..." I couldn't complete my thought. "Glisette must have been very upset."

"Do all elicromancer tantrums end so badly for mortals?"

"It wasn't a tantrum. She...she must have had her elicrin stone taken from her." I hated giving them this vital piece of information. But I hoped what I told them wouldn't matter.

"Then how did she cause the snowstorm?"

"Elicrin magic is hereditary," I explained, shifting potatoes around with my fork without looking at him. The more he thought he had broken my will to escape, the better. "Glisette had power before she came into possession of an elicrin stone. Raw magic. It's unruly without an elicrin stone, which allows precision and control."

"I see," he said. "So without it, she is more dangerous in some ways and less in others?"

"Yes, I suppose."

He looked up, studied me briefly. He plucked an empty cordial glass from the tray at his elbow. "This is pomati, made from the pomace after the grapes are pressed." He placed the glass in front of me, seeming almost pleased. He preferred his captives and employees docile.

What was the most natural way for me to act after watching them drag Lucrez to her execution? Should I be timid and compliant? Or eager to offer them anything in a bid to win freedom?

I decided to just drink the pomati for now, as it required me to say nothing. The spirit was stronger than I expected—too strong. A couple more of these and my head would be spinning.

"If you are able to help us recover the princess, I will consider releasing you," Orturio said.

This was the first time he had used the language of a captor. He thought I was desperate enough to believe his promise. He thought my hopes depended upon his willingness to do as he said.

"The huntsman's neighbor said the princess and the elicromancer left the village with the huntsman and his family in the early morning. The huntsman told the old man that if he felt unsafe and wanted to join them at the hideout, he could meet him at the edifice in Enturra at noon the day after tomorrow, on Sun's Benediction. The huntsman must expect that the crowds will help give him cover from us and the queen's guards."

"So you want to follow the old man and ambush the huntsman when they meet?"

Orturio shook his head. "He's in no state to take the huntsman up on his offer. Viteus nearly killed him. Thankfully, there's a priest in Enturra, one of our allies who helps us protect religious artifacts. He says he knows the huntsman's face. He will be on the lookout. We can follow the huntsman to his hideout, where you will approach the group, establish trust, and make sure that your friend allows the princess to come with us. If that happens, we will release you. If anything goes wrong—if Princess Navara gets hurt or you fail to secure her in our custody—the deal is off."

"I understand," I said.

The uncle shook his fist. "And if we find out that unbelieving huntsman has violated her—"

"Uncle," Orturio said in a placating tone. "She *will* be the pure queen who restores faith to Perispos, as the ancient scriptures foretell. Our mission is to protect her and continue her mother's work of raising her on the path of virtue. She will strike fear into the hearts of those who reject the faith."

Repressing a shudder of disgust required all of my resolve. The young princess's "purity" was far from the business of middle-aged men mired in views of bygone centuries. If they had their way, Navara would return Perispos to the age of violent religious conquests and heretic executions.

Any of my elicromancer friends could kill Orturio with a flick of their pinky fingers. But I needed to do it now, before he could hurt anyone else, before he could sink his claws into Navara and make the future queen an enemy of elicromancers, a punisher of unbelievers. The Uprising's influence would be felt throughout the world if they succeeded.

Orturio grabbed the bottle to pour us each another drink. I watched him splash more liquid into the glasses and felt the small reassuring pressure of the perfume bottle between my ribs.

It was time.

They were large men. The full dose of tincture would probably knock one man out, but splitting it two ways was a gamble—and that was only *if* my plan to distract them actually worked.

But I didn't have a choice. It would be now or never. At least the uncle was older. I could give Orturio most of the draught.

I faked a chill that visibly shook my shoulders, rubbing my upper arms for warmth. "I feel the cold again. Do you think the snow has returned?"

They both hurried to the window. With calm movements even though my heart was raging, I slipped the perfume bottle out of my bodice. The stopper made a tiny pop as I removed it, but they didn't notice. I reached to splash most of the tincture in Orturio's drink and the rest in the uncle's. Hopefully, the pomati would disguise the taste. If not . . . I didn't want to ponder if not.

I barely had enough time to hide the empty bottle in my lap before Orturio turned around and said, "It's not snowing again, thank the Holies."

Orturio settled back down and drained the clear liquid in the glass, blinking a little in surprise at the taste. I drank mine, resisting the urge to search his face for a sign that he knew what I had done.

Frowning, he poured himself another. He would either recognize the difference or wash the taste away and shrug it off. He looked at me as he drank. I averted my eyes and stabbed a potato.

I didn't anticipate it would be enough to lull two large men to sleep within minutes, as it would me. I could only hope it was enough to cloud their senses. I ate slowly, taking small bites and watching through my eyelashes as Orturio complained to his uncle about what the snow would do to his harvest and ultimately, his product and fortune. I thought his blinks seemed heavier, longer, but it could have just been wishful thinking.

Faith in my plan wavered when I finished the last bite of my meal. I hoped Orturio wouldn't lose interest and send me back to my chamber.

He continued rambling about how the poor weather would ruin them. "But I believe we stand to recoup some of it when we install the princess on the crown—"

I looked up in surprise at his mistake. He hadn't noticed, and neither had his uncle. The tincture was affecting them both now, undoubtedly helped along by the pomati.

I nearly offered to pour another round, but decided I was better staying put, inessential to the increasingly incoherent dialogue. At last, Orturio blinked a few times, his head lolling slightly to the side.

The uncle snapped in Orturio's face to try to wake him before settling back in his chair, unsuccessful. He grumbled something that made no sense, slurred by the pomati and the tincture.

A feeling of urgency sprang upon me. I set the perfume bottle on the table and slipped out of my seat, eyeing the fire iron at the hearth. The weakness of my injured ankle would make this a difficult fight. I steeled myself for a struggle.

"What are you...?" The uncle garbled his words as his lazy gaze tried to follow me to the hearth. The fire iron felt powerful in my grip.

The uncle's back was turned to me—an easy target. Orturio sat in profile at the head of the table, his head resting on his chest. I debated a moment before deciding that it was Orturio I had to take down first. He posed the greatest danger if he recovered consciousness before I could make my escape.

I circled around the head of the table, the slipper of my unmaimed foot sliding along the floor as I favored the other. I looked at the uncle; his mouth was open, his breathing heavy, his eyelids barely flickering.

I raised the pointed fire iron, found my balance, and gritted my teeth. The weapon whistled through the air as I brought it down and struck Orturio's broad crown, denting his skull, spraying blood over my knuckles.

Orturio roared and thrashed. My second blow only glanced off his skull. The uncle jerked awake and lunged for the iron, swaying so heavily that he dragged us both backward as we struggled, sending knives of pain through my sprained ankle. We tumbled together, and his large body broke my fall. He tried to wrap his thick arm around my neck, but I slipped away from his grip and snatched my weapon again, swinging it down to meet his groin. He cursed and howled.

Orturio staggered from his chair. He swiped to knock me down, but the head wound and the tincture slowed him enough that I was able to land another solid, bloody swipe to the side of his head, which sent him barreling to the stone floor.

The maid who had cared for me since the other's death hurried in, gasped, and exited. She might summon the guards or the other servants. I had to finish this now.

The uncle gripped my maimed ankle, squeezing the swollen knot with his massive fist. I issued a sound that was part sob, part scream, and fell against the table. My elbow crushed the tray of cordial glasses and the bottle of pomati. Glass stung my skin, but I'd managed to cling to the fire iron. I turned to find the uncle getting to his feet. If he caught me, it wouldn't take much for him to overpower me. I couldn't give him the chance. I whacked him hard in the basin between his shoulder and neck, then swiped up and smacked him across the face. He roared like an angry bear as he stumbled back and fell, fatally striking his head on the stone mantel.

Orturio lay on the ground in an unmoving heap. I flung away the fire iron and dug into his breast pocket for his key ring.

"The Uprising won't die with us," Lord Orturio said, his wide eyes darting to and fro.

Clenching the keys in one fist, I extracted the iron effigy of the Holy of Loyalty from the pouch sewn at my waist. I slid it into his breast pocket and patted it. "We'll see about that."

I waited only a moment before his broad chest ceased its frantic rising and falling.

Victorious, I started my limping trek toward the cellar door before any of the servants could discover the carnage and try to stop me.

The corridor seemed to stretch to eternity, and the pine cellar door seemed so far away.

Behind me, I heard a shuffle and a deep groan. I looked back to find Orturio careening after me, blood gushing over his face. Had he pretended to breathe his last breath, or had rage reanimated his battered body?

With a wail of fear, I limped faster. I fumbled with the keys, my hands quaking. My ankle collapsed beneath me, and I rammed my shoulder into the wall, knocking down a lyre on display. Its strings made a discordant noise as its hollow body bounced across the floor. I strove on, but Orturio bellowed with anger and the lyre flew past my head, breaking to pieces on the cellar door.

Just a few more uneven, halting steps, and I would reach it. My pulse hammered as I found the right key. I slammed against the door, jammed the key into the lock, and heard the click. But before I could open the door, a hand wrenched back my shoulder.

I turned to face my wild-eyed enemy, my controlling captor. The blood leaking from Orturio's wounds made me queasy. He reeled back to strike me, but over his shoulder I saw the same stoic maid who had brought me my tincture. She held a kitchen cleaver in her grip. Its wide blade winked in the dim light.

Perhaps Orturio knew how to make servants obey, but he didn't know how to earn their loyalty.

Setting her jaw, the woman buried the cleaver in the middle of her master's back. Shock turned to pain as it passed over his features.

Turning my back on him, I swung open the cellar door and locked myself in the dark on the other side. I listened to the heavy thud of Orturio's body slumping to the floor, and then the soft, careful steps of the maid finishing the job. A wet *shink* let me know she had dislodged the weapon from his back, and another announced the final, deadly blow. Orturio's last breaths gurgled out.

I fled clumsily down the dark stairs and ran to the shrine, so focused on my destination that I forgot about the table and rammed into it with my left hip, letting out a yelp. I groped the idols until I found the round shield boss and flicked the panel open.

The thought hadn't struck me until now: What if Orturio had moved the maid's body and my elicrin stone after last night, threatened by the idea of anyone sneaking around in the cellar? Or worse, what if he had disposed of Lucrez's body here, too?

When I yanked the shrine away from the hidden room, I felt the barrel at waist-level and the blood squelching on the floor. I pried off the lid and plunged my hands into the blood bath, refusing to think about the cold tangle of limbs and swath of matted curls. I whimpered in disgust at the vague odor that had begun to emanate from the corpse. But finally, finally, I felt something hard and small. A grunt of joy burst out of me when I lifted the elicrin stone from the muck and raised it high, its bloody chain dangling.

"May you live on in the land of light," I whispered to the maid's dead body. Then I clutched my elicrin stone. *"Carathin har,"* I said. Light spilled through my fingers.

I slipped the jewel around my neck with my blood-slicked hands and searched the shelves of the secret room by its comforting light.

I found a large leather satchel of gold coins and slipped it over my shoulder. I also spotted a dagger with an elaborate sheath and belt, which I lashed around my waist. I turned to go, but a gaudy silver cylinder perched on an overhead shelf caught the light: a scroll case. A round gold emblem depicting the four-horned ram winked at me.

Could this be the sealed scroll, the one that Ambrosine had

burned that entire edifice hoping to destroy? If it was worth something to both Ambrosine and the Uprising, I knew I couldn't leave it behind. I dropped it in the satchel.

The large door on the other end of the cellar beckoned me. I hurried down the aisle of wine barrels. Through the keyhole, I saw the two dogs pacing, wary.

I crouched to position my weight beneath the heavy plank barring the door, growling against the waves of pain that throbbed through my swollen ankle. I saw stars, but I managed to lift it and toss it away.

Shoving open the massive doors, I heard the dogs bark and scramble toward me. I could cut them down with *umrac korat*, the slashing spell, one of the few I'd practiced. But I knew I wouldn't need to. The smell of blood and death lured them straight to the secret room. They didn't mind me at all.

I snuck out of the cellar unnoticed, limping up the green slope and into the open twilight.

TWENTY-SEVEN

GLISETTE
THE NEXT DAY

A PEARL of sweat dripped along my jaw. The spring sun had emerged to thaw the ice and snow blanketing the woods. My skin warmed beneath my borrowed wool tunic as I helped Navara practice a basic sword-fighting maneuver.

"Hips toward me," I reminded her, as Devorian's instructor had reminded me so many times. I used to flutter my eyelashes and beg him to give me lessons even though Mother scolded us every time she found out.

Navara adjusted her stance and tightened her grip around her branch. "Like this?"

"Lower your dominant hand. You'd be squeezing the blade right now."

"I'm useless," she said, shaking her head. "How can I lead my people if I've never even held a weapon?"

"It's more symbolic than anything," I reassured her, lifting my own branch. "Your people think of you as a girl, not as a young woman ready to take command. You probably won't need to know how to fight, but you need to look the part. The hair helps, I think."

"Does it?" she asked, combing back a tangled lock. The blunt cut paired with her tattered dress had made her look young and helpless. But now, while wearing one of the boys' winter tunics, she looked older, tougher, more resilient. Short hair drew attention to her regal, dimpled chin and acute dark eyes. She truly was a rare beauty.

"Yes," I replied. "Now if we can set you atop a saddle and hand you a real sword without toppling you, we have a warrior queen in the making."

Navara laughed, but when she resumed her stance, she was serious and determined to learn.

Her earnestness reminded me of Perennia, and I struggled to believe my sister was truly gone. Had Ambrosine held a funeral yet? What did Devorian think had happened that horrible night? A tracking map would take weeks to create, but I felt almost certain he would use every resource to find me.

"Are you all right?" Navara asked, searching my face. I realized my magic had stolen the warmth from the breeze.

"Fine," I said, lifting the hem of my tunic to shimmy out of it. Perhaps pretending I was too warm might somehow make the cold disappear. Underneath, I wore only my tight linen chemise tucked into breeches, both of which were in need of rigorous laundering.

I looked uphill toward the hideout to see if anyone had noticed the chill. Sev's father's cabin was built into a hillside in the depths of the forest, earth-sheltered and cloaked in green. It was even smaller than the family's cottage in the village and there were no windows, not even a chimney. But it provided us with basic necessities and crouched a safe distance from any roads or woodland trails.

"My father used to poach these lands to keep us fed," Sev had explained to Navara and me when we arrived early yesterday morning. His brothers and sisters had started playing games in the middle of the only room, the younger ones chattering giddily as though this were some fun adventure. Sev, his mother, Stasi, and Jeno did a fine job of protecting them from even the fear of danger. "This was his hideout from the king's foresters."

"He was a poacher?" Navara asked, surprised. "How did he become my father's head huntsman?"

"He heard about king's foresters hunting for a thief who stole two horses from a nobleman," he said. "My father caught the thief and the horses and delivered them to the king. He asked for no reward but steady employment and modest pay, and your father obliged. Years later, after they had become friends, my father confessed to having been a poacher. The king just laughed." Navara had smiled at this.

No one came trotting down the hill in reaction to the cold, so I resumed the lesson. "Now, if someone is reeling back like this"— I picked up my branch to demonstrate—"you're going to want to come down on their right shoulder. It will block any counterattack, and you've landed a solid blow."

"I see," Navara said, trying out the motion.

"Let's say someone attacks you like this," I went on, lowering my branch to mimic jabbing her with the tip. "You're going to want to lean into your back foot to evade, as it's harder to block a head-on offense of this manner than to just avoid contact."

"Like this?" she asked, shifting her weight.

"Yes, then recover with a more decisive block once you're less vulnerable. So swing your blade down with strength." Our branches clashed.

"Wait . . . if this is just for appearances, why are you teaching me this?" she asked.

"You have a target on your back," I said. "It's good to know how to defend yourself. But if you have a choice, always run away rather than engage. Running gives you the best chance of survival."

Navara bit her lip. "How did you do it?" she asked, lowering her branch. "You stormed the Moth King's tower. Were you not afraid? I want to be a leader like you, but I'm so afraid."

A dark truth came reluctantly to mind: my elicrin stone had made me brave. Knowing ancient magic waited at my beck and call had prevented fear from governing my actions. Without it, I didn't know whether I could be courageous in the face of death.

For the first time, it struck me how terrifying it must have been for Kadri to accompany us, how bold she had been to refuse to let Mercer turn her away.

"Maybe see it as doing what you feel you must, one small choice at a time," I said softly. "You've already started your perilous journey; you endangered your life asking me to meet you in the edifice. Today, you're learning to wield a sword—"

"A stick."

"A sword," I insisted. "So that you can fight for your people. And tomorrow, you'll do something even more courageous. You're no less brave, and no more terrified, than I was."

"Hmm," Navara said, pursing her lips. "That makes sense. You learn courage as it's required of you."

"Exactly. I used to be perfectly content spending my days at social events, drinking wine, gossiping, and dallying with boys I didn't even fancy just to feel a thrill. When my brother accidentally awoke the Moth King, it awoke something in me too. A sense of purpose. A calling to right his wrongs, for the sake of my kingdom and my family's honor. You have the same love for your kingdom and family. You will find the courage you need."

Navara smiled a small smile. "I'm sure Commander Larsio will be reluctant to put me in danger, but I hope I'm brave enough to defy him if I need to."

"I don't want any mortals to have to see battle," I said, regret heavy on my heart. "The Realm Alliance started this, and we need to finish it."

I mentally retraced the letters of the urgent missives I'd left with the village dispatcher yesterday morning. Mortal messaging was so inefficient. If we'd been able to establish magical missive routes across the sea, the others might already be on their way. I hoped they were regardless—that Mercer had seen a vision, that he and Valory would use the portal to come directly to Halithenica.

Had Devorian found a way to contact the Realm Alliance? Had Ambrosine stopped him from reaching out, or worse, did he believe her version of events? Had she imprisoned him within his own mind, like Myron? Had she shown Devorian the lovely, heart-rending visions she had shown me of our parents, our family made whole again?

These possibilities made a bitter cold comb through the wind. Suddenly, I could see my breath.

I knew someone would come check on us after such an abrupt change in the air. And sure enough, by the time I straightened, Sev was treading through the melting snow toward us, his leather boots quiet on the forest floor despite his confident stride. He had left the hideout last night to seek out the commander who had resigned. I'd slept with a lump of worry in my throat. What if Ambrosine or the Uprising captured him?

I expected to feel relief at his return, but I didn't expect it in the form of heat flaring through my chest.

"Did you find Commander Larsio?" I asked, before Sev could question if everything was all right.

"Right where I expected him," he replied with a smirk. "In the gambling den in Lorganti. We're meeting him at an abandoned edifice in two days. He seemed relieved to have something to do."

"Are you sure it's safe to involve him?" I asked. We had discussed this already, but I hadn't warmed to the idea. I trusted the Realm Alliance and the people at this hideout—no one else.

"The commander knows everything about the royal army," Sev reminded me. "He knows any strategy it could use, every weakness it has. He will know what to expect from your sister's forces. And he knows how to ready an army. We need him."

"My friends will come—"

"What if they don't?"

His sharpness lacerated what little sense of calm I felt.

"He was my father's commander for twenty years," Navara added gently, lowering her branch. "I trust him. Even when the elicromancers do arrive, it won't hurt to have him on our side."

Sensing I was outnumbered again, I fell quiet.

"So you know how to fight without spells and magic?" Sev asked me, skeptical. He folded his arms and leaned against a tree. A ray of sunlight shot through the leaves and painted the tips of his tousled raven hair gold. "Or are you two just playing with sticks?"

I let out a harsh laugh before I realized he was serious. I could have explained to him that it was tradition in Nissera for boys in royal families to learn the arts of warfare, a tradition that began back when kings were mortals and the few living elicromancers were just hermits in the mountains. I could have explained how I'd defied my mother to learn, or that wielding a sword in addition to my elicrin magic made me doubly deadly as a foe. Instead, I glared at him. "If you think I'm playing, why don't you join the game?"

"Pff," he said, and gestured dismissively.

"Come, now. You think I'm helpless without magic? Let me show you just how helpless." I jerked my head at Navara. "Let him borrow your sword."

"Stick," Sev said.

"Sword," Navara corrected, raising an eyebrow at him. She held out the branch.

"Very well," he sighed, unfolding his arms to accept it.

I snatched up my tunic, used it to dab at the sweat on my neck, and tossed it over a tree limb before brandishing my weapon. Sev adopted a fighting stance, but the corner of his mouth quirked up in amusement.

We each shifted our weight before I lunged. He reacted quickly and blocked a high strike that would have come down on his head. I ducked his answering thrust and swiped sideways at his knees. His branch collided with mine with a loud crack that made birds scatter from their perches overhead. We both reeled back, but he was first to recover. His next swipe was pitiful, perfunctory, and I dodged it easily.

"Don't hold back," I growled.

"I'm not—"

"Don't hold back!"

My command barked through the quiet. Freezing air swirled

around us, streaming my hair and toying with the sleeves and hem of Sev's loose brown tunic.

The bitter cold made me realize that I was desperate to prove to myself that I didn't need magic—that I could be strong without it.

Sev stared me down for a moment before he set his jaw and reengaged. This time, he attacked first, and he was swift. His blows were hard, aggressive, but graceful. Sweat dripped down my temples as I ducked and jumped and twirled out of the way, breathless. He put me on the defense; it was all I could do to evade his strikes. When I managed to outmaneuver him, my blows were weak. The need to release my rage was my only fuel as we struggled on. I did strike him once in the ribs and he answered by blasting my thigh with bruising force. When I grunted in pain, he apologized, and the annoyance at his pacification helped me recover my waning strength. We parried until our branches tangled over our heads. The next thing I knew, he had spun me in place, dropped his weapon, and taken hold of mine, which he used like a bar against my sternum to trap me.

"Let's call it a draw," he said. I could feel the rise and fall of his hard chest and the warmth of his panting breaths gusting over my ear.

Twigs snapped in the distance, and I looked to see Stasi hiking toward us, hopping over snarls of thorns in her path. "Stew's ready," she said.

Sev and I disentangled. I wanted to glare at him, but the fight had depleted my anger.

Navara shot me a quizzical expression before I turned and led the way back to the cabin. All of us gathered around the campfire, where a large cauldron of rabbit stew bubbled. Many pairs of busy feet had melted the snow around the hideout. It had been a relief to see the children shedding their patched-up cloaks as we journeyed here, with Sev leading the three youngest atop his rouncey, Orfeo.

"What sort of magic spells do you know?" Eleni asked me as we ate in a large huddle.

"Oh, all sorts," I replied. "I could put out this campfire and start it up again with only a few words. I could cut our firewood without lifting a finger. And that leather strap in your hair? I could make it look like a pretty ribbon, at least for an hour or two. What's your favorite color?"

She bit her tongue as she thought. "Blue."

"I could turn it blue, whatever shade you like."

She grinned. "Could you make this dress into a fancy gown?"

"It would be hard work, and it would probably only last a few minutes," I said. "But one of my ancestors could make anything look like anything else. She was beautiful, but she could make herself look like an old man with warts on his face."

The younger children sniggered.

Sev plunked down his half-finished bowl of stew and stalked around the corner of the cabin. Frowning, his mother watched him leave before flashing Navara and me apologetic looks. Shortly after, I heard the sound of Sev's axe splitting wood.

The children turned their attentions to Navara, allowing me to finish my meal quickly and follow Sev. I found him tossing split logs onto a growing pile. I could practically see the anger pulsing in the lean muscles of his forearms and hands.

"Do you need something?" he asked, lifting his collar to wipe sweat from his forehead. He said it like I was just another mouth to feed, a burden on his back.

"Can I help?" I asked, trying not to sound indignant.

"No." He swung down the axe so hard it made me jump. He cleaved the log cleanly down the center. One of the pieces landed near my boot.

"Did I say something to upset you?" I asked.

He bent to retrieve it and tossed it on the pile, effortlessly hauling a fresh log onto his chopping block. "You're making elicromancy sound harmless."

"Some of it *is* harmless," I contended. "I think your people have vilified magic enough."

"No one needs to vilify it. Even before we had a wicked elicromancer queen, we heard news from Nissera. No mortal with sense wants anything to do with your kind."

Each word was strained with animosity. *This* was why he had glared at me when I had first arrived at the palace. And the moments of kindness since then, had they been inspired by guilt over nearly killing me? Pity?

"You sound just like the people who killed your father," I snapped. I wanted to revoke the words as soon as they came out, but instead I crossed my arms and stood my ground. "You're no 'elicromancer sympathizer,' are you? You're tolerating me to get what you want. I bet you wish your father had never followed the king's orders to kill my parents' murderers."

"Well, he's gone, your parents are still dead, and the Uprising is stronger than ever. What was the use?"

"Justice," I said, even as tears blurred my eyes.

"That must keep you warm at night." His muscles tensed dangerously as he swung the axe again, splitting another log. I bared my teeth at his back, repressing a growl of frustration that I knew would rip through the wood as an icy wind, making the children cold and miserable again. I turned and walked away before he could elicit an emotional outburst we would both regret.

I sat by the stream downhill from the cabin, watching hunks of melting ice float past. I loathed how the cold came and went with my mood. It made me feel exposed, vulnerable. I could not lose hold of my temper for even a moment.

Sunset smeared ruby clouds across the sky. Noticing the hour, I pushed myself up and traipsed to a blackberry bush. If I returned empty-handed, the long absence would reek of a childish tantrum.

As I piled the berries in my tunic, a sharp thorn pricked my fingertip. Jerking back, I sucked on the pad of my finger and tasted blood. I switched hands to pluck an overripe berry, and the bruise-black drupelets burst in my hand. But instead of the usual purple-pink, the juice staining my skin glared the distinct shade of fresh blood.

I touched the tip of my tongue to it and spat in disgust. It *tasted* like blood, metallic and tangy. I tried another and almost gagged. I shook out my tunic and watched the rest of the bad crop tumble to the ground.

A cold whisper brushed across my nape, along with a sound like jagged knives scraping together. *Vengeance can be yours.*

Gasping, I whirled around to see who had snuck up on me. But I saw nothing—only the forest with its slightly unfamiliar flora, lit by slanted sunbeams.

Something tickled my elbow. I looked and found that the tiny wound from the thorn had somehow gushed blood from the tip of my finger to the crease of my elbow, staining my sleeve.

I pressured the pricked skin to stop the blood, but it only surged harder. Soon, so much slick blood covered my hands that I hurried to plunge them in the cold stream.

The stream turned red.

Tamping down a sense of panic, I sprinted back to the cabin, the tiny wound still gushing. I barged through the door, startling everyone, and darted to grab a dishrag from the back of wooden chair where Navara sat.

"What's wrong?" Sev asked, flinching toward his weapons. I didn't fool myself that his concern was on my behalf.

Without answering, I clenched the cloth in my fist, expecting blood to rapidly soak the fabric.

But when I examined the cut, the blood was gone. Only a tiny dab of it stained the cloth.

"What is it?" Sev rounded the table to look. "Oh, just a prick."

"There was blood everywhere," I said, high-pitched and slipping briefly back into Nisseran. "It was running down my arms...and someone spoke to me..." I looked around the room. "Were any of you down by the stream a moment ago?"

Everyone shook their heads and exchanged bewildered glances. "Did you see someone?" Sev strode to his stash of weapons propped against the wall, taking up his axe.

"No, I didn't see anyone."

Navara sank her teeth into her lower lip. She took my hand and turned it over. "You said you saw blood everywhere?"

"Yes. All over me, and in the river. The blackberries were filled with it too." I shuddered in horror, but Navara merely looked somber.

"Do you remember in the edifice, when I told you about the last chapter of the Book of Belief?" she asked.

I gripped the table to steady myself and closed my eyes to wade through the mire of that night's tragedy. "You said it foretells that the Fallen will try to claim earthly vessels. When all four succeed, humanity is doomed... or something dour like that."

"There's a reason why Nexantius claimed Ambrosine," she whispered. Her hands clasped mine. They were cold. "A reason why she stirred him, or summoned him, or whatever she did by entering one of our sacred places. It's long been thought that the Fallen will seek out elicromancer vessels because they're more capable than human vessels. More *like* the Fallen, some would say, though I don't believe that myself."

"What are you saying?"

Navara's brown eyes met mine, swimming with dread. She whispered the name, as though fearful it could act as a summons. "Themera."

"Cruelty?" I whispered back, and I could almost taste the tang of blood again.

"Like the Holies, each of the Fallen has their own symbol. Nexantius has mirrors. Robivoros, teeth. Silimos, mold. And Themera, blood."

"You think she's trying to claim me like Nexantius claimed Ambrosine?"

I didn't want to entertain the possibility. Nexantius encouraged Ambrosine's most wicked inclinations and augmented her power for mirror illusions. Their unholy union had been both as unlikely and inevitable as a lightning strike. If Themera was trying to claim me, what did it mean that she had chosen me as her vessel?

"Maybe we should go outside," Sev suggested, reminding me that Navara and I were not alone. "My family doesn't speak Nisseran, but they know the names of the Fallen."

I looked up and found all seven of his siblings watching us with rapt attention.

The children whispered as the three of us slipped out into the twilight, the door squealing shut behind us. The insects that had survived the winter storm whirred and chirped their nighttime songs. I searched the shadows of the forest, repressing a shiver. "I think I should leave," I said. "None of you are safe with me."

"You'll be more vulnerable out there, alone," Navara said. "A Fallen can't cross into the mortal world without a willing receptacle. As long as you deny her, she cannot hurt us."

"Are you certain?" I asked. "It sounds so farfetched."

"Ambrosine's union with Nexantius did nothing but strengthen my faith," Navara explained. "Now I know that what the Book of Belief says is true. And I know that we have to defeat them, or the four scourges will come and innocent people will suffer and die."

"How?" I asked. "How do we stop them?"

"I don't know. The answer is in the sealed scroll." Navara dropped her head in her hands. "And it's probably long gone."

"Why is it sealed?" I asked. "Wouldn't the high priest want everyone to know how to defeat the Fallen?"

"Even though it's written by the same prophets as the rest of the Book, it's considered apocryphal," Navara said without looking up. "My father has said before that its contents would shake the people's faith. Instead of picking and choosing what to share, our high priests and rulers keep the whole thing secret."

"And you think Ambrosine took it?" I asked.

She peeled her hands away from her face. "The day after she killed the high priest, she interrogated me to see if my father had ever told me what it said. Thankfully, she could tell I wasn't lying. I'm sure she's destroyed it by now."

"Or maybe not," Sev said, his brown eyes radiant. "Not if she never found it."

"What do you mean?" Navara asked.

"The day before Father Peramati died, he summoned me to run an errand. He said he needed someone fast and dangerous and that I had permission to kill anyone who tried to stop me. He gave me a sack and instructed me to bring it to where the Arreneos River crosses the road outside of Enturra. An old man in a hood met me there, and I passed it on to him. I never looked inside—Father Peramati told me the Holies would curse my family, as ridiculous as that sounds. By the weight and shape, it could have been a scroll case. Ambrosine questioned me about it the next day. She wanted to know who met me, but I barely saw his face."

"There's an old priest in Enturra named Father Frangos who collects Agrimas artifacts," Navara said. "My grandfather paid for him to build a secure vault in the Edifice of the Fallen in Enturra to expand his collection. Maybe Father Frangos agreed to safeguard the scroll when Father Peramati realized it was in danger. Do you think the man you met was a priest?"

"I don't know," Sev admitted. "But I'm going to Enturra tomorrow for more supplies, and to meet our neighbor Yannis in case he needs to hide with us. I could look around the edifice while I'm there."

"I'm the only one with a chance of convincing the priest to let me see it," Navara argued. "It may not be time for me to inherit it, but the knowledge of the scroll is my birthright."

Sev shook his head. "It's too dangerous for you to go."

"Ambrosine is powerful even by elicromancers' standards," I said. "With Nexantius, I don't know what more she's capable of. I've been assuming Valory Braiosa could defeat her, but she's not here. We are. If there's something that tells us how to defeat them, we need it."

"And you need me to get it," Navara said, satisfied.

"Everyone is watching for both of you—" Sev started.

"Oh!" Navara interrupted. "Tomorrow is Sun's Benediction! This is perfect."

"Why—?" Sev tried again, but she cut him off.

"I have an idea." She hurried back inside, leaving Sev and me alone. I remembered that we weren't exactly charmed with each other at the moment.

"I'm going to check the perimeter," he said gruffly.

I took a deep breath, not quite ready to rejoin the curious children who had seen me lose my composure over the prick of a thorn.

"Do you want a second set of eyes?" I asked.

"If you want," he agreed. I fell into step beside him, our feet crunching leaves that should have been green but had crumpled in the frost. We were quiet for a long time. Sev seemed thoughtful.

"It's easy for me to blame your family for what happened to my father," he said softly. "And for my family being in danger now. But this isn't your fault. There are people who deserve the blame. Ambrosine, the Uprising..."

"It's easier to blame me."

He made a vague, affirmative sound in his throat.

"Is this an apology?" I mused.

He looked at me sideways.

I sighed and kicked a pebble from my path. "I'll forever regret arranging Ambrosine's marriage to Myron. It's fair for you to blame me for that."

"You wanted to give her a chance at redemption. A new start."

"I thought that an auspicious marriage to a decent man might allow her to begin anew...to reclaim something that I'm not sure she ever possessed." I glanced down at Sev's fidgeting fingers. "What effigy do you keep in your pocket? Some virtue you lack? Certainly not honesty."

He chuckled, but his face turned grim as he fished out an effigy and showed me the likeness of Hestreclea with her dog. "Loyalty. The Uprising left it beside my father's body. They were trying to send a message. Someday, I'll bury it with his killer." He didn't speak for a moment as his dark eyes explored the twilit trees. "I always thought of the Holies and the Fallen as symbols rather than real beings. I began to question that when Ambrosine changed."

He sighed. The way his eyes searched the woods told me he knew them well, that he regarded the trees and trickling streams as friends and confidants.

"Ambrosine and I had become friendly before it happened. I like King Myron, and they seemed fond of each other. She made him laugh. And then shadows came over her, over the palace, and it felt to me like they were consuming everything."

"Why didn't you leave?"

"The day she ordered me to kill you wasn't the first time she threatened my family. When she asked me about the high priest's errand, she tried to seduce the truth out of me. When I gave her nothing, she threatened me instead. Strangely, I could tell she didn't *want* to threaten me. She didn't enjoy it. And she let me go."

The twinge of irritation I felt was a bit of a surprise. Had Ambrosine succeeded in seducing Sev? He didn't say. He may have had no answers for her, but that didn't mean nothing had happened when she'd sought them. I thought of the way Ambrosine had fawned over Sev's successful hunt when Perennia and I first arrived, and I took comfort in how cold he had seemed toward her. *If only I could go back to then*, I thought, *do this all differently.*

"Do you think there's anything left of your sister inside her?" he asked.

"Don't call her my sister anymore," I said coldly, looking up at the night. "My only sister is dead."

TWENTY-EIGHT

GLISETTE

OUTSIDE the cabin Navara adjusted the dark-blue fabric over my face and topped it with a crown of twisted branches. She'd spent all night laboring with needle and thread over her ruined gown only to produce...a veil.

"How is this not conspicuous?" I demanded.

"It's Sun's Benediction Day," Navara said, as though it was an explanation. She tucked my blonde hair beneath the draping. She had repurposed the lacy overlay to cover my face, while opaque fabric covered my fair braid.

"That doesn't answer my question."

"You look like a bride," Sev remarked, striding past us to prepare Orfeo for the trip. He grinned at Navara. "Very clever.

"I'm sorry—it's clever for me to prance around with sticky saplings on my head?" I asked.

"They're supposed to be flowers, but..." Navara winced. "You killed all the flowers."

"Sun's Benediction is a blessed day to hold a wedding," Sev explained, more to the point. "Many couples have waited all year for this day. There will be weddings at every edifice around Halithenica."

"Unless Ambrosine cancelled the celebrations," Navara said, crestfallen at the idea. "But hopefully, she'll be too distracted looking for us to mind if a few people get married today." She finished fitting my veil before stepping back to admire her work, regaining her cheer. "The bride wears a veil and the groom doesn't remove it until they consummate the marriage."

"It would be unthinkable for anyone else to remove a bride's veil," Sev added. "You'll be safely disguised."

"So you'll be the groom," I said. "Will the queen's men not recognize you?"

"I don't hunt this far east of the city. The local foresters won't know me, and even guards who had been stationed at the palace probably couldn't pick me out of a crowd. I'm more worried about the Uprising."

"What if Ambrosine gave them a description of you?" I asked. "She's not openly hunting you down because that would contradict the kidnapping narrative, but..."

He brushed it off. "There's nothing remarkable you could say about my appearance to set me apart."

I guess "handsome, irritatingly so" wouldn't find its way into an official description. Then again, Ambrosine had included that bit about my scar.

I turned to Navara. "What's your disguise?"

"Your maid," Navara replied with a curtsy. "She also wears a veil so as to ward off the groom's lust. While you two are waiting for your turn, I'll sneak away to see Father Frangos. He's very old and doesn't perform the ceremonies anymore."

"Our turn?" I echoed.

"Your ceremony. Don't worry. You won't have to do or say anything. A priest will just pray over you, and that will be it."

I scoffed. "This is foolish. Can't we simply break into the edifice vault?"

"I don't know how we would do that without drawing attention," Navara said. "The vault is impregnable. My grandfather entertained fanciful fears about elicromancers trying to destroy our religious history, and he wanted to protect the treasure Father Frangos had acquired."

I looked to Sev to supply an argument. Certainly he didn't think we should endanger ourselves—and his family—only to learn that the sealed scroll was not in the vault, or worse, that its contents were useless.

Perhaps Sev could not resist his princess. Or perhaps Ambrosine's dalliance with darkness had deepened his belief in the lore of the Holy and the Fallen, as it had Navara's. He said nothing except, "However we get it, it would be nice to have something to bring to Commander Larsio tomorrow. He's a brilliant man, but that won't be enough to defeat an elicromancer possessed by a Fallen deity."

Capitulating in spite of my reservations, I went to wriggle into Stasi's best dress, green linen with sunflowers embroidered around the collar. The seams shaping the bust were a tad constrictive, and the hem hit just above my ankles. But Navara said poor and rich brides would be getting married today, and no one would think anything of an ill-fitting dress.

Sev exchanged his brown tunic and leather jerkin for a cream tunic with blue accents. He gave me one of his smaller hunting knives and a holster, which I fastened to my stocking-clad thigh.

At first, we journeyed through the woods on foot, leading Orfeo behind us, snapping to attention at every creak of lofty branches swaying in the wind. At one point, I heard a twig break and reached for my knife, but it was only a mother doe and her fawn.

When we neared the road to Enturra, Navara rearranged my veil and donned her own. Sev patted Orfeo's storm-colored withers and waved me over.

I hiked up my skirt and set my foot in the stirrup, but soon realized the impossibility of mounting a horse in a dress. I'd always worn riding clothes. Today, I would have to ride sidesaddle. Watching me struggle, Sev offered his hand.

"Oh, all right," I said, and he gripped either side of my waist, settling me into the dip of the saddle.

"Anything for my bride," he said with a playful smile as he grabbed the lead rope and started toward the road. Navara crossed her hands primly and followed us.

My eyes began to ache from straining to see the forest through the lace pattern of my veil. I settled for staring at Orfeo's dappled neck and dark mane until Sev stopped suddenly, on high alert. I looked up and saw two figures.

"Foresters," Sev whispered over his shoulder. "Stay calm."

As the men drew closer, I could make out their brown livery with the purple tree of Perispos on their chests. They carried bows and full quivers.

One of the foresters hailed us. Sev waved at him.

"Happy Benediction," the stranger said, observing my bridal garb. "We don't want to delay you on this blessed day, but we must stop everyone we see. Have you crossed paths with two young women in the woods? One blonde?"

The other man peered through our veils, but lost interest after registering our peasant's clothing.

"No, but we've been watching for them," Sev answered. "We've been praying for the princess's safety since we heard, Holies keep her."

"Yes, Holies keep her," the first man replied gravely.

"If you see anything suspicious, let the royal guards know," the other said. "There are four stationed in every village."

Sev nodded dutifully.

"Blessings," the first forester said with a wave at me. I waved daintily back with a gloved hand, holding my breath until they disappeared.

We journeyed on. Before long, Enturra appeared at the horizon. Though hardly bigger than Sev's village, it seemed more affluent, with newer buildings and broader streets. I tensed on the saddle as we crossed a river bridge and passed royal guards stationed at the other end.

The atmosphere of festivity felt unmistakable, yet subdued. A few girls wore coronets like mine, sadly deprived of flowers, and vendors flaunted discounts on vegetables whose limp leaves had browned in the frost.

We passed another bride and groom escorted by a whole wedding party that smiled and waved at us. "May Orico bless you with many children!" a drunken member of their party yelled our way.

As in Sev's village, the domed edifice was at the center of the square, but this one had a courtyard with rows of towering hedges and cypress trees. A crowd had gathered to watch a priest pray in monotone over a couple at the altar.

Sev clenched my waist to help me dismount. I felt unsteady and surrendered my weight to his sturdy grip, relishing the momentary relief of trusting someone besides myself to be strong.

"I'm going to see if Father Frangos is in the parish," Navara whispered, standing on tiptoe to point to a stone outbuilding covered in ivy. Before I could hiss a warning to be cautious, she had slipped through the crowd and hurried off.

"I don't like this," I whispered to Sev as he passed off Orfeo's lead to an altar attendant in gray.

"It will be fine," the huntsman said near my ear. He caught my hand and brushed a kiss on the back of my glove. This affection came mysteriously naturally to someone whose behavior ranged from surly and wry. "Everyone adores Navara, especially the clergy. They'll do whatever she asks."

I nodded and watched the other couple leave the edifice to cheers from the crowd. It was strange, not knowing whether the bride was grinning beneath that veil or mourning her former life.

The crowd shifted. Newcomers arrived to watch the next modest spectacle while others wandered off. The priest waved us inside with a liver-spotted hand. If he was the young one, Father Frangos must have been a true antique.

When I reached the threshold, I couldn't force myself to go any farther.

Suddenly, it felt like midnight again. Shadows filled the sacred place. The carvings of the Holies, removed and cold and unhelpful, made me want to smash the chipped marble altar.

"No," I whispered aloud, struggling to breathe, ready to rip apart at the seams.

Sev smoothly turned my Nisseran protest into a Perispi explanation for the priest: *"Nontrus eggigaris ta incini tis nedo, pre ti vitero,"* he said. *We wanted her mother to be here, but she died recently.*

Only Sev's firm grip kept me from remembering Perennia's weight in my arms, rocking her while the Holies slept through a violent starlit night.

I forced myself to enter the edifice by imagining that those marble faces were hers, at least the soft ones: Lovingkindness, Honesty, Generosity, Humility. If anyone lived as a deity of virtues in the heavens, it was Perennia. If anyone could brighten that velvet-black expanse, it was she. People had tended to lump Perennia in with the rest of us Lorenthi siblings—scathing-witted and spoiled. But there hadn't been a haughty bone in that girl's body. She had deserved more, deserved better. She had deserved happiness we could never attain, malcontent as we were. She had been like Mother, someone who grew and helped things; if Mother ever restricted us, it was for the hope of trying to steer us true, like training wild ivy to climb a trellis. Perennia had been the same way, always drawing out the best of us.

Both of them were gone.

As Sev and I stepped before the altar and faced each other, a raw, bitter wind arose from nowhere, swirling through the edifice. It tugged at my veil, but Sev caught it between two fingers and stared intently into my eyes.

"This again!" the priest cried as the crowd gasped in dismay.

The huntsman interlaced the fingers of his other hand with mine, and even through the leather glove, I felt warmth to counter my cold.

Perennia would want me to protect Navara as I had tried to protect her. If I ruined this now, the guards might drag the princess back to her doom at Ambrosine's hand.

Sunshine poured through stained-glass windows, and I imagined that it was Perennia offering her encouragement to do what needed to be done.

I squeezed Sev's hand. He gave me a nod.

The priest opened his book and began a prayer.

❧ TWENTY-NINE ❧

KADRI

AFTER my escape I trudged through muck and melted snow, hoping to see the shadowy outline of a village against the clear night. Now that I was free, I knew I would be remiss to risk my safety materializing. But the tenderness of my injury, exacerbated by fighting Orturio, slowed me down and exhausted me. Without the tincture, the pain grew worse. I gave up for the night, veering off road to shelter under an oak tree.

When morning came I awoke to the ruckus of a rickety wagon rolling by. The driver appeared to be a farmer, so I flagged him down. The amiable man offered to take me to Givita, which he explained was on my way to Enturra—the village where Viteus and the priest would be looking for the huntsman. The name Givita bumped around my foggy, pain-addled mind until I recognized it as the huntsman's village, the one he fled with Glisette and Princess Navara only yesterday morning.

Now that they were gone, this fact was of little use, but the farmer said there was a folk healer there who could help me. Then he spent the remainder of the journey lamenting the terrible weather and blaming elicromancers for dragging Perispos into their personal conflicts.

My elicrin stone stayed snug beneath the neckline of my dress.

We bumped along for about half an hour before we reached Givita. The farmer pointed me to the folk healer's cottage and went on to sell what was left of his healthy spring crop. I thanked him and winced as I limped to the healer's door and knocked.

After some shuffling and inquisitive back-and-forth, a middle-aged woman opened one shutter to the breezy day.

She observed my expensive, dirtied gown and my crooked stance. Her keen eyes narrowed to survey the damage. "Can you pay?"

"Yes."

She slammed the shutter, unlocked the door, and grudgingly admitted me to her cottage, where dried herbs and copper pots hung from the low ceiling. A curtain partitioned off the far end of the room. "Go sit on the empty cot," she said, salty, and shut the door.

I hobbled across the room and pulled aside the curtain, with-holding a gasp. On one of the two cots lay a gray-haired man who had been beaten to death's doorstep. His face was a purplish knot of cuts and bruises, and magenta splotches covered his ribs and stomach. A boy who shared features with the woman dabbed at his wounds with a cool compress.

I sat on the empty cot. "What happened?" I asked the boy.

But I already knew. The Uprising had happened to him. This must be the neighbor whom they had questioned, the one Viteus had nearly beaten to death.

"Mind your business and we'll mind ours," the woman chided before the boy could answer, appearing with a tray of bottles and bandages, but the old man spoke over her.

"I knew that beautiful girl was trouble," he muttered feverishly. He turned his head to look at me, his swollen eyes probing my face.

"Taking advantage of a good family's kindness. Winning them over with sweets and visits. Leading bad men to their door."

My hands clenched into fists. He didn't know that Lucrez had lied to save the huntsman's family—and lost her life for it. But just in case Viteus returned to inflict more abuse on this poor man, I couldn't risk telling him what I knew.

Grief pierced through my anger, and I sank onto the cot.

"You just rest, Yannis, you old troublemaker," the woman teased fondly, though when she turned away, the impish smile she'd donned for his benefit fell into a frown of deep worry.

She knelt next to me and clucked over my swollen ankle.

"This needs rest," she said in a strident tone after a quick examination. "For twelve diromi I can treat you here for three days, meals included."

Hissing against the pain, I dug out two of the gold coins from Orturio's treasure room.

"Those are a century old," she marveled. "They have King Coriander's face instead of King Myron's. Where did you find them?"

"Mind your business and I'll mind mine," I replied.

She narrowed her eyes. "Fair enough."

"I want treatment through tomorrow morning, fresh clothes, supplies for a letter that you will deliver to the dispatcher, a map, and enough meals and pain tinctures for three days on the road."

"At your service," she said, plucking the coins from my hand and tucking them into her apron pocket.

She offered to help me change out of my filthy dress and into a gown, but I asked for privacy in order to keep my elicrin stone hidden. I tucked the pack with the scroll case and coins under my pillow. After all I'd endured, I wouldn't let anyone thieve anything from me ever again—not my spoils, not my freedom, not Rynna, if she survived.

After I changed, the healer bandaged my ankle and offered me cabbage bean soup. I ate it with haste and slid under the blanket, waiting for her to close the curtain. When she did, I looked at the old man's battered face.

Satisfied that he was sleeping deeply, I slipped the scroll case from the satchel under my pillow. My hope was that this would be the sealed scroll Orturio had mentioned, and that it could tell me more about the scourges from the Book of Belief. Perhaps the Uprising had stolen the scroll to keep it safe from Ambrosine, or maybe they had wanted it for their own nefarious purposes. Either way, it was mine now.

The case was intricately stylized with foliage motifs. Most that I had seen contained a thin pull-tab that would unroll the retractable parchment within, but this one didn't. I pressed on the gold ram emblem and nothing happened. Scowling, I turned it this way and that, attempting to unscrew both the top and bottom. I supposed it made sense for such a purportedly precious scroll to be difficult to open.

After giving it a good shake to make sure it even held a scroll, I huffed, stuffed it back under my pillow, and started my letter to Rynna.

My words emerged more frantic than I'd intended. I wanted to soothe her worries, but my fear and fury seeped into the ink. When

I reread the message, my request for her to hastily send whomever the Realm Alliance could spare sounded deeply alarming.

I co-addressed it to Mercer, admitting that a dark corner of my heart wasn't sure Rynna had survived the Jav Darhu attack.

After giving the folk healer the letter to bring to the dispatcher, I decided to do as she instructed. Though it was not even midday, I would rest—rest without hearing locks turning in my dreams, rest so I could be of sound mind to find my friend, rest knowing that I would never let anyone take my freedom again.

The folk healer clearly found my charity suspicious, but still accepted two more gold coins to cover Yannis's treatment. She wished me a blessed Sun's Benediction as I departed from her home before sunrise. It struck me that this was the holiday King Myron had invited Fabian and me to attend. We had discussed it a lifetime ago and a world away.

Wearing a simple woven cotton dress and carrying a pack of food and medicine, I set out toward Enturra. I needed to reach the village before the huntsman set foot in town. Viteus and the local priest might already be watching for him.

The sun beamed bright, melting the remaining clumps of snow. The muddy road made for a wearying journey, but it heartened me to catch sight of modest bridal parties en route to the village edifices.

I wondered if things were as bad as Orturio and Mathis had claimed. Maybe Ambrosine hadn't been responsible for the edifice burning. Maybe she hadn't killed the high priest. Orturio could have lied about everything. I would have had no way of knowing.

But one thing I did not doubt: nearly every priest and altar attendant in and around Halithenica was complicit in the Uprising.

That reminder darkened my thoughts as a domed Edifice of the Holies rose up from the hills after a long morning on the road. Unlike the ramshackle villages I'd passed between here and Givita, Enturra's streets were paved with cobblestones, and the cozy village square was crowded with revelers.

In spite of this, the hairs on my nape bristled when I crossed the river bridge to the village. The folk healer had given me a scarf, which I'd used to cover my head so that Viteus wouldn't recognize me. I could only imagine what sort of torture he would inflict if he knew what I had done to Lord Orturio.

I reached the sparse market stalls and combed the streets, mentally revisiting my final conversation with Orturio. Viteus did not know the huntsman—Severo Segona, Lucrez had called him—by appearance. But the old priest, Father Frangos, knew him. Studying the layout of the village square, the domed Edifice of the Holies, the passage that I believed led to the underground Edifice of the Fallen, the towering trees, and the changing crowd, I decided Father Frangos would need a high vantage point to have any hope of scrutinizing every face. Viteus would likely remain at street level in order to act quickly on a signal from on high.

There was a priest performing the ceremonies at the edifice altar. Was this Father Frangos? He did not seem to be watching the crowd at all. From the edge of the courtyard, I watched him recite lengthy prayers without looking up from the couple in front of him.

Had the plans changed? Had Viteus returned to the estate and discovered the truth of his master's violent death? What if he was hunting *me* now?

Or maybe I had been too preoccupied with serving Orturio the tincture to commit that vital conversation to memory. Maybe I'd scrambled the details. The time? The town? Or perhaps the huntsman's neighbor had lied to protect him, just like Lucrez.

The thought of boarding a ship back to Nissera tempted me. I couldn't leave Glisette, but if the huntsman didn't show, how else was I supposed to find my friend? Barge into the forest and call her name? Follow every stray gust of cold wind? A tracking map required expertise, time, and magical resources I probably wouldn't be able to find in Perispos even if I knew exactly what they were. Maybe the only way to rescue Glisette was to hurry home and ask the rest of the Realm Alliance for help.

I sighed and swept my eyes around the square, studying windows, terraces, roofs, and finally, the tiny cupola perched atop the edifice's dome. A macerated old man peered through one of the arched openings, surveying the crowd in the market.

Ah, Father Frangos, you stealthy old bastard.

I watched him as noon drew ever closer. Two weddings had already taken place on my watch. A large bridal party escorted the second couple, and their jubilant, rambunctious reveling staked me with sudden homesickness for my friends.

A man in their group shouted, "May Orico bless you with many children!" at an oncoming party of three. There was only the veiled bride, the groom, and one maid.

I remembered the Perispi ambassador's daughter mentioning

that Sun's Benediction was her favorite holiday because she liked seeing so many joyful couples joining in matrimony. But this bride didn't seem joyful. She looked stiff and afraid under that veil, and I found myself glaring at the handsome man accompanying her. But he gazed on her with admiration, and she seemed to take comfort in his touch.

The veiled maid whispered to the bride and left to knock on the door of a small building between the two edifices.

Realizing I'd let myself get distracted, I shot my gaze back to Father Frangos in the cupola. His withered hands gripped the banister as he squinted down at the courtyard. Something had caught his attention.

Meanwhile the ceremony began, and the bride's maid was following an altar attendant down the stairs to the underground edifice. He looked back as he went down, finding Father Frangos. The old priest gave him an unmistakable nod.

Something was happening. I didn't know where Viteus was, but I couldn't risk missing the chance to act on a signal from the priest.

I started to follow them to the Edifice of the Fallen, but the memory of the cool, dark wine cellar threatened to overwhelm my senses. I felt cold, and the scent of sour fermentation mixed with gore seeped its unwelcome way back into my mind.

I took a deep breath. I was an elicromancer now—again—facing mere mortals.

And I couldn't let the Uprising hurt anyone ever again.

Touching my stone through my collar for encouragement, I wove my way through the courtyard crowd to the mouth of the staircase. I limped quietly down, arriving in a candlelit underground corridor. Stone pillars engraved with winding thorns led the way to a table holding a bowl of ashes and folded brown rags. Beyond that, a stone archway opened into a temple with an immense mirror and disturbing murals. Talva, the ambassador's daughter, had described the dim, subterranean edifices, but this was more unsettling than I had imagined. From where I stood at the threshold, I could see two of the four Fallen deities reigning over suffering supplicants. Depravity was more beast than human, a monstrosity of teeth and exposed muscle. Apathy was a gnarled woman whose upper body was wrapped in sheer cobwebs. Her lower half had been overtaken by rampant gray vegetation.

Directly ahead, the altar attendant and the girl stood before the mirror in profile. The girl had lifted her veil in the seclusion of the edifice, revealing short brown hair and an older version of a pretty face I remembered from a ball in Yorth years ago.

Princess Navara.

Anticipation rushed through me. If the priest recognized the huntsman, and the princess had come with him, did that mean Glisette was here too?

"I'm so looking forward to seeing Father Frangos's famed collection," Navara said, clasping her hands.

"It's here, Your Highness," the boy said, swinging the mirror away from the wall to reveal an iron door with a bolt lock. "But only Father Frangos has the key."

"And you summoned him?"

"Yes."

"Could you tell him to hurry?"

"He's eighty-six years old, Your Highness."

Navara huffed and crossed her arms. Her impatient gaze slung back to the staircase. She gasped when she saw me poised at the entrance.

The altar attendant slammed the mirror back into place. "Who are you?"

"*Nagak!*" I shouted. A burst of white light and magic jolted out of my elicrin stone and rammed into him, thrusting him against the mirror. Navara screeched and reared back in surprise. The glass shattered and the boy dropped on the floor.

"Oh! That was stronger than I expected." I peeled the scarf from the lower half of my face. "Navara, I'm Kadri Lillis."

"I remember you! My father and I came to your engagement celebration in Yorth. Did the Realm Alliance send you?" she asked, hopeful.

"I am with the Realm Alliance, but I'm the only one."

"Wait a moment. You're a mortal. How—?"

"We have to go," I said, seizing her elbows. "That boy and Father Frangos are working with the Uprising. Come, before their agents find us."

"I can't leave until I get what I came here for," she insisted. "If you're the only elicromancer who's come to help us, that means we still need it. It will take more than one of you to defeat Ambrosine and Nexantius."

"Nexantius?" I repeated, bewildered.

I heard footsteps and turned to find the old priest descending to the edifice.

"Father!" she called, hurrying to meet the old man. "I'm looking for something that I think may be in your vault. Will you help me?"

"Of course I will help you, my blessed princess," the old man said, patting her hand. "We are going to keep you safe."

That *we* resounded menacingly in my mind. *We* meant Viteus and his henchmen. *We* meant an entire network of clergy members who were eager to claim the princess as their champion, as the restorer of Agrimas.

"The Holies have provided for us on this day." Father Frangos looked beyond the princess and his smile fell. He narrowed his eyes at the shattered glass and the boy lying unconscious on the floor. "What happened here?"

"He touched my arm," Navara explained. "My friend here thought he was trying to hurt me and...overreacted."

"Stupid boy," the old man wheezed. "He should have known not to lay a finger on you. He won't bother you again. We will keep you safe."

"I *am* safe, Father," Navara argued. "I only need access to the vault. I believe you possess an artifact that will help us overthrow the usurper queen."

"Someday, all the treasures in my keeping will be yours," he said, clearly placating her. "But for the moment, you will be going to a secure hideout with worthy comforts. You will remain there until Ambrosine Lorenthi is no longer a threat to your life. These men will take you there and protect you."

He gestured behind him. Viteus jogged down the stairs, that same treacherous knife that he had used to murder poor Lucrez bumping against his thigh. The other two men from Orturio's estate followed him.

A primal fear set my heart thumping. It didn't matter to my

racing pulse that I had recovered my elicrin stone, that powerful magic now coursed through my veins. This cruel, violent man knew no limits.

When Viteus noticed me, he didn't seem surprised. He must not have known about Orturio's death or about my escape. He probably thought Orturio was still using me to make sure Glisette allowed Navara to leave with them.

"Your Highness." Viteus brushed back his slick swell of hair and bowed to Navara. "I am delighted to see you alive and well." He gestured at me. "Our associate here will put your companions at ease. They will be relieved to no longer bear the burden of protecting the precious jewel of Perispos. But we must hurry before the queen's guards find us."

His ingratiating words made my skin crawl, and I wasn't alone. Navara looked to me, uncertainty clouding her expression.

"Plans have changed," I replied, fury taking command of my voice. My fear dissolved in the heat of my anger. "She's not going with you, you reprobate puddle of piss."

Tension filled the air between us. Viteus flexed his knife hand, but he merely sneered at me. "When Lord Orturio hears about this—"

"Oh, he won't," I laughed darkly. "I killed him. And his uncle."

"You're lying," he said.

"I'm afraid not." I removed my elicrin stone from its hiding spot and watched him register the turning of the tables. I raised a hand. *"Nagak!"*

But I missed Viteus, instead hitting the man behind him. He flew back, striking his hip and shoulder against one of the thorn-engraved pillars. His bark of pain echoed up the passage. I cringed, hoping we wouldn't draw any guards down here. I tried the spell on Viteus again, but he jolted out of the way and the spell hit the wall. I had seen elicromancers block plenty of spells but had no idea that dodging one was as easy as sidestepping waste tossed from a window.

He drew his hooked knife. My vision blurred red as I remembered Lucrez struggling and screaming before she died at his hand.

More steps thundered down the stairs. I looked up and saw the groom from before. He stopped and scanned the edifice, taking in Viteus and his naked blade, Father Frangos, Navara, me, and the unconscious altar attendant. As the tall, veiled bride followed him, he splayed his arm out in a protective motion that made me wonder if they were indeed who I thought they were. Maybe they were real lovers stumbling into an unfortunate situation.

But then the bride ripped off her veil, revealing flaxen hair only slightly mussed by the pins clinging to it.

"Kadri?" Glisette asked in utter disbelief.

❧ THIRTY ❧

GLISETTE
A FEW MOMENTS BEFORE

HE priest almost put himself to sleep with his liturgy. I would regret it later, but I gripped Sev's hand like floating driftwood in a violent storm.

The comfort didn't last long. I felt him tense up. He had witnessed some sort of disturbance through the edifice windows over my shoulder. His eyes darted about in alarm. What was happening?

He shifted his weight from one foot to the other, restless, before leaning in and uttering in a low voice, "With all due respect, Father, could we make this quick?"

The old man blinked at him. "Goodness, young man! Are you that anxious to consummate?" He squinted through my veil, as though a certain degree of beauty might explain Sev's eagerness. I wanted to shrink down, to become invisible. Thankfully, the opacity of the fabric thwarted his gaze. He cleared his throat and said, "I'll skip to the end then, I suppose."

At last he tapered off and wished us healthy children, muttering that we would have many, eager as we were. People cheered as we exited the edifice, but soon shifted their attention to the next eager party in finer clothes.

"Navara followed an altar boy down to the Edifice of the Fallen,"

Sev said in my ear, leading me by the hand. "I saw him signal to someone."

A distant shout carried over the noise of the crowd. It sounded like it was echoing up from underground.

Sev pushed his way through the heedless revelers. When we reached the top of the stairwell, I could feel the pull of something unnatural that willed me into the cavernous underground temple.

I followed Sev down. He jerked to a halt at the bottom of the stairs, and when I drew even with him, I saw why.

We had stumbled upon a standoff. After registering the weapons and the number of possible opponents, I noticed Navara, who stood at the apex of this odd formation, and beside her...

It couldn't be. I ripped away the veil and blinked at my friend. "Kadri?"

It *was* her.

I couldn't think of a time when I'd been happier to see a familiar face.

She wore a necklace that looked suspiciously like an elicrin stone, gradient violet and sapphire. I had only ever seen comparable colors in the fay dwelling, where everything had been so saturated and vibrant.

The stone held a faint glow of lurking magic, which the untrained eye might not see.

But how? What did this mean? Had Valory—?

"No bloodshed is necessary," the old priest said, shattering the fragile silence.

"He's right." A young man with slick dark hair and keen eyes said. He shot a glare at Kadri. "You know our mission is to protect Her Highness. She will be safer with us than with anyone else."

How would Kadri know these men? Why was she here??

"Safe in some ways," Kadri agreed. She shifted her weight, and I noticed her favoring one leg. "But not in others. She will not be free to think for herself." Hatred flamed in her eyes. Kadri was typically bright-humored and full of grace. This man had committed some unforgivable act.

"Princess," he said, appealing to Navara instead. "We have resources, and deep roots in the faith—the faith your mother raised you to hold sacred. Elicromancers have their own plans for this world. They don't care who sits on your throne. But we, the Uprising, are devoted to seeing you crowned."

"They want to use you, Navara," Kadri said.

"To persecute anyone who does not follow Agrimas," Sev added.

"Do you know who was a member of the Uprising, blessed princess?" Father Frangos asked. "The high priest, Father Peramati. *Every* priest is, except for those who have strayed from their calling. They are lazy. They do not guide the flock. They drink wine all day and watch the faith crumble. They are guilty of Apathy, unlike those of us who fight to preserve the old ways—who fight to protect you."

Navara swung an uncertain glance at each face in the edifice. "I cannot bring hope and help to my people while safely hidden away."

"Nor can you bring hope and help if you're dead," the priest replied. "Once you are safe, we will provide whatever resources you desire, whatever you need from my collection." He gestured at the vault. "Just say the word. I will send anything you request. But you must agree to go with these men."

Navara's eyes swept over the ghastly murals on their way to look to me for guidance. I was touched to see such trust in her eyes. I shook my head, my fingers longing to touch my hidden blade.

"I suppose it is foolish to stay on the run when there's a safe hideout waiting for me," she said, surprising me. "If the guards find us, the queen will kill me, and my people will have nothing."

Was this a ploy to get inside the vault? It couldn't be—the priest hadn't promised her access to it until she was "safe." It was more likely she was trying to spare us a bloody brawl. But she must know we wouldn't let her sacrifice her safety for ours.

"What are you doing, Navara?" I asked.

She ignored me. "My friends have taken care of me," she continued, confirming my fears. "I will only go if you swear on Eulippa's gentle hand that you will not hurt or hunt them."

"We swear on Eulippa's gentle hand," the younger agent said, placing his hand over his heart, but his sycophantic manner made his attempt at sincerity sound quite the opposite.

Navara nodded and dutifully crossed the edifice to join him. He gave her a thin, oily smile.

Oh, Navara, don't do this, I thought, still restive with the urge to unsheathe Sev's knife from the harness at my thigh. *There's a difference between courageous and reckless.*

But Navara never stopped walking. As soon as she reached the Uprising agents, she slipped through their ranks and bolted straight for the stairs. Sev and I stepped aside to let her pass. *Good, clever girl,* I thought, hiking up my skirt to at last draw my weapon.

"Take Orfeo and ride hard!" Sev called after her. He unsheathed his knife and attacked the man who lunged to chase her.

Sev wielded his weapon like an extension of his body. He shifted his stance once, and again, light on his feet. He dodged a swipe at his chest and cut his blade in every direction to create his own sort of shield.

The smarmy leader sprinted to the exit to run after Navara.

"Nagak!" Kadri called, clipping his shoulder with her spell. She needed mentorship, but the spell held power, enough to slam him sideways against the wall, to slow him down.

Father Frangos doddered unsteadily toward the smashed mirror and patted the altar boy hard on the cheek to wake him. The boy groaned and pushed himself up from the broken glass. Father Frangos unlocked the vault and dragged open the door. The boy joined him, and Father Frangos locked the both of them safely inside.

That left me to engage the third man. The exhilaration of battle made my scar tingle with the memory of the blade that had rent my flesh. I had faced more frightening enemies than these, but my elicrin stone had always allowed me to maintain a little distance. Now I had no shield to erect, no spells to cast, no control over the magic that had already brought misery to the innocent people of Perispos. I didn't even have a sword, my weapon of choice.

But I would have to make do.

The man lunged for my gut, and I resisted the urge to try to block him, as I would with a much longer blade. Instead, ducking under his elbow, I slid the knife beneath his ribs, ripping the bust of Stasi's dress clear up the seam in the process. The cut into his flesh was long but shallow, earning only a grunt before he whirled on me.

Taking a cue from Sev, I danced around unpredictably. In my periphery I could see Sev wrestling with his opponent. They had suspended each other's knife-wielding hands and were jabbing with shoulders and knees to try to regain the advantage.

The leader recovered and made another dash for the exit, desperate to catch Navara. Kadri chose a more appropriate spell, *umrac korat*, but her aim was so haphazard that the bright light struck the wall far over his head, carving out a divot.

"I'm sorry! I didn't have a clear shot!" she said to me.

"Use *praenthar ilmen*!" I yelled. The spell would erect a stone barrier to stop him. She repeated it and a wall of stones appeared from thin air, but it was too late. He was gone. It only barricaded us inside with our remaining opponents.

The distraction cost me. My adversary pounced closer and seized my wrist, turning my knife away from him. I bared my teeth, struggling against his sheer strength. He spun me around and shoved me against the wall. My cheek smashed against a painting of a woman suffering at Themera's feet.

"Glisette!" Sev yelled. Even in the midst of my terror, there was something so powerful about hearing him call out my name.

"Got any more knives hidden under there?" my assailant whispered in my ear, his breaths grazing the back of my neck. His greedy hands, damp with sweat, bunched up the folds of my skirt as he felt along my thigh.

Fury burned like a wall of fire in my chest. I smacked the hard back of my skull against what I could only hope was his nose. He released me and stumbled away.

Kadri intervened with the slashing spell. I heard a guttural noise. When I faced my opponent, he was swaying on his feet. He fell with a hard *thwack* on the stones.

Kadri stared at the deep, bloody carve marks crossing his back. Those magic-etched, murderous slashes...the edifice...

The searing, horrid memory of Perennia pummeled me. I felt like I was falling, drowning in icy darkness. I needed to get control of myself. Guards waited at the entrance to the village, guards seeking any sign of me or Navara, who was alone and exposed.

My untethered magic, driven by grief, would not respond to the small voice in my head that tried desperately to soothe. But Kadri was already here, catching me in her embrace, bringing the kind of warmth and love that had previously felt as distant as Perennia's smile.

I wept into her shoulder. I didn't realize I'd spoken my sister's name aloud until Kadri said, "I know. I'm so sorry."

Concern for Sev and Navara yanked me back to the present reality. I realized how oddly quiet the edifice seemed now, following the shouts and cries of pain.

I looked through the blur of tears and found Sev standing over his fallen opponent, his brow shimmering with sweat. He had jammed his knife deep into the man's chest and now ripped it out, trailing fresh blood as he dashed toward me and knelt.

"Are you hurt?" He didn't touch me, but I could see the instinct to do so pulsing in the raised veins of his strong and slender hands.

"No, I'm all right." I waved him off and pushed myself up, reclaiming my knife and lifting my skirt to sink it back into the sheath. Was it my imagination, or did his eyes follow my movements? "Let's go find Navara," I said, and looked at Kadri. *"Praenthar sarth.* That will undo the barrier."

Kadri repeated the spell and disintegrated the stone block-ade. Bitterness wreathed her words as she said, "We can't let him take her."

THIRTY-ONE

KADRI

HE huntsman and Glisette were fast, their soles pounding across the courtyard as they dodged and shoved their way through the throng. I bumped against someone, rocked back on my ankle, and squealed as it throbbed. I pined for the vials of tincture rattling around in my satchel.

The huntsman made an agile leap onto a ledge. "She's riding away," he said, peering at the road. He looked down at Glisette. "I'll run ahead. Take your time so the guards don't pay you any heed."

Glisette nodded. "Be careful, Sev."

The huntsman leapt off and ran through the market. Glisette secured her veil, but a few liberated locks waved like banners in the breeze. I did my best to stash them away as we walked.

Viteus wasn't like a royal guard following orders. He wasn't basic sword skills and a love of country stuffed into livery. Devotion to Agrimas and a thirst for blood drove him. Orturio might be dead, but with the princess in his grip, Viteus might step into the role of leader and keep the Uprising intact.

As we neared the river bridge, the sight of the guards in purple livery made a rising panic roil inside me. Surprisingly, they were more of a boon than hindrance; they had stopped Viteus and taken his knife. They appeared to be questioning him, their hands resting on their sword pommels.

"They must have seen him chasing a girl and not known who she was," Glisette said. "Should we wait? He might tell them who I am."

"He won't," I said. "He wouldn't risk leading them to her. The last thing he wants is for Ambrosine to capture Navara."

"Let's go, then," Glisette said. She linked arms with me and slowed her pace. I followed her lead, forcing myself to look nonchalant and smile. Another bridal party trailed behind us and we ambled back to join their group. Viteus held us in his furious gaze but did nothing. I wanted to meet his stare, though I knew the meager satisfaction wasn't worth drawing attention.

As soon as it felt safe, we hurried, knowing the guards could set him loose at any second.

My ribs felt bruised from breathlessness, and my ankle was in agony by the time we caught up to the huntsman and the princess. They had waited for us in the nearby woods. They were relieved to see us, and for the first time since the Jav Darhu had kidnapped me, I actually felt safe.

"That was not what I expected," Glisette said, rasping for breath. It was so strange to know she was momentarily mortal, to see her without that cloudy lilac stone at her throat. "Kadri...how did you get here? How in the world did you get tangled with the Uprising? And why did Valory give you an elicrin stone without telling us?"

"The king of Erdem found out about my elicrin stone and sent mercenaries to kidnap me," I explained, catching my breath. "But a man named Rasmus Orturio bought me out from under King Agmur. He and Mathis were working together to overthrow the Realm Alliance—"

"Uncle Mathis?" Glisette clarified.

"Yes. They thought I could help them. If I couldn't or wouldn't, Lord Orturio planned to kill me. Mathis just wanted to weaken our influence, but Orturio wanted all elicromancers dead. He was the leader of the Uprising."

"I knew it," the huntsman said darkly. He was a handsome fellow, as far as those things went. The way I caught him looking at Glisette, coupled with the knowledge that Ambrosine had trusted him and Lucrez had risked her life to protect him...well, it made me wonder if he looked at all women that way. "It was Rasmus Orturio all along."

"Yes." I pulled my gray skirt to untangle it from a gnarl of thorns that had latched on to my hem. "But I killed him."

The huntsman—Sev—looked at me with wild eyes. "You killed the leader of the Uprising?"

"I did," I said, wary, resituating the pack on my shoulder. I patted the outline of the bottles to make sure they were still intact.

Sev's face changed. He'd been wearing the detached expression of someone trying to stay alive. Now his brown eyes shimmered with an emotion so raw I couldn't name it. Awe? Sadness? Anger?

He stalked back toward me, and I felt the urge to back away. But he took my hand, looked at me squarely, and said, "You've won revenge on my dead father's behalf. You've ripped out the Uprising's radical hatred by the bulb. For that, I owe you. I will do anything you ask of me. Thank you."

"Um, you're welcome," I said, overcoming my surprise. "I actually... I did it for Lucrez. To my understanding, you and she were... familiar?"

"Were?"

I bowed my head. "They found out that she warned you they were coming. They killed her for betraying them."

My words had never broken anyone like this before. His eyes filled with tears.

"The man chasing Navara was the one who did it," I said. "His name is Viteus. Orturio gave the orders, and Viteus carried them out." I almost mentioned the neighbor, Yannis, but bit my lip. The huntsman already looked angry enough to turn back and kill Viteus with his bare hands.

"She was my friend," he said. "She loved my siblings like they were her own family. She never told me the truth about the man she worked for, but... only because she knew what would happen if she did. And she was right."

Now I felt broken. I shut my eyes against the memory of Viteus manhandling Lucrez, gleefully dragging her outside to put her to death.

"I'm so sorry, Sev," Glisette whispered. "She seemed like a lovely person."

"She was... and clever too," he said. "She fooled me. And she saved me."

"She saved me too," I whispered.

"What kind of help did the Uprising want from you, Kadri?" Glisette asked.

"They thought they could convince me to turn against the Realm Alliance, to undermine you. Based on the truth...that I disagreed with one of our first decisions."

Glisette stared at the dirt under her fingernails, and then rubbed her forehead, not meeting my eyes. "I could tell you wanted a harsher punishment for Ambrosine, but I didn't acknowledge it. I held our pardon of Rayed like a shield against my guilt...."

"I should have spoken up—"

"No, *I* was the problem, Kadri," she said through her teeth. "I was being selfish as usual. I found it difficult to punish Ambrosine, partly because Perennia wanted to think she could change...." She trailed off, grimacing against a flood of tears. "It was easier to answer Myron's marriage offer than to face the truth that my sister was irredeemable." She sighed and offered me a small smile. "I can't believe you're an elicromancer. Valory shouldn't have given you the elicrin stone without asking us."

"I know. And I shouldn't have taken it."

"But...you deserve it, Kadri. More than most of us who entered the Water."

I stared at her for a few seconds before throwing my arms around her shoulders. She laughed and returned the embrace.

"Perhaps we should make changes to the Realm Alliance when we return," I suggested. "More mortals. And maybe...maybe Valory should take a step back. There's too much power in our group. The stakes are too high for new leaders trying to find their footing."

"I think you might be right," she said.

"And I'll give up my elicrin stone if I need to. So mortals don't think we're using Valory's power for our own gain."

"What's your gift?" Glisette asked, stepping back so her blue-green eyes could examine my elicrin stone again.

"Marksmanship," I said with a crooked grin.

She dismissed me with a wave of her hand. "As if you need that anyway."

"We should move on," Sev interrupted. "He'll try to follow us. Kadri, is it? You can ride Orfeo."

I nodded and limped over to pat the great gray beast, who flicked his tail at me. I mounted my healthy foot in the stirrup and managed to launch myself onto the saddle with help from Glisette.

"We risked our lives for nothing," Navara grumbled as we started off. "Sorry, Kadri. Not for nothing. But we were supposed to get that scroll."

"Scroll?" I asked. "Is that what you were looking for in the vault?"

"Yes," Navara sighed. "The sealed apocrypha that will tell us how to defeat the Fallen."

I slipped my hand into my bag and extracted the silver scroll case. "I don't want to bring false hope, but Orturio had a cellar of treasures and I found this. I tried every which way to open it. I don't know what's inside it, but I know that both the Uprising and Ambrosine want it. Orturio told me that Ambrosine burned down an edifice to try to destroy it."

I handed the artifact down to Navara. She frowned, turning it over, and noticed the gold seal of the four-horned ram. "By the Holies," she breathed. "This is it. Unless it's a duplicate."

She searched for a pull-tab, just as I had, and then scowled and tried to twist both ends.

"The high priest must have passed the scroll to the Uprising through Father Frangos," Sev said. "To keep it safe from Ambrosine."

"The Uprising didn't tell me why she was looking for it," I said. "What interest does she have in destroying an Agrimas scroll?"

"She's a vessel for one of the Fallen deities," Navara explained. "Nexantius. He's living inside her, and the scroll is supposed to tell us how to banish the Fallen should they manage to claim human vessels."

I looked down at Glisette, expecting to see skepticism, but found only resignation on the graceful planes of her face. Could the ambiguous connection I'd begun to draw between Wenryn's plight and Apathy's scourge be real? If so, why was a Fallen plaguing Nissera?

Eerie echoes of Mercer's warning at the Realm Alliance meeting reverberated through my mind just as they'd reverberated through the meeting chamber back home: *Whenever deep magic is eradicated, it leaves a gap, a hollow place of power. It presents an opportunity for another supernatural force to establish dominion.*

"So…" I started, "do we believe in the Holies and the Fallen now?"

It was a genuine question, but Glisette dipped her head in embarrassment. "To an extent," she admitted. "There's undoubtedly a dark being inhabiting Ambrosine."

"And you're sure she's not dark on all her own?" I asked.

"She is. But she's encountered something even darker."

Navara huffed in frustration. "Now if only we could get this thing open, we could defeat both of them."

"Or...all three of them," I ventured.

I began to explain my growing suspicions about the scourge of Apathy, gaining confidence when I realized they were taking me seriously.

"Is that why the rest of the Realm Alliance hasn't come to help us?" Glisette asked. "You think they're facing a Fallen of their own?"

"To my understanding, Silimos would need a willing vessel to inhabit, one with the capacity to hold extraordinary power," Navara said. "Granted, I don't know much about the Water, or the hollow place it left. There's so much we still don't know. If only we could see this twice-damned scroll."

Sev looked over his shoulder in surprise. "What?" Navara asked, but he didn't answer, smiling as he again trained his eyes on the path that only he knew.

Glisette reached up to take my hand in hers, intertwining our fingers.

Stranded between my two countries, I had found a bit of home.

THIRTY-TWO

GLISETTE

THE aroma of smoking venison made me salivate as we neared the cabin. Sev had hauled back a fallow deer before we'd left this morning. He and his mother made a fine team putting food on the table to feed so many mouths.

The younger children nearly took Sev down like wolves attacking a bear, then noticed Kadri and asked her how long she'd be staying and whether she lived in a palace too. They had clearly acclimated to royal guests.

Sev and Stasi herded them away as we gathered in the large room to eat. I felt the sensation of eyes on me as I set my empty plate on the floor and shamelessly licked grease from my fingers. When I looked up, I found Sev watching me.

Melda clucked over Kadri's bruised ankle. Thankfully, Kadri had tincture with her and threw it back like it was liquid salvation.

When we finished dinner, Stasi coached the children through washing the dishes, and Jeno went outside for his shift as watchman. Navara rinsed her hands before extracting the scroll case from Kadri's bag.

"Is it some sort of puzzle box?" I asked her. Kadri pulled out a chair and sat, watching.

"Maybe." Navara pressed on the gold emblem to no avail. "My

father told me a riddle about the sealed scroll. It mentions a key, but there's no keyhole here."

"What was the riddle?" Kadri asked.

"It's a reference to the Holy of Honesty," Navara explained. " 'I carry the candle and the key. I bear the burden of truth.' "

With a metallic click, a tiny pull-tab popped out of the scroll case. Navara gasped. "It's not a riddle. It's a password!"

Kadri and I exchanged glances. Kadri mouthed, "Magic?" I nodded.

Navara pulled open the tab and peeked at the edge of the scroll. The ink had been well preserved, exposed to only hints of light and traces of dust over the centuries. I could almost smell the secrets it contained.

"This is breaking the law," Navara said, suddenly on the verge of panic. "I'm not supposed to know what it says until I'm queen. Maybe I should do this alone so the Holies don't curse either of you. Yes, that sounds best." She shooed us off. "Go sit over there. I'll read it and let you know what I find. That way, I'm the only one in danger of being cursed. It was my idea, so here I go."

The two fingers that held the pull-tab trembled.

She unrolled the first page of elaborate, ornamental writing, flinching as though it might burst into flames. As Kadri and I walked away, I braced myself, wondering if there really was some kind of curse on this scroll. With magic involved, there was no telling.

But nothing happened. Navara released her bated breath and began to read.

Yawning, Kadri went to stretch out on her pallet. I searched the room.

"He went outside," Navara said from behind me.

"Who?" I asked, looking over my shoulder.

"Sev." The hint of a canny smile tugged at her lip.

A more bashful girl might have blushed, but I just narrowed my eyes at her and strode to the door, casting a conspiratorial smile her way as I pulled the latch.

The night breeze was crisp and smelled of smoke. I saw Jeno sitting by the waning campfire with a crossbow. Sev rounded the corner, carrying the armful of firewood that he had chopped in a rage yesterday. He wore his hunting knife and a hatchet on his belt.

"Too cramped inside?" he asked, stalking the rest of the way to the fire and dropping his burden.

"A bit." I joined them in the shuddering ring of firelight. Jeno's dark brows furrowed as he studied the woods. Sev had said he took his role as lookout very seriously. Something told me Jeno was ready to grow up, and knew whom he wanted to be like when he did.

"I wanted to thank you," I said to Sev. "For helping me keep calm during the ceremony when I..." I trailed off, hoping he understood.

"I couldn't have you falling apart when there was urgent consummating to be done."

I laughed, a curious warmth unfurling behind my navel. Even though I hadn't known him long, it felt like a legendary accomplishment to have cracked his dispassionate façade, especially when I remembered the initial disdain in his eyes. To him, I'd been nothing but a haughty, foreign elicromancer queen who had inflicted my vicious sister on his mortal nation. What did he think of me now?

"What is consummating?" Jeno asked, peeling his eyes away from the woods to look at his older brother.

Sev laughed. "Walk the perimeter, would you?"

Jeno complied with only a little protest.

I stepped closer to the fire, crossed my arms against the cool night, and realized I was still wearing Stasi's ripped dress.

"So, your friend," Sev said, bending to set a log on the dimming fire. "She's not one of the all-powerful elicromancers we've been waiting for."

"I'm afraid not. The rest of us have undergone extensive training, but Kadri is new at this."

"Does she have any chance of defeating Ambrosine?" he asked.

"She can help, but Ambrosine is probably the most powerful of us all—except Valory Braiosa, who doesn't count. Ambrosine is older than the rest of us and has been an elicromancer the longest. She gets what she wants, whatever it takes."

"Not always," Sev said.

"What do you mean?" I asked, my voice trembling a little. I looked him in the eye. His dark curls were thick and tousled, cutting an exaggerated shadow on the ground.

"I mean that I gave her nothing, in case you were wondering. Neither the information nor the...other thing she sought."

I smiled in relief, not caring that it would make my feelings obvious. "It's hard to believe anyone could reject her," I said, collecting my thoughts. "Her heart is rougher than a pumice stone, but she's objectively ravishing."

"Yes, she is." He took a deep breath. "And you resemble her."

I looked askance at him. "So I've been told."

"But you're nothing alike. She's a shadow wearing your skin."

I tilted my head as my mind did its work parsing the strangely poetic words into Nisseran. Firelight accentuated the tailored lines of his face, the angular jaw and pronounced cheekbones.

This wasn't the first time that I had thought of touching him, but it was the first time I had wondered whether my body would act of its own accord and bring me near him, make good on its own silent, daring promise. It would be too easy to fall into the refuge of a strong body, the warmth of another person.

I wondered whether there might be more to this unforeseen desire than that. The way I'd grasped his hand in the edifice to stay afloat frightened me a little. Still, fear like that meant I could feel something other than sadness. It meant that I was alive, and that maybe there were joys worth living for.

Without breaking our gazes, I stepped closer, testing him. He didn't shift back to maintain the distance between us, but he didn't help me close it either. He just stared, searching my face. Then his warm brown eyes drifted down to my lips. He swallowed, his throat bobbing.

That ended my silent deliberation. I neared him, leaving only enough space for a closed fist between his chest and mine.

Inhaling a soft breath, I gradually splayed my fingers along the rough fabric of his shirt where it covered his solid midriff, giving him ample opportunity to stop me if he wanted. But he didn't. Flicking my gaze back up to his eyes, I raised my chin, slow and calm as melting ice, stopping just short of touching my mouth to his.

For a second or two, he stood as stiff and lifeless as that iron effigy in his pocket. Doubts fired through my mind. We barely knew each other. He'd been so cold at first that I'd misread his kindness as something else.

But then he sighed against me and parted my mouth gently with his own, his warm bottom lip drifting over mine. Delight charted a course through my every nerve. He grasped my elbows, bowing me against him, intensifying the kiss. My emboldened hands explored the muscular contours of his stomach, chest, and arms, indulging in the strength I'd seen displayed during the fight.

Suddenly he pulled back, and I braced myself for him to change his mind, dooming us to another irritable argument. But he glanced over my shoulder at the cabin, stepped sideways toward the dying campfire, and kicked a spray of dirt over the feeble flames to cast us in darkness.

I smiled. We didn't have long before Jeno returned, but Sev seemed to want to make the most of what little privacy we could claim. His fingers laced through the hair that tumbled down my back as he brought his lips back to mine.

A wild thought struck me, and I blinked up at him. "Are we *actually* married after today?"

He cocked his head. "According to the law, yes. But I won't tell if you don't. Although…" He took on a feisty, crooked grin that made my blood burn hot. "Does this make me the king of Volarre?"

I scoffed playfully. "More like the queen's consort."

That wasn't exactly true; Hubert and I still needed to convince Father's other advisors to change the statute. I couldn't appoint their replacements until they died.

Sev didn't need to know that, but there was something I needed to know.

"You got so angry when I talked about magic," I said. "If you're not fond of elicromancers, why are you…?"

"Fond of you?" he supplied, his fingers still combing through the long tendrils. "I'm sorry. I was taught that elicromancers were different from mortals, that you looked down on us. Ambrosine only reinforced that, and you looked like just another powerful, rich elicromancer when you arrived. I thought perhaps tales of your bravery had been exaggerated—a scar didn't prove anything. But then you volunteered to give up your life for Navara. It confused me. I've been trying to make you fit the mold of an elicromancer so that I didn't have to confront my feelings. Now I've surrendered to the truth that you may be powerful and immortal, but you're human. A brave, selfless, beautiful human."

I crushed my lips against his again, more fiercely than before. Those words completely disarmed me, deepened my desire, and I relished the warmth of his skin through the thin barrier of his shirt.

But the cabin door swung open, and we jerked apart.

"Glisette? Sev?" Navara called, peering at the moonless night.

"Coming!" I called over my shoulder. Sev and I shared a muffled laugh before we walked back to the moss-cloaked cabin.

Inside, Navara was scowling at a section of the scroll. Kadri rose from her pallet on the floor and tiptoed around Margala and Eleni, who made their dolls fight with toy wooden swords.

"What's wrong?" I asked Navara as the three of us gathered around her.

She blew a harsh breath from her nostrils. "This scroll is non-sense. It's absurdity. It's *blasphemy*."

"What do you mean? It doesn't say how we can defeat a Fallen?"

"It does. But we can't trust anything it says. There's a reason it's considered apocryphal, a reason why my ancestors only allowed two people at a time to know what it contains." Navara blinked the shine of tears from her eyes. "It says the Holies and the Fallen were once creatures who roamed the earth and drank freely from the 'pool of power in the west.'"

"You mean...the Water?" I asked. "In Nissera?"

She nodded grimly. "Eight of the creatures used their powers wisely, and so the pool gave them magical stones of varying shapes and colors that increased their power and virtue. Jealous, the other four tried to claim the pool of power for their own, growing more and more selfish until they embodied evil itself. The eight Holies banished them to infinite darkness in Galgeth, the netherworld. The Holies remained on earth for an age, making"—she looked at the text and quoted—"'holy union' with one another until they decided to stop drinking from the pool, give up their stones, and age. Their children lived among mortals to spread magic to mankind. The word *Agrimas* is a modern translation of an ancient Perispi phrase meaning 'gods on earth.' I've never heard that."

"That's what *elicrin* means in Old Nisseran," I said.

"If this is true, then Agrimas is just an elaborate fantasy." Navara indelicately fed the ancient document back into its case. "If this is true, elicromancy isn't an offshoot of Agrimas, as I've always been taught, and elicromancers didn't spawn from Nexantius. They are the descendants of the Holies. The Holies were elicromancers. It's all the *same.*"

I looked up to find Melda staring at us over her darning work. The children had been caught up in their games and spats, but the older ones noticed Navara raising her voice.

"If this is true, it means that the edifices, the effigies, the prayers, the pedantic scripture...they're just a way to frame elicrin magic," she went on. "They're a way to control the people of Perispos, to define what it means to be a moral and obedient citizen."

I shifted uncomfortably and looked at Sev.

"This was kept secret for a reason," she said sharply. "It's blasphemous. Why do they even safeguard it? Why didn't my father or the high priest burn it already? In fact..." Navara gritted her teeth, pushed back her chair, and snatched up the scroll case.

"What are you doing?" I asked. "Navara!"

She left, slamming the door hard enough to make Margala and Eleni jump. I followed.

When I stepped outside, I found three dark figures.

I froze in fear as my eyes adjusted to the low light of the fire that Jeno must have stoked back to life.

The Uprising agent—Viteus—pressed a knife against the column of Jeno's throat. In his other hand, he held Jeno's loaded crossbow. Navara stood motionless by the fire with her hands raised in surrender, the scroll case in her grip.

Sev appeared beside me, brandishing his axe. Kadri stood in the doorway. Muted white light illuminated her elicrin stone.

"What is it?" little Margala asked from inside. Kadri shushed her and told Melda to gather the children in a corner of the room.

"Let him go," Sev commanded, his voice low and dangerous.

"I will." Viteus's eyes were crazed and bright, his hair mussed by leaves and branches. "If the princess and the scroll come with me."

"I'll go with you," Navara said. "Don't hurt anyone."

"We made this bargain last time, Princess." Viteus raked his menacing gaze over me. "Find some rope to bind her wrists. No more tricks."

I hesitated, but he pressed the point of the knife against Jeno's throat and made him cry out. "Do it!" Viteus barked.

I shoved past Sev and searched through his hunting supplies. I found string in his pack and swept my eyes over the clump of frightened children, sheltered behind Melda at the back of the room. We should never have brought our trouble on this family.

I hurried back outside.

"Tie it tight and show me your work," Viteus said. Navara offered me her wrists, but Viteus said, "Behind your back."

Navara turned in place. The string quivered in my fingers as I wound it around her wrists. My mind reeled as I tried to scrape up an idea to get us out of this.

"Glisette, we can't allow the children to get hurt, no matter what," Navara whispered over her shoulder. "I have to go. Without me, the Uprising wouldn't even be looking for any of you."

A tear slipped down my cheek. The responsibility to protect Navara from the threats prowling on every side had offered me a new purpose when I had lost mine. More than that, I cared for Navara. She was *good*, open-minded and unsullied by the political cynicism that sometimes plagued me, yet mature enough to act nobly and bring hope to her people.

"Commander Larsio will help you," she continued. "But this scroll says a thousand armies could never defeat Nexantius."

"Finish up!" Viteus commanded. "No more talking."

Navara ignored him. "You have to offer yourself as a vessel to one of the Holies and banish Nexantius back to darkness, as the Holies did before. Then you and the other elicromancers can kill Ambrosine."

"Bring her here!" Viteus said.

I secured the knot and led Navara to him.

"Good enough," he said. "I'll take them both and release the boy when we've traveled a safe distance. If any of you follow us, I'll slit his throat." He looked over my shoulder at Kadri. "You can assure the others this is not an empty threat."

"They agree to your terms," Navara said. She looked back at me. "Use the elemental ritual to summon a Holy. It's in the first chapter of the Book of Belief."

"Stop talking!" Viteus shouted, and reared back the crossbow as if to strike her with the metal stirrup. He didn't, but it was too late. He had revealed how he truly viewed his divinely appointed leader—as an object to control. "Follow close behind me, Princess."

He backed away, using Jeno as a shield. Navara followed. But as they moved, Jeno saw an opportunity to grab Viteus's hand and yank the knife down and away from his throat. He slipped under Viteus's arm and stepped out of the way, pulling Navara with him. Sev reeled back and flung his axe. It flew through the air and lodged in Viteus's thigh.

Viteus screamed and dropped the knife as blood spurted over his breeches, but his left hand managed to cling to the crossbow. He clumsily pointed it at Sev and released the lever.

I heard the slender bolt whistle by, followed by the wet noise of it sailing through flesh and muscle. I pivoted and saw Sev gripping his upper arm. Dark blood stained his sleeve. He bared his teeth and staggered back against the doorframe.

My voice sounded far away when I called his name. I covered his hand with my own, pressuring the wide wound where the bolt had passed clean through. We sank to the ground together.

His blood leaked between my fingers, pooling in the basin of each knuckle before dripping down in jagged stripes along the back of my hand.

I can help you.

The disembodied whisper tickled my ear. I shook it off, pressing my skirt against the wound. But the whisper came back on the other side, and then it hummed inside my head, passing from ear to ear until I felt surrounded.

Is this what you want? it asked.

I heard a scuffle behind me. I turned to find Viteus yanking off Jeno's quiver of crossbow bolts. He pushed the boy to the ground and stepped into the stirrup to reload the weapon. Navara screamed at him, her hands tied helplessly behind her back.

Kadri cut in front of me, her elicrin stone bright. Favoring his injured right leg made Viteus sway a little, but he managed to heave up the crossbow and loose another bolt.

It went clean through Kadri's chest and over my head, embedding in the cabin door next to the one that had struck Sev. She flailed and sank to her knees.

This can't be real, I thought. I couldn't move. Anchored in place, helpless, I watched my dearest friend die.

Jeno was next. The bolt sank through his chest as though his body were a pin cushion.

Viteus reloaded the crossbow yet again and pointed it at Navara. "We don't need a faithless queen," he said, and buried a bolt in her belly.

I knew this couldn't be real. If this were real, I would be able to move, to fight, to scream and sob. Instead, I was frozen in horror. It was like the blood running down my arm and filling the stream.

Viteus tossed the crossbow and empty quiver and collected his knife. He limped past the fire toward me, but I couldn't so much as reach out to catch his leg. He stepped over Sev's body and entered the cabin.

I heard the pleas of Sev's mother and the cries of the children as he cornered them. I tried to close my eyes, but I couldn't. I couldn't escape the horrific nightmare.

After the slaughter, Viteus trudged out of the cabin.

Tears blurred my vision as I looked back down at Sev. His mouth hung open. His eyes were vacant. My dress was drenched in blood. It had dyed the green fabric a dark brown and stained the cheerful sunflowers a savage red.

I heard someone stirring inside the cabin.

Margala shuffled to the doorway, her white nightgown soaked red. Blood spilled into the whites of her eyes, as though every vessel inside them had burst and flooded in lightning-shaped rivulets. The irises were black yet bright, like burning coals.

"Is this what you want?" she asked, gesturing around. It was a woman's voice—deep and ancient, underscored by vicious whispers—emerging from the little girl's mouth. "This is what will happen if you don't let me inside you."

She took a step toward me. I was desperate to scramble away, but I couldn't move.

"The Holies won't answer your call. They don't care what

happens here on earth," she said. "But I do. I can help you win. You don't have to watch more loved ones suffer or die."

"Themera?" I whispered. Finally, I could speak again. "Is any of this real?"

The chorus of whispers weaving around her voice silenced as she stood over me, her small face level with mine. With blood-encrusted fingers, she combed back my hair. "If you don't let me inside you, it will be."

THIRTY-THREE

AMBROSINE
THREE WEEKS AGO

THE sea wind whipped my hair into tangles. On the map, the weather-beaten islet of Alonnides looked like an accidental inkblot off the Perispi coast. But as our rowboat labored closer, the formation jutted up from the blue waves like a rock beast with verdant growth trailing along its spine.

The other islets were more like sea stacks, stark and uninhabitable. Merchant vessels were too large to navigate this stretch of water, and human life had long ago forsaken this ragged coast.

That's why it's perfect, I thought.

Damiatta grunted as she rowed us through the gentle waves toward our destination. She had helped me choose this lonely islet as the meeting place.

I knew Valory would answer my message. Well-intentioned people could be so easily fooled.

I had used my enchanted mirror to speak with Perennia. Our weekly chats were perfunctory and stale, but reliable.

This time I asked to see a servant about shipping some of the belongings I had forgotten in Nissera. When Perennia left the room and the servant came, Nexantius and I manipulated her. Everyone wanted something. We showed the servant a version of her that was beautiful enough to catch the eye of a wealthy, handsome duke, whom I promised to contact on her behalf. We convinced her that the duke only needed to notice her, and he would defy his family to marry her. In turn, she wrote down my anonymous message for Valory, which she would send via magical missive routes.

Valory would never ignore someone asking for help, and she was too powerful to fear going alone.

The task of scaling the gray rocks to the islet's plateau proved arduous. At the top, I wiped the sweat from eyes, grimacing at the memory of those few weeks spent laboring to launch Glisette's ridiculous food assistance program. My body was not designed to haul grain sacks and collect grime like a second skin. Subjects didn't *want* to see their sovereigns working like peasants. The dignity of our kingdom rested on the way we presented ourselves.

I caught my breath and surveyed the tiny islet.

Would this work? What would Valory do to me if it didn't?

Could Nexantius protect me from her? Could the power of the Fallen match hers?

Focus on the deception, Nexantius reminded me. *If you don't fool her, our plan will fail.*

Clouds obscured the noonday sun. It shouldn't be long now, unless Mercer had seen a vision that had compelled him to warn Valory against answering the mysterious call.

But several minutes later, a prism appeared out of thin air, expanding like blown glass. Through the portal, I glimpsed a bare stone chamber inside the wing of the palace in Arna that used to house the elicromancer academy.

Valory stood at the threshold of the portal.

Dark half-moons hung under clever eyes of amber green. The

wind from my side tossed her auburn-tinged brunette hair and the cloak around her shoulders. The points of the gold crown she wore had been fashioned to look like antler prongs. I had built her up in my mind, but she was still the same, small and slight.

She looked tired. A prick of empathy pestered me. She had come to her power by accident, and it was no minor burden to bear. The politics were undoubtedly complicated. How do you convince the world you're not a threat when you can hardly convince yourself?

"Ambrosine? Was it you who messaged me for help?" Her inflection revealed suspicion.

"Yes, and I know you probably think this is some sort of trick," I said, my hands splayed in a peaceful gesture. "That's why the message was anonymous. I needed you to meet me, face-to-face, without any preconceived notions. This is too urgent to allow our petty differences to stand in the way."

"Petty differences?" she demanded. "You refuse to see the scope of the harm you've caused."

I had to bite my lip hard to keep from retaliating.

"What is so urgent?" she asked.

"You may not believe me, but Nissera is under a new threat. The Water's absence has created a power vacuum. That pool is and always has been sacred, and elicrin beings of long ago drank from it—centuries before our kin. That place has a connection to the beyond that even you could not possibly sever."

"I don't doubt that. But how would you know anything about the Water's state? You can't materialize, and it's quite a journey to the Forest of the West Fringe."

I stepped forward. Valory's wary eyes narrowed, but she held her ground, relaxing her shoulders to show that she was not threatened by me.

"Listen," I said. "A being who was once banished to eternal darkness possesses mirror magic not unlike mine, and he has been attempting to communicate with me, to *use* me. He and his kind are looking for a way back to this world, and the Water is their gateway."

"What is your game here, Ambrosine?"

The connection I was about to voice had struck me suddenly in the night. I knew it would be my most salient argument and that Valory would not be able to dismiss it. "Think about the gate to the netherworld out in the Marav Sea, the same gate Tamarice's supernatural army breached. What do legends say it's made of?"

"Black rock," she said, impatient.

"And after you dried up the Water... what was left?"

"Black rock," she admitted.

"Even though the floor of the Water had been like the bottom of any other lake when it was full..."

A pause. She considered.

"What if it's a ripped seam in the fabric of our world, like the gate to Galgeth?" I asked, hitting a panicked pitch that wasn't entirely manufactured. "Through those gates have come war, destruction, death. Our grandfathers fortified the gate, but the Water is unguarded in the middle of the forest."

Valory swallowed hard. A slight pallor washed over her face.

"Use your portal. We'll go there now and make sure nothing has already passed through. And then, for the sake of the realm, lay every enchantment you can think of to sew those seams back up. If

I'm wrong or you feel that I'm deceiving you, you can take what's left of my power."

The following seconds seemed like minutes. The wind tore at my hair. It would take an age to comb it smooth again.

Focus, Nexantius reminded me.

"I know I made a mistake, ignoring signs that Lord Valmarys meant ill," I pressed. "I mean, the Moth King. But the truth is that I *do* know what that mistake cost. I don't want to make another. I don't want the being that's been haunting me to find another way into this world. And that's why I'm coming to you."

Valory sighed. The angles of her face softened. Everyone loves a well-told tale of repentance and redemption.

Even so, I could hardly believe it when she stepped through the portal and turned her back to me, *trusting* me. The portal shrank to the size of a jewelry case before expanding again, revealing the Forest of the West Fringe on the opposite side.

The scene in the frame was oddly quiet. No breeze or birds whistled in the tops of the timeworn trees. The sun was no friend to this stretch of forest. It wasn't raining, but dampness, dense and cool, draped over the air.

I followed Valory. My inward gloating ceased when the smell struck me—like wet stockings, mushrooms, and rotting wood all stewing in a cauldron.

"By Queen Bristal's grave," I swore. "That's vile."

Valory cut a look over her shoulder.

"What? I can say that. She was my great-great-grandmother too."

She shielded her nose and mouth with her sleeve and took

several steps into the forest. "That looks like the clearing up ahead," she said. "Where the Water was."

Leaving the portal open, she wended her way through the trees and ferns, reaching the clearing before I did. I heard her gasp.

When I drew up behind her and peered down into the pit, I found an incursion of sickly gray moss and lichen, a forest of cup-shaped fungal growths with mouth-sized pores that leaked a clear, tacky substance. There were many trapped insects and even a few birds and rodents.

At the center of the pit sprawled a complex web of grayish roots that resembled long, spindly fingers. The way they branched outward sent an unbidden shiver up my spine; it looked as though something had dug into our world from another. *An invasion.*

Yes, Nexantius hissed.

Valory hunkered down at the edge and made a disgusted sound. "I think you're right. The Realm Alliance needs to know what is happening here."

Are you sure about this? I asked Nexantius.

You underestimate us.

I took a fortifying breath and stepped up behind Valory. Like those creatures in the ooze, Valory was trapped in my deception. I almost hated to shatter the idea of me she now held: contrite, helpful, even transformed. For a moment, I fancied that I might be rewarded with my full power, might win forgiveness from my sisters and brother. Instead of treating me like a traitor, they would welcome me back. Warning them of a rising evil in Nissera would more than compensate for my mistakes.

I could simply release Myron from the grasp of illusion and

delusion, and Navara would be too relieved to ever speak a word against me. I could reclaim my old life.

It's a fantasy, my magnificent consort. You and I shall never be parted. We have made promises to each other, dreamed dreams we must fulfill. Claim your prize before it's too late.

My nerves prickled with the thrill of crossing that line, shattering the deception. I flinched toward Valory, hesitated, steeled myself, and finally planted my sole between her shoulder blades.

She cried in shock as she tumbled into the putrescent pit. Her crown flung away and bounced with muffled clinks. She managed to land on her hands and knees, and when she looked up at me, I saw the fire of battle in her wild eyes.

Fear pummeled me like a punch to the gut. What if Nexantius had underestimated her?

A ring of fire flared up around her, the blistering flames licking high. This had to be one of the dozen powers she had stripped from elicromancers whom she had deemed worthy of punishment.

The fire hungrily climbed the walls of the pit and rushed at me like a wave. I lurched back and threw my hand over my face to shield myself from the heat, knowing my end had come.

But swirls of cool, bright silver painted over my flesh, beginning at my fingertips, coating my fingers and hands and arms like armor.

The fire should have claimed me. But I didn't even feel it.

What is this? I asked Nexantius.

Your reward for doing what I asked.

When Valory realized the flames would not hurt me, she relented, and the flames snuffed out. I dropped my hand to stare deep into her eyes.

She looked unsure, maybe even afraid.

The image seared itself into my memory. Forevermore, it would bring me comfort and delight.

The wolf had become the helpless lamb.

She bared her teeth and struggled to stand, but the sticky substance slowed her down. The fire had not damaged the other-worldly infestation. If anything, her attack seemed to strengthen it. The collection of varying growths seemed to breathe in and expand like diseased lungs.

I heard a *whoosh* behind me and spun to find a second, identical Valory. So she had confiscated the elicrin power from a Duplicator as well. "What an intriguing assortment of stolen gifts," I mused. "Mercer must enjoy this one."

This new Valory began to generate an armor of her own, made of sparkling, faceted crystal—the enviable gift that had once belonged to her first cousin Ander Ermetarius, before she killed him. Her diamond-hard fist struck me across the face and set my head ring-ing, but my armor from Nexantius made us equals, and the effect was no worse than if she'd struck me with her naked fist.

I'd never fought anyone with my hands before, but I reared upward, slamming a hard fist down on her shoulder. The suppos-edly impenetrable crystal of her armor cracked like glass, and both iterations of Valory cried out in pain. I reeled back to strike another blow, but the duplicate flickered and disappeared.

I turned to the pit and found Valory mired in the growth. The roots, which I'd imagined breathing only a moment ago, slithered their way around her calves. But she wasn't done fighting. Spikes protruded from her limbs, sharp and pale. They were made of bone. Yet another gift she had curated, another elicromancer she had oppressed and robbed.

The growth in the pit recoiled a little, hissing and squealing as her spikes punctured its tendrils and spilled more ooze. But the sentient growth recovered, lashing around her wrists and pinning her against the earth.

Panic set in, and I relished it. Instead of relying on the sophisticated elicrin gifts in her collection, Valory resorted to her crude, unruly power of sheer destruction. Screaming, she curled her fingers and thrust her hands upward, ripping the roots from the earth without touching them.

Nexantius . . . what's happening? She shouldn't be able to escape.

He didn't answer, but I felt his thoughts agitating.

Valory snapped her head up and looked at me. Her right hand rose, fingers tense with the potential to wreck and kill. She jerked her wrist, and magic erupted out of her.

No elicrin stone, all power.

The mighty trees around us cracked as though struck by lightning. I heard them sway and one fell right beside me, a hand's breadth from crushing me. The impact shook the earth beneath my feet, but I remained still, solid and unmovable, like one of those iron effigies come to life.

Valory screamed as she tried and failed to break me, destroying everything around me instead.

When it stopped, I opened my eyes and found her panting, lines of despair etched across her somewhat-pretty face. The roots she had torn up squirmed back to life and seized her with new determination, dragging her to the center of the pit. One of them slithered into her mouth in spite of her fierce struggle, sliding down her throat like a snake, staking her in place. They trapped her so completely that I could not tell where she ended and they began. Her wide eyes stared in horror.

"The only power you can truly call your own is the power to cause discord," I called to her. "Deep in your heart, you know this. The world will be a safer, fairer place with you restrained."

I turned my back on her and hiked over felled trees to the portal, my silver armor retreating. After I stepped through to the deserted island, the portal shrank into a tiny wooden case again, small enough for me to pick up and carry back down to the shore, where Damiatta waited for me.

Silimos would crumble Valory's will and possess her.

Nexantius and I had ideas for the other two Fallen. Soon all four would have vessels, and we would be unstoppable.

From now on I would obey no laws and bow to no authority.

☙ THIRTY-FOUR ❧

KADRI

S soon as the bloodshed erupted outside the cabin, swift and brutal, I was ready. Viteus had struck Sev with the crossbow, but he wouldn't hurt anyone else.

The spell came to me not from memory of the battles I had fought alongside my elicromancer friends. Instead, I'd found it while thumbing through the book Valory had given me. It was non-violent but deadly. If I missed and caught the wrong person, I could simply release its hold.

As Glisette lunged to help Sev, I stepped toward the fire, taking her place. My elicrin stone had begun to learn from me, to sense my thoughts. I could feel it pulling from the magic Valory had infused in my blood, asking me what I wanted.

It lit up before I even uttered the spell.

I looked Viteus in the eyes, thinking of Lucrez and the sacrifices she had made for this family and for me, the sacrifices that had resulted in her murder. *"Bereth caranwen,"* I whispered.

The magic flowed out of me, and the strangling spell took hold. His eyes went wide and his lips parted as he gasped for breath. He doubled over and dropped the crossbow to claw at his throat.

The struggle lasted longer than I anticipated, my magic lapsing for a second as doubt overcame me. But finally, he choked and fell dead.

Good riddance.

When I turned to help Sev, I found Glisette lying prone on the ground beside him, colorless and convulsing. Sev's mother ventured out of the cabin to press a cloth to his wound.

"What's wrong with her?" Sev gasped, rapidly losing color himself.

I dropped to my knees and brushed hair away from her face. "Glisette?"

She jerked awake as if from a trance. She looked at Navara, back at me, and then at the children inside the cabin. She found Sev and let out a sob, rolling up onto her elbows to crawl toward him.

"I'm all right," he said feebly.

"Let's get you both inside," his mother said.

One of the boys helped her lift Sev. At least the bolt had gone clean through his arm. If it had been barbed, it would have lodged in the muscle and made a downright mess of the wound.

Depositing Sev on a pallet, his mother calmly doled out orders to the children to bring her supplies. She had to slice Sev's shirt to get at the wound. I did not envy her the delicate work ahead.

Jeno cut the string binding Navara's wrists, and she smiled at him. "Thank you," she said, and the boy's cheeks darkened a few ruddy shades.

Navara and I sat Glisette at the table. Navara fetched her a ladle of water, and she drank obediently.

"No one but Sev is hurt?" Glisette asked.

"No one," Navara answered. "Kadri saved our lives."

"What happened to you?" I squeezed my friend's hand. The puckered skin of her scar caught the light as she looked up at me. "I've never seen you like that."

"Themera," she said, and looked at Navara. "I think blood provokes hallucinations from her. Yesterday I pricked my finger on the blackberry bushes, and she came. This time she warned me that if I don't let her use me as a vessel, I will lose everything and everyone. She sent me a vision. She made me think all of you had been slaughtered."

Navara grimaced. "That's horrible, Glisette. I'm so sorry."

Glisette nodded, casting a glance toward Sev, who moaned in misery.

Navara traced her fingers over the surface of the knotty wood table. As though she'd been avoiding it, she lifted her eyes to look at the silver scroll case poised at the center. "At least we know what to do now...to banish Nexantius."

"I thought you said it was blasphemous," I said.

"I was just scared. To learn that everything I've always believed—everything my mother taught me—was based on lies. But feeling helpless just then made me even more scared. I don't want anyone to die. And if the only way to save innocent people is to admit that my faith is rooted in magic"—she shrugged—"then so be it."

I clasped her hand, and she squeezed it hard.

"The only thing I don't understand is how my father could let my mother and me go on believing in Agrimas when he knew the truth. He knew that it was all a story. No wonder the leaders claimed a curse would befall whoever reads the scroll without divine appointment. Its contents would undermine their leadership." She dropped her face into her hands. "And no wonder my father was so keen to promote friendly ties with elicromancers. He knows your magic isn't an unholy abomination. It's just...a force."

"A force made good or bad by the people who use it and the choices they make," I offered.

Navara nodded and brushed her short hair behind her ears. "I think I always knew that."

Glisette's cheeks had recovered their natural blush. She placed a hand on Navara's shoulder. "It shouldn't change the way you see your mother, Navara. If she was virtuous, then she was virtuous, whatever the reason. Your people loved her, and they will love you."

"They will love you, not because you lead them to the altar," I added, "but because you lead them."

"Leading well is hard," Glisette added, sitting taller. She looked at me. "Kadri and I have not been queens for long. We've already made mistakes. We've had to set aside our pride. But I think either of us would endure embarrassment over our failures and frustration over being underestimated again and again just for the chance to do something good in this world. It won't be easy, but you will be the best queen Perispos has ever known."

Navara looked at her through her dewy eyelashes. A tear slipped down her cheek, but she nodded. "Then let's defeat the worst."

In the cool, quiet hours of the morning, we set out west to meet Commander Larsio. I hoped that what the scroll said was true, that there was a way to separate Ambrosine from the power inside her.

Otherwise, even the largest army in the known world might not be able to take her down.

The others seemed to have confidence in this commander, so I decided to set aside my worry until I heard his ideas.

The huntsman was hardly in a state to travel. The fresh dressing his mother applied would help, but she worried aloud about the risk of infection and begged him to wait another day. Only after Glisette promised to continue cleansing and rewrapping it every several hours did she finally concede.

Melda would not accept the coins I'd stolen from Orturio's cellar, so I pulled the oldest girl, Stasi, aside as we prepared to go.

"Are you sure you will be safe here?" I asked, pressing several outdated gold pieces into her palm. "And have enough to eat?"

"This will help," she replied. "And I can hunt too. My father stashed an old bow and quiver here somewhere. Thank you."

I offered her a sad, knowing smile. Perhaps her early childhood had been different, but in the absence of a father, her mother needed her. Her eldest brother provided and the second eldest protected, leaving her to parent. Were the family more secure, she might have been permitted to learn a trade. I'd been fortunate enough to practice archery as much as I wanted, and to read and study and explore the city at will. But it wasn't as though Father and Rayed had never underestimated me, had never closed a door on a conversation when they saw me peeking in. I hoped a promising future awaited Stasi.

Navara uttered a sheepish goodbye to Jeno while Glisette, Sev, and I watched, reining in smiles. We left the gray rouncey in the family's care and departed the hidden cabin on foot.

For a quiet moment before dawn, the clouds cleared and the

stars sparkled. They stayed put even as a rosy sunrise fanned out over the towering oaks, beeches, and evergreen firs.

We didn't talk much, instead keeping our ears alert for any signs of foresters. Sev took us on a meandering path to help us avoid them, but we did spot a pair at the top of a wooded hill once. We hid behind a rock until long after they were gone.

By afternoon we glimpsed the ruins of the abandoned edifice through the trees. It was a relief; Sev's face had turned gray and his bandages were soaked. As soon as we were safe, we could both partake of the remaining tincture in my bag.

Nature had reclaimed the sacred building for its own. Moss and ivy slithered along the walls. A young tree reached its branches through the shattered stained-glass windows as if seeking shelter. Ivy coiled around the ornate stone columns of the entryway, and the steps had cracked with the pressure of strong shoots pushing their way to sunlight.

We approached twin wooden doors hanging crookedly on rusty hinges.

"This is it?" Navara asked, peering inside. "It doesn't seem like an ideal place to hide out and plan a coup." She turned to Sev and whispered, "Was Commander Larsio drinking when you found him in the gambling den?"

"Only enough to fool the other players into thinking they could best me," a stranger's deep voice said.

I whirled. A middle-aged man with black hair, a clean-cut beard, and clever hazel eyes clapped Sev on the shoulder, earning a wince of pain. A quality sword hung from the man's belt, but he gave no inclination that he planned to draw it on us.

"Commander!" Navara said. "I'm sorry, I—"

"No need to be sorry, Your Highness." He smiled and bowed to her. "Your Majesty." He bowed to Glisette, and then turned to me. "Sev didn't mention a third companion."

"I'm Kadri Lillis," I replied.

"Ah, Your Majesty," he said, offering another bow. "A pleasure. I am Gian Larsio, former commander of the King's Army. Please, come with me."

With a dignified stride that suited his status, the commander led us around the back side of the crumbling edifice.

Two guards in purple livery stood at attention outside an ivy-covered iron gate leading to the underground edifice. Navara and Glisette stopped in their tracks, and Sev flinched toward his knife. The warmth of live magic filled my chest.

"It's all right. They're retired soldiers," the commander explained. "And they're on our side."

Sev's eyes remained sharp and attentive, but I relaxed. The soldiers did look older, and their faded tunics bore a slightly different design from those worn by the soldiers in Enturra.

Commander Larsio swung open the iron gate and gestured for us to descend. The hairs on my arms prickled at the thought of being trapped underground, maybe even ambushed. Our best knife fighter was injured, and I didn't know if I could take on more than one person with my elicrin stone and live to tell the tale. But Navara proceeded without hesitation. Glisette, Sev, and I followed.

What we found below was a torchlit Edifice of the Fallen much like the last one, with a mirror and unsettling scenes painted on the walls.

"Why *did* you choose this place to meet us, Commander Larsio?" Navara asked.

The commander detached the mirror frame from the wall. "Just as the king and the high priest have their secrets, the king and I have ours."

Beyond the mirror lay another iron door, but when the commander opened the bolt lock, he revealed something far more ambitious than a secret room of religious treasures.

A long underground tunnel stretched before us, harboring hundreds of swords, shields, spears, axes, bows, and collections of armor glinting in the torchlight. There were crates with cans of food, grain sacks, bottles of lamp oil, fur cloaks, vials of curatives... supplies for survival.

"What is this place?" Navara gasped.

"A reserve armory," the commander said. "It was built in case of a siege on the capital. It's been here for hundreds of years, one of the best-kept secrets of Perispos. Even my former deputy, who's now leading the queen's army, doesn't know about it."

"In case of a siege..." Glisette mused, peering down dark passages that branched off from the armory. "Does that mean these tunnels go all the way to the palace?"

"Indeed. There's also a path leading to the coast, where ancillary war vessels are kept underground."

"Manmade tunnels vast enough to accommodate war ships?" Sev asked in disbelief.

"When your neighbors have magic, you need ingenuity." The commander clasped his hands proudly. "Settle in and we'll talk."

We dragged crates into a circle and sat. Glisette found a

stringent curative and fresh bandages to treat Sev's wounds while Navara inspected the food stores. "These aren't hundreds of years old, are they?" she asked, holding a jar of packed venison to the torchlight.

"No, Princess," the commander answered. "Sour stomachs would only make a siege more difficult to endure. Before the stores spoil, I bring them to local edifices to distribute to the poor."

"And the priests don't know where it comes from?" she asked, nervous as a doe at the snap of a twig. "They don't know about this place?"

"They have no idea," he assured her.

Navara had kept a cool head during both of our encounters with the Uprising, but now I could see how thoroughly the group had terrified even the object of their devotion. Viteus's promise to protect had rightfully rung hollow in her ears.

Selecting venison, green beans, and potatoes, Navara returned and passed the food around. Sev and Glisette were naming the resources and players at our disposal: one injured Marksman elicromancer with novice skills; an experienced elicromancer who lacked an elicrin stone; a capable hunter and fighter who was wounded; powerful allies who may or may not be on their way to help; and a princess with political sway.

"And whichever Holy we decide to call down," Navara said when they had finished.

"Navara..." Glisette said.

"What? Now that we have weapons and supplies and a leader, you've lost faith?"

"I never had faith. Not like you did."

"Do," Navara corrected. "I can reconcile what I learned. If anything, I'm more convinced that a Holy will answer your call."

"Planning well is the best way to keep innocent people, *your* people, from getting swept up in Ambrosine's wrath," Glisette said.

Navara thought for a moment and nodded.

"It's true. We are facing an elicromancer enemy with little regard for mortal life," Commander Larsio said. "With your permission, Princess, we will prioritize protecting the civilians of Halithenica."

"Of course," Navara said.

"That means we don't storm the city, even if additional forces from Nissera join us."

"I agree," Sev said. "Ambrosine doesn't care about her people, but she knows that we do. If the battle happens within the city gates, that gives her leverage. She could terrorize her citizens to try to win concessions from us."

"The tunnels, then," Glisette said. "We catch her off guard."

"It's an option," the commander said. "But that still brings the battle close to innocent people. We need to lure her out of the palace and away from the city."

I thought of the labyrinth of mirrors within the palace that Glisette had described, and how easily Ambrosine could use them to her advantage. "How?" I asked.

The commander took a thoughtful swig of ale and set his flagon aside. "Before the sun sets tonight, Princess Navara will go to one of the towns and give a rousing speech, inspiring those who are able to join her rebellion and fight for us. That will lay the foundation of our deception: that we're mounting a large-scale resistance to directly attack the city. But in truth, we're planning an ambush."

"Why would we want Ambrosine to think we have a strong army when we don't?" Navara asked.

"A few dozen retired soldiers and an elicromancer without an elicrin stone will not draw her out," the commander explained. "But if she believes we are a growing army gaining numbers by the day, with elicromancer allies, she and her army will meet us. The new commander will want to avoid defending the capital at all costs. It's destructive and expensive."

"But their forces are so much stronger than any civilian army we could gather," Sev said. "Even a clever ambush would fail with those odds. Our hands are tied without real help from Nissera."

"Nissera's help would be ideal," the commander admitted. "But Navara's rallying cry will pick off soldiers who waver in their loyalty to the queen."

"If they recognized Ambrosine for what she is, wouldn't they have defected already?" I asked.

"As long as the king is still signing decrees, the soldiers might feel they have to obey their orders, regardless of the circumstances. But when Navara calls them to action, they will know they can defy the queen without breaking their oaths to crown and country. Those who do not abandon her when they have opportunity and reason should be considered complicit in her evils."

The commander's rationale and wisdom chipped away at the fear that had been steadily mounting. But as the only elicromancer here, I might have to be the one to defeat Ambrosine—and that scared me to the bone.

"The first element of our strategy is the inspiration and illusion," the commander said. "That is your part, Princess. Tonight, you will raise the banner of your cause and make the queen believe we are planning an invasion. The second is false information. We need an informant to feed the queen secrets, secrets that she will believe we don't want her to know. If we make our plan too obvious, she'll recognize the deception for what it is. She has to think she is outsmarting us."

"An altar attendant who used to work for the Uprising now works for Ambrosine," I said. "The Uprising fed her false information to test her, and she took it straight to Ambrosine. I can force the priest in Enturra to put me in contact with her. He'll do it—he doesn't want to see Ambrosine triumph over Navara any more than we do. When I speak to the informant, I'll pretend to be an Uprising agent who still believes she's our ally on the inside."

"But why would an Uprising agent know about our plans for rebellion?" Glisette asked.

"The Uprising lacks a leader. It would make sense for them to unite with our resistance to defeat a common enemy."

"Excellent," the commander said, rubbing his hands together. "The third element is battlefield advantage. The forest is a prime location for an ambush. But we can boost that advantage with unpredictable conditions. I can feel in my knees that the summer rains will come soon." He looked at Glisette. "You could turn them into a winter storm, a storm for which we are prepared, and they are not. A storm that allows us to hide traps under a fresh layer of snow."

"I don't have my elicrin stone," Glisette reminded him. "I have no control."

"That leads me to the final element," the commander said. "The theft. We need every elicromancer ally we can get, including you, Your Majesty. Sev knows his way around the palace, and we have a tunnel leading right to it." He gestured at a dark passage leading north. I couldn't contain my shiver. The thought of roaming in the dark, getting lost, getting trapped, going mad down here made me want to drag open that vault door and never set one foot underground again.

"That is far too risky," Glisette said. "Ambrosine could have tossed my elicrin stone in the ocean by now."

"She wanted trophies as proof of your deaths," Sev reminded her. "You think she'd ask for a lock of your hair but toss away your elicrin stone?"

"She will kill you on sight, Sev!" Glisette cried. "And it could be for nothing. We have no proof she kept it."

"Well…" I started. Glisette was going to kill me for this. "She took it from you before she ordered Sev to kill you, right? She may have kept it to monitor your status."

"Status?" Sev asked.

Glisette sighed. "An elicrin stone separated from its master burns to the touch, but only if the master is alive. It's a bond that can only be severed by death or willing abandonment. She could have known I was alive with or without your proof. I didn't tell you that because I wanted you to spare us."

"I was always going to spare you," Sev said softly. "Why do you think I waited until you regained consciousness? I just needed one of you to talk me out of my orders."

Glisette smiled crookedly at him. Sev grinned back, but the smile slipped away when he looked at the commander. "I'll go now."

"I'll go too," I volunteered. "Glisette can teach me the concealing spell so I can hide us both."

"You and *I* should go, then," Glisette said to me. "There's no reason for Sev to risk his life for my elicrin stone."

"You don't know the palace like I do," Sev argued. Neither of them seemed to want to admit outright that they were trying their best to protect each other. "Where the guards are stationed, how to navigate the mirrors..."

"And I need you, Glisette," Navara said. "I could use another lesson before I carry a sword in public."

"The commander would do a better job—" Glisette started, but Navara held out a finger to shush her.

"And most importantly, there's a deity you need to ask a favor of."

THIRTY-FIVE

GLISETTE

AN hour later I walked a distance with Sev down the north tunnel to see him off to the palace. The passage yawned at us, so dark that my mind could imprint whatever fears it wanted onto that stretching abyss.

It was easy to imagine a woman with a crown of knives whispering in the dark, or a creature wrought of teeth and muscle waiting to tear me apart, or even Ambrosine herself, watching me with wicked eyes like newly minted coins.

Sev's hand brushed mine as we walked. When the armory was far enough away that we could claim some privacy, he stopped. We hadn't truly spoken since before our kiss—not about the matters that animated my heart, otherwise thriving on only grief and revenge.

He turned, his dark eyes soft but intense. In the faint light from the armory, his face looked wan and tight.

We had only known each other for a few tempestuous days, but I felt attuned to the slightest change in his stolid expression and sensitive to his every gesture, whether meaningful or not.

"You should wait until the bleeding's stopped," I said.

He frowned at his bandage. "I'd imagine living without your

power feels a bit like being wounded. You suddenly can't do things that were easier than breathing before."

I nodded. "I felt so helpless yesterday."

"So did I. My brothers and sisters are my responsibility. And I thought I had failed them."

That word, *failed*, carved a hole in my chest.

But the rough warmth of Sev's hand settled against my cheek. "Glisette," he whispered, waiting until I looked up at him. "That kind of love—the love you have for Perennia—reaches across death."

The levy broke and I fell into his embrace. His arm tightened around me, the other hanging limp at his side. I wept, crushed against soft leather and the scents of the woods. We resided in that moment, wishing we could cure each other's pain. And the wishing itself was enough to ease it, if only a little.

Wiping tears from my eyes, I stepped back. He dug the iron effigy out of his pocket. "I'm going to find your elicrin stone. And until we meet again, we'll each have something that belongs to the other."

His touch lingered as he placed it in my hand.

Twisting torchlight at the mouth of the tunnel diverted our attention. Kadri stared past us at the path before her as though it was the gullet of a monster ready to devour her. "I don't know if I can do this," she called out.

Sev's deep voice boomed back at her. "I have a map of the tunnels and everything we need in case we lose our way," he said, patting the satchel at his hip. "Commander Larsio said there's an emergency opening at the midpoint."

Kadri nodded, determined but not enthused, and limped toward us.

"You're sure you can do the concealing spell?" I asked her. "Remember, you have to be touching Sev for it to cover him. And it's *seter inoden*, with emphasis on the—"

"I *know*, Glisette. Remind me not to take you on as a tutor when we go home."

Home. I had hardly thought about home in the days since Perennia's death. What would home be without her?

"Please, be careful," I whispered. I embraced Kadri and then watched my two wounded friends venture into the darkness. The thought of losing anyone else made my heart feel like glass waiting to be shattered.

I turned and stalked back to the armory, finding it empty. After her swordplay lessons with the commander, Navara had gone to gather materials needed for the elemental ritual. According to the apocryphal scroll, it would call down one of the Holies. I had reservations about the ritual and tried not to pin all of my hopes on its efficacy—which was easier to do now that we had the commander's acumen and, possibly, my elicrin stone. But it wouldn't hurt to try.

I started toward the stairs, but as soon as I crossed the threshold from the armory to the run-down edifice, a harsh chorus of whispers cut around me, like a thousand knives whirring past my temples. They overlapped, growing more sinister with every step I took toward the light.

The Holies will not come.
I am the only one here to help you.
You are making a mistake.
You cannot win without me.

You need me.

You are mine.

The dark declarations intensified until wordless shrieks of suffering and wails of mourning wove through them like bloodred strands in a black tapestry.

Cold dread filled the pit of my stomach. If half of the Fallen had already come to our world, the other two would be even more desperate to join them. I could feel that powerful desperation as the spirit of Themera crashed over me like a frozen river.

Whom would Robivoros try to claim?

One of my friends? Devorian?

Devorian. If Ambrosine had been vulnerable to Nexantius due to her vanity, did that mean Devorian's proclivity for overindulgence made him vulnerable to Robivoros?

I clutched Sev's effigy, feeling the fading warmth of his closeness. I reached the stairs and took them three at a time until the whispers fell silent.

The fresh air and the presence of the two guards calmed me as I rounded the derelict Edifice of the Holies. Commander Larsio sat on the base of a broken column at the entrance, making a charcoal sketch of what appeared to be a trap.

"How did she do?" I asked, slipping the effigy into my pocket. "She won't slice any of her own soldiers' heads off, will she?"

He chuckled. "Her mother always said that Kromanos had gifted her determination and spirit. I think that will have to suffice."

"Thank you for helping us, Commander," I said. "I know it must not be easy to plan an attack against your own men."

"The ones who will heed Navara's call have been listening all along. They should know a true leader from a tyrant."

"I hope so," I said, and picked my way over the cracked steps to the edifice entrance.

Pale gold sunlight fell through the high windows onto a lush, crumbling landscape of ruin and rebirth. Navara knelt at the altar at the center of the room, whispering prayers. She had positioned clay bowls in a tidy line at the feet of the Holy deities.

She rose and turned. "It's ready for you," she said.

I wove through the path of weeds toward the imposing marble structure, crossing through shafts of sunlight where dust motes swirled like stardust.

Each bowl contained something representing a Holy. For Honesty, the burning tip of a candle. For Moderation, salt. Humility, dirt. Lovingkindness, a feather. Diligence, seeds. Generosity, wine. Loyalty, stone. And Courage, metal.

There was also a knife, laid suggestively in the foreground. Of course—most magic rituals required pain and blood.

"What do I do?" I asked.

"Draw blood and drip it into the bowl of the Holy you wish to call down," Navara said. "You're supposed to pray, but... you should just do what feels right. Don't be disingenuous."

I held in a snort. "Which one should I ask?"

"Lekdytos, Humility, is the foil of Nexantius," she said. "But Atrelius is the warrior god, and his sword and shield are said to have powers of their own. Honestly, you should follow your instinct. I'll leave you to make your choice. The commander and I are going to the city."

"Are you sure you don't want me to come with you?" I asked, hoping she would say yes. I believed the Fallen were real and present, but it was harder to believe the Holies would come at our beck and call. I didn't want to disappoint Navara or, admittedly, myself.

"I mean no offense, but I'm sure my people are a bit miffed about their ruined crops. They might not want to join the movement if they know you're—"

"Understandable." I waved her off, but my inner guilt was more difficult to dismiss. "Good luck, Navara."

She smiled warmly. "Blessings, Glisette."

When she was gone, I looked up at the once-vibrant blue ceiling, painted with stars, curved into a dome like the sky above.

My heart felt as hollow as this forsaken temple, but I nudged my doubt aside and dropped to my knees. Looking up into the hard face of Atrelius, Holy of Courage, I decided he was the most rational choice.

I took up the knife. It would be foolish to slit my palm days before a battle. Then again, this seemed to be some version of a sacrifice. I had to actually sacrifice something.

Bracing myself, I rested the sharp point against my palm and dug in. A hiss of pain escaped through my teeth. A jewel-red stripe intersected the lines running across my flesh, and I closed my fist to trap the pooling blood.

"Atrelius," I whispered. "God of Courage, or whatever you are. Ancient elicromancer, it seems. I, um…I offer myself as a vessel. The Fallen have begun to invade our world. We need your wrath and your might to drive them out, to banish them to darkness as you did once before."

I let my bleeding hand drift toward the clay bowl holding the piece of metal, a steel chape from the tip of a scabbard. But as the blood drops grew ripe and ready to fall, I jerked my hand toward the bowl holding the feather. A few stray drops landed on the steel chape, but I let the rest fall before Eulippa.

Lovingkindness, the foil of Cruelty—the foil of Themera.

"Eulippa, I call you down in Perennia's honor," I said, my voice rising, strengthening in conviction. "She was the kindest soul I knew in this world. And she deserves to be avenged. Rip your enemy out of Ambrosine so that I can destroy her for the evils she has committed."

My blood began to pool at the bottom of the bowl, staining the gray-brown feather. The birds outside whistled their tunes as the streaks of sunlight grew warmer, brighter. I laughed in disbelief.

Eulippa had heard me.

But clouds passed over the sun, stealing the warmth from the crown of my head and the tops of my shoulders. A cool wind blew, and with it came distant whispers that raised gooseflesh on my arms.

"Are you here, Eulippa?" I whispered as I looked up at the statue.

I felt the silence like the drop of a mighty hammer.

THIRTY-SIX

EATH had stolen the color in my sister's cheeks, but her beauty endured.

Her honeyed tresses had been gingerly arranged to cascade over her shoulders. The butter-yellow dress I had commissioned from the clothier for her welcome banquet softened the scarlet of her painted lips.

Even under the sunrays falling through the windows in the throne room, Perennia's hand felt as cold as her engraved stone bed. I had the instinct to try to warm her fingers with my own, just like when she used to tiptoe to my bedchamber, begging to climb into bed with her eldest sister. I had promised I would protect her from night beasties, such as the old hag who hid in the wardrobe, waiting to steal your youth and beauty while you slept. She would cut you and bleed you until she had enough blood to paint her skin. If the hag succeeded, she would host a ball and prance around in your clothes. *You* would then wake up as an old hag and haunt wardrobes until you managed to steal another girl's youth and beauty.

I told Perennia I would stay awake and protect her from danger. But I never told her the danger wasn't real, that I had invented the story myself. Glisette persistently tried to convince young Perennia it was fake. Perennia wanted to believe her, and in the daytime she always did.

But at night, she believed me.

She had outgrown her fear of the hag years ago. But sometimes I thought back to that story and wished I had been the kind of sister who lied to protect, never to harm.

The hand that rested over Perennia's curled into a fist.

Glisette. Always making herself the arbiter of right and wrong, the voice of reason when a plot had gone too far. Glisette and I used to agree on almost everything, but there was an invisible line I could not cross without crossing her.

I never thought that line would become a rift so vast and jagged.

I never thought I would order her execution.

I told Sev to do it as quickly and painlessly as possible. My plan to frame Glisette for Perennia's death was not hatched out of spite; I needed to explain Navara's disappearance. Glisette would be at peace and would not know or care that I had made her a villain in the eyes of my subjects.

I had no choice. After last night, nothing would ever be the same. Glisette would have run back to the Realm Alliance, roaring that Perennia's death was my fault. They would believe her. They would challenge me, wage war against me. I would have to waste my mortal army and my resources fighting. I would lose Devorian. The cost of letting Glisette return and tell her story was simply too high.

Now I would get to tell Devorian *my* story.

Perennia's rose elicrin stone lay lightless in my hand. Beyond her Solacer gift, she had never developed much of an affinity for elicromancy. Her power was distinct enough that she had received her elicrin stone after only a few years, despite not mastering many spells. Glisette and I had always competed with each other, driving us to diligence in our magical studies. But Perennia was excellent at only one thing when it came to elicromancy: taking away sorrow when it became too heavy to bear.

A tear slid down my cheek and splashed on the cloudy pink surface of her stone. Ironically, I needed her gift now more than ever.

"Shall I plan the ceremony while you rest, Your Majesty?" Damiatta asked. "I can order her favorite flowers."

"I've sent for my brother. When he arrives, we will hold the funeral."

"But that could take—"

"I don't care how long it takes," I snapped. "She's been embalmed. We will wait."

"I'll ask the undertaker to move her back to the mortuary until he arrives."

"No," I barked. "Leave her."

Damiatta bowed her head. A crew of men entered the throne room, carrying the glass case I had requested. It was from the beloved late queen's funeral. The people had wanted to bid the queen farewell one last time, but Myron wanted no one to touch her. So a glass case with gold scrollwork accents had been constructed for a procession and viewing.

The princess's tutor had told me this. She had brought up the dead queen at every opportunity. Now she was dead too.

"It's perfect," I said, ushering the men into the throne room. They placed the prism over Perennia's body.

"Leave me," I said when they finished, and everyone, even Damiatta, hurried out.

But I was never truly alone.

The silver mask appeared in the reflected light glancing off the glass. The comforting touch of a disembodied hand alighted on my shoulder.

For so long I have only known the tedium of eternal darkness, Nexantius said. *Now, through you, I feel pain again. I remember what it means to be alive.*

You're the only one who understands me, I told him. *I wish you could step outside of my mind and the mirrors. I wish you could stand beside me, rule beside me instead of through me.*

I know that you are grieving. But you should know that there is a way.

A way for what? I asked, a ray of hope puncturing the darkness like a bold new star burning to life. Nexantius was my only true ally, the being who saw every corner of my soul and still embraced me.

A way for me to become my own man, to take on my own vessel, he replied. *But all of the Fallen must return to this world first. That is the only way we will have the power we need to emerge from our human vessels. We are waiting for Silimos to break down Valory's will. And while we wait, we must continue searching for willing and worthy vessels for Robivoros and Themera. Devorian is a man of appetite, is he not?*

I suppose... I answered, cautious. *Why?*

Robivoros would delight to have such a vessel.

Isn't he more monster than man? I asked. *I agreed that Themera and Glisette would make a good match. But I've seen the paintings of Robivoros, and—*

They're exaggerated. Nexantius brushed me off. *Meant to stoke fear. Besides, it's only temporary. When we have each gained enough power through our hosts, we can choose any flesh vessels we desire, even those without the capacity for magic or extraordinary power. You could choose one for me. You enjoy the huntsman's appearance. Imagine me wearing his form, ruling this world at your side. We would be loved and admired by all. Now that Navara and your sisters are gone, you will be the fairest creature alive, renowned in every corner of the world.*

"Your Majesty?" Damiatta asked, cutting through the magnificent fantasy Nexantius had spun for me.

"What?" I snapped.

"The huntsman has returned."

"Oh." I laid a hand over the place where I'd felt the ghostly touch on the shoulder of my black mourning gown.

Severo Segona would not dare return if he had failed to do what I asked.

That meant Glisette was dead. An unexpected loneliness burrowed in my gut, but I clung to Nexantius's promise that he and I could be together, beside each other. "Send him in."

Damiatta bowed her head and swung open one of the double doors to admit Severo.

A bloody game bag swung in his grip. Strange, gleeful horror overcame me. I had nearly forgotten I had asked him for Navara's lungs and liver as proof of her death. I had uttered this demand in a frenzy, realizing I could hardly trust someone so principled—even under threat of harm to his loved ones—not to release the targets to the wild and tell me he had done the deed.

"The proof you requested," he growled.

"Damiatta, wrap this up and bring it to my private chamber before he makes a mess," I said.

Damiatta did as I asked, unburdening him of the bloody sack and hurrying away.

"And the hair?" I demanded.

Jaw set, the huntsman strode forward and offered me a lock of golden hair, most assuredly ripped out by the roots, judging by the flecks of blood and flesh.

My own sister, gone, just like the other.

"Am I dismissed?" he asked, glaring at me.

"Yes." I waved him off. "Go kill something worthy of a funereal feast."

As soon as he departed, I ascended to my private chamber. The game bag waited on the hearth stones, wrapped in a second, cleaner sack. Damiatta had left, and there were no signs of any servants but for a tea tray left on my vanity.

I deposited the lock of hair beside it and took a breath, steeling myself to cross the room and glimpse inside the sack. Once there, I hunkered down on the hearth stones and turned my face away, peeking out of the corner of my eye.

A bloody mess of organs filled the sack.

I could have started a fire in the hearth and burned them. But morbid curiosity got the better of me. I slipped a hand inside the sack, grasping at the feel and texture of the spongy remains. I lifted the liver with fingers covered in dark-brownish red.

Thinking of the old hag, I laughed. I knew I looked mad, but I felt the opposite—enlightened, invigorated. Perhaps Perennia's death had ruined my mind, or maybe ordering the execution of my other sister had dealt the last blow to my sanity. Maybe it was the being I had allowed inside me who was making me mad, tearing me apart.

But the glee persisted through the madness. Navara was dead.

"You specimen of beauty," I whispered. "Now you are finished."

Cackling, I dropped the liver and smeared the blood on my face. Her youth I didn't need, but beauty I would take. It would compound mine, multiply it until mortals could not bear to regard me.

Someone knocked. It had to be Damiatta—she was the only one who would dare disturb me. "Your Majesty, your brother has arrived," she said. "I took him to the throne room to visit your sister's remains."

"He's here already? How?" I asked. What had I done? Now I would have to win him over with a tale of innocence wearing traces of the princess's blood on my flesh.

"Yes. Now you can give her a timely farewell."

I stood and peered at the mirror, at the creature I had become. "I'll be down shortly," I called.

All evening Devorian wept at Perennia's side while I made funeral arrangements for the morrow. He didn't seem to note Myron's absence, and he certainly didn't catch any cues about the high priest's death or Commander Larsio's recent resignation. He didn't care whether Perennia's death was my fault or Glisette's. He brushed off my account of the story and wept, wept until he sank to the floor and didn't rise.

After a good while of trying to comfort him, I showed him his chamber and retreated for the night. Devorian didn't want to hear my defense, at least not right now.

Before falling into a fitful night's sleep, I removed the portal box from my drawer to look in on Valory. My nerves had become more agitated than a nest of hissing snakes, and seeing her held captive while Silimos tightened her clutches would soothe them.

I tied a cloth around the lower half of my face to subdue the smell before unlatching the box. Since it had been created for Valory, it would only open to the last place she had wished to go.

A forest overgrown with gray lichen and oozing fungi lay ahead of me. The sulfuric, moldy stocking scent had become so overwhelming that I would soon need to stop visiting altogether.

But there she was—trapped at the center of the pit, cocooned in flossy strands of ooze. Her flesh resembled mold at the bottom of a forgotten cup of tea. Her limbs were twisted, arthritic, pinned close to her body. Roots splayed out from her mouth and grew from her fingers like unpared nails. Even more so than before, I had to strain by the light of my elicrin stone to see where she ended and the growth began.

I had to think that she would surrender to Silimos soon in order to escape this prison of mind and body. From what I could tell, no one had found her, or at least no one had succeeded in freeing her if they had. The forest would become less welcoming each day. Her only way out? Agree to invite the Fallen inside her body and soul.

Comforted and exhausted, I stumbled into bed without even visiting the edifice to spin fantasies for my mad, pathetic husband.

Clouds shrouded the sky the next day. I rose late and donned mourning attire again. Devorian and I sat in an open-top carriage in the damp, warm air, following Perennia's procession on a loop through Halithenica as rain began to fall.

My subjects emerged from their clay-and-brick homes and cramped, dim shops to see her. Some openly admired her beauty, but no one offered me anything beyond perfunctory condolences with downcast eyes. Many frantically reached for the iron trinkets in their pockets as if to ward me away.

This procession was a bad idea. If Devorian noted their apprehension, he might begin to weave a tale of his own, different from the one he'd barely given me a chance to tell.

"I wish the Realm Alliance could be here," Devorian said. "Or just a few of Perennia's friends from home. None of these people know her. They're being kind for your sake, but tomorrow they will move on. We could have at least waited for Glisette—"

"No," I said. "It was her spell that killed Perennia. She was so ashamed that she threw away her elicrin stone and fled."

"That's not what I heard at the port. The criers are saying she went mad, murdered her own sister, and kidnapped the princess."

"Gossip," I said, waving it off. "They don't know her. They invent their own stories."

"Where is Navara then? And King Myron?"

"The king has suffered digestive woes for weeks, and the princess is traumatized. She witnessed the altercation. It would never have happened if Glisette could resist being so suspicious of me. She got it into her head that I violated my probation. How? They put restrictions on my magic! She's determined to think the worst of me, and it has broken our family."

A sudden, cold blast of wind tore through the city streets. Its frigid fingers tugged off my headdress. The rain turned to hard sleet and the people fled to shelter. Trying to escape the sudden onslaught of cold, miserable weather, the coachman snapped the reins and our carriage jostled roughly over the cobblestones. But we could only go so fast following a carriage carrying a glass coffin and a lifeless body.

"Glissy," Devorian breathed. He extended his palm and watched the sleet turn to snowflakes.

"What?" I asked, my heart dropping to my heels.

"It must be her . . . unless it snows here on the cusp of summer?"

"Not that I'm aware of," I breathed, crossing my arms against the biting wind.

"I have to find her," Devorian said. He craned his neck to see how far we were from the palace. His nose and ears were already bright pink from cold.

"Why? She ran away. She doesn't want to be found."

"Maybe not by you," he said in a dark voice. Then he sighed, his breath fogging the air. "I'm sorry. We shouldn't turn against each other right now. I made that mistake with the three of you after Mother and Father, and I don't want to do it again. I'll leave after the ceremony and return to collect Perennia's remains before I go home. Do you have Glisette's elicrin stone? I'm sure she'll want it back after..." He gestured at the wild winter weather.

"I don't know what happened to it," I lied.

We fell silent, impatiently waiting for the procession to end.

As soon as we arrived back at the palace, Devorian stormed away to collect his luggage. I ran to my quarters to yank open my vanity drawer and rummage for the purple chalcedony. An elicrin stone that had been unwillingly surrendered—and whose owner still lived and breathed—would revolt and burn to the touch.

A vile curse tore out of my lips as the stone seared my skin. I threw it back into the drawer and slammed it shut. Angry red blisters rose on my fingertips.

Glisette was alive.

Severo had defied me. He had spared Glisette, and probably Navara too. He wouldn't release my sister only to let his princess perish.

What had he given me, if not Navara's lungs and liver?

He had probably fled, taken his family into hiding, thinking he had outsmarted me. I didn't even know where he lived. I had manipulated him with idle threats.

But they wouldn't be idle now. Within minutes, my men would be hunting down the spineless huntsman and the two girls he had failed to kill. I had already told the deputy commander to send out a few royal guards to look for the princess, feigning concern for her. Now my men would hunt in earnest, scouring every town, and every forester would be on the lookout for the three of them.

I would not rest until my commands were carried out.

I would not rest until my soldiers dragged the princess back so I could slaughter her myself.

✤ THIRTY-SEVEN ✤

GLISETTE

BACK in the armory, I found myself wishing I had insisted on accompanying Navara to inspire the people. But she was right; my snowstorm had surely stoked the anti-elicromancer sentiments that Ambrosine's tyranny had set aflame. Even if we banished Nexantius and defeated Ambrosine, the people of Perispos would never trust elicromancers again.

Solving problems our kind had created didn't exactly make us heroes.

Where was Valory? Mercer? Tilmorn? I would happily take even Melkior if it meant having another elicromancer ally. Who had the Fallen of Apathy claimed in Nissera?

I sat on a crate, tapping my heels with impatience and worry, absentmindedly picking at the cloth tied around my bloody hand.

Part of me wanted to pursue Sev and Kadri down that tunnel. At least it would give me something to *do* besides stew in my many failures. Maybe the apocryphal scroll wasn't the problem. Maybe it was me—my heart, my soul, my tendency toward harshness and derision, which I had to beat back constantly like a swarm of flies.

Desperate for a distraction, I snatched the commander's sketches and notes. I took my time digesting every detail. It seemed that the ambush would take place where the northern border of the Borivali Forest intersected a road leading south from Halithenica. Thanks to the false information, Ambrosine would think our army was on the move from much farther south and would march her army to intercept us in a valley that offered her high ground and favorable conditions. They would think they were surprising us, but we would be waiting for them before they even reached the forest.

After I had read and memorized the commander's notes, I stood up, stretched, and wandered through the aisles of weapons. I withdrew a sword from its pegs and tested it. It was standard-issue but well balanced. The scabbard slid off with a satisfying *shing*, and I raised the blade, pointing it at an imaginary opponent.

One of the guards shouted outside. My blood beat a deafening rhythm in my ears. Had a forester stumbled upon us? Or worse, had Ambrosine discovered our location?

Seizing the hilt in both hands, I ran, my boots pounding up the stairs.

When I reached the surface, I saw the two guards pointing their swords at three men—all blond, all wearing elicrin stones.

Devorian raised his hands to show he meant no harm. Mercer flanked him on the left, a tracking map in his hand, and Tilmorn followed close behind.

My sword dropped to the grass. I staggered into Devorian's arms. Even the cool, hard pressure of his magenta elicrin stone against my cheekbone brought me comfort.

The guards must have stood down. It felt like Devorian and I were the only people left on earth, tethered to it by our shared grief and love.

A freezing wind swirled around us, but he spoke softly to me until my power calmed. "Perennia's at peace now," he said. "I helped put her to rest. She looked so beautiful. After all this, we'll take her home with us."

"I was worried that Ambrosine would trap or tame you and make you do her bidding," I said through tears. I stepped back to look at him. He had braided his shoulder-length hair, which reminded me of Father.

"I cannot be trapped or tamed, Glissy. You should have known better." He frowned up at the ruins of the edifice. "Is this where you've been hiding?"

Leave it Devorian to criticize the accommodations.

"It's more than meets the eye." I turned, smiling through sniffles, to greet Mercer. He scooped me off my feet into a fierce embrace.

"You're a sight for sore eyes," I said.

"So are you."

When he set me down, I met the one eye that was golden-brown as wheaty ale. He looked grim, maybe even a little thinner than when I had seen him a fortnight ago. Long, unpleasant sea voyages could do that to the hardiest among us, but I knew it had more to do with worry.

"Valory?" I asked.

"I found her. She's alive. But it's...hard to explain."

"We're safe here," I said. "Come inside and tell me everything."

As we turned to descend, I found my way to Tilmorn for a quick embrace. He noticed my bloody bandage and placed his thumb in the hollow of my hand to heal me.

"Remember, not the scar," I said.

Power surged from his murky gray elicrin stone and traveled under my skin, closing up my cut.

The old soldiers' mouths dropped open. One of them found the courage to ask Tilmorn if he could heal the leg he had injured saving Navara's grandfather from an assassination attempt. Tilmorn may not have understood his words, but he understood the nature of the request—he received the same everywhere he went. Beneath that stoic, intimidating exterior lived the heart of a Healer, which Melkior had never really possessed. Valory had done the right thing giving them each new gifts. In fact, Valory had done a lot of things right. But the world feared her and always would.

"Right this way," I said, picking my sword from the overgrown grass and leading them down to the edifice. "I think you'll be pleased by what you find."

A Holy had not come, and Navara would be disappointed by that. But this was far better.

Kadri's kidnapping had initially brought Devorian to Perispos. Rynna, who had barely survived the attack, had gathered that the kidnappers planned to take Kadri to Erdem. Devorian had immediately set sail with supplies to make a tracking map for Kadri on the way. He planned to meet up with us at the palace and send Perennia home so that he and I could search for Kadri together.

Mercer and Tilmorn had remained behind with Melkior and Fabian to continue fighting the invasion in the forest, but Mercer had quickly made a connection between the spreading disease and what was happening here in Perispos. Fabian and Melkior stayed behind in Nissera to govern and offer shelter to Rynna's people as the rot spread and worsened. Mercer and Tilmorn had reached the Perispi shore a few hours ago, equipped with tracking maps for all three of us. They'd found Devorian first, who had departed from the palace and was materializing from village to village, asking about me. He had not been able to complete his tracking map for Kadri thanks to a storm that had covered the full moon at sea.

When the three of them reunited, they set out in search of Kadri, who appeared to be closest. According to the map, they had crossed paths with her but had never seen her. Now, looking at the extensive underground tunnels, they understood what had thwarted them.

"When did you make the connection between Ambrosine and the forest rot?" I asked Mercer.

He ran a hand over his tired face and raked it through his sandy hair. "When we found Valory ensnared in the pit. We tried to cut her out, but the growth had become a part of her already. It would have been like cutting off a limb."

"It smells like the bowels of Galgeth," Tilmorn said, tracing his thumb absentmindedly along the scars the Moth King had carved on his face—scars that even his gift could not heal. "The very air is toxic. We could only stay minutes at a time before materializing away. The growth was trying to latch on to us, just like it did to the fay."

"I knew the hollow place left by the Water might attract something," Mercer said. "But how could Valory have been overpowered so easily?"

I saw deep love engraved into the lines of worry on his face. Months ago, I might have averted my eyes, ignored the unwelcome ache in my heart. Now I forced myself to gaze upon it, like staring at the sun, and found it no longer burned.

"The moment we found her, I saw a vision of Ambrosine using Valory's portal to visit the Water," he explained. "We think she lured Valory there and used dark magic to entrap her."

I felt weighed down, like I had swallowed an anchor. Valory may have been mysteriously absent, but the knowledge of her invincibility had nested at the back of my mind, a comfort in the darkest hours. She would get us out of this mess as soon as she could. Nothing could overpower her. She would come to Perispos and end it all with one flick of her wrist.

That sense of safety had been stripped away.

This must have been what Ambrosine meant. *My plan has already been set in motion, but I want you to help me. Help me and be even stronger than Valory.*

Kadri was right. One of the Fallen had invaded the Forest of the West Fringe. It was all part of Ambrosine's plan.

"I could tell Ambrosine was using dark magic," Devorian said as he perused the food options, picking up jars and plunking them back down with a grimace. "In fact, I'm embarrassed to admit that she frightened me."

"She's not *using* dark magic," I said. "The dark magic lives within her. And his name is Vainglory."

After I explained everything to them, I curled on my pallet next to Devorian's and stared at the red dot on Kadri's tracking map by the light of a candle stub. She and Severo had not yet left the palace.

I didn't remember drifting off, but I awoke to Kadri yelling from deep inside the tunnel. I jerked awake, fumbled for my sword in the dark, and ran to the mouth of the passage.

Had someone pursued them from the palace? The convenience of the tunnels came with drawbacks. If even one person on the other side found out about the underground network, this whole operation would be compromised. The commander had considered my elicrin stone valuable enough to risk such danger, but that was before he and Navara had returned to three elicromancers ready to fight for the cause. Their arrival would be nearly enough to temper Navara's disappointment when she found I had not succeeded in summoning a Holy.

I heard the shuffle of distant footsteps—it sounded like two people, thankfully—but I couldn't see what state they were in.

"Kadri?" I called. "Sev?"

A groan echoed down the tunnel. "Help us!" Kadri called.

Behind me, I heard three spells light three elicrin stones. Tilmorn pushed past me and ran to meet them. I sprinted after him.

"Oh, Tilmorn!" Kadri gasped. "Help him! He's lost so much blood."

Tilmorn blocked my view, but as I ran, I caught glimpses of Sev's bare torso and a bloodied dish rag clamped against the wound. His face was greenish-gray, the color of death.

If Tilmorn hadn't come…

I couldn't even ponder it.

"Ambrosine came in while we were searching her bedchamber," Kadri explained, doubling over to catch her breath. "She started talking to her mirror and didn't seem to be leaving anytime soon. We tried to sneak out, but she saw the door open and called for her guards. Sev and I lost hold of each other as we ran. There was a fight, and Sev got stabbed before I was able to cloak him under the spell again. We barely made it out."

"Did anyone see you open the passage?" Commander Larsio asked.

"A guard who stabbed him followed us, but I killed him and dragged him into the tunnel with us," Kadri said.

"Blood trail?" the commander asked.

She shook her head. "Just a bit before we stifled the bleeding. It wouldn't lead them to the passage."

Tilmorn alleviated Sev's pain and restored him to health. Sev searched the faces standing over him, blinking at the ones he didn't recognize.

But when his probing gaze landed on Devorian, he bared his teeth and lunged.

"Sev!" I shouted. "What are you doing?"

Tilmorn held him back, claiming the slightest edge in pure strength, but Sev was more agile. He ducked under Tilmorn's arm and locked a grip around Devorian's throat. Devorian, for his part, did not retaliate with magic. Tilmorn and I were able to drag Sev away.

"He tried to kill me at the palace!" he cried.

"That was his uncle!" Kadri yelled over the commotion. "Elicromancers don't age, so the two look alike."

"It *was* Devorian you saw a few days ago," I explained, gripping his arm in case he planned to attack again. "But he left the palace soon after."

Sev looked from Devorian to Kadri to me, his sweat-slicked chest heaving. Kadri's words sank in. "Why was Mathis there?" I asked.

"When he left the Uprising, he must have realized Ambrosine was his only ally," Kadri said. "She wants to cripple the Realm Alliance as desperately as he does."

"Typical Mathis," Devorian muttered. "Doing whatever is politically expedient without regard for the consequences."

"So, you didn't get the elicrin stone?" I asked. My first hope was to see them return alive, but the disappointment at their failure to retrieve my stone dug deeper than I expected.

"Oh, we did," Kadri said, reaching into her pocket and pulling it out by the chain. She dangled it over her finger. "I probably should have led with that."

THIRTY-EIGHT

GLISETTE

THE summer rains did come, just as Commander Larsio's knees predicted.

For three wet days, we dug and rigged traps where the road met the border of the forest according to his sketches. Larsio traveled from town to town, recruiting trustworthy warriors. He sent some farther south to set up camp. That would be the decoy army, comprised of retired soldiers and inexperienced civilians.

Meanwhile, the commander had discreetly led the young and experienced soldiers to the armory rather than the campsite after rigorously testing their loyalties. Even with elicromancers and the element of surprise, our ambush needed muscle.

Kadri had deceived the Uprising informant about our "plans" to attack the city. We expected Ambrosine to send a scout and ready her troops.

That scout would find an army of hundreds helmed by Navara, Mercer, and Devorian. But when Ambrosine's troops marched to meet them, we would spring our attack. Mercer and Devorian would materialize to help us, and Navara would lead the decoy army onward to reinforce us. Since she wasn't trained to fight, Navara would double back to hide in the armory until the battle's end.

The traps we set at the ambush site were simple canvas-covered pits containing sharpened stakes. My snowstorm would hide the coverings.

When those were ready, sentries stayed behind to keep a lookout while the rest of us returned to the armory. Weapons, waterskins, and stores of food and ale were distributed. By our estimation, Ambrosine's army would be on the march by tomorrow morning. There was little left to do besides wait.

Mercer and I huddled with Kadri to try to teach her whatever spells she might need, but her marksmanship gift would be more useful than any spell.

"I told Glisette she can't be my tutor back home," Kadri said, eyeing me. "She's too bossy."

"Glisette? Bossy?" Mercer cocked his head.

"No matter what conditions I survive, you will always imagine me as a spoon-fed, demanding brat, won't you?"

Mercer laughed his deep, resounding laugh and threw an arm around my shoulder. "I see the Ice Queen still hasn't learned to tolerate jokes at her expense."

I flicked his ear, surprising him. "And the Prophet still can't predict what's coming next," I retorted playfully.

Mercer feigned hurt at my retaliation and Kadri laughed. She'd been cheerful since she'd learned that Tilmorn had been able to heal Rynna from the Jav Darhu's poison.

I wandered over to the casks of watered-down ale to refill my flagon, weaving around clusters of young soldiers who couldn't pry their eyes off of me. Whether it was my beauty, my resemblance to Ambrosine, or both, they studied me like a newly discovered specimen.

My fingers trembled as I turned the spout. I had survived the raid on Darmeska, but I was just as frightened now. The nightmares had never left me, and I wouldn't forget the pain of the injuries that Rynna's nectar had healed. Diversion seemed to be the only tool to assuage my fears. Tipping my full flagon back, I took a gulp and looked around for Sev.

I found him sitting on a crate, sharpening his hunting knife. But he wasn't paying as much attention to the task. Instead, he was watching me.

I smiled. He returned a half smile and refocused on his work.

I made my way over to him and nudged his boot with the toe of mine. "Are you worried?" I asked, claiming a nearby crate.

He pursed his lips. "No, not really."

"Then why are you so quiet? You've avoided me all evening."

He studied me for a moment before shooting his steely gaze to Mercer. "You chart your course by him like he's the North Star."

"No, I don't."

"I see you looking for him whenever he leaves your side."

I shook my head. "If I'm looking for anyone, it's you."

He scoffed. "You have your life, and I have mine. Maybe it seemed otherwise for a few days, but it's just the truth."

"He is a dear friend to me. Nothing more."

"Are you sure of that?"

"More than ever," I said. "For a time, I thought I loved him. But it was because of what we went through together."

"And what about this?" he asked, gesturing between him and me. "Is it temporary? A diversion from the fear and pain? Will we return to our lives and forget?"

"I don't want to," I said, my face heating. I thought of the way I had clung to him in the edifice when I pretended to be his bride, the way he kicked dirt over the fire so we could kiss in the dark. "But you're warm to me one minute and cold the next. If there's any hesitation on my side, it's because I don't know whether you desire me or are simply going along with it because circumstances thrust us together—"

He stood up. I thought he would storm off, but he caught my hand and led me down one of the long aisles. We stopped in front of baskets overflowing with fur cloaks, which we would most certainly need on the morrow when I brought the freezing weather.

After making sure we had privacy, he turned to face me. "I didn't mean to be cold. I just wanted to give you space with him, if you wanted it."

"I don't want it."

"Glisette," he breathed. "I care for you, and I have from the moment I realized you were different from Ambrosine. You've surprised me every day since."

"I have?"

He nodded.

"You've surprised me too," I said. "I thought you were rude."

"I can be."

"And humorless."

A smile crossed his lips. "Only to people who don't know me. But you know me better than most already."

I leaned back against the shelf, planting my hands on my hips. This time, I wanted him to come to me. I blinked up at him, letting my eagerness show on my face.

He stepped closer and propped his hand on the shelf above my head. "I'd like to kiss you again," he said softly.

"By all means."

His callused fingers streamed through my hair as he pressed his lips against mine. A moan escaped and I kissed him back, tugging him flush against me in the shadows.

But a flagon bounced off the ground, jarring us, and several soldiers responded to the gaff with rowdy laughs. No one could see us, but the ruckus served as a reminder that we weren't alone.

We gradually pulled apart, Sev's breaths heaving with desire and his starry eyes studying my mouth.

"That should give you something to fight for," I said. "I mean, other than your seven brothers and sisters, your mother, your princess, your kingdom—"

"My what?" His voice rumbled against my mouth. "I've forgotten everything but the taste of your lips."

I grinned. We stole every second that we could but eventually forced ourselves to rejoin the others.

"Enjoy yourself?" Kadri asked quietly as I sat beside her.

"What do you mean?"

"You're glowing."

I laughed, though worry hedged out my momentary joy. Tilmorn had returned from healing everyone who had the slightest ache or ailment, but Navara, who had been following him around to watch him work, was nowhere to be seen. "Where's Navara?" I asked.

"She said she was going to pray," Kadri answered. "Poor girl. She's frightened."

Yawning, I stood up. I would need to rest for tomorrow,

especially to generate a powerful storm. But until everyone else started unrolling their pallets and snuffing out the candles, I wouldn't be able to sleep.

The vault door was cracked open. I decided to slip out and find Navara in the abandoned Edifice of the Holies, perhaps make one more attempt to call down a deity.

When I stepped into the Edifice of the Fallen, the dark whispers returned.

But this time, they laughed. A thousand voices mingled as one, all laughing at me.

I spun around to the portrait of Themera to stare her down, tell her I was not afraid. I half expected to find her bloodred lips parted in laughter.

But I found Navara sprawled on the dirt floor of the edifice, her eyes a bright, reflective silver.

"Navara!" I tried to shake her awake while the guards trampled down the stairs at the sound of my cry. I set my head against her chest to listen for a heartbeat and whimpered at the sound of silence. Her skin was so cold, and her irises glinted like salmon scales.

A breathy chuckle made the hairs on my neck prickle. I looked up at the edifice mirror, standing open on its hinges, and found a shadowy outline of Ambrosine surrounded by a dark glow, like the ring around the moon during an eclipse.

I could have used the same shattering spell I'd used while trying to escape Ambrosine's illusions in the palace. But I reeled back and drove my first into the glass, roaring with anger.

The mirror burst into shards. The laughter stopped.

Navara heaved a breath like she'd been drowning and finally surfaced. She blinked away the silver from her wide, wild eyes, and one of the guards helped her stand.

"She tricked me," she gasped. "I thought it was real."

"Thought what was real?" I demanded.

Navara stumbled forward and clutched my sleeve. "She looked like an old woman who approached my parents and me on the street when I was a child. She offered me a perfect apple, but I was afraid of her because she was bent and covered in warts. I was so young and I didn't know better. So I said no and ran away. Later, Mother told me that I couldn't be a true leader if I did not look upon everyone with kindness." She coughed and massaged her throat. "I always regretted not taking the gift. It used to make me think I would be a terrible queen. I hoped my parents would have a son so I wouldn't have to be."

I rubbed her shoulder and thought of the twisted memories Ambrosine had shown me in the mirrors. Myron must have told her this story.

"I didn't want to make the same mistake again," Navara said. "So when the old woman offered me the apple, I took it. I had a bad feeling, like before, but I knew my mother would want me to. I took a bite, and then I couldn't breathe. I was choking. The woman's face changed to Ambrosine's. That's the last thing I remember until you came."

"You were a child, Navara. That moment didn't mean anything." I took her hand in mine. "You have already made a good and valiant leader. Come, let's go back inside."

As I stepped over the glass to lead her in, an icy fear pierced my heart. If Ambrosine could find Navara in a mirror, did that mean she had found our army? That she knew of our plans? Or perhaps all she knew was that Navara was hiding in an Edifice of the Fallen. The whole country was full of them. Surely, she wouldn't be able to tell one apart from the other.

Did Themera, who pursued me so relentlessly, know where I was, or was she reaching out blindly from the darkness to which the Holies had banished her?

If Themera knew where I was, I decided, Nexantius and Ambrosine would have found us by now.

Hopefully, Ambrosine had found Navara in the mirror because she could not find her in person. Hopefully, she had had merely chanced upon her nemesis on some other plane, the shadow universe of reflections that she and Nexantius ruled together. Otherwise, she would be here.

I resolved to finish this, to make sure Navara survived no matter what it took from me.

But it would not be easy. Navara was growing in power and beauty, and Ambrosine's envious heart would not rest until one or both of them were dead.

❧ THIRTY-NINE ❧

KADRI

I TESTED the draw of the bow from the armory. Compared to the gorgeous bow Rynna had given me, it was lousy. But everything crafted by human hands seemed lousy by comparison.

Despite the early summer rain, the dawn was too warm for the heavy furs, leather gloves, and winter boots we wore. As the squadron gathered around and prepared to move out for the ambush, sweat beaded on my brow and raindrops tickled my scalp.

I stood next to Glisette, a quiver packed with arrows slung over my shoulder. Her brows sketched a rigid line, and there was worry in her eyes.

Our scout had reported that Ambrosine's army was indeed on the move, marching south on the road from Halithenica.

Sev stood beside Glisette with a crossbow in his gloved grip and several knives strapped to his belt. He wore his weapons as naturally as Glisette wore flowing dresses—like he had been born wearing them.

In front of the broken edifice steps, Navara mounted a bay courser the commander had brought from camp. She looked like a little girl, straddled across the twitching muscles of the warhorse's broad back.

But when she drew her sword to speak to the anxious, sweating warriors, she seemed to fill out, to grow taller, stronger, and less afraid.

The elicromancers were satisfied to stay in the shadows and let her give off her own light, brighter than any elicrin stone in the eyes of her people. The army seemed wary of us anyway—especially of Glisette, who looked too much like Ambrosine.

"An impostor sits on our throne," Navara said. "I refuse to let my great kingdom fall at the feet of a liar and snake. The people of Perispos will rise up and reclaim what belongs to us."

This earned a cheer from the soldiers. She punched her sword in the air, feeding on their enthusiasm. As she led the horse back and forth in a jaunty, proud parade of one, the wet wind raked back her short hair, showcasing her lovely features and the fire in her deep brown eyes. I could see her arm trembling with the weight of the sword, but I doubted her admirers cared a bit.

"The people of Perispos are strong," she went on. "We are warriors at heart—sons and daughters of Atrelius. We may be mortals, but we will long outlive the queen's tyranny."

The responding cheers and hollers were so loud I felt them vibrating in my chest.

"She's good at this," I said to Glisette.

"She is," she agreed.

When Navara finished, we wished good luck to her, Mercer, and Devorian, who were going off with the decoy army. Glisette clung to her brother for a long time, long enough that we had to run to catch up with the rest of the soldiers following Commander Larsio to the ambush site.

Many of our fellow ambushers carried short spears that could be easily thrown from treetops or bushes, while others, like me, carried bows and quivers. Glisette carried a sword. But armed with her elicrin stone, she probably wouldn't need it. I remembered the wall of ice she had created to break down the bridge at Darmeska, and the fluttering fear in my belly stilled for a moment.

We moved stealthily, hiking for an hour through mist-shrouded forest hills before we had to navigate around the traps at the ambush site. The high-branching beech trees with smooth gray bark had been stripped of some of their leaves in Glisette's first storm, but the silver firs crowding around them offered enough cover for us. I tried to toss my rope around a strong limb and succeeded on the fourth try. I bit off my gloves so I could tie a secure friction knot like Sev had shown me, then looped the rope into a makeshift harness and hoisted myself high, mounting a strong branch. Grateful for the strength in my healed ankle, I reeled in the rope and tucked it into my pack.

A few dozen other soldiers did the same, while many others took their places in the low brush. I saw Sev claim the tree next to me and watched Tilmorn cross to the other side of the road.

Glisette approached the edge of the forest. I looked out from the green boughs to the rolling hills and found the outline of Halithenica, a tiny shadow at the horizon.

Even this far away, I could distinguish a mass of warriors marching down the road.

My heart sank to my bowels, and my grip on the sturdy branch weakened. I had survived one battle, but what if that was thanks to sheer luck?

Glisette stood next Commander Larsio, waiting.

It seemed an agonizing eternity before the army drew close enough that my eyes could separate one soldier from another.

Most of the army was infantry. A small cavalry pulled up the rear. Their ranks formed a long, thin line that snaked down the road, which was ideal for an ambush; we could engage small numbers of them at a time. Some might even turn back or scatter when they realized they had encountered an attack. We had planned for that.

I had told the altar girl, Damiatta, of our plans, pretending I hadn't noticed how her eyes sparked with cunning. Thanks to her information, Ambrosine and her commander thought they had no reason to be alarmed. They thought they would beat our army to the valley beyond the woods. They anticipated a pitched battle that would give them the upper hand.

Glisette and Commander Larsio exchanged glances. The time had come.

The battle was beginning.

I closed my eyes and thought of Rynna, of Rayed, and of Valory, who suffered in stillness and despair. I thought of all the homes I had known and loved, from the lush, stormy Erdem to the sunny beaches of Beyrian, to the mystical beauty of Wenryn. I thought of Lucrez, who had been so brave and unexpectedly selfless, and Perennia, who had died trying to hold her fractured family together.

When I opened my eyes again, Glisette had lifted her hands, preparing to bring wrath down on her sister's army.

Hunkered in the high branches, I sank into my furs for warmth, bracing myself for what would come.

The biting wind howled in my ears until they ached. The rain turned to hard sleet, and then to swirling snow. Glisette shaped the storm with her gestures like a potter shaping clay.

It stalled over us, churning until I had to shield my face. When I dared look again, a thick layer of snow covered the ground.

With a great thrust, Glisette pushed the storm out from the forest toward the fast-approaching infantry.

Helmets flew off, and even a few crest-shaped shields caught gusts and blew away. Most of the cavalry dismounted and tried to harry their horses onward, but the beasts preferred turning their rumps to the freezing wind.

Good. The infantry would be exhausted by the time they reached us.

Glisette backed into the forest and let her arms drop, palms down, as though taming a wild beast. The winds dissipated. The fresh snow settled down quietly around us. Then the precipitation turned back from snow to misty rain.

Ambrosine's army regrouped as much as possible and pressed on. I repositioned myself in my tree to find the best firing position. My fingers brushed the fletching of an arrow in my quiver, anxious to send it flying, anxious for this to be over.

I nocked it, relishing the creak of the string and the magic pumping through my veins—my Marksman gift was more ready than I was.

I aimed at the road and waited for the front row of soldiers to struggle through the deep snow. An inconspicuous stake in the ground marked our attack zone.

I set my sights on one of the frontrunners, aiming for his heart.

His arm had tired of holding the shield against the wind. It drooped, leaving his chest exposed.

As soon as my target passed the stake, I let fly. My arrow struck its mark.

Several other archers hit their targets, while others struck shields or snow. Chaos erupted in the enemy ranks. The outer ends of the first two rows began to collapse like metal folding as it melted, their cries of sudden anguish revealing their surprise.

To avoid trampling the victims, the rows behind them split and veered off the road. The traps waited for them beneath the cloak of snow.

I nocked another arrow while the second group of archers let fly. I set my sights on a mark and struck him in the neck. Killing meant silencing a small voice in my mind that said all war was evil, no matter the cause. But these weren't helpless civilians or people who had been magically forced to do the Moth King's bidding. They had chosen their fate.

If we didn't defeat Ambrosine, the scourges of the Fallen would devastate this world until nothing remained but miserable souls.

Blood spattered over the pure, bright snow. As the bodies piled up at the front ranks and the hidden traps on their side of the road were revealed, the second group of enemy soldiers fanned out along the edges of the woods.

Glisette took one side of the road and Tilmorn the other, each sending spells that wiped out clusters of soldiers before they could even cross into the forest. I had used the thrusting spell to good effect already, but my uncertainty had given it only a tenth of the intensity that these two could muster. When they yelled *"Nagak,"* entire groups of armor-clad men soared for several yards and landed hard.

As our ambush split the front ranks like an axe splitting a log, the cavalry pushed to the fore. With Glisette and Tilmorn protecting us from the wave of oncoming soldiers, I had the perfect chance to reach a better vantage point for the next phase: targeting the mounted warriors.

I retied my rope and shimmied down, leaping into the snow and sinking deep. The shots from the trees were thinning out, clearing a way for me to duck and run to the pile of bodies without fearing friendly fire. I collected stray arrows from the snow on my way.

Approaching the heap of bodies in chain mail, I dropped to one knee and slid my bow off to load an arrow.

The cavalry tried to break through the ranks of struggling foot soldiers, many of whom were fleeing back toward the city. I couldn't blame them; Glisette and Tilmorn made a fearful sight, their elicrin stones as bright as stars behind the gray curtain of misty rain, their spells discarding enemies like pieces on a game board.

I blinked the rain from my eyes and stretched my bowstring, aiming for the frontrunner of the cavalry, who steered his horse around the disorganized groups of foot soldiers. The commander had explained that the army's chain mail could be penetrated with enough force and precision.

My elicrin gift wrapped around my ligaments and muscles like warm fibers. I closed my eyes to release the arrow, trusting my magic to take over.

When I opened my eyes, the leader of the cavalry toppled off his horse in a spray of blood. My shot had struck true.

But before I managed to secure another arrow, a hard force hit my side and flattened me on the ground.

It was an enemy warrior. An arrow protruded from his left shoulder, but his right fist wound back to strike me in the face.

"*Sokek sinna*," I rasped, erecting the glimmering shield just in time for him to break his hand on its solid surface. He shouted and clambered off of me. I let down my shield and leapt to my feet, but he had already grabbed a nearby sword and slashed at my thigh, splitting the skin. I yelped and clamped down on the wound, nearly losing my wits before I used the slashing spell to tear the flesh across his throat. He gurgled for breath and collapsed.

I limped to retrieve my bow and arrow, looking for something to bind up the gaping wound. But I needed to slow down this cavalry before it was too late. Screaming through my teeth, I dropped to my knees to take cover again, my hands shaking as I nocked another arrow.

Someone gripped my shoulder, and in the dizzying clamor and confusion, I saw Mercer leaning over me, rain dripping from his face and hair. His bone-white eye served as a devastating reminder that even triumph didn't prevent us from carrying battle scars for the rest of our lives, both outside and in.

Mercer tore a piece of his black tunic and said, "Just until Tilmorn can get to you."

I nodded and accepted the strip of wool, knotting it tight around the open cut. Mercer sprinted to join Tilmorn at the front lines.

When I looked up, the other elicromancers had wiped out half of the foot soldiers and the cavalry was charging. Pain somehow sharpened my focus, and I took out one mounted fighter after another, my aim consistently truer than any mortal's could have been—although I would have done a fine job as a mortal. Sev joined me behind the barricade of bodies, his wet face and hands streaked with blood. He abandoned the crossbow for a longbow and took several shots that synchronized with mine and struck accurately most of the time, although he did hit horse instead of rider twice.

Finally, Ambrosine's army broke up enough to allow hope that this battle might end soon, at least as far as mortals were concerned. These soldiers didn't stand a chance. Glisette could probably drive most of the remaining men away with another torrential snowstorm.

But there was Ambrosine to contend with, and maybe even Mathis. I knew which side had better odds; five elicromancers versus two was almost a sure bet for us, especially considering Mathis's and Ambrosine's elicromancy restrictions. But with Nexantius involved, it was more complicated. I had no idea what would happen next.

As the army thinned out, I glimpsed Ambrosine at the rear of the procession. She rode a black warhorse and wore scant metal armor that revealed too much of her ivory flesh to offer any protection. Glorious blond braids whipped behind her, wet from the snowstorm, and even from afar I caught flashes of silver in her eyes.

She drew closer, and those flashes became swirling streaks, spilling over every bit of exposed flesh to coat her contours in intricate designs of reflective metal.

A carriage with iron bars and wooden slats rolled alongside her, pulled by two black horses with wild, frightened eyes, steered by an even more frightened soldier.

Was this some kind of beast Ambrosine planned to unleash? A prisoner she would use to manipulate us? Land of light—what if she had somehow caught and trapped Navara?

Ambrosine signaled two fingers at the driver. He dismounted from the carriage seat and unlocked the peg latch of the iron cage.

The door swung open.

❧ FORTY ❧

GLISETTE

T HE creature that crawled out of the shadows of the cage was far more frightening than the edifice murals could ever convey.

Its flesh looked like what should lie *underneath* flesh—red, raw, sinewy, stripped down. Short, sharp teeth lined an unnaturally wide mouth and longer, tusklike teeth jutted from its skull and knotty knuckles.

Somehow both gaunt and muscular, the monster crept out of the cage on four limbs... and lunged to devour the man who had set it free.

I shut my eyes to the horrible sight, but I couldn't shut out the screams.

Robivoros.

When I opened them, the beast had consumed its fill, leaving nothing but picked bones. It stood on its hind legs, revealing an open maw in the middle of its belly, lined with two rows of needle-sharp teeth.

There was only one person Ambrosine could have convinced to become a vessel for this being, just by flaunting the promise of power. The vague similarities—the height, the stride, the stray fair hairs clinging to the red scalp—proved that this was, or used to be, Uncle Mathis.

My stomach heaved and I bent double, but I managed to swallow back the sickness. I had no choice.

Ambrosine had set her sights on me.

She dismounted, trudging through the snow, trampling over the bodies of her fallen soldiers.

Mercer and Tilmorn charged to fight Mathis while Kadri took several clean shots at him, lodging arrows in his chest and even one in his forehead to no avail.

Devorian drew even with me, his magenta elicrin stone glowing, ready to unleash an arsenal of spells on Ambrosine.

"Her armor can deflect spells," I told him.

"Lovely," he muttered. "Our odds are excellent. Think we can appeal to her sense of familial affection?"

"I'd say it's a bit late for that. I'm going to try something. If it doesn't work, we're only stalling the inevitable."

"I like your optimism. If you survive and I don't, do you promise to take care of Larabelle?"

"Better than you ever could." I managed to smile at him. "If you survive and I don't, will you care for Sev's family?"

"They'll be drowning in wealth. Suffocating."

"Let's see if this works."

I stretched out my arms, inhaled a sense of calm, and summoned my elicrin power.

The rain fell in a continuous mist, but my wind made the drops change directions and swirl into a funnel. The temperature plummeted and I drove the freezing water at Ambrosine, encasing her in a column of ice as high and thick as a tower.

But after a few beats of quiet, her silver-plated fists broke through the ice, shattering it as I had shattered her mirrors.

This would be the end. Kadri's gift and mine were the only ones suited for the battlefield. If Ambrosine could deflect every spell, then Devorian, Mercer, and Tilmorn couldn't do much. Even Kadri and I would only be able to slow Ambrosine and Mathis down.

As Ambrosine gained ground, I readied the shielding spell on my tongue. But Devorian panicked and uttered the thrusting spell first in an effort to keep her at bay. She raised an arm to deflect it and it rebounded, striking me hard in the chest.

I flew back and crashed through the snow, landing hard. The brutal fall beat the breath out of my lungs. I was fortunate that I hadn't smacked into a tree or an armored corpse, but the pain was agonizing.

I *told* Devorian it wouldn't work.

With a groan, I coaxed myself up and found Devorian erecting a shield. But Ambrosine, swiftly approaching, bared her teeth and punched the barrier. Instead of breaking her hand, as it would anyone else's, the barrier became flexible, bending with her force. She struck Devorian hard across the jaw and he collapsed where he stood, knocked unconscious, maybe even...

No.

The rage I felt nested so deep in my soul that my entire body shook with the need to destroy her.

"Pull back!" I heard the commander call to whoever was still fighting in the woods.

Now it was only us—the elicromancers who had allowed this to happen. The elicromancers who had to finish this or die trying.

Accepting my fate, I let anger conquer logic and strategy. Logic and strategy would do nothing for me anymore.

I drew my sword and charged at Ambrosine.

Roaring, I swung my blade down on her shoulder. It broke to shards. My arm bounced back and our bodies collided with bruising force. The momentum was on her side, and we tumbled down together.

My head careened, and stars twinkled in my vision. Before I could blink them away, Ambrosine smacked me across the face, the armor coating her hand more rigid than a gauntlet. Warm blood filled my mouth and nose. But I realized I was still gripping the hilt—all that remained of my broken sword—and slammed it into her jaw.

The sound was of metal hitting metal. She didn't even flinch.

"You aligned yourself with the wrong people," she said, pinning both of my wrists to the ground with her iron grip. "Family used to come first, but you changed."

"*You* changed," I barked through the blood pooling in my mouth. I could feel that my nose had been jammed off-center, the bone and cartilage crooked. I squirmed beneath Ambrosine. Her knees locked around my hips like a vise, trapping me in place. I tried to materialize, but her armor gave her the power to anchor me there. My shoulders strained at their sockets and I halted the attempt before it ripped me limb from limb.

One more blow to the head and I would likely cross that veil of death, forsaking this world to the hands of the Fallen.

But not without a better fight than this.

My power answered my summons, and the falling raindrops flocked together and froze into icicles with points as sharp as knives. I flicked my finger and drove them down her spine, but they shattered on her armor just like the sword.

The thunder of a cavalry approaching from the woods made her loosen her grip on one of my wrists so she could look at the road. Our reinforcements had arrived.

I used the distraction to try the most desperate thing I could think of—attacking her vanity. I gripped a generous handful of her fair hair and yanked as hard as I could, ripping a whole patch out by the roots.

When she squealed, she sounded exactly like the Ambrosine I knew, the Ambrosine who could be more easily manipulated by threats to her beauty than threats to her life.

The diversion allowed me to kick her away and stagger to my feet. I had to warn our reinforcements to turn back, to take up shelter in the armory. I had to tell Sev and every other ambusher left alive to go with them, to keep resisting, to try to find another way to banish the Fallen.

I materialized to the tree line and stumbled into the shadows. So many bodies sprawled over the battleground, and I was afraid to see a familiar face among them. Most of the ambushers had retreated and scattered to hide in the forest. Had Sev left too?

Setting my back to a tree, I peered at the road and saw that Navara was leading the reinforcements. I spat a curse. She was supposed to have doubled back and returned to the safety of the armory. Why hadn't she? She wasn't ready for this.

"Glisette!" I turned to see Sev kicking through the snow toward me. Watered-down blood stained his face and neck, but he didn't seem to be wounded, at least not gravely so. My heart leapt with joy at seeing him alive, but fear gripped me anew. He needed to go back with the other mortals.

When he reached me, he cupped my jaw and winced at my face. "That bad?" I asked.

"You can't outlast her," he said. "We have to retreat and regroup."

"I have to stall them while you get Navara and the others to safety."

"I'm not going to—"

"Go!" I splayed a hand on his chest and pushed, but he didn't budge. "Go, or it will be too late for everyone. They need you, Sev."

He shook his head, but I could see my words wearing down his obstinacy. We both knew there were things far more important than the way we felt about each other.

With a sigh of surrender, he gently kissed my bruised, bloodied lips and ran off to intercept Navara and the reinforcements.

Buttressing my resolve, I turned and saw traces of a glimmering magical shield through the trees. I materialized back onto the open field and found Devorian, Kadri, Mercer, and Tilmorn combining their elicrin shields to protect the mortals in retreat.

It wasn't a strategy for victory. None of us had a plan other than to try to mitigate the damage. This was a losing battle, and it would be over soon.

I hurried to join their ranks, coaxing the shield from my elicrin stone with a whisper. It expanded like a beautiful starflower in bloom and reached out to meld with Devorian's.

His face looked worse than mine felt, but through his swollen, broken skin, I could read the meaningful look he turned my way: this was the end, and if we had to die, at least we would die fighting together.

I looked over my shoulder to see the ranks of reinforcements riding away. From behind the heaps of carnage on the road, Navara met my eyes before she guided her courser around, the last one to retreat.

Ambrosine glared, singling me out to face her wrath first. Mathis prowled at the other end of the chain, blood slinging from his sharp teeth as he crept on all fours toward Tilmorn, a predator ready to lunge at his prey. Kadri's arrows studded his flesh, but they didn't seem to be doing much to slow him down.

"Go get the girl like I told you!" Ambrosine shouted at him. Though she hadn't recognized signs of our ambush, she saw this shield for what it was: a stalling tactic. Mathis growled at Tilmorn but tore off down the tree line to skirt around the shields, moving faster than a rabid wolf. Tilmorn and Mercer materialized away to give chase.

Not Navara. Not those innocent people.

It was I who was most responsible for offering Ambrosine lenience, for letting her wed a king instead of sending her to wallow in a prison cell.

Ambrosine charged at my shield. I separated mine from the others' and made the cold wind howl until the rain began to freeze in sheets around Kadri and Devorian. The dense silver-blue ice rose up like a blockade, gleaming in the low light, shutting out the sound of their protests. I knew they didn't want my protection, but they were going to get it.

Ambrosine's armored fists collided with my shield. I reinforced the spell, calling every ounce of magic in my blood to the fore to resist. It held, bending only a little, but the sheer strength of Ambrosine's newfound powers drove my heels through the snow like a plow until we had returned to the shadows of the winter forest.

Both of us cried out with the effort. I couldn't hold her for long. When she reeled back a fist and slammed it into the shield, this time it broke through and rammed into my chest.

The blow struck me like a runaway carriage. I hit the trunk of a tree, collapsing onto the cold, soft ground.

A metal shield left by one of the enemy soldiers lay half buried in snow nearby. The steel reflected a warped, blurred view of my face, unrecognizable from abuse.

It also reflected movements behind me, and I heard the grunts of a struggle. I turned to find Commander Larsio attempting to help a gravely wounded mortal soldier retreat.

Above them, in the treetops, the creature Ambrosine had helped create prowled.

I shouted a warning from where I lay. The commander looked up and shielded his face as Mathis lunged. But Tilmorn intervened in a blur of strength and speed, catching the brunt of the attack while the commander and the wounded man escaped.

Mathis's teeth went to work. Tilmorn tried to heal himself even as the flesh was ripped from his bones and limbs were torn asunder.

I screamed and turned my ravaged face away. After all we had survived, Ambrosine would bring our downfall.

A strange peace fell over me, as soft as falling snow but as warm as sunshine. It was time to say farewell to this world. It was time to die.

Two twinkling golden specks bloomed in my vision like newborn stars. One was bright as a lantern and nearly within reach on my left side, right where the enemy shield had been a moment ago. The other speck waited beyond the border of the forest, flickering like a distant candle flame. I watched them blink, wondering if they would lead me to the land of light if I followed them.

Ambrosine towered over me, blocking out the distant light. She spoke, but her voice sounded far away. The quiet was thick in my ears, the light of the nearest golden speck growing brighter.

Curious, I reached out a trembling hand to touch it.

My fingertip bumped something solid. It was still the metal shield, lodged halfway in the snow. But it was no longer steel and crest-shaped, a discarded piece of enemy armor. Instead, it was round and golden as the sun.

I stretched to claim it, seizing its rim and raking it over the snow toward me. "That's not going to save you," Ambrosine said through a laugh, her voice echoing from somewhere distant.

The strap settled over my hand, a perfect fit, supple and warm beneath my touch. Ambrosine lifted her armored foot to strike me hard in the face. I swung up the shield to block her, expecting it to dent or break or crumble to dust just like my sword.

But it held.

"Where did you get that?" Ambrosine demanded, panic rising, as though she could just now see the glow of magic beaming from the shield. I heard the overlap of Nexantius's deep voice with hers. Perhaps, for the first time, the Fallen felt he had something to fear.

My gaze shot to the other golden glow, the distant one. Blood clogged my airways and my eyes were beginning to swell, but if I could just make it there, to that light, I knew what I would find.

Gritting my teeth, I drove the shield at Ambrosine, shoving her out of the way as I rose up.

I ran, leaping over fallen soldiers, kicking up bloody snow. I stumbled, but I saw that the light awaiting me in the distance had taken the shape of a sword, and I pressed on. The hilt was the same ordinary one I'd carried into battle and abandoned when Ambrosine shattered the blade. But the blade had regenerated, like a Healer's gift regrowing a severed limb. The new one glowed as if fresh from the forge, the glaring gold of pure power.

I heard Ambrosine calling out behind me. I lunged for the sword, scooped up the hilt, and found it lightweight and easy to wield despite its massive size. Like two old friends meeting, the golden sword and shield belonged as a pair.

My strength and hope renewed, I whirled just in time to block Ambrosine's incoming blow with the shield. I swiped the sword and she ducked. I swiped again and she evaded, but this time she stumbled and fell on her back in the snow. She had never been a fighter.

"Glisette, wait!" she cried, but her voice did not belong to her. It was Nexantius who cried out. They were one and the same.

The crisp sound of snow beneath my boots seemed deafening as I stepped up and stood over her. I raised the golden sword and, in spite of her protests, I jammed it deep into her chest.

A piercing, horrid scream tore over the battlefield.

Ambrosine's body quaked. Her flesh and bone wrestled with itself until she choked and a black substance dribbled from her lips.

She gagged and coughed out more of the dark bile, which collected in a pool and sank into the snow like ink.

Her silver armor turned to sparkling dust and blew away. The liquid silver drained from her eyes, leaving them blue green and fearful.

I yanked my sword from her chest. It left no visible wound.

The Mathis-creature came tearing out from the trees, slinging gore as it charged at me. I tossed the hilt to change my grip and threw the weapon like a spear. It sank deep into the gaping mouth in his belly and shot back out, the hilt landing squarely in my grip.

Another scream, another convulsion, and both of the creature's mouths spat out black bile. Robivoros retreated, leaving Mathis gaunt, pale, and shuddering.

Kadri jogged toward us and shot an arrow straight through his throat.

Mathis collapsed, never to rise again.

Ambrosine palmed away the black bile from her lips and knelt. "Glisette," she whispered. "What's happened? I don't remember anything. I only recall a dark haze—"

"Stop lying!" I roared.

"I'm not—"

"You have terrorized the people of Perispos. Your time is done."

I raised my sword to strike her down, but I couldn't bring myself to deal the final blow, to end her life.

I saw Devorian out of the corner of my eye. He stopped in his tracks. He could have said a spell, almost any spell, to finish her. Yet he couldn't do it either.

Now I understood why Ambrosine had commanded Sev to murder me instead of doing it herself.

But Navara stepped out from the trees, her fur cloak and cropped black hair catching the wind. She unsheathed her sword and approached Ambrosine from behind.

I offered her a nod, giving her permission to do what I could not.

Navara swung her sword point-up and closed her eyes, as if praying for Ambrosine's soul, or for preemptive forgiveness. Then, without a moment's hesitation, she reared back and pushed the sword between Ambrosine's shoulder blades.

I forced myself not to look away as the blade ripped through her, the sharp point jutting out from the wall of her chest.

My strike had ended Nexantius. Navara's would end my sister, forever.

As Ambrosine caved into the wound, breathing her last breath, I dropped to my knees in the snow and buried my face in my hands.

When I lifted my eyes, I found a smooth landscape of snow reflecting golden sunlight. There were no dead warriors or scattered weapons. No Ambrosine, no Navara.

Instead, a woman in brilliant gold armor stood before me. She had gray-streaked black hair, eyes like liquid gold, and softly glowing skin.

"Hesper?" I asked in disbelief.

"Atrelius," she answered. "We came as soon as we could."

"We?"

Another figure stepped into view. Warm tears filled my eyes and spilled over.

Her eyes and hair were the same shade of molten gold, and she wore a fluid dress that looked like it had been knit out of morning sunrays.

"Perennia," I breathed.

"Perennia is at peace," the newcomer answered.

"She's...in the land of light?" I asked.

The golden woman in the gown nodded, her eyes soft. This was Eulippa. I'd called them both down when I had spilled my blood in the clay bowls at the abandoned edifice. "The journey beyond takes time if the bonds of earthly love are strong, and we had to wait for the two pure souls who had died at our altar to cross over. We do not share a body with another soul, or take what is not freely given."

"Glisette!" Devorian cried from a world away. I felt him shake my shoulders.

I blinked and the vision of Perennia, or Eulippa, was gone, and so was Atrelius.

I collapsed in his arms, weeping. Weeping because Perennia was gone again, and because she was never really here. Weeping that the Holies could not have come sooner. Weeping for Tilmorn because I knew in my heart he had not been able to heal himself rapidly enough survive the attack, and for Mercer, who had only reunited with him months ago.

For Ambrosine, for who she used to be and who she might have been.

❦ FORTY-ONE ❦

GLISETTE

GRIEF hung in the air, sharper than cold and thicker than snow.

Or maybe it only seemed that way to the four of us.

The mortal soldiers celebrated Ambrosine's defeat. The unused reinforcements were happy to help clear the road, drag the enemy dead to trenches, and care for our wounded soldiers so that those who fought could rest.

Mercer wept while Commander Larsio and Sev prepared Tilmorn's remains for the pyre. They discouraged us from looking at him until the flames began to consume him. But after seeing Robivoros's other victims, I had an all-too-clear image in my mind. Devorian, Kadri, and I laid our hands on Mercer and wept alongside him. I cried until I had no more tears.

We held a ceremony for Tilmorn, bidding him farewell. Mercer would return to collect his ashes, but none of us wanted Valory to suffer a moment longer than necessary, Mercer least of all.

I offered him the glowing sword of Atrelius. "Go get her," I whispered.

He planted a kiss on my brow and materialized to the palace to find the portal box Ambrosine had stolen.

Devorian and I leaned on each other, pressing packs of snow to our wounds.

Word of our victory had spread to Halithenica like a grassfire.

A parade awaited Navara in the streets. Her people tossed garlands in her path and shoved one another aside so that they could touch her boots, or even just a hair of her horse's tail. She was their divine leader. They would hear the story that she had slain Ambrosine herself, and it was the story they needed to hear.

Navara accepted the praise gracefully, punching her sword high. But I could see the tension between her shoulder blades, the desperation to reach her father.

Once inside the palace, she ran to the Edifice of the Fallen. Kadri, Devorian, and I followed, smashing mirrors to banish any lingering foul magic.

Everyone we encountered looked relieved beyond belief; any willing ally of Ambrosine's would have fled to escape punishment.

I thought Navara might lead us to some dark underground passage, but instead she ran straight for Ambrosine's bedchamber, where we encountered Mercer and Valory. Their fingers intertwined, turning white from the ferocity of their grips.

Ambrosine may have overpowered Valory, but even so, I didn't believe there was a force in the world that could sunder that grasp.

Valory clutched her portal box in the other hand. Pallor haunted her ivory flesh, and I shivered looking into her eyes. I could see every dreadful hour of her captivity written across her face and knew she would have rather fought the battle a hundred times over than endured the slow, slithering horror of that pit.

She and Kadri embraced in a way that Valory and I never would, but neither of us minded. We communicated in our own language.

"Glisette," she whispered, those sad eyes tracing the swollen, horrid lump of my face. That she would pity me after what she had endured spoke to how awful I must have looked.

"Commission a portrait while you can," I joked, but no one laughed. I was too ghastly a sight, apparently.

Valory didn't let me duck under the emotion of the moment as she usually did. She cupped my elbow as though I were a fragile thing she feared to touch. "Thank you for saving me. Mercer said you manifested the sword."

"More or less," I croaked. Even though Eulippa had been just a glittering, golden effigy of my sister, an otherworldly imitation of her physical form, I still wished she could have stayed longer. "But I can't help blaming myself for Ambrosine."

She nodded. "We made a mistake."

Mercer handed me what was left of the sword. The golden blade had faded to ether, leaving only the hilt.

Together, we followed voices through a door hidden behind a tapestry in Ambrosine's chamber, down winding stone stairs that led to an Edifice of the Fallen.

"Is it really you?" I heard King Myron ask. He sounded like a broken man, but I heard hope in his voice.

"Yes, Father, it's me," Navara said.

When we arrived at the bottom of the stairwell, we found King Myron fettered by chains that gave him only enough slack to roam the room. He was even more gaunt and hollow than when Ambrosine had shown him to me. A tray of food on the floor sat untouched. He had been prepared to fade away.

When he saw me, he cried out and tried to push Navara behind him to keep her safe. "It's all right, Father," Navara soothed, cradling him. "That's not her. She's gone forever."

I didn't know what awaited me back home after the heroes' reception that Navara was planning. Would people still be rioting in the streets of Pontaval? Would the fledgling Realm Alliance recover from such a grave error?

All I knew was that leaving would be more difficult than I ever expected.

The reception gave Navara an excuse to hold us hostage, but I didn't mind. Kadri and I shared a chamber and slept for nearly two days. I woke once and found Sev at my bedside, but he whispered me back to sleep, leaving me with the scent of spruce and soap. Later, a physician came to set my nose. It hurt so badly that I wanted to break his in retribution. At another point, Devorian strolled in to tell us that Valory had brought Fabian and Larabelle through her portal and asked if we wanted to bid them hello or if we planned to rot here. We both yelled, "Rot!" and pulled the covers over our heads.

The deep sleep failed to hedge out the horrible dreams. I eventually decided that being awake, in pain, and hideous was preferable to sleeping.

This time, Kadri was already up and about, eating biscuits and drinking cold tea. Navara had left us gowns to wear to the reception, which was now somehow only a few hours away.

The soft, layered dress of sky-blue silk was kind to my wounds, and even though mottled bruises ringed my eyes and swollen cuts marred my nose, lips, and cheeks, I found the courage to descend to the throne room.

Other than Navara and King Myron, who looked thin but rejuvenated, Sev was the first person I noticed. He had traded his usual leather jerkin for a dark-purple one with leather buckles, but a belt of weapons still hung around his hips.

The reception was a bit of an embarrassing show, with seats of honor for the elicromancers, plus Sev and Commander Larsio, as well as honorary seats for Tilmorn and Perennia. Thankfully, most of the attention fell on Navara and Myron, who announced that every priest and altar attendant found to have been involved with the Uprising would be imprisoned, and that they would handpick their replacements.

Sev's family had donned their best clothes to accept Navara's invitation—except Stasi, whose first best dress I had accidentally ruined. I would need to repay her for that, and more.

Sev sat across from me, his deep eyes set on mine, more comforting than a warm summer dusk.

"I want to thank all of you for holding strong in my absence, for protecting my daughter and my kingdom," Myron said. "We have made mistakes here, every one of us, including me. My wife did not claim control over me without my consent. She could not have crawled inside my mind without exploiting my undeniable weaknesses."

Navara looked like she wanted to interrupt, but he held up a gentle hand to shush her.

"That said, every decree I signed since the day before Father Peramati's death will be undone. And we will not, regardless of the temptation some may feel, shrink away from elicromancers in fear. These heroes have proved what my daughter and I always knew to be true: the hearts of elicromancers are no different from the hearts of mortals. While they are capable of great destruction, they also have the power to do great good."

He lifted his glass, his weakened hand trembling. "To every hero here today, living or dead. And to my brave daughter."

"Hear, hear!" the guests called. They were much livelier now than when Ambrosine was their host.

I smiled at Navara. Our friendship had strengthened the Realm Alliance's rapport with Perispos. I looked forward to seeing her grow as a leader.

"Commander Larsio and I have one more announcement," the king said. "As of tomorrow, Severo Segona will no longer be the royal huntsman. He will begin training to take over the post of king's commander, and someday, queen's commander."

We toasted Sev. I raised my glass the highest.

"This way," I said, leading Sev by the hand through the woods. The glorious sunset splashed scarlet and gold across the summer sky.

At dawn I would return home. But tonight belonged to us.

"I have no idea what to expect," he admitted.

"Good."

"Since you made me dress like this, I at least know it will be cold," he said, indicating his fur cloak and gloves.

I led him up a hill and around a rock formation, listening for the sound of water. At last I found the cave of dazzling ice, which I'd built beside a gushing waterfall in the forest.

The sunset sparkled across the impeccably smooth walls of the cave. I had taken my time crafting it, imagining the fleeting, wonderful moments Sev and I could spend together in this temporary place of beauty. It represented us, in a way.

"You made this?" he asked in awe.

"You saw me destroy so much," I said. "I wanted to show you what I could build." He looked at me with wonder in his eyes. "Go inside!" I urged.

I had shaped a raised platform where I had piled dozens of warm furs. I even made a table for a silver tea service, which I'd materialized here a few pieces at a time.

Sev shook his head in disbelief. "This is *almost* the most beautiful thing I've ever seen." He caught my hand and pulled me toward him.

"Is that so, Commander?" I asked, splaying my hands on his chest. Delicately, he held my face. I tried to resist the urge to shy away from him, aware of how dreadful I looked.

But Sev didn't let me shy away. The heat of his desiring gaze burned over my skin despite the cold that made white wisps of our breath. He nudged my chin up with his knuckle, stepped closer, and brushed my mouth with his.

I stole a deep breath and responded with little regard for my cuts and bruises, little regard for anything but the comfort of his nearness.

I wished he could come with me, but I didn't dare ask. He had a family to care for, a king to serve, and the promise of a distinguished new position.

Separate paths stretched before us. They would inevitably intersect, but our only promise was here, now, in this beautiful, transient place, and I forbade my thoughts from taking me elsewhere.

❧ FORTY-TWO ❧

KADRI
DOGHAN, ERDEM
THREE WEEKS LATER

CLAY roof tiles shifted perilously beneath my boots as I crouched to wait for my quarry by the full moon's light.

Nighttime in Doghan was exciting, more so than any Nisseran city. Thieves prowled. Beggars plucked songs on poorly tuned instruments and laughed their toothless laughs. Street vendors stayed out late to overcharge drunken revelers and gamblers. Dancers and dishwashers alike practiced other occupations in the wee, black hours of the morning.

The tracking map I had meticulously created to find Lucrez's son had brought me here, to the wool factory, where the clacking of pedal-driven looms did not halt until long after sunset, when the overtired factory workers retired to their cramped bunks.

The first time I had used Valory's portal to come here, I planned to only watch, listen, and learn. My gut feeling was that Sami had never held a prestigious scribe apprenticeship, although it was possible he had simply been turned out on the street when Orturio stopped paying his tuition, and then got plucked up by this vulturine factory owner who worked his poor laborers to the bone.

I hadn't known which little boy Sami was until I watched him sneak out. The tracking map showed him peeling off from the group of workers clustered in the living quarters next to the factory. Then I saw his dark head peek out from a side door. He tiptoed down the steps to the alley to feed dinner scraps to a mangy gray street cat. My heart nearly burst with adoration.

I had tried to approach him without scaring him away. But when he saw me, he was even more skittish than the cat, which morphed into nothing but a streak of gray hair as she darted down the alley.

"It's all right," I had told him before he could run inside. "Your mother sent me."

I hadn't planned what I would say to him. At that moment, I'd realized I needed to tell him the truth.

I had rocked him as he cried and screamed silent screams into his trembling hands so no one would hear.

And then he told me what had happened when he arrived for his supposed apprenticeship.

Orturio had never paid a single coin for Sami's care. Instead, he had sent the boy to work in the wool factory, for which he received a commission from the owner. An older boy had helped Sami write the letters and lie to his mother according to instructions left by Orturio.

To get Sami out of the horrible situation with as little trouble as possible, I had paid the factory owner a good sum right then and brought Sami home with me. But after seeing the children's dirty faces, their meager food and lousy lodging, the hopelessness in the eyes of the mothers and fathers and grandparents, I couldn't leave them to pay their sweat to such a crooked man.

I had planned to return.

Sami had never seen any magic and feared stepping through the portal. He had not learned to trust me yet. But when he saw the palace at Beyrian, the opulent bedchamber awaiting him, the feast that could have fed ten growing boys, and the view of the infinite ocean, he hesitantly warmed to the idea of calling this place home.

He still wanted his cat. And I wanted to end this corrupt operation for good.

So here I was, back at the factory, watching and waiting for the owner to retire to his study for the evening.

I had gleaned that he often lent money to the poor and forced them into labor when they struggled to repay the debt on time. He offered his services in seasons of desperation and set these poor people up to fail.

As for seizing what he claimed he was owed, he had struck a bargain with Captain Nasso; the Jav Darhu would visit families who had missed their payments and personally deliver them to the factory to work off their debt. The factory owner would skim off the top of the workers' wages to pay the Jav Darhu for their services, thus making it even harder for any of the debtors to repay him.

After retrieving Sami, I had come one more time to watch and listen. I'd heard them discussing a delivery that would happen tonight, less than a quarter hour from now.

Greedy bastard, I thought as I watched the owner retire to his study and cozy up to the desk to frown over documents—probably contracts on which people had signed their lives away.

Tiptoeing down the slope of the roof, I leapt over the narrow alleyway, landed on a broad concrete ledge, and pinned myself to the exterior wall to catch my balance. From there, I planted my palms on the windowsill and whispered *"erac esfashir"* to break the glass.

The factory owner gasped and nearly fell out of his chair.

"You!" he said as I swung my legs over the ledge. "You're back. Why? I let you take that boy."

I stalked over to perch on the edge of his desk, toying with the trinkets and shuffling a stack of coins. "I'm here to politely ask you to cancel the debt of every person who works for you and let them go free," I said.

He laughed in response.

"I amuse you?"

"They signed contracts," he said, opening the drawer and flinging a stack of parchment on the desk. "They knew what they were agreeing to."

I smacked a hand on top of the contracts and slid them over, peering at them as though giving them a once-over. Instead, I tore them up and smiled at him. "The polite part is a one-time bargain."

"The Jav Darhu are making a delivery tonight," the man grumbled. "I don't know who you are or where you got the money to buy that boy, but you had better hope you're gone by the time Captain Nasso arrives."

I pursed my lips. "I think I'll stay. I was going to track Nasso down, but this saves me the work. I have plenty, seeing as I am the elicromancer queen of Yorth and the newly appointed leader of the Realm Alliance. I'm quite busy."

I lifted my elicrin stone out of my collar. The man balked.

"I'll give you a week to cancel your workers' debts and set them free," I went on. "You will make sure every lone child in your care has a guardian. You will employ people who *need* work and pay them a dignified wage."

"It is not against the law to demand what you are owed," he growled, growing flustered. "I will appeal to King Agmur to overturn whatever authority you claim to have here. Go back to Yorth and make your own laws."

A downstairs door opened and shut. The factory owner looked me in the eye, tilting his head, thinking that he had surely called my bluff. Everyone in their right mind ran from the wrath of Jav Darhu.

The longer I waited him out, the more he squirmed. When footsteps trampled to the landing outside the study door, I crossed my hands and waited.

The door flung open. Captain Nasso and two of his men escorted a middle-aged man and his daughter, who looked only a few years younger than me and terribly frightened.

Captain Nasso's unflappable expression changed to surprise. "Kadri Lillis," he said sedately. "I heard Rasmus Orturio was bludgeoned to death with a fire iron."

"You heard correctly."

The creaks behind me signaled that the factory owner was again squirming in his chair.

Nasso flicked his brown eyes to the elicrin stone around my neck.

"Let's talk," he said. "What do you want?"

"You cannot bargain with me, Ardjan Nasso."

"The kidnapping was not personal," he said, as though that made it any less heinous. "I delivered on a promise. It's what I do. You should be angry with King Agmur."

"Oh, I am angry with him. But it's very important that *you* know, Captain, that people do not belong to other people, even if your clients' pockets tell you otherwise." I looked over his shoulder at the man and his daughter huddling in the corner. "You're free to go and your debts are cancelled."

They turned to take advantage of the opportunity I had given them. The two mercenaries behind Captain Nasso began to draw their curved swords to block them from leaving the room—ever protective of the goods to be delivered.

I nocked an arrow and sent it straight through one's shoulder. The other, I hit with the thrusting spell. My next arrow went through Nasso's calf. He yelled through his teeth.

The man and his daughter ran.

I strode toward Nasso and stared him down.

"I have a tracking map with your name on it," I said. "If something happens to it, I can make another. I can stalk you, haunt you for the rest of your days, which won't be many if you cross me." I clamped his broad, bearded jaw. "You will find other employ, Ardjan Nasso, or your torment of me will look charitable compared to what I do to you."

The summer sun baked the sand and salt water onto our skin. Rynna and I reclined on the beach, watching Sami's fastidious attempt to build a sandcastle that looked like the real palace.

Rynna's slender fingers traced my palm. The scar from the scourge in the forest marred her wrist, and she was not the only one of her people who bore such a mark. Over the past weeks, I had found myself pressing my lips to that scar out of gratefulness that this trial was over, that the Fallen were banished, that I had been able to return to this life and to her.

"When they took you, I feared I might never see you again," Rynna whispered, playing with my tresses, which were hot as coals in the midday sunshine.

"You had to know I would do anything to come back to you."

She nodded. "I knew."

"Why do you love me?" I asked. I had never asked her this, though I wondered every day. "You've lived a much longer life than I have. Your people don't care for mortals *or* elicromancers."

She sighed. "Over the centuries, the fay nearly let Nissera tear itself apart time and time again without ever revealing ourselves or stepping in to help. Mercer was right; we only intervene when it benefits us. That's probably why the scourge of Apathy threatened to destroy us so swiftly and completely—it fed off of our own apathy. We lent it power."

She raked the sand with her fingertips, thinking. "I was drawn to you because you cared," she said softly. "You cared so deeply.

About your mission, your friends...about saving innocent people. You may have been a mortal, but you set out to take down Emlyn Valmarys like you had every chance in the world."

She flicked the cylindrical elicrin stone resting at my sternum. It was beautiful, no doubt, but not nearly as beautiful as the long-lashed periwinkle eyes that blinked up at me. "You're modest and kind, but you're not going to give up that elicrin stone simply because it stirs controversy. I love your spirit." She leaned on her elbow and hooked her other hand around my waist, dragging me through the warm sand toward her. "And your beauty drives me mad."

When she opened her lips against mine, they were softer and sweeter than rose petals. Every touch had already been precious before the Jav Darhu yanked us apart, but now they were scorchingly soft, unimaginably dear, never enough to satisfy, yet somehow everything I ever wanted.

"I love you, Rynna," I whispered.

"I love you, Kadri," she replied. "Are you sure Fabian approves of this sort of public display?"

"Since when did you care if he did?"

She nudged my shoulder. "Since I cared that you cared."

"Well, he doesn't," I said. "We've decided that we're not going to hide anything. We love each other; that's not a lie."

"Plus," she purred, "you're the leader of the Realm Alliance. You do whatever you wish."

I snorted. "Sure, within reason, and if the majority agrees with me, and if—"

She shushed me with her lips, not for the first time, and we both laughed.

I didn't know how the Realm Alliance would govern now, what we would do about the mortals flocking to ask Valory for power or the precarious relationship with King Agmur of Erdem.

At least now I understood what home meant to me. It was not Wenryn or Erdem, but the best parts of each, nestled in this warm and peaceful place between.

EPILOGUE

VALORY

For hours, days, weeks, the creature hovering at the edge of my mind tortured me until I longed for death.

I couldn't sleep and therefore couldn't dream. I saw Mercer, but I couldn't speak to him.

And he couldn't set me free. When he tried, it felt like he was ripping me apart.

I began to fade, and the creature filled what empty space I left behind.

Say yes say yes say yes say yes, it chanted without ceasing.

Someday I would succumb.

No soul could endure this.

When Mercer returned with a golden blade and leapt into the pit, I thought I had at last gone fully mad.

Or maybe Mercer had returned to end my misery somehow. Yes…instead of hacking at the roots around me, he lifted the sword high.

And sank it between my ribs.

The roots recoiled. I choked and sputtered and finally gasped a breath of life anew.

Mercer scooped me up and rocked me, untangling me from the receding mass of roots. He kissed my forehead and cheeks and eyelids and lips with fervent love. I hoped this wasn't a dream.

Within minutes the invasion had retreated beneath the black rocks. Mercer carried me out of the pit. The forest around us was scarred, gray and barren, but no longer insidious and alive.

"I was so scared," he said, tears shining in his eyes.

"Ambrosine?" I asked, my tongue thick, dry, lazy in my mouth.

"She's dead."

I rested my head in the hollow of his throat and wept with relief.

He wanted to carry me, but I mustered the strength to stand. The battle wasn't over.

Before Mercer helped me limp back to the portal, I stared down at the bald black rocks, seeing the empty Water pit for what it was, for what I had helped it become when I touched it without permission:

An opening.

A passage.

A tear in the fabric of the mortal world.

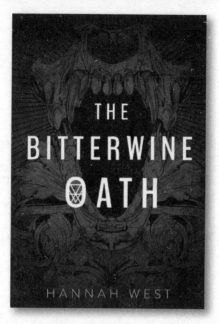

ACKNOWLEDGMENTS

Writing this book was a lonelier labor than usual, but that only made the people who were a part of the process all the more valuable. To those who have been patient through my (sometimes tearful) struggle to wrangle my creativity into the confines of publishing deadlines, bless you.

Thank you to my husband, Vince, who has been so supportive of my passion. I can't imagine sitting down to write every day without the backbone your encouragement.

Thank you to Sarah Goodman. Your critique partnership is as valuable today as when we were clueless querying writers teaming up to take on the world, and your friendship is far more precious than even that.

Thank you to my parents for always investing in my creativity and providing a foundation of love and acceptance. I know there have been many times when I took that for granted.

Thank you to Sally Morgridge, my saint of an editor at Holiday House, who fielded a 4:00 a.m. freak-out e-mail with such grace. Every stroke of your proverbial pen has done nothing but make the magic shine (shimmer, scintillate, glitter, glimmer, glisten, glister, glint, gleam, glow) brighter.

I also want to thank the other talented, hardworking people at Holiday House who have championed this series, especially Hannah Finne, Eryn Levine, Terry Borzumato-Greenberg, Michelle

Montague, Emily Mannon, Faye Bi, Cheryl Lew, Alexa Higbee, Nicole Benevento, Asharee Peters, Miriam Miller, Derek Stordahl, Kevin Jones, and Mary Cash. Thank you to hawkeyed copyeditor Pamela Glauber, my one-woman comma cleanup crew. Thank you to Kerry Martin and the design team, cover artist Daniel Burgess, and illustrator Jaime Zollars for enriching these books with stunning artwork.

Thank you to Jeff Goodman for your wise counsel on all things hunting and bow related that were not easily Googleable.

Thank you to my many supportive friends and family members. I appreciate you more than you know. And thank you to the readers who have shared this series with book clubs or recommended it to fantasy lovers at libraries and bookstores.

And thank you to young readers—the empathy you learn from books will save the world.